Redemption's Lullaby

A NOVEL

Toshii K. D. Cooper

This book is dedicated to Universal Truth and all of my ancestors. I am who I am.

Acknowledgements

First, I give thanks and praises to the Great I AM. For IT provides constant mirrors that keep me humble and forever evoluting. I am truly blessed.

Thank you to my parents, Mwikali B. Hayes and Joseph A. Cooper, for showing me, in your individual ways, how not to settle, to strive for greatness. You have been two of my greatest teachers. I love you both INFINITELY.

Thank you, Shonell Bacon, my editor. Though some of your feedback was challenging to receive, I am forever grateful for the guidance and direction you provided.

Thank you, Torry Holmes, for gifting me your beautiful painting, *Redemption,* and allowing me to use it for the cover of *Redemption's Lullaby.* You rock!

Thank you to Alexis Hightower, Imani Jones-Ratcliffe, Dylon Killian, Chaun Walker-Grainger, and my mother, Mwikali B. Hayes, for taking the time to read my pre-edited book and providing invaluable advisement and urging.

Thank you, Kisha Lawson Elder, for the plethora of information you shared with me about rape victims' experiences at hospitals - from the physical examinations and counselling resources to reporting the crime and explaining treatment options for sexually transmitted diseases and pregnancies. I am also grateful to the Dekalb Rape Crisis Center for everything I learned when I worked as a volunteer on their rape crisis hotline.

Thank you, Julia Blues, for being a listening ear, supporter and encourager, as well as a source of inspiration as I witnessed you become a published author.

Thank you to my Auntie Barbara Wright, my sisters Winifred Yancy and Rhonda Cooper, my cousin Jonathan Lason, LaShawn Brinson, Tim Brown, Earla Duana, Nicha Cumberbatch, Erin Parks, and all of my friends and family who either allowed me to talk their ears off about my fears, my joys, scenes from my life, and or who would periodically ask me or say, "so, what's going on with your book" or "I'm looking forward to reading your book." Thanks for rooting for me. I love y'all to the moon and back...

New Moon

New thoughts, new ideas, new opportunities, new relationships. Expect new, expect change…

Prologue

The only way for me to sum up my interpretations of my life's experiences is through a mental video of rare, collected photographic pictures of me in portraits drawn in still life's and non-still life's works of art. I am the muse, the sketch, the celebrated body of work, the scenery, the observer, and the artist, all at the same time. It's like a series of never ending flashes of imperfectly crafted black and white, and sometimes colored, snapshots are forever embedded within my mind's eye for recollection upon my need to laugh, cry, smile, learn, or heal from. I don't feel like my existence is unlike any other's – just interpreted like no other's.

And with that, here's some of my video.

The whole concept of yin and yang has never really dwelled in my mind for more than a few minutes until, just now, ya'll. Ya see, I happened to be in the very presence of the definition of masculinity stunningly crowned with a head full of long, thick locs, a smile to die for, and so much cool fillin-me-up swag that a Mother Superior might question some of the decisions she's made. So, to say the least, I'm a lil throwed off (yeah I said throwed) and am finding it a tad bit challenging to produce coherent, audible sentences at the moment. Humph, so, I guess it's a good thing he's takin a moment to think about the conversation we're having so I can, hopefully, collect my thoughts, or at least find a damn vowel.

But, damn! How can I think about something as trivial as letters at a time like this when o' boy's presence alone is poetically screaming that he's the yang to my everything that is yin – the dresses, purses, and stilettos in my closet, the frilliness of my boudoir, the tenor in my voice, and the decorative lace that makes up the thong discretely concealed beneath my jeans, just to name a few of my everything? Dare I say that he just might be the omega to my alpha, the sun to my moon, and the fire to my water? Or, am I narrow-mindedly missing any evidence of real connectedness becuz my physical eyes are undividedly fixed upon what I feel is the epitome of all that is 'Oh my damned' fine (pronounced foine) to the nth degree and it's fillin up the doorway to my bedroom with such a perfect stance that I'm soulfully frazzled at the conversation I've clumsily stumbled into - that I have to have – the one that has him in thought right now. Funny. Just a few moments earlier we were entangled within an organic, tasty, ravenous tongue dance. But, I'm cool. I'm patient. Or am I?

Shit! Really!? I wish that I could jus lift myself up from my seated position on my bed and walk over to 'yang' with such a sway to my hips and confidence-inflated stare that he'd unconsciously start to unbutton his plaid button-down shirt, revealing his very nicely sculpted chest etched through his white T, accented by a hangin golden lion head medallion just in time for me to softly caress it upon approach. Yeah, but that's just a wish at the moment given my plight. Shit, I'm liable to trip and fall over the fuckin oxygen in the room if I got up from my bed right now with all this throwed-off-ness up inside of me at the moment. Yeah, sittin is my best bet.

And I guess I should apologize for my inability to stop continuously describing my observation of 'yang'. But, who says a pair of jeans can't precisely sag on a tall, slender build in the most phenomenal way bringin just enough attention to some new Timberland boots that make a chick like me pinch her legs together from the street sexy embracing her vision and wild imagination?

Uh-oh! Wait, ya'll! His expression is changing. But since I haven't a clue of what he's thinkin, I am finding it extra hard to think of something clever to say to fill the silence in the room while nonchalantly dimming the light on the topic at hand.

Oooop! Aw shiiit! How bout he's walkin toward me with that confident-inflated stare I wanted to put on him just a few minutes ago. Unh! You betta go boy! I quickly counter his move by brushing my antique white, ruffled, DKNY pillow shams, neck roll, and square pillow off the bed and onto my hardwoods where I figured they'd be more protected from body oils, perfumes, and hell, just plain ole dirt. So, with that same thought, I fold my matching duvet and quilt back where they're barely hangin on the bed to make sure they're safe, too. Hey, call me anal if you want, but I like my frills clean.

Okay, so, can I just say that I don't know what it is about dark-skinded guys (yeah, I said skinded) that tug at the inside of my core? I mean, just lookin at this smooth, extra dark chocolate, coating before me got me forgettin…things. See? I wasn't gone say things ya'll. Nanh, don't get me wrong. He's a creative mastermind when it comes to the composition of music and an intellectual philosopher when it comes to digestin life's circumstances. And though I inwardly question the honesty of his spirituality at times, I lust after the immediate aforementioned description just as much as I do his physical. Hahaha! No, I can't say that I lust after him yet cuz, well, we've only been talkin for a couple of months and I'm not sure if I've met him yet. So, I can only reference his description for now. Plus, I'm sure that he'll be pretty guarded for a while, as will I, given the current circumstances, in which, our paths are crossing. Hence, the reason why I'm stallin, a lil, instead of (humph, real talk?) in the missionary position for real. Hahaha! Or better yet, on all fours with the quickness. You feel me?

But gettin back to that physical. Oooh la la, with some hot melted butta on IT! Can you understand me?! Unh, unh, unh. I just love lookin at his thick lips, especially the way the upper ridge of his top lip kinda curves up. Unh hunh. To me, that particular feature adds eroticism to the mechanics of his facial muscles when he talks, which tend to throw me off, just as much as his presence, when we're up close and personal. Like now, for instance, his lips were just movin, and I know sound was coming from him. But for the life of me, I haven't got a clue of what he just said cuz my attention was and still is on that upper ridge. Shiiittt! It's like I'm simultaneously caught up in his unadulterated expression of raw sexy, my present urgency to be intertwined up in it, and the inner conscious me who's questioning the questions of my motives. So, to say the least, I's a lil perplexed at the moment. Yep, just a lil bit. But knowin that perplexity wasn't invited to this party, I force my *self* to get a grip and be in the NOW with his description. Yes, I can do this.

Ready? Set? ACTION!

"So, we're good, Black?" Hahaha! Y'all like my nickname for him?

"Yeah, Baby. Why you lookin like that? I wanna be wit cho fine ass. Shit, I ain't seen you in over a month."

Smiling and basking in the focus of his undivided attention, which happens to be me, I purr, "I know baby. I've been thinkin bout you, humph, hell, and this moment, like crazy for a minute now."

After unconsciously, visually and mentally, travelling to an unknown place for a moment, I'm accosted by Black's stance and stare when I return. And, though most of me is in a serious mood right now, my facetious counter-mind is amused at how he's perched up on the pillows I left at the head of my bed like a big ole bad black wolf ready to devour its prey – lil ole me. Hmmm, this is kinda scary lookin.

"Oh yeah? Well…"

Wait, the wolf is sayin something. Focus, Corin. "I'm sorry, baby, what did you say?"

"Just that I'm gone need you to stop talking and come here."

Aw shit, I just felt a tingle between my legs. Sexually aroused and a lil excited about what's to come, I reply, "Make me" in my most seductive voice, look, and pose. *(wink, wink)*

Quickly reacting to my command, Black pulls me toward him and removes my blouse and bra right about the same time this piercing alarm goes off in my head, *DING! DING! DING! Umm, Corin, girl, are you sure you wanna let him inside of you right now? I mean, yeah, y'all been talking for about two and a half months. But, he's been on the road, for let's see, ummm, nine weeks of that statistic. Think, girl! You know you need to get to know him better. Let him take you out on at least one date. Damn! Omega to your alpha, hunh? Child please!*

Shit! There goes that intuitive monitoring system that I'm about to ignore, again, like so many other times in my life. Yeah, yeah, yeah. I know. I am being warned, like most women, when we're about to jump into a sexual/intimate/want a relationship situation with a man who hasn't vested any substantial time, interest, or minimally measured mundane gestures toward us. And it's so incredibly unfortunate that though I know that something is not quite right, I'm gonna proceed forward as if this is not the third time I've seen him in two and a half months. Yeah, see, I'm gonna give myself a break cuz we've, at least, been talking on the phone almost every day for the past month or so. I know, or at least I've convinced myself, that I have to be flexible if I want this man – I mean, he is a driver for a living, for heaven's sake, who travels extensively throughout the U.S. So, it might be a little tricky at times, in regards to spending time with one another, but we can make this work. Yeah, everything'll be okay. Sooo, comfortably moving right along, I take an inward breath and continue placing oblivion in full effect within the forefront of my mind while pushing common sense into the back drop.

Hmmm, now that all of that is said and done, I can redirect my attention to the seductive collision that's about to occur. OMG! I really want to laugh aloud when I focus in on Black. He's on top of me just sort of lookin down at me. Though I don't see any drool coming out of his mouth, it looks and feels like I will feel a few drops on, or near, my left nipple any minute now as he voraciously swallows my breasts with his eyes. I'm wondering, damn bra, when was the last time you had sex, or saw a naked woman's body, even? Oooh please don't huff and puff and blow my temple down. It's the only one I got.

DING! DING! DING!

Ignoring that annoying alarm in my head a-gain, I literally have to catch myself before I start laughin. I almost feel like I should verbally reassure him that the kitty's all his tonight, and, indefinitely if he's a good boy. But instead, I decide to show him as I let him tenderly fondle me in all the right places. Yeah, the wolf actually has a tender touch. In fact, after a few moments, I realize that my baby has some skills. Awe shhiiitt! I can't help looking up toward the ceiling as I salute GOD with a silent thank You. Wait! With a slight smile on my face, I ask myself, did I just think of him as my baby? Hmmm, I guess I am relaxing into the concept of me and him, now, even though I'm quite aware that he's still just a description.

Oooh, suddenly reacting to a delectable placement of his teeth and tongue on my body, I exclaim, "Oh, yes! Right there, baby. Damn, how did you know to do…aawww!"

"Oh yes!" I am definitely enjoying our playful physical banter – his tongue, teeth, hands, hot breath versus my words (dirty talk y'all), hands, grind of my pelvis, and tongue where I can get it. It's like we're using everything to grasp one another's bodies in raptured pandemonium. Unh, unh, unh. When I tell you that you don't understand what I'm going through right now, I need you to sorta understand. It's like the acuteness of pleasure that my body is experiencing is loudly rebelling against HIM EVER STOPPIN what he's doing as he successfully besets my sexual senses. Yes, this is what I'm talkin bout. I think everything's gonna be okay. He's actin like he wanna git it, git it. "Oooh yeah…UUUUnnnnhhh!"

All of a sudden I feel like all of the worrying I did before Black arrived was in vain. I mean clearly he's cool with everything. Feeling better about us/we/he and I, I allow my assuredness to propel me to grab two fists-full of his thick, long, ropy locs and pull his head toward me at an angle so I can commence to kissing and licking his neck and ears, signaling to him that it's his turn now.

I hear him say, "Aaawww. Keep it comin, Baby," as I move down to his chest and lick and bite on his nipples.

Gettin off on the fact that I'm gettin him off, I begin to let loose, even more, and proceed to give his body a tongue bath – lingering in places that cue his arousal.

I'm trippin, cuz like me, he really gets into the foreplay. I mean, I'm so loving his verbal, "UMPHS", and the way he grips my ass. Oh, YES, ya boy got my walls nice and moist. The steam between my legs is gradually opening up the pores all over my body, lettin an unfathomable amount of lust in. Shiiiit, by the time he stops me and says, "Now you again," I feel as though my entire dark-hued body has turned completely fire-red from the heat transferring between us. I mean, he really doesn't have to reciprocate the tongue bath. Hell, ya girl is officially in heat. MEOW! But, hey, don't get me wrong. I am lettin him linger on my nipples for jussst a lil while longer. In fact, I feel myself unconsciously pulling him back to their keen sense of bliss as he reaches for a condom. Shiiit, all I can say is that his soft kisses coupled with an occasional bite and suckling has me in another dimension thinking I am two sweet, juicy mangos that are tantalizing his palate into ecstatic euphoria. Ooooh, did I say that he's good? UNDERSTATEMENT! And, YES, I am sooo lookin forward to our on-the-spot choreographed romped-inflamed sexual encounter in my playpen. I have a feeling that he won't disappoint.

DING! DING! DING!

Whatever.

Waxing Crescent

Pay attention to your life. Feed your
interests with Divine intentions.

Trick Or Treat

36 hours later

"Whad up, Queenie?"

"Nothin, girl. You still at the day spa?"

"Yeah. I have one more massage in twenty minutes, and then I'm out. Been a crazy long day."

"Oh yeah?"

"Yeah."

"I would ask if you wanna hang out later, but I know with Black in town, the answer's no."

Thinkin back to Friday night, I begin blushin and noddin my head like Queenie can see me. "Humph, you know it. A sista's gone have to get wit you during the week my sweet dawlin! Hahaha!"

"Dang! It's like that, Corin? You just gone push ya girl to the side like that? Ha!"

Sittin back on my stool pushed up against the wall, I lean my head back and close my eyes as I fill my thoughts with Black. "All I can say is girrrlll, I's gone need you to understand."

"Ha! Girl, you crazy! So, what cha'll gettin into tonight? Or need I ask?"

Damn, I can't stop blushin. "Shut up, Queenie!"

"I'm just sayin, the way you told it, sound like y'all barely came up for air."

"Humph." Smiling as I think back to Friday night, I try to ignore a familiar emptiness approaching my mind, my gut. But, it's gradually filling my body, one cell at a time. Trying to ignore it, I continue to clown around with Queenie. "All I'm sayin is that a sista's pushin REWIND with the quickness."

"Hehehe! Look at Corin. Girl gettin her groove on and stuff. Me like!"

Tryin to give a convincin giggle, I barely hear Queenie edge on with, "I ain't mad atcha, girl. Not mad at all."

Man, I know I need to just relax and think positive, but it feels like history's about to repeat itself. FUCK! Suddenly, Queenie's voice sounds like background noise in a scene of my life that I half wish didn't include me. I'm thinking, yeah, Friday night was off the chain, but what about now? Today? I hear my girl talkin, but I can't stop from zoning out to the emptiness of right now. Shit, why can't the fun ever last for me? I mean, when is this horror within this part of my life gonna turn into a romantic comedy? I really like romantic comedies – even realistic dramas. But, the horrors have to go.

"Corin?"

One by one, I slowly remove protective layers of concrete-structured feelings as I finally begin to unblock thoughts that I've been ignoring all day.

"Hello? Corin?"

In a small, hoarse voice travelling from a remote space in time, I answer my best friend, "Yeah. I'm here."

"Damn, girl. What happened that quick? You sound like the end of the world is lookin you dead in the eyes."

"Hahaha!" Laughing at how incredulous I find my own moods, I try very hard to snap out of the one I'm in now. "Naw, girl. It's not the end of the world. My mind just went somewhere."

"Oh yeah? Where'd it go?"

"Somewhere in Black's mind."

"Umph, you betta get outta there quick, girl. Ain't no telling what you'll find."

Hearing myself giggling unconsciously, I wonder why do I do that – giggle or laugh unnecessarily. I guess it's my way of filling uncomfortable spaces within conversations.

"Corin!"

"Yeah, I'm hear."

"Well, talk then. Shit, I'll let you go if you want to walk through Black's mind."

"My bad, Queenie. You know?" Ooooh, now my stomach's starting to quiver.

"What?"

"I don't know. It's probably nothing."

"Unh unh. Don't start, Corin. You know I hate it when you do that shit. Whad up, girl?"

"Umm. I don't know. It's just that I haven't heard from him since last night."

"Oh. It's probably nothing, girl. You know how you jump to crazy conclusions."

Thinking that she's right, I do jump to conclusions a lot, the little girl in me responds to her with a sad, "Yeah. I know."

"Have you called him, yet, today?"

This damn quiver in my stomach is on blast now. Damn!

"Corin?"

Talkin to myself, I encouragingly command my mind to think positive.

"Get it together, mama. Don't jump to any conclusions, okay?"

Trying to respond to my girl, I find it hard to find my voice.

Recognizing the delicate space I'm in, Queenie softens her voice some as she attempts to get me to snap out of the space I've entered, "Corin?"

With a dry mouth, I barely am able to answer Queenie. "Hunh?"

She repeats her previous question. "Have you called him yet today?"

"No. Not yet." Making another strong effort to snap out of it, I try to crack a joke, "Humph, I guess I was lettin him sleep in and do him cuz I assumed I'd be doin him tonight."

"Girrrl, you know you crazy, right?"

The faint laughter in her voice is telling me that she's acknowledging my weak attempt to snap out of it in addition to adding her own effort to lighten me up. And oooh, how I wish it was workin. But, it's not. Chuckling a little…Damn, there I go filling space again. Any way, my mind partially journeys to dreadville, USA, as I matter-of-factly continue with the conversation. "Last night, ummm, he hung wit his boyz at a jam session uptown. And we never made plans for today."

"No?"

"Unh, unh. As a matter of fact, let me call him before I start my last client." I guess courage is claiming my voice. "He ain't call me all day."

"Humph."

"I'ma talk to you later all right, girl?"

"All right, mama." Knowing me so well, Queenie advises, "Don't start trippin."

"I won't."

"Breathe, Corin. I know you."

"I'm good, Queenie. Peace."

I guess my anxiousness has gotten a hold of me because I hung up before I heard Queenie say goodbye. As I dial Black's number, I feel the quiver turn into a sinking feeling in my stomach while inevitability creeps into my consciousness. Shit, he's only in town for the weekend and I haven't seen him since yesterday morning. I feel my heart racing with my crazy thoughts as I listen to his phone ring. Oooh, if he don't answer, I'm gone loose it. Come on, Black! Answer your phone!

Just when I begin to give up hope and prepare to leave a message, I hear him say hello.

Letting out my breath that I didn't know I was holding, I feel my heart beating a familiar fast rhythm. Wait a minute. Something's not right. He said hello. He never answers my calls with just a hello.

"Hello?"

Shit, there it goes again. Feeling out of sorts, I take a breath and fake some pep in my voice. "Hey you. What's up?"

"Hey. What's up, Corin?"

Lookin at the phone, I'm thinking, did he just call me Corin? What happened to Baby? Shit, somethin's definitely up. But, I'm gone act like nothing's wrong – that his greeting is normal. "Ummm. So what's up with you today?"

"What you mean?"

Tryin to control my emotions, but increasingly feelin crazy uncomfortable with his unspoken words and dry tone, I begin to taste apprehension. Shit. What could have possibly happened between last night's phone call and now? I mean, damn! Wait, Corin. Stop overreacting. Get it together, mama. Hearing Queenie's last words, I attempt to breathe.

"Corin? Hello?"

Tryin to sound light while feelin hella heavy, I play it off by lying, "Yeah, I'm here."

"Oh."

"Yeah, my bad." Searching for a lie, I ramble on with, "My coworker just stuck her head in my room to let me know that my last client just arrived."

"Oh. All right, then. I'll let you go."

Almost cutting him off, I blurt, "No. Wait." Shit what am I gonna say? "Ummm, so what's up with me and you later?"

"I don't know. I'm at T's right now. And we're going to a spot in a few."

"Oh, so I'm not gonna see you on your last night in town?"

"Naw. It don't look like it."

Standin up, I mentally go off, unh, unh. No he didn't. Wait a f-in minute. He couldn't have just wanted the panties. Could he? But, wait, why am I mentally going off and not verbally. What am I afraid of? Not knowing where the courage is coming from, I silently tell myself to just say what's on my mind. "Okay, so I'm a little confused. What's up with you? You were all over me the other night, blowin my phone up yesterday, and now you're acting all funny." While he took his time to answer me, the apprehension I was tastin a moment ago, became thick and bitter. I knew what he was gonna say before he said it – well at least some of it.

"Well, I'm not diggin what you dropped on me the other night."

Humph, I knew it. Damn! *Why me, GOD? Not again. Pleeeaaase! Not again.* Wait, get it together, Corin. *Please accept my apologies, GOD. I mean, I know me saying, "why me" is questioning you and I was told never to do that. But, hey, honestly, how am I supposed to grow if I don't ask you a question every now and then. I mean sometimes shit is confusing. But, I think I need to speak directly to Black right now before he thinks I hung up.*

"Hello?"

Ignoring the fact that I've been speechless for a few moments, I pick up the conversation like there wasn't a break. "What are you talkin bout, Black? You were cool with it then."

"Well, I'm not now."

I'm not sure if I'm angry, hurt, or relieved that he spoke it. "Okay, so

I'm still confused. If you're not digging it, or maybe I should say, or dug it the other night, then why did you have sex with me?"

"What you mean? You tricked me. What else was a I supposed to do? Hell, I had a rock-hard dick that wanted to be inside of you."

"Wait, wait, wait, wait, wait a minute. What? I tricked you?"

"You heard me."

Chuckling and shaking my head, I'm thinking this dude has lost his mind. "How did I trick you, Black? What are you talkin bout?"

"You knew I was gonna say I was cool with it. Any man would have in that position."

After inwardly repeating what he just said, *any man would have in that position*, my mind quickly rewinds to Tyrone, this dope artist/painter I dated for a short time, and I say to myself, no, that's not true. Tyrone didn't. This is some bullshit. "Okay. Wait a minute! Didn't you tell me that you have two female friends who have herpes, and that you talk about it with each of them from time to time when they need somebody to talk to?"

"Yeah."

"And didn't you say that because of y'all conversations, you were comfortable with being with someone who had it and that you still wanted to be with me?"

"I know what I said, Corin. But…"

Not caring that I'm interrupting him, I ask, "So what? You really didn't mean that you wanted to be with me? You just wanted to put your dick at ease?"

"At the moment I thought that I did want to be with you. But I've had time…"

Oooh, that hurt. So, now he doesn't want to be with me. Humph. Now I know what I was afraid of earlier – rejection. Cutting him off again, I'm in utter disbelief that he thinks I tricked him. "This is so incredibly crazy to me. You're mad at me cuz you had sex with me?"

"Look, stop cutting me off, Corin! I'm mad at you cuz you tricked me! You could've been told me that you had herpes! But you gone wait until the other night – after I've been on the road for more than six weeks! You knew I was feelin you! And you gone pull some shit like that?"

"But, how could you..? Wait, my bad. Go head."

"I spoke to one of my friends who has it, and she told me that she does this kind of shit all the time – especially if she ain't had none in a while. She said that no man has ever denied her once she got him all hot and at that point of no return."

Silently conversing with myself, I ask, why am I trembling? Somewhere inside of me, I answer, ummm, Corin, cuz this is worse than rejection. "Obviously, I don't know your friend, Black. But I'm sayin, based upon what you know of me, does that even sound a little bit like me?"

"I don't know what you'd do for a lay."

Exasperated, I yell into the phone, "What?! You don't know what I'd do for a lay?"

"You heard me! Wait, hold on, someone's calling me."

As I listen to the sarcasm and innate disrespect drippin from his every word, I clasp my hands together to make them stop shaking. Then I realize that it's my entire body that's shaking. I can't believe this shit. He really thinks I tricked him? Naw, this is his way of bailin. Tricked him? I don't have to trick nobody to have sex with me. Do I? Wait. Hell no! What am I askin myself? Ooooh, how do I wake up from this nightmare – this horror flick?

"Yeah, I'm back."

Confused, hurt, and feeling extra-rejected with a dose of self-pity and shame (Where did the self-pity and shame come from? Oh yeah, dreadville, USA.), I start trying to explain my side. "Okay, so first of all I'mma need you to lower your voice when you talk to me. And you're trippin if you think I have to trick anyone into sleepin with me." In the back of my mind, I ask myself again, did I trick him? I mean, me and Tyrone was in a similar situation when I told him. Damn, and now that I think about it, I remember feeling like my whole body was covered in sores by the way Tyrone initially looked at me and backed away from me when the truth left my lips. I mean, even though we were sitting on his bed, fully clothed, within inches of one another, in Indian-style, I felt like I was in a movie where the camera zoomed me clear across the room, placing light-years between us. I remember wanting to run down the stairs, out of his brownstone, and straight to the 'A' train. Shit. *GOD help*!

"Hello!"

"I'm here. Just was thinkin bout something. But any way, nanh, I admit that the other night may not have been the ideal time for me to drop that on you. But, honestly, I've never found any time to ever be a good time to tell anyone that I have herpes. I mean, think about it. If I share it too soon, I risk scaring a brotha off. And if I share it after we've spent time together, I risk him saying why didn't I tell him earlier."

"What chu talkin bout, Corin? That's crazy. I've been knowing you for, like, a year and a half, now. You could've been told me!"

"Ummm, okay. I know you're upset now. But, come on, Black. Yeah, I've been knowin you that long, but we've only been datin for about two and a half months. Before that, we just used to say hi and bye to each other with an occasional lingering look."

"What about those two nights we listened to music in my car outside your apartment for hours? Or the last time I was at your house? Or, hell, any time on the phone? We talked damn near every day for the past six weeks."

Bitin back angry tears and dreading that I'll have to end this phone call, unresolved, in a minute to go and greet my client, I speak from the only place I know right now, my heart. In an even tone filled with regret I annunciate, "Tone. Pitch. Volume. I'm gone say this one more time. Watch how you talk to me, Black. Nanh, first of all, I'm not tryin to share no news like that over the phone. I need to be in the person's presence to feel their reaction. And that was kind of hard to do with you cuz you were always on the road. And yeah, those times in your car would have been cool if we'd been seein each other longer. Hell, that's why I didn't let you come up to my apartment.

I was tryin to create space and time, between us getting to know each other, and us becoming sexually involved. I mean hell, think about it. This thing we got goin is crazy. You're always on the road – talkin bout how you have to make that money to pay child support for your daughter. We've never ever gone out on a date."

DING! DING! DING!

I push that alarm to the side and continue, "And before Friday night, I've only seen you three times in two and a half months."

"That's bullshit, Corin. Hell, I was sharing shit wit you – telling you bout when I was in jail and the shit I went through growing up. Shiiit, I don't tell just anybody that shit."

Feeling horrible about the points he just made; the fact that we're having this conversation; the truth of me not seeing him tonight; and the reality that I have to go and get my client, I quickly contemplate how to end the call. Do I apologize? Wait. For what? I'm not goin out like no punk. (Or is that too late?) "I have to go and get my client. Will you be around in an hour or so to talk?"

"I don't know."

Knowing damn well I should be saying, 'you know what, Black? Fuck you! Think what the fuck you wanna think'. Instead, I allow that damn self-pity and shame to get the best of me as I think of a way to get him to understand me so that he'll call me Baby again or at least so he doesn't think ill of me. Can you say grow a spine, Corin? Humph, feeling rejected is a motha. So, I lighten my voice with a flash of a smile and respond, "Okay, I'll call you back. Peace." I press end and put my phone in my purse and commence to ignore the agitation within my body. But, it doesn't work. I feel like my thoughts, future words, feelings, and limbs are all knotted up and rolling alongside a tumbleweed in a desert with nowhere to go except for the direction in which the wind blows. I know I can't deal with this alone. So I call upon my rock, GOD, as I command myself to be still.

Divinity In Motion

*G*OD, *please help ya girl calm down. This is so not a good look – especially since I have to give a massage in a few minutes.*

It feels like GOD instantaneously answers my plea cuz I immediately feel a shift occur, lessening the tension I didn't know I was holding in my face, and I give thanks. *"Thank you, GOD.* First, silence embraces the room, and then it embraces me. It almost feels like I'm waking up from a nap. I, unconsciously, stretch my arms into the air and notice that some of my muscles feel achy – stiff. So, I stand up and stretch them in the air, again, before I bend over from my hips to stretch the back of my legs. I begin to feel dizzy while my head is pointing downward, so I immediately bend my knees in a squat position, lower my head between my legs, and slowly catch my breath as the dizziness dissipates. I slowly raise my head and notice that my vision is a little blurry and begin blinking and widening my eyelids to refocus my eyes. Once I'm comfortable with their clarity, I slowly stand up and check my bearings before I sit on my stool again. Chuckling out loud, I think of how I wouldn't want to find myself on the floor because I missed the stool altogether. I can see it now. Headline reads, 'Woman, with Herpes Cracks Tailbone after Man Accuses Her of Tricking Him into Having Sex'. Yeah, so not a sexy look.

My mother pops into my mind once I realize that I've been staring at nothing for a few moments. She always jokes about how, since I was a child, she'd always find me staring off into space for no apparent reason. Hahaha! I can hear her now, "Corin to earth, Corin to earth. Come in Corin." Well, I guess that's a good sign – me thinking of a warm Mama moment. After a moment or two, I allow numbness to capture my feelings

12

as I mentally prepare myself for my last massage session. "Okay, baby girl, take some deep breaths," I say aloud to myself. "Everything's gonna be all right." Briefly pausing and questioning that thought, I wonder, really? Will it ever be all right?

Ummm, yeah, a small voice answers. *As soon as you begin to heed the warnings that you always receive, things will get better.*

Again, silence. Through my periphery, I observe my chest and abdomen rise and fall as I breathe. I can actually hear and feel the rhythm of my heart beat slowing down, lessening its pace back to normalcy. *GOD, thank you. I know that no matter what the outcome is, everything will be just fine. The key is overcoming me and listening to You.* Satiated with that thought, I stand and walk toward the door. But, before I open it, I cross my hands over my chest for a few moments while looking at my reflection in the mirror on the wall next to the door. I notice the clock's reflection behind me and realize that I should have gone to greet my client three minutes ago. Damn! Before I open the door to leave my massage room, I silently give myself one last pep talk. *You can do this. Go get this woman with a smile on your face. She's here to relax.* Then I force a smile at myself in the mirror, and go to the lobby to greet my client. I am relieved to find a woman completing an intake form. *Yes! Thank You, GOD, for padding the time for me.* If this is my client, then I'm on time according to her.

Given that she's the only one in the lobby filling out a form and the fact that I just saw my colleagues escort their clients to their massage rooms, I make the obvious assumption that this woman is my client. Once she looks up, after signing the form, I inquisitively say the name, "Heidi?"

She matches my smile with a smile and answers, "Yes" as she shakes my extended hand. We proceed to my room engaged in small talk.

the massage

Positive affirmations are to the mind like free weights are to the physical body. They both strengthen your ability to carry life via consistent exercise and conscious breathing. *I am worthy of happiness. I am worthy of happiness. I am strong. I am strong. I believe in myself. I believe in myself. I am normal and natural.* I have to repeat these affirmations because it's important for me to keep my energetic vibrations high while I'm working. And affirmations are the perfect weights to keep me in energetic shape. They're another way I summons GOD, aside from prayer, when I get caught up in my head. Now, don't get me wrong. I am as human as they come – I haven't shoved my conversation with Black into the ethers of my mind. No, not at all. In fact, it's almost as if I'm two people right now. For instance, I'm the hurt woman who feels rejected and a little shamefully dirty (where did shamefully dirty come from?) and I'm the massage therapist who loves to help people alleviate their stresses.

DING! DING! DING! HELLLLLOOOOO! Massage therapist stressed out here!

On a side note, sometimes I feel bad for people receiving massages from massage therapists they don't know because they have no idea the actual mental state that person is in during the massage session. Humph, cuz let me tell you, though some of my co-workers at this day spa I work at are mad cool, there are many who are happily depressed, confused, and just plain ole dark. Shit, I get a shivering chill just imagining anyone from the latter group lightly grazin me with the corner of their pinky. Ugh!

Please understand that I am a firm believer in the power of the invisible space/energy between two people and how it affects them either positively or negatively. Oh yes, a person's thoughts, feelings, emotions, and energy overall, can affect your mood without them sayin a word.

That's why it's so important for me to constantly protect myself through prayer, affirmations, meditation and light therapy throughout my every day goings on of life. Right now, ignore the concept of 'light therapy'. Maybe I'll explain it a little later. I don't know. But, anyway, some of you might say that you don't care what your massage therapist is going through as long as they're giving you a great massage. But, the reality is that if they're in a negative state of mind, like sad, heartbroken, angry, or vindicating to the point of wanting to kick somebody's ass, then please trust me when I say that you won't receive a great massage. Their unsolicited negative attitude started with negative inward emotions and thoughts that can affect you, even if they don't outwardly express it in some way or another.

Thus, I feel it's important to know your massage therapist as much as possible. And you know what? Real talk? You probably should get to know everybody, to some degree, whose work involves touching you, like your barber, hairstylist, esthetician, nail tech, doctors, for examples. Talk to them from time to time. If you were referred to them by someone, then ask that person what they know about 'em – why they like 'em so much. Find out, if you can, if they're having a good day, or not, before they touch you. Try to discern their persona before you become vulnerable to their energy because it's that invisible stuff/energy that links us all together – that we use to feed, stimulate, and/or dismantle one another with.

Think about it. Your defenses are down as you relax into a state of being created by your superbly skilled massage therapist. Now, you've allowed yourself to be open to whatever energy, positive or negative, your therapist is experiencing.

Ya see, I'm human and I have moments, like most humans, when I get in my funks. My affirmations assist me, my clients, and everyone I come into contact with. They help me stay in the moment, away from past experiences like having sex with Black that have caused ill-feelings within me, so that I can be a conduit of phenomenally pleasing physical and energetic massages.

Like I said earlier, it feels like I'm two totally different people right now as I massage this woman. I feel like I'm teeter tattering between victimization and love in motion - Divinity. For instance, even though I took time to calm myself down, I am still hurting from Black's accusations and rejection of me. Yet if the spa coordinators out front knew the conversation I just had with Black, they'd vie to call my name for me to walk across the stage of life to retrieve my award for best actress in a f'n horror flick. Clearly, I am either the best actress that I know who doesn't work in theater or on screen, or prayer really works, my dawlins. Cuz I don't know how I did it, but I managed to greet my client with a cheerful, professional demeanor that belied interest and concern as she shared her preference for light pressure and the areas of her body she wanted me to focus on - when, of course, it could have been much easier for me not to pay her any attention while I dissected and replayed my conversation with Black in my head, over and over again. The trick for me is to remain cautiously aware of my feelings and thoughts because right now as she inquires if I feel this obviously hardened knot near her left shoulder blade, a very small part of me wants to say, *will you please just shut up while I continue to strengthen my inner muscles and figure my life out? Damn! Thank youuu!?*

I am loved. I am loved. I am strong...

But, of course, I'm a professional. My clients never need to know, via my actions or words that I'm not in a good space. With that in mind, I envision my aunt's face, and think, good thing she taught me to value and respect my clients by removing my ego and personal energy from all my massage sessions as I invite GOD in through prayer and affirmations to work through me. Otherwise, ain't no telling what kind of shit I'd be passing on to this lady right now as she talks about how stressed out she is at work. I know that right now is not about me or what happened in the past, whether it's a moment, day, or a year ago. Right now is all about Heidi. So, I respond light-heartedly, "Trust me, I can pretty much feel all the knots that you feel when I touch them. And this one's a doozy." I jokingly add, "It has your job written all over it."

"Oh, I know. That area, where you are now, bothers me every day, especially at night when I'm trying to sleep. What is it, exactly?"

Okay. Here we go, as I playfully roll my eyes back into my head – the infamous massage therapist and client conversation. "It's your muscle tissue that's stuck together due to a lack of oxygen flowing through that area."

"Really?"

"Yeah, when oxygen isn't flowing fluidly throughout our bodies, it allows toxic substances like calcium deposits, lactic acid, and more to accumulate within certain areas in our muscles which may cause achy knots."

"Oh."

You know what? I ain't mad at this conversation. It's actually a nice interception for keepin my thoughts of Black at bay. *Thanks, GOD!* "Yeah, that's one of the main reasons we encourage people to drink lots of water after they've received a massage. Ya see, we're helping to break up the toxins by manipulating the muscles with various massage techniques. It's up to you to flush the toxins out of your body by drinking water afterwards. Otherwise, they'll just move around your body and settle somewhere else, either to contribute to another knot, cause a headache or the beginning of some other type of ailment."

"Wow! I never knew all of that. Thanks!"

Oh so grateful for the distraction, I humbly tell her, "You're welcome" as I send up a silent thanks to GOD.

"You're a gem, Corin. It feels good knowing that you're getting rid of that thing for me so that I can sleep better from now on."

As I shake my head at what she's assuming I can do in one session, I wonder to myself why people seem to always want a quick fix when it comes to the health of their bodies, alleviating pain, releasing weight, etc.

Looking down at my client's back, I focus more intently on her troubled knot.

I'm cracking up inside because this woman really thinks that I can get rid of this hump in her back that resembles the beginning stages of a new arm in one massage session. Shaking my head, I put a cheezy grin on my face, wanting desperately to laugh out loud at my joke. Oh, how I love what I do.

But, wait. In all seriousness, this knot does not feel new. And before I continue, let me just say, for now, that I'm more than a massage therapist. Much much more. But I'll get into that a little later. Okay, so as I palm the area between Heidi's shoulder blades, her wings I like to call them, I sense that this tension has been here for a very long time. "Heidi, how long has this knot been causing you discomfort?"

"Whew. I don't know exactly - maybe two years or more. Why do you ask?"

I know not to tell her that I sense that it's an old ache that stemmed from a deep emotional pain from the past which makes me want to physically cry, like for real cry, for a couple of reasons. One, it'll either open up a can of worms that I don't want to get into right now. And truth be told, that information, me knowing more than what she's told me through my intuition, might either frighten her, and or, enhance the pain, that she's currently feeling, from her reliving the traumatic event that caused it. So, instead, I answer her justly, eliminating some details.

"I was just wondering because this knot's pretty big and, though, I may be able to alleviate some of the pain and help to diminish a small portion of it today, it will definitely take more than one massage session to get rid of it completely, especially since you don't like deep pressure."

"Oh. So how often do you think I should get a massage?"

"Well, that depends upon your discretionary income. Once a week or every two weeks is ideal. However, if you receive a massage once per month and supplement your sessions with some form of daily exercise, eat foods rich in oxygen, and create quiet time to just breathe, then that can help you feel better as well. Ya see..."

Cutting me off, she asks me, "What foods are rich in oxygen?"

"Green, leafy vegetables and some fruits. And it's imperative to drink plenty of water daily – a minimum of sixty-four ounces."

"Ummm, okay..."

"Ya see, what I was gonna say earlier is that although it's important for us to increase the circulation within our bodies, we have to supply our bodies with oxygen, via food, water, and conscious breathing from breathing exercises, as well, so that the increased circulation has a boost of fuel to feed our cells with nutrients and not toxins."

"Wow! I'm learning so much."

Though I enjoy educating my clients on how to take care of themselves in between massage sessions (it actually gives me a rush), I do not enjoy dominating my sessions with conversations, even if it's helping me not to think about Black. See, I prefer quiet sessions so that my clients can relax, be in the moment of receiving comfort, so that they experience the maximum effectiveness a massage can provide. So, with that, I respond with "That's wonderful! I'm glad to be of service. I'll abbreviate the points on a card that you can take with you when we're done."

"That'll be awesome, Corin! Thanks!"

"My pleasure."

Oh, great! Silence again. Now I'm back to blocking thoughts and images of Black with affirmations as silence fills the empty spaces in the room. *I love and approve of myself. Oooh, damn, why does my chest feel tight? Hmmm.* I mentally shake it off like it's nothing. *I love and approve of myself. I am happy with every aspect of me. I am normal and natural. Present-moment awareness can heal the mind, body, and spirit in wondrous ways.* Hmmm, where did I hear that saying? I guess it sounds good, and all. But again, practicality is another issue. I mean whoever said that must have never had a care in the world. Yet and still, starting right now, I's gone be a trooper. So, I'll keep practicing 'stayin in the moment' until it sticks. *Breathe Corin. Breathe, girl.*

Just when I get into an even breathing pattern, Heidi decides to share how nervous she is about a blind date she's going on tomorrow. Chuckling to myself, I realize that my back-and-forth battle between being the victim, divinity in training, and the professional massage therapist is becoming a little comical. I admire my ability to listen and respond to my client with intrigue and interest as I do a two-step-jump-back move to the absurdity of music playin in the backdrop of my mind. This is such a crazy state I'm in right now. I mean, this woman has no clue that if I don't maintain focus on most of her words, consciously breathe, and silently affirm inward strength, that I could easily burst into untamed tears. Urgh! I so need to get a grip. *But thank goodness for you, GOD. Humph. I know you're with me right now cuz one, you're embodying my mind with laughable thoughts, and two, I'm actually balancing on my two feet sharing this beautiful gift of healing, through massage, that you have given me instead of taking off running across the country like Tom Hanks did in the movie 'Forrest Gump' when life threw him a curve ball.* Since watchin that movie, I always found delight in a sayin that his mother, played by Sally Fields, used to say – 'Life is like a box of chocolates. You never know what you're gonna get.'

But hell, my take is more like what I'm thinking is like a box of chocolates. Wait! No, it ain't even fuckin candy. It's more like a box of mirrors forcing me to look at myself from different angles. In other words, what bullshit am I gonna continue to feed myself or allow others to feed me? When am I gonna pay attention to me and act accordingly? I mean, the signs were bold and the alarms were loud from, I think, the first phone call with Black when I honestly look back on it. *But, no, me takin heed to any of Your warnings would've been too much like right, GOD.* Unh, unh, ya see, I chose to bury all of that so that I could convince myself that all was good within me, within him, and that there could be an us. *Thank You, thank You, thank You, GOD, for holdin me up during this massage and forcing me to go inward.* I know, in all honesty, that I can't get mad at Black. This is my stuff. He's just acting out his part in my drama so that I'll overcome the weaknesses of self-condemnation. This has to be my wake-up call for me to figure out a way to live with all of who I am, unconditionally. But, on a surface level, from my most human ego-laden, underdeveloped conscious side, SCREW THAT MOTHA! Who the hell does he think he is - talking to me all crazy, disrespectful, and accusatory and shit? Clearly he has lost his motha fuckin mind. Couldn't tell me none of that shit to my face like a grown ass man. Naw, he gone bail out on the phone. Shit, and I had to call him to find this shit out, too? What an asshole.

Whew! Now that felt pretty good. I think I felt one of my vertebrae slide back into place. Shiiiit! Sometimes cursing is better than a chiropractic adjustment and massage put together.

But you know what? Oooh weee! Karma is a motha. Believe you, me. It's so funny, though. The way a lot of people are livin in this world make you think that they don't have a clue about karma. Either that, or they just don't care. But, see me, life's experiences have proven that I'm nobody's neophyte when it comes to the repercussions of karma. I've been on the givin and receivin end of that truth a many of day. The question is was Black creating it or paying me back? Seein that karma spans across lifetimes, who really knows that answer? All I plan to do, at this point, is to start creating some good karma in my life. Cuz this right here is not cool at all. *GOD, I pray that I diligently follow your guidance and direction after I cry my eyes out for the next few days or weeks.*

Oh yes, my dawlins. Like I said earlier, I am as human as they come. I'm not gonna hold this hurt, or experience, in my body so that I can fall victim to ulcers, cancer, hair loss, irregular menstrual periods, or any other ailment because I didn't shed the necessary tears before I commenced to really healing myself.

Oh, shoot! Was that a tangent I landed on? Damn! How long was that one? Five minutes? *I'm, so, beggin You, GOD, to please help me get out of my head so that I can be present with…* Shit! You've got to be kiddin me. Tell me I didn't forget this woman's name? How could I forget her name? Is it Heather? Holly? Oooh, unh, unh. This is so not a good look. I guess I let that victim part of me get the best of me. Oh, how I pray that none of my stuff/emotions/confusion have seeped through to this woman. She deserves to leave this massage feeling uplifted and rejuvenated, not self-depleted.

DING! DING! DING!

I know. I'm gettin it, GOD. No more hitting the snooze button to Your wake-up calls.

How Now Came From Then

two months later

Eew! Though it's cooled down some, it's still hot as hell. And even though my sundress is stickin to my sweaty body from the humidity, I don't want to be anywhere else but sittin right here on Mama May's porch right now. You see, I'm a summer baby - one of its daughters, actually. My mother used to joke about how the summer of '70 gave birth to me, not her. Seeing that neither her nor my father ever really cared for the summer, she never understood how anyone, more so, a child of hers, could prefer a fan over an air conditioner in 80 degree or higher weather. And honestly, I haven't a clue why I'm like this. I just know that I don't like to be cold and that I prefer hot and humid weather over dry heat or chilly temperatures any day. I guess, in a way, the humidity reminds me that there's substance to The Invisible, whether I'm conscious of it or not, that embraces every crevice of my body. So, this moment right here is heaven on earth for me. Hmmm, I never thought about it before, but maybe the stickiness I feel on my body from the humidity reminds me that I'm real – that I'm here. Sometimes the reminder is right on time. And sometimes, well, not so much. But right now, it's perfect.

Humph! I think I might have cried for eight days straight after that initial heartbreaking phone call between me and Black. And I'm sure that the few times I anxiously and in-depthly entertained our bootleg conversations after that day didn't help the daily rejection I put myself through when I was awaiting his decision of whether or not he still wanted to kick it with me. I know you're thinkin, "Damn girl, you still wanted to be with him?"

In my mind, I hear the lyrics, BASE! HOW LOW CAN YOU GO? Who knew that a line from a Public Enemy song would be so profound in my drama? Humph!

And yes, he decided to leave me alone completely. Hahaha…that's not even funny cuz I think I went beyond the core of the earth, I got so low and down on myself. Pitiful, right?

So, why did I just laugh? Well, that's easy. I yearn to laugh it all off and pretend that there's nothing mentally wrong with me. But, I know that the reactions from the rejections I feel when men break it off with me, at times, aren't normal. It's like their heartbreakin words or sudden lack of interest in me can feel like blows from a crow bar continuously pounding on my upper back forcing my shoulders to curve inward while beating down my self-confidence. And, that the organ commonly called heart feels distant in a far away place unknown to conscious man as opposed to a vital instrument supplying me with life. Humph, I know that that's not normal cuz I've never witnessed any of my friends get as low as I do when they break up or experience rejection from men.

Yeah, so even though the pain I just described has subsided tremendously, I have to explain to you that whether I'm feeling the metaphoric pain on my back or the absence of my heart, that *me, myself, I'm* nowhere to be found even if you can reach out and touch my flesh. Unh, unh. I'm in a corner of hell especially carved out for *me, myself, and I* created by a myriad of thoughts stemmed around rejection. So, oh yeah, it feels real good to feel me right now in this moment. I welcome the stickiness with open arms. I need to feel *me* again so that I can heal.

In fact, the south is just the medicine I need right now. There's nothing like chillin outside at the end of a hot, lazy summer day away from the noise of life. And trust me when I say that the noise I hear daily, back home in New York, commuting between Manhattan and Brooklyn, going to and from work, is on blast all of the time. So, please pardon me if I repeat myself, but I welcome the peace here. The only sounds I hear, right now, are the sweet melodies of crickets along with other creations of nature. My fascination with trees is always heightened when I visit the south because they're so abundantly commanding in a lovable kind of way. And right now, as I stare at their familial stances in Mama May's front yard, I almost think I can hear them communicate what GOD is.

Wow! There's nothing like sittin within the serene stillness of nature. I mean, take this time of the day, for instance. My awareness becomes so enthralled when the sky is not quite black - when its vast canvas is brushed with beautiful purples, pinks, oranges, and some yellows surrounding the white light emanating from the moon. It's in these moments that I allow my thoughts to quiet down as I contemplate on the comeliness of GOD. Funny, though zoning out at this time of day has been a ritual of mine since I was a little girl, I'm always pleasantly surprised and delighted to find myself, suddenly, in the presence of billions of stars patiently awaiting my attention and wonderment. *GOD, You are splendidly beautiful. Thank You.*

Mama May's porch is a comfort zone for me. It consoles me like I imagine a soft, fluffy baby blanket consoles a sleeping baby. There's so much peace here that I'm always saddened when it's time for me to return home. I give thanks that she's still around for me to enjoy the peace within and around her. I love to hear her stories of yesteryear, way back when she was a young woman, because I enjoy piecing together circumstances from her life, from my lineage, as I witness wisdom and depth in motion within her eyes. Her presence is TRUTH and her absence is my evolution to the TRUTH. Meaning, when I'm not around her, I'm flipping, turning, and mirroring her teachings together with my stories, lessons, and conclusions back and forth within my mind until I'm able to digest everything within my consciousness of TRUTH or not. Hey, I'm human. And in comparison to her, I am a pre-neophyte on the path to enlightenment. But, on the path nonetheless.

Sometimes I like to engross myself in other people's stories so that I can take a break from my own. But, don't get me wrong. I don't believe in shoving things. I know that I have to adhere to all of the light bulb moments I had when I was massaging my last client on that crazy day Black put a mirror to my face with his words. I know that I have to find love within myself and nurture it so that I can love me unconditionally - infinitely. Yes, I am aware of that. But, I just arrived here yesterday morning. I know it may take some time, but my goal is to focus on the best of me, or at least pull it out of the abyss of confusion that lies within the consciousness of me. Shoot, while I'm here, it's all about immersin myself in the beauty all around me and, hopefully, learn and heal along the way.

Oh, how I love Mama May. She's really my aunt, my mother's older sister. But, for some reason, everybody calls her Mama May, even my mother, Mary Clementine Rivers, who's only two years younger than her. The way she got her nickname, putting Mama in front of her name, was never clear. But, once you meet her, you'll find that the title Mama is befitting. She's a soulful expression of love that people are instantly and excitedly drawn to. And I guess, her siblings, my mom, uncle Thaddeus, and twin uncles, Terrell and Terrance Williams, easily settled into that name, or shall I say that title, because it probably soothed their woes and brightened their paths to healing after all of the losses they endured at such young ages.

Humph! But, don't get me wrong. Though her love may have provided an anchor for them to hold onto on this physical plane during their sorrowful moments, I'm sure that it was their innate strength from GOD that had to have brought them through the roughage to astounding lead characters within their own well written life scripts. Oh, yes, they more than survived the pain. They surpassed its haunting veil of defeat triumphantly. And you know what? It feels good to know that I come from a family of warriors, that I am a warrior, as well, because they birthed me. Our inward strengths and tenacious spirits carry us forward as we write, record, and be within this universal production called life.

You know? Before I continue, I think it's only fair that I share with you that my uncle Terrell died tryin to save a man from drowning in Lake Ponchartrain back in New Awlins, (a.k.a. New Orleans) about three years ago. *GOD, bless his soul.* Yep, he used to walk the levy, back and forth for about a half an hour, three to five times a week. According to witnesses, he unselfishly removed his shoes and shirt and jumped into the lake when someone pointed out that it looked like a man was in trouble. And the man didn't survive either. Well, anyway, his absence is still so raw to me that I don't like talkin about it or him much. So, forgive me if I don't speak about my uncles much. Once I think of one, I think of them all.

You'll soon realize that one of my characteristics is one of nostalgia. Yep. That's me, all right – always reminiscing. I don't know if it's a good thing or a bad thing because lots of times, like now, it takes me away from my present circumstances. But, all I know is that when I observe myself writing, recording, and being the Best Lead Female within my life's script, I often reflect upon my supporting cast and how our collective discernment of TRUTH and experiences assists and or hinders our progression through time. For instance, though I never met my grandparents, I love them so much from the stories I've been told about them that I can almost smell their personal bodily scents. Yep, you read that right. I imagine that my grandfather's scent was like a woodsy spiced undertone while my grandmother's whispered cinnamon and orange. That's deep, right? And, even though I didn't step onto the set, or main stage, until they were long gone, their lives have directly impacted mine through the impact they've had on their children, my mom, Mama May, and my uncles, inclusively. In fact, thinking of my grandparents, Ruth and Carl Hayes, always saddens, fascinates, and intrigues me, all at the same time.

Ya see, in 1960, when my mother was 15 years old and Mama May, 17, their parents were killed by a drunk driver while they were walking home from a friend's party. At the time, my grandparents, mother and her siblings lived in the Caliope projects on Rocheblave Street in New Awlins, Louisiana. They had some friends, Mr. and Mrs. Baptiste, who lived on Louisiana Avenue Parkway between South Galvez and South Roman streets, who threw card parties every third Saturday night. Together, my grandparents and their neighbors, Mr. and Mrs. Washington, affectionately called Miss Betty (her first name was Betty) and Mr. Butta (his nickname was Butta), would walk to the Baptiste's party once a month anticipating some good music and dancin, throw-down finger-suckin food, and lots of shit-talkin, from the men, mostly. At least, that's what Thelma Baptiste, the Baptiste's older daughter, would tell Mama May at school every Monday, following the parties, during lunch time. I guess it was my grandparents' and their friends' way of releasing and escaping some of the ills of being black in the south.

Well, anyway, according to Mama May and my mama, who got the story from the only witnesses, Miss Betty and Mr. Butta, this one ill-fated night after the Baptiste's party, my grandfather and Mr. Butta had gotten tipsier than usual. So they were walkin a lil slow, a few feet behind my grandmother and Miss Betty, talkin and actin crazy. They were all walkin on the neutral-ground, the grassy strip of land that divides South Galvez Street. When they got to Fourth Street, Mr. Butta called out to his wife that he wanted to stop by his brotha's house and holla at him for a minute. Given that it was close to 2:30 in the morning, everyone knew that that was code for he was too tired and, perhaps, too drunk, to continue walkin back to the projects. And, even though Miss Betty didn't feel like going to her brother-in-law's house, she knew her husband had already made up his mind. So, it didn't make sense to argue with him about gettin home, so she could sleep in her own bed that night, especially since she knew it would be an up-hill-no-win battle. Plus, she knew that their three daughters, Lola May, Inez, and Yvette, were in good hands with Mama May, who, like many other Saturday nights, was babysittin for them while she looked after my mom and uncles as well. Thus, Miss Betty obliged her husband's demanded request by slowing her pace and lettin him catch up to her so he could put his arm around her shoulder – partly out of affection and partly to help hold him up.

Thankful that she'd worn some comfortable shoes to walk to and from the party in, Miss Betty said she remembered sayin, "All right baby, lean on me if you have to, but let's get to movin cuz I'm tired." Before crossing from the neutral ground to the side walk to proceed half a block down Fourth Street toward Claiborne, Mr. Butta asked my grandfather if he and my grandmother wanted to come along. Mama May and my mother said that no matter who was retelling the story, Miss Betty or Mr. Butta, they'd always stare off into the distance as they recounted my grandfather's cheerful response, "No thank you my good man. I promised this pretty lil lady that I'd walk her home tonight and that's what I'ma do." They said that he warmly tipped his hat toward my grandmother as she blushed and lightly tapped him on the shoulder before placing her hand in his.

Apparently, those were the last words they heard my grandfather speak and the last display of love and tenderness they witnessed between their two friends before they hurriedly crossed the street upon hearing an approaching car. Both Miss Betty and Mr. Butta said that they don't know what made them turn around first - the loud cry that my grandfather made as he accidently stepped into a hole, probably twistin his ankle, or the sound of the car, they heard earlier, crashing into a car on South Galvez Street. Shaking their heads as they relived the events, they'd say that it all happened so fast. By the time they turned completely around to see about my grandfather, a midnight blue 1957 Chevy Bel Air, had spun out of control after hitting the car on the street and careened onto the neutral-ground, killing my grandparents upon impact.

Yeah, that was some fucked up shit, right? Ordinarily, I'd ask you to excuse my profanity, but sometimes there aren't any other words which can express the sentiment you're tryin to convey. To top it off, if that's possible, the man who killed them was a member of one of New Awlins' prominent mafia families. So...as the story goes, no one reported him out of fear of the mafia retaliating. Can you imagine knowing who killed your parents, but not being able to tell a soul? It's something that I've never been able to digest ever since I was a little girl, when I first heard the story. In fact, my stomach always gets a little queasy when I think about it. Like right now, I'ma have to stop telling this part of the story before I throw up. But let me say this before I move on. The man who killed them was brutally killed about ten years later from, apparently, a drug deal gone bad. Oh yes, karma is a motha. Believe that!

Sooo, now are you seeing what I was talkin about earlier? Only warrior energy could get anyone through such a terrible experience. Shoot, I feel like losin my own damn mind just thinking about that craziness. But, the peace I'm feelin while sittin on Mama May's porch keeps me in check. "Deep breath in, Corin." Huhhh! Haaaaa! That was a nice exhale. Okay, I'm a little better now.

Well, after the deaths of their parents, my mother, Mama May, and the twins, who were twelve at the time, went to live with Cousin Lily, their mother's aunt, and her daughter, Alma, who happened to have lived within walking distance of the projects on Fourth Street between South Galvez and South Miro Streets. I figure that had to have been a huge blessing because they didn't have to change their schools or make new friends. But then again, wait a minute. Maybe that wasn't much of a blessing cuz that means they lived, and went to school, within walking distance of where their parents died. Damn! I just thought about that. Shit! Talk about reliving a nightmare. Damn! Well, I guess it's a good thing that they had lots of love and support then. From what I've been told, between their oldest brother, my uncle Thaddeus, who was livin in Texas with his wife when everything happened, my grandfather's people, especially his mother and father, grandma Cresie and Pops, and Cousin Lily's friends and church members, my mother and her siblings didn't want for anything except, of course, maybe a hug from their parents or even just to hear their voices. In fact, speaking of wanting to hear their voices, even til this day, every now and then, Mama May would say that she misses her mother's voice. She said that my grandmother had a lovely singing voice, that she would bring everyone to tears every time she'd sing a solo at church. And that what she missed most about her mom was hearing her hum and sing while she was cookin, especially in the mornings. She said that her mother's voice was her alarm clock that felt like a feel-good hug every morning. And that it was in the mornings, during the first year following my grandparents' deaths, that she'd wake up in tears at the alarming silence coming from Cousin Lily's kitchen.

Wow! That right there is one of the reasons why I like and love Mama May so much. She talks about her life easily and effortlessly – even the hurtful parts. Even though my mother has shared bits and pieces of her past with me, she keeps a lot of stuff to herself, buried. I mean, almost every time I ask her about her childhood or my grandparents, she annoyingly tells me that she either doesn't remember and to go ask Mama May, the griot of the family, or to stop concerning myself with the past – that the present and the future is what's most important right now. So, to say the least, I learn most about my family's history from Mama May than anyone else. Wait, let me not say that. I compare and contrast information I've received from her and what I received from my uncle Terrell before he died. But, obviously now, it's all from my auntie.

Anyway, sometimes I wonder if my mother has really forgotten, if she has unconsciously blocked out her formative years because of the pain the memories trigger, or if she does remember, but just don't want to relive the pain by reminiscing. Either way, my heart genuinely goes out to her. I can't imagine breathing without reminiscing every now and again.

Wait y'all. Been drinking a lot of water and need to tinkle. I'll be right back.

I pause for no apparent reason as I step back on the porch. Though I'd like to just hop back into my story, unconscious unwanted memories seep into the pores of my thoughts, causing ill effects upon my feelings. It's like I'm abruptly caught in an angle of shame and a wave of self-pity as I wonder how long it's gonna take me to heal my mind of sabotaging thoughts, my body of herpes, as well as mend the puncture in my soul which is the summation of what I just mentioned and a lil more. Perturbed is the operative feeling of the moment given the thoughts that just crept in. And mysteriously on cue, I begin to repeat affirmations to myself in a soft whisper, "I am Divine. I am Divine. I am Divine."

Well, well, well, I guess the exercises I've been doing to positively change the way I look at myself are working cuz that affirmation just rolled off of my tongue automatically. *Thanks, God!* "I forgive myself for not paying attention to my life. I forgive myself for not paying attention to my life. I forgive myself for not paying attention to my life. I love and approve of myself." Shit! There it goes again. Why can't I say that affirmation without feeling a tightness in my chest? Looking up at the stars, I say to God aloud, "Please teach me how to love and approve of myself. Please."

As I sit back on my favorite chaise lounge, I take some deep breaths, and for about five or so minutes, I visualize my body filled with a calm pink light massaging all of my cells, nerves, organs, muscles, bones, etc. "I love and approve of myself. I love and approve of myself. I love and approve of myself. I love and approve of myself." *Okay, now those felt a lil better than the one a few minutes ago.* Whew, self-work ain't no joke, ya'll.

I know ya'll probably thinkin, "Damn girl, haven't two months past? You not over Black yet?" And the answer is yes and no. Ya see, I'm over Black in the sense that I don't think of him any more romantically. But, there's a part of me that wonders if he still thinks I tricked him into havin sex with me AND if he's told anyone that I know, personally, what happened between us – mainly that I have herpes. And if so, what do they think of me. AND, really, let it be known that somewhere between my surface self and the core of my center, I wonder if anyone will ever love and accept me completely. That wonderment right there is a motha fucka.

Nanh, don't get me wrong. There are a lot of things that I know. Like, I know I shouldn't care about what anyone thinks of me, especially Black, but I do. And I, also, know that as long as I care about what the next person thinks of me, I have to continue to enhance my self-value, love, and respect so that I'll eventually not care – hence, the affirmations. I mean, think about what I said a moment ago. I want someone to love and accept me completely. But, in the conceptual scheme of it all, I know that script doesn't exist right now cuz, presently, I'm unable to do it for myself. Clueless is my operative sentiment of how to accept all of me all the time. And so, sometimes I wonder what right do I have to want love and acceptance from another when I'm not authentically loving and accepting myself. Shoot, if I was all about me right now, I wouldn't care what anyone thought of me, especially oh boy. I know I just repeated myself. Just makin sure I feel the understanding that's guiding and directing the breakthrough of my inner muck. That's why I'm here at Mama May's - workin on me. I know that I have to release the anger, shame, and sadness that's been livin in me for over a decade now. This existence is some deep shit.

"I love and approve of myself. I love and approve of myself. I love and approve of myself." Okay. Now those felt better than the last few. It's called baby steps, ya'll, coupled with consistency.

Now, don't think I'm ignoring my story when I start reminiscing. It's all a part of healing for me. You'll see. Hmm, now where was I? Oh yeah…

So, though my mom, Mama May, and my uncles lived with Cousin Lily, their mother's aunt, primarily, they often spent weekends and some weeknights during school holidays at Grandma Cresie and Pops', William Hayes Jr.'s house – my grandfather's parents.

They were fortunate in not ever needing anything like clothes, food, money, etc., before or after the accident, no matter where they laid their heads. But, they were always privy to more luxuries in the form of clothes, toys, anything they wanted to eat, within reason, money, and no house chores when they were at Grandma Cresie and Pops' house. However, apparently, there were prices they had to pay for the luxuries, which, some might call blessings as well. For instance, every time they visited, they had to select a book from Pops' extensive library, if they didn't bring one of their own, and read for a minimum of two hours a day. Mama May told me that Pops believed that the mind is a muscle that needs to be flexed, via reading and writing, continuously in order to achieve access to opportunities. So, every month, all of them had to write book reports on one of the books they read in addition to discussing the book orally, with either him or Grandma Cresie to enhance their comprehension of the book as well as their presentation skills. Impressive right? Well the prices didn't stop there. They also had to learn and adhere to proper southern etiquette in the form of posture, table manners, dining and conversational skills, and party etiquette, in which they practiced every Christmas season when Grandma Cresie threw her annual holiday party, and, when she hosted various luncheons throughout the year, which were, merely, social gatherings for her and her friends to hob nob at.

Hob nob I say? Unh, unh, unh. Oh, how I love my family history. It's so juicy and fascinating to me. Here I go – deepening the reminiscence by way of Mama May and Uncle Terrell. But, hey, I have nothing but time sittin here on this porch. So humor me with your attention.

Pops was a pharmacist and Grandma Cresie was a socialite who was very caught up with family and professional images in addition to the status quo. Unh hunh. I hope I haven't confused you or anything. Yes, I am reflecting on Old New Awlins, back at the beginning of the 1960's. And yes, everyone I've spoken of thus far are black/colored, except for that member of the mafia, of course. And yes, my great grandparents were considered black as well. But, they were a part of the small elite community of well-to-do negroes in New Awlins who were, and still are, commonly referred to as Creoles. They prided themselves on their obviously mixed genealogy based upon the color of their skin (light-skinned/high yellow/red bone/shit colored is what we call them). Some almost passing for white while many did. And let's not forget the smooth, wavy texture of their hair, some even having straight hair just like white folks. Well, no one seems to know about Pops' parents. However, I'm guessing that at least one of his parents was pure white/Caucasian and the other Creole, with a lot of white blood, because based upon a picture I saw of him in one of Mama May's photo albums, he looked like a straight up white man. I mean, it's amazing how much that man could have passed for white. I remember wondering to myself, "Who is this man?" when I first saw his picture and why was he in the family album.

Well, based on the stories I heard, I'm sure the color of his skin assisted him in attaining education, his pharmacy, and home amongst other privileges. But, privileged or not, he was still a black man living in the south. And though I was told that he was a very smart, highly intellectual man, I believe that inward strength, warrior energy, must have posed as his best friend in order for him to attain the successes he achieved in the guises of career and lifestyle. I say posed because it couldn't have been deeply ingrained within him given that he was an alcoholic as well. Unh hunh, I know you weren't expectin to hear that but, hey, don't forget he was a privileged black man in the south. Who knows what he had to endure to maintain his guises.

Now, from what I understand, Grandma Cresie was more Native American than anything else. Back then, and even now, people in New Awlins would say that she was Indian, or that she had Indian in her.

She undeniably loved my grandfather, her only son, who never completed college or amounted to anything worth bragging about in her eyes. And she also loved his children even though, according to her standards, he married my grandmother, who was beneath him – or shall I say beneath her.

Rollin my eyes up in my head, all I can think of is, hilarious. Yep! My great grandmother never accepted my grandmother because she was a dark-*skinded* woman with nappy hair from an impoverished background with a child, my uncle Thaddeus, out of wedlock. Plus, she didn't always sing for the Lord, if you know what I mean. Yes, yes, yes! My grandmother never had a chance, and from my understanding, Grandma Cresie reminded her of that continuously by the way she condescendingly spoke to her and how she dismissed most of everything my grandmother had to say. Humph. Unh, unh, unh. It's a damn shame how a person's character back then carried little weight in comparison to the shade of brown they wore in conjunction with the coil of their hair.

Smile! And now shake your heads cuz you've just received a dose of the ill-norms of old and present New Awlins.

Though I don't think it was right how Grandma Cresie discriminated against her own daughter-in-law, I can't hate her cuz her mother, and the way of the times back then, conditioned and validated her actions. Now, let me tell you this. It didn't matter that Grandma Cresie didn't grow up wealthy herself – that her mother, who was one hundred percent Native American (Indian), raised her and her sister, Aunt Lucinda, by herself cooking for two different white families during the week, in which she was a mistress to one of the husbands (after their father left her for another woman) while delivering babies from time to time as a midwife. And get this, what's fascinating to me is that she was a seer, someone who can see into the future. But, none of any of what I just mentioned mattered. No, unh, unh. What mattered most is that both Grandma Cresie and Aunt Lucinda, who were red-boned/light-skinned (compliments of their Native American ancestry), were taught to marry Creole and rich. Their skin complexion, naturally long, wavy hair, and their mother's many affiliations, from her midwifery and 'fortune tellin' skills which were highly sought out by the white elite, afforded them privileges within certain societal circles that women, like my grandmother, never could experience because of the complexion of their skin, texture of their hair, and economic background.

On a side note, I wish I knew more about my great great grandmother. Prophecy always intrigues me.

Life is so crazy to me. You know what I mean - that 'doesn't-make-any-kind-of-sense' concept of discriminating against others, especially those within your own race kind of crazy? And what's even more mind boggling is that things haven't changed much. But, let me not digress.

Even with all of the discrimination, I still think it's kinda awesome, and I'm sure that some of the folks who knew my great great grandmother, probably thought something similar, too, that she did okay by her daughters. Mama May told me that Aunt Lucinda married a doctor, Dr. Duncan, who was one of the founding members of Flint Goodrich Hospital, the only private *colored*, African-American owned hospital in Louisiana. Yep, both Grandma Cresie and Aunt Lucinda married well – within the black elite. But, I wonder if Grandma Cresie would agree that marrying well came with a price. Sure, she and Pops were able to shower their grandchildren materially, hob nob with the elite, and take advantage of educational opportunities that weren't afforded to the average person at the time. But, was it all worth it? Remember I told you Pops was an alcoholic and Grandma Cresie, well, it didn't seem like she was one to accept folks that were unlike her. Which, to me, says that she didn't completely accept herself. And, please pardon me, but I don't know much about Aunt Lucinda.

Get this. Even though my mom and her siblings were exposed to more affluence when they visited Grandma Cresie and Pops, who loved them deeply, they collectively chose to stay with Cousin Lily, on a permanent basis, out of a deeper love and respect they held for their mother. Don't you just love the idiosyncrasies of family bonds? I'm sure, to a certain extent, Grandma Cresie was perplexed by that decision. I wonder if she ever realized the effectual prices of her personality or way of life.

On a higher note, I'm glad that my mom and nem had Grandma Cresie and Pops in their lives cuz they provided exposure to another way of living, being, existing. And exposure, whether one labels it as good or bad, provide colorful, in addition to black and white, bench marks for us to experience as we play out our individual roles within our *scripts*.

Shoot, some exposure we happily weave in while others we urgently rip out.

The Veil Of Pickin Cotton

Oh when the Saints (BOMP BOMP BOMP)
Go marchin in (BOMP BOMP BOMP)
Oh when the Saints go marchin in (bomp bomp bomp)
Oh I want to be in dat numba
Oh when the Saints go marchin in...

The fullness of my roots excites and motivates me. Plus, my recollections are affording me the opportunity to get away, for just a lil longer, from my personal story – the reason I'm at Mama May's in the first place. But, don't worry. I'm not gonna leave you hangin. I'll share everything in due time. I promise. For real.

So, have I mentioned, yet, how much I absolutely love New Awlins? Oh yeah! Me love me some New Awlins. I'm telling you that even though I try to express my feelings about New Awlins from time to time, I feel like the words within my personal vocabulary bank are incapable of successfully completing the task judiciously. I mean, I really don't feel like there are enough words in the English language that can truly express this undefinable love and connection I have for my hometown. And, what's so crazy weird is that I rarely visit these days. But, whenever I do, I instantly feel like I'm a fetus in its womb being nourished through an ancient multi-dimensional umbilical cord that makes sure I'm always attached to the core of its protection and indirect guidance. Hahaha! You're probably thinking how can I, or anyone for that matter, feel protected by Sin City, The Big Easy, The City That Care Forgot? Humph, like I said, I can't describe the connection nor understand it for that matter. I kinda feel like something's gonna be revealed to me one day that'll explain this unbreakable tie between us – me and New Awlins.

Like, I might run across some old family documents that'll reveal something mystically ethereal about one of my ancestors, or that I'm gone find out about a miraculous, magical event within the city that occurred during the same moment I was conceived. I mean, something has to explain the excitement I feel just thinkin about New Awlins.

Get this! Once I remember thinkin that it feels like, as soon as I enter New Awlins' frequency, rather by plane or car, that I feel the sound and radio waves abruptly change. It's like they begin to vibrate at an intensity that effectively slows my mind, increases the beating of my heart, and excites the cells in my body, all at the same time, for no other reason than I'm near home. And I feel like I have these invisible antennas that all stand at attention along with the fine hair on my arms and legs alerting me that I'm entering into my original realm of existence on this earth within this lifetime. Shit, maybe all of my lifetimes. Now, that would be a trip. Any way, if I am asleep during this entrance, then something wakes me up – similar to an invisible nudge of some sort. And as I drive around the city and vibe with my family and friends, in person, or even long distance on the phone, I instantly accept and take in everything from the good, the bad, the neutral. So, actually, I guess, when I really think about it, it doesn't matter if I'm travelling there physically, vocally or mentally, I still feel a heightened sense to my total being – like now. I really have goose bumps right now and ya'll know I just described it as hot and humid where I am. But, I will say this, it's definitely more pronounced when I'm their physically.

My nose is wide open to all of what New Awlins is to me, its history, my lineage, my history, my experiences, the Lakefront, crawfish, poverty, daiquiris, the Calliope Projects, unknown memories, Mardi Gras, the sweet dialect, Canal Street, Creoles, North Tonti, The Second Line, Catholicism, the Mississippi River, secrets whispered, Gert Town, bayyy-bey, St. Peter Claver, my ancestors, the Huey P. Long Bridge, old interest-bearing money, gossip, South Galvez, Café Dumonde, sittin on the front poach (porch) waving at everyone that walk by, my grandparents' murderer, pralines, goin to the country – (Greensburg), hurricanes, The Superdome, St. Charles Street Car, the river-front, potato chips and pickled pig lips, The Garden District, pool halls, Esplanade, Tipitina's, the mafia, jazz, makin groceries (as opposed to buyin them), City Park, playing double dutch with telephone cords, Split Second, jubilee music, hide and go get it – tee hee hee, cold dranks, voodoo, southern hospitality, Bayou Classic, Now and Laters, Jimmy's in Pigeon Town, sin, Xavier, shrimp po boys, Magazine Street, gumbo, The Saints, the twinkle that's reflected from my eye to its rhythm and much, much more. Whew! There's so much more - I'm tellin you. It's an **UNCONDITIONAL LOVE** that automatically surfaces though I'm still actively searching for it within myself *for myself.* Rationally, I wonder how can that be – loving something more than I love myself? Damn! Is it love, then…

Hmmm, here's a thought. What if that protection that I feel so strongly from New Awlins is coming from my ancestors? Ooooh, I just got a chill.

Oh, I want to be in dat numba

Oh when the Saints go marchin in…

Well, gettin back to my family. If you think that what I told you about Grandma Cresie and Pops was interesting, then check this out. Remember when I told you that Cousin Lily was my grandmother's aunt?

"Corey! Co—rey!"

Ooooh, wait, ya'll. That's Mama May callin me. She calls me Corey sometimes. "Ma'am?"

I hear her walking toward the front door. She waits until she opens the screened door before she responds. "Are you okay out here?"

"Yes, ma'am. You know me. I'm just out here soakin in all this beautifulness as I let my thoughts run free."

"Un hunh." She looks at me for a moment with a wrinkled brow determining that I'm not sayin all that's on my mind. "Well I noticed you haven't eaten the dinner I prepared, and I haven't seen you eat anything since that piece of watermelon from this morning."

Briefly realizing that I haven't eaten since then, I stammer a little, not lookin at my aunt in her eyes, "Oh, I'm fine. I guess I've jus been in my head. But I was gone fix me a plate in a lil while. It's only 7:30, Mama May."

"Now don't get sassy with me, young lady. I know how to tell time."

Ooop! Did I upset her? "Oh, my apologies. I didn't mean to offend…"

"Yeah, well, I'm gone go ahead and put the food up. Now that I know you're gonna eat, I'll leave some out for you."

"No wait. I was planning on puttin the food away and washing the dishes. Please let me do that."

"No, I'm up now. You stay right where you are. Your eyes are tellin on you, Corey. Something's haunting you."

Embarrassed that she can read me so well, I look away from her.

"You know where I am if and when you wanna talk about it."

Lookin down in my lap, I barely here my voice express my respect. "Yes, ma'am. I know. Thanks."

As she turns back to walk to the kitchen, I feel completely naked and a lil relieved. I mean one thing I can always count on Mama May for is respecting my space. Hence, the relief. If that same conversation occurred with me and my mother, it would be a whole notha story with my mother leaving angry and disappointed that she didn't know what was goin on with me. But, Mama May respects spaces regardless of her x-ray vision.

Hmmm. Okay, ya'll. I'm not gone leave you hangin. But I need a minute to just breathe. It's amazing how Mama May can see through me so well. Hell, I wouldn't be surprised if she already knows what I'm goin through.

I love my aunt so much. I look forward to the day when I can tune into myself like she can tune into others, it seems, instantly. Wait, wait, wait, wait, wait. You know what? That's a lie. I'm already in tune with myself – with You, GOD. I think we all know my issue is learning to take heed to my inner promptings and messages.

Deep breath in. "Hunhhhh. Haaawww. Hunhhh. Haaawww. Hunhhh. Haaawww." Conscious breathing works wonders. Okay, ya'll. I'm 'bout to get back to the story. Now, where was I?

Oh yeah. Okay, so remember when I told you that Cousin Lily was my grandmother's aunt? By the way, her name was Lily Parker. Well, apparently, my grandmother never referred to Cousin Lily as her aunt. She was accustomed to calling her *her* cousin – hence, Cousin Lily. Hahaha! Oh, the tales of Old New Awlins. Okay, get this. My grandmother's father, Papa, or William Parker, and Cousin Lily were brother and sister. So, you would think that my grandmother would refer to her as her aunt, right? Well, no, she couldn't do that cuz Papa didn't, or couldn't, call her his sister. He had to call her his cousin becuz Cousin Lily looked just like a white woman and he, on the other hand, was black as night. And though it happened all the time, it wasn't right acknowledging blatant white blood being that close to blatant black blood. Ha! Oh, yeah, both sides of my mama's folks, paternal and maternal, displayed all the creepin that went on amongst them slave masters. Hahaha! I mean, those cream-colored/pink-tinted (white) men loved them some dark chocolate-pecan-honey-butter toned women. Hence, the class of Creoles. Hahaha! You gotta laugh at it to keep from cryin.

It turns out that Clementine Parker, a mixed slave (Creole) from Haiti was Papa and Cousin Lily's mother. Papa was the product of her and her slave husband while Cousin Lily was the product of her and the slave owner, a man by the name of Jean Alverez Latorre. No one knows Papa's father's name.

I was told that my grandmother described Papa as a prideful man who was tall, inwardly and outwardly strong, and dark-skinned. He was both respected and feared amongst the community in which he lived. Apparently, like Grandma Cresie's mama, Papa had the gift of prophecy, too. According to my grandmother by way of Mama May and Uncle Terrell, people used to come to Papa on a weekly basis to hear and experience his gift. She told my mom and nem that once a person would tell Papa what they wanted to know, he'd graze the pages of a closed bible with a coin, and wherever his hand was guided to stop, he'd open that page of the bible and read the passage which always answered the question or addressed the situation at hand. He was so on point that, once, a man came to see him cuz his daughter had been missing for a few hours, and Papa prophesied that the little girl had been killed. Papa's reputation of always being right caused the man to begin screamin hysterically before he ran away, grief-stricken by the prediction. And yes, the little girl's body was found a few days later behind a dumpster in an alley. Like I said, he was feared and respected – what a gift to have.

Well, given the circumstances he was born into, I'm glad that Papa was an inwardly strong man. I mean, I can't even imagine having to refer to my blood sister as my cousin based upon the color of our skin. No matter what the circumstances that would cause such a family secret, and that one right there was a doozy for sure, I'm sure there lies some

degree of internal damage to *EVERYONE* involved especially, if one of
the siblings, Cousin Lily, in this instance, was given more opportunities,
materially.

Can't help but wonder if Cousin Lily lived in the Big House, or in
the house with Papa, her brother, Clementine and her slave husband, or
other quarters? How was she received among the other slaves and their
children, or her stepfather, and half brother, Papa, for that matter? Was
Papa given a little more like Cousin Lily may have been given because
their mama was the master's mistress? If that was the case, did the other
slave children resent them both, or just Cousin Lily because she looked
like a white girl? Was Jean Alverez Latorre married? If so, did he have any
kids, and how did they receive her, if at all? Was Cousin Lily accepted by
anyone? If yes, did that mean Papa was ignored by everyone?

And what about their household within the slave quarters? Did Papa's
father resent Clementine? Did he beat her? How did their marriage endure
day-to-day, if it did at all. Neither my mother nor Mama May know
anything about Papa's and Cousin Lily's upbringing. But, I'm pretty sure
that it wudn't nothin nice.

Was Clementine Parker raped by Jean Alverez Latorre? Was she afraid
of him? Did she want to sleep with him? Did she want to sleep with Papa's
father afterwards?

Questions, questions, questions.

By the way, I heard that Cousin Lily didn't pay a dime for the duplex
she lived in because her father deeded it, along with a second single-family
shotgun house that sat behind it, to her. Talk about a blessing, right? Unh
hunh. And although, according to Mama May, Cousin Lily was generous
to all of them after the deaths of my grandparents, I can't help but be a
little curious about the level of elitism, if any, that resided in her toward
them because they were a product of Papa. Hey, I'm just bein real. Hell,
or maybe even a little negative. But, the times they grew up in promoted
such attitudes, right?

Well, in any case, that old house uptown on Fourth Street is still
standing. Our family never sold it. Though no one lives there full-time
right now, it's a place of refuge for friends and former tenants' family
members who are in need of a temporary place to stay who aren't afraid
to live in the hood. Humph, though it's smack dab in the middle of the

ghetto, we take attentive, good care of it because it's our unique carving of history etched out within this INFINITE universe.

My New Awlins is my sunshine bursting with love, deceit, family secrets, GOD, mysticism, my history.

First Quarter

To thine ownself be true…

The Magic Lady

According to Mama May, it was a sad day in uptown New Awlins when Cousin Lily, a staple in the community who was loved by many, passed from a stroke, three years after my grandparents' deaths. She said that during the entire year following Cousin Lily's death, it felt like someone was pouring salt on open wombs that covered her entire body every half hour, and that she prayed more than any other time in her life thus far – that she was lookin, searchin, and seekin The Hand Of GOD constantly and encouraged my mom and uncles to do the same. In fact, every Sunday evening around 6:00 p.m., for eight to ten months after Cousin Lily's death, Mama May told me that all of them, including cousin Alma, held hands in a circle and prayed together. Hence, the strong bond we all have with one another today.

. Everyone, including cousin Alma, continued to live in Cousin Lily's house after her death. They said that it took years for them to come to peace about my grandparents' and Cousin Lily's deaths, but they had each other plus the support of other family members, friends, Cousin Lily's church, who donated clothes, food, and a little money every now and then, and Grandma Cresie and Pops, of course. They were fortunate to have so much support and love, of which none of them took for granted. Everyone talks about how they all chipped in to help pay expenses - my mom babysitting and playing the piano for the church, her brothers pullin weeds, cuttin grass, and maintainin paper routes here and there, and Mama May cleanin houses during the day and takin in ironing on the weekends until she finally agreed to attend Dillard University's Nursing program through Grandma Cresie's brother-in-law, Dr. Duncan's connection with Flint Goodrich Hospital. From what I hear, it wasn't easy. But they had each other. Though Grandma Cresie tried to give them more, monetarily and materially, she admired and respected their closeness and how cousin Alma assured her that, financially, nothing would change, that they were home with family - her. And I'm guessin that Grandma Cresie recognized that cousin Alma needed them just as much as they needed her.

I was told that Cousin Lily's house was always a place of refuge for family, friends, and neighbors. Every day somebody was sittin with her, at the kitchen table, ingesting her wisdom and loving spirit. Everyone says that Cousin Lily had a way of making you feel good about yourself.

Now, you know what I found interesting? I was told that people continued to go to Cousin Lily's house after her death. It's almost as if that house was a sanctuary of some sort. And even though cousin Alma was ten to fifteen years older than Mama May, people came to the house to visit Mama May more than they did her. My mom and uncles told me that, for some reason, everyone, including the kids and adults in the neighborhood, always turned to Mama May for guidance, encouragement, a warm hug, or just a listening ear even though she was only twenty years old when Cousin Lily passed away. They said that those old folks, back then, used to say that Mama May was an old soul – that she'd been here before and was wise beyond her years. And it's so weird to me that no one knows when, exactly, that people, including her siblings, stopped calling her May and began calling her Mama May. And, apparently, no one really questioned it either. It just became her name like breathing air – a natural instinct. And since she was an innate nurturer, my mom and her brothers naturally fell into the rhythm of the affirmed name, Mama May. Her name is so profound that other family members, acquaintances, colleagues, friends, etc., all, call her Mama May til this day. Well, my mama goes between May and Mama May.

Right now, she's 75 years old and still gets around like a young woman in her forties. She says it's her love for God and being true to herself in all situations that keep her young. Her honey-toned face is smooth and soft with no descript wrinkles. Light laugh lines appear around her deep-set slightly slanted eyes and the corners of her mouth when she smiles and laughs. She stands about five feet six inches tall with a slender-to-medium build. She has salt and pepper locks that used to hang to her thighs in her sixties. Everybody was shocked when she shaved her head on her seventieth birthday. To me, she looked radiantly beautiful with an ethnic appeal. Less than a year later, she began growing her locks again. Now, they reach her shoulders.

Those old folks were right when they said she was an old soul because anyone who shares a moment with Mama May, instantly recognizes that she is a different kind of person - highly evolved. Her evolution stems from her strong connection to GOD and her interests and respect for Universal laws and the spirit world.

Shortly after starting college, I asked Mama May who introduced her to GOD and metaphysical concepts. I found it interesting that my mom and uncles weren't really into metaphysics like Mama May was. In fact, my uncle Terrence doesn't go to church at all, and my uncle Terrell, when he was alive, I guess, followed in my mom's footsteps by being a 'born again' Christian. I remember Mama May smiling like a little girl whose dad had just pinched her on the cheeks and told her that she was the prettiest and sweetest little girl in all the land when she told me that her dad, my grandfather, used to talk to her a lot about GOD. She told me that he had some books on metaphysics that he got from this rich family he worked for. Apparently, the husband, who was a descendant of an oil tycoon, always talked about how everything in the universe is made up of the same stuff, or energy, vibrating at various levels affecting everything else – even inanimate objects like homes, furniture, and/or rocks.

She said that my grandfather would become excited and childlike when he talked to her about his philosophy about life. Once, Mama May shared that he always talked about how the majority of humans vibrate at very low levels – that they are unable to hear, see, feel, taste, smell, and live out their purposes because they were dead – they were comfortable following and being the status quo; and that his optimum quest from self-study was solely to qualify his vibrations to such high intensities that he'd be able to travel between worlds and download pertinent information from higher beings and the Source, GOD, in order to help mankind thrive on this planet instead of die of ignorance. When Mama May told me all of that I was thinking, Wow, my grandfather was a cool dude and Grandma Cresie hadn't an inkling of who he was. Oh, how I wished I had known him personally. Funny how society refers to all of that as New Age thinking when, not only did my grandfather resonate with it, but people from thousands of years before him did, as well.

My apologies for digressing. But don't you think it's awesome that my grandfather would share various concepts, from time to time with Mama May after noticing her genuine interest – especially since, back then, adults rarely talked in depth with their children becuz children were supposed to be seen and not heard. It was ironic that she beamed as she told me how childlike he'd become, he was so excited, every time they had one of their little talks becuz I imagine she witnessed from him what I witness from her every time we have one of our little talks.

Apparently, my mother and her brothers never showed any interests in my grandfather's books. I guess they consciously and, maybe even, subconsciously took my grandmother's side which was that she didn't believe in no hocus pocus – that all she needed was Jesus to see her through.

Well, years of research, self-study, and her love of GOD led Mama May to write some books of her own. To me, her books are soulful commentary about living a fulfilled life. They are based upon her relationship with GOD, Spirit Guides and angels, astral travel, the divinity within meditation, the healing powers of touch, as well as a few fictional novels. People all over the world are always inviting her to speak and/or lecture on her books.

As the years progress, I continuously admire my aunt's keen mind, phenomenal health, and calm disposition. When she's not traveling, she makes sure that she walks three miles per day. And, no matter where she is in the world, she practices Zhan Zuang – a form of Chi Kung, for an hour, and sits in quiet contemplation or meditates for at least an hour after that, every day. Aside from a piece of grilled fish every now and then, her diet consists of mostly fresh fruits and vegetables, peas and beans, and nuts and berries. She rarely eats sweets, and primarily drinks water. She's a retired nurse practitioner and massage therapist. She retired from nursing when she was sixty years old and decided, five years ago, that she wanted to rest her body altogether. So, she stopped taking massage appointments and referred all of her clients to a young girl she was mentoring back in New Awlins at the time. But, she still teaches meditation classes, lectures on five published books she's written, four of which are best sellers, and provides healings on rare occasions.

You're probably wondering about that last statement - 'provide healings'.

Well, you see, Mama May has a gift from GOD that allows her to heal people by just touching them. And get this, they don't even have to be in her presence for her to heal them. You might be thinkin that doesn't make much sense. Humph, but, it's the truth. When I was a little girl, I used to always call my aunt the magic lady cuz when I would fall down and hurt myself, the pain would always go away within moments of her lovingly holding me and tending to my wound. And the wound would be gone by the time I woke up the next day with no scab. So, even though I was very young in age – around five years old, I began to notice that my mom could hold me the same way, kiss my tears away, and tend to my wound with the same care. But even though she'd help to calm my spirit down, I'd still feel the sting and/or pain of the cut or scrape and it always developed a scab.

Nanh, check this out. I kid you not that what I'm about to tell you is a true story. In fact, I guess you can say that it was my pivotal ah ha moment that my aunt was more than the magic lady, that she had a gift. Ya see, once, when I was in college, I experienced Mama May's healing hands, hmmm - maybe, for the first time since I was a little girl. I remember it felt like a crazy weird moment becuz so much time had passed since I'd hurt myself around her that I think I might have temporarily forgotten all about her being the magic lady. Well, anyway, some times back in my early teens, every now and then, I'd lose my voice. I mean, literally, I could not speak. And this would happen to me at least once or twice a year until my sophomore year in college. Well, one day, during that sophomore year in college, Mama May called me while I was studying. I knew that if I didn't answer the phone or call her back within a reasonable time that she'd become concerned. So, I went over to her house with paper and pencil to let her know that I had lost my voice. She looked at me with a worried expression and asked if I was sick. I wrote on my pad, no, that I lose my voice from time to time and that I should have it back within a few days. With that, she ushered me to her massage/healing room and told me to lay on the table face-up. I did as I was instructed and closed my eyes to relax. I felt Mama May's hands first on my head, then my forehead, and lastly my throat. Now, this is the honest truth, and I'm bein for real when I tell you that I don't lie. When she told me to get up, not only was my voice back to normal, but it never disappeared again. Amazed and shocked at hearing my voice that day, I asked her what she did. She explained to me that my fifth chakra, this energy field located at the center of my throat, was closed. And becuz I was opened to receiving assistance, she was able to open it and help it spin normally – enabling me to voice my thoughts.

Now, at the time, I was familiar with the seven major chakras in the body, their location, color associations, and what they represented. So once she brought it to my attention, I knew that my lost voice represented me feeling powerless in some aspect of my life, becuz the fifth chakra, located at the throat, represents the seat of expression and communication – the center that helps us manifests our existence through verbal communication. And when we are unable to express ourselves verbally, there's usually something going on in our lives in which we feel powerless. And I knew exactly what that something was given hurtful circumstances in my personal life at the time. Okay, okay, okay. My boyfriend had just broken up with me - amongst other things. But, I'll fill you in on that a lil later.

So obviously Mama May knew the essence of my lost voice, but not its cause. However, that day, she taught me a meditation exercise that helped to keep my throat chakra open and spinning. Afterwards, I noticed that I spoke up for myself more than before, projected my voice more confidently when I spoke, and made sure that I communicated as efficiently as possible in *most* situations. And truth be known, like I said earlier, I've never lost my voice since then (knock on wood).

A lot of people are unable to comprehend Mama May. But, I must say, they sure do love and respect her and the gift she has cuz she's either healed them or one of their loved ones. People come from all over the world just to hear her speak, receive healings, or just to be in her presence. She's the most genuine, humblest person I know in spite of her popularity amongst the masses.

"Corey!"

Startled, I jump at the sound of Mama May's voice. "Ma'am?"

"Girl, what you jumpin for? I swear you'll jump at your own shadow."

I chuckle at a memory of me in my brownstone in Brooklyn. "Hahaha! You're right, Mama May. I have jumped at my own shadow lots of times. My mama always make fun of me for that, too."

"Huh huh huh! I know. Huh huh huh! We gone have to get that fear outta you, girl."

"I know. I'm lookin forward to that day. But, in my defense, I was caught up in some thoughts and didn't hear you walk up."

"Yeah, I figured so cuz I jus looked at you for a moment before I said yo name – wondering where you were."

The human psyche is amazing to me. I have excellent hearing and, becuz the fear that Mama May just mentioned surfaces from time to time, I am very much aware and in tune to my surroundings. But, there are times, and I'm sure you've experienced this as well, that I feel as if I must take trips into other worlds and/or dimensions becuz I'm either startled by someone callin my name or I faintly here someone calling my name repeatedly until I slowly come to, or focus in on them – like waking up from a nap. "Funny you should appear at this particular moment becuz I was just reflecting on your healing abilities and how you helped me gain my voice back when I was in college."

"Oh yeah?"

"Yeah."

"Well, you must hold that memory dear because you had a peaceful smile on your face."

"Really, Mama May?"

"That's what I said, hunh?"

"Yep, that's what you said. And, yes I do hold it dear."

"Well, I just wanted to let you know that I'm gonna read a lil and turn in shortly after."

"Oh, okay. Are you feelin all right? It's only eight o'clock and it seemed like you napped for a while earlier."

"Yeah, I'm fine. I guess I'm just drained from workin out there in my vegetable garden earlier today."

"Yeah, today was a hot one."

"Tell me about it. I'ma take it easy for the next couple of days. I have some help comin on Thursday or Friday. I have to check my calendar."

"Oh yeah? Who?"

"My landscaper is scheduled to be here this week. I just like to get out there, on my own from time to time, to allow my hands to intimately work with the earth. You know me. I like to physically ground myself as much as possible."

"Yep, I know you. Hahaha! But that's good, Mama May. I'm glad that you have some help comin this week."

"Yeah, well, so, be sure and turn everything off before you go to sleep."

"Yes Ma'am."

"I love you, Corey. Know that everything will be all right."

It's amazing how tears can surface instantly when a particular string of words are arranged in a certain way and coming from a particular person. Humph. At the sight of my tears, my aunt steps onto the porch and kisses me on the forehead.

"You have a strong spirit, Corey. And you know that GOD is always with you."

"I know. And I love you, too, Auntie Mama May."

"Hahaha! Girl, you know you's a fool."

Laughing at my childhood name for her, she goes back into the house. Even after ten minutes have passed, I can feel that she's still smiling or, at least thinking back to yesteryear from me calling her Auntie Mama May. Yep, my radar is usually on when it comes to her. I bet if I walked into her room right now, I'd find her smiling and looking off into the distance. Hmmm, I wonder what our connection was in past lives, if we knew each other at all.

Who's That Girl?

Though I have come for a three-week visit, it just might turn into a two-month summer visit. The extended stay will be all right. I have the time at work because I rarely take time off. And right now, I really need to be with my aunt, around her, and feel her nurturing spirit throughout her surroundings. Basically, a sista's in need of a psychological hug rolled up in a redemptive embrace. I've always valued my special relationship with Mama May. And a series of events in my life, of which a fraction of them you witnessed a couple of months ago, has led me here to, Conyers, Georgia, Mama May's home right outside of Atlanta.

She lives in a yellow, ranch-styled home that has a wrap-around screened in porch with white accents. It sits, along with two separate loft offices, on two acres of a gated picturesque landscape that has seven uniquely themed gardens. Her love of flowers, trees, and water is evident all over her property. She has a waterfall that flows into a swimming pool filled with salt water that reminds you of a creek. Right now, lavender is planted around the perimeter of the sitting area around the pool which is decorated with beautiful statuesque pieces of amethyst crystal along with various potted plants and the most comfortable outdoor furniture I've ever lounged on. There's a walking bridge that crosses over the pool that flows into a path that leads you to a labyrinth outlined by perfectly manicured trees that stand about seven or eight feet tall. She lives here with her husband, my Uncle Charles. They moved here about five years ago from New Awlins. Both of her children, my cousins, Mya and Kyle, live outside of the United States right now. Mya lives in Jamaica with her husband and three kids while Kyle, her twin brother, lives in London with his wife and child. Mama May and Uncle Charles are made for each other. Uncle Charles is a poet and writer by passion and spiritualist by birth – he was born with a veil. In fact, a lot of people in his family were born like that – they can see spirits and have premonitions about stuff. So, yeah, it's always a treat to visit Mama May and Uncle Charles cuz if you're opened to it all, you leave spellbound from Uncle Charles' visions and trips into the spirit world, and Mama May's premonitions, that I'll speak on a little later, and healings. Oh, and my Uncle Charles tells the funniest stories. Right now, he's in London marketing his latest Sci Fi novel. So, it's just me and Mama May right now. What I love about them is that they are happy. They're in love with one another and with what they do. They don't have to work, write or market another book, or lecture on one as well. Financially, they are better than all right. But they continue to do what they do because they can and it's so a part of them. They are the healthiest seventy-five-year-olds I know.

Aw! I'm telling you, there is so much peace here, ya'll. And heaven only knows that right now, ya girl, meaning me, needs some peace. Last night, after Mama May turned in, I sat here, on the porch like I am right now, for an hour, in my favorite chaise lounge, soaking in the stars, moon, and the hum of the evening. Let's just say that I enjoy getting my nature on. It feels good to be outside, feel completely safe, and comforted with peace. I feel like this getaway is exactly what I need to calm my spirit, heal my wounds, and help me move on with my life.

Like I eluded to earlier, Mama May has no idea why I'm here. She knows that I'll tell her in my time. Maybe. It depends on how Spirit moves me. Or, you know what? She might figure it out on her own, knowing her and her visions and shit. Hence, the downfall of being in the company of psychics. Yeah, like Papa, her mother's father, and Grandma Cresie's mama, she too, has the gift of prophecy at times. I say, 'at times', because she doesn't experience it a lot. Every now and then she'll talk about a premonition she received through her thoughts or dreams, or sometimes a faint voice from what she calls her inner ear. She calls it her inner ear cuz whenever she has one of those experiences, she knows that no one physically around her can hear what she hears. But, then again, maybe she experiences prophetic moments more than I know, but she just don't talk about them much. I do know that she's more into defining herself as a healer even more than as a writer. But, never a psychic. Naw, in fact, I remember her tellin me that she never knows when stuff will come to her and that it's easier for her to see stuff about strangers than those close to her. She said that she thinks that her emotional connection to loved ones may prevent it.

But who knows. Regardless if she knows or not, she won't say anything unless I say it first. She respects people's privacy and space. I mean, I can't overemphasize the lack of pressure imposed upon me here when it comes to my business in my life.

I think that though I have a great relationship with my mother, sometimes, I feel pressured to make her proud. Humph, you know what, though? That might just be my ego talkin. You know, me puttin unnecessary pressure on myself – always tryin to keep the peace.

But I don't know why it is that I'm just different with Mama May. And I feel like she's different with me than with my cousins, Mya and Kyle. We share openly and honestly with one another when Spirit prompts us to. I'm not saying that we never disagree. I'm just saying that my relationship with her is easier than with anyone else.

Everyone knows that I'm an extremely private person. I don't consciously keep my life a secret. I just don't feel that all of the daily nuances of living need to be shared. Both, my mother and Mama May, say that idle chatter is a distraction from living a purposeful life. And I'm in total agreement with that concept. I wonder who taught them that – my grandmother, Grandma Cresie, Cousin Lily? Who knows?

Though I share a lot of my triumphs and some disappointments with Mama May, I've never shared what I'm going through right now with her because it's been very hard for me to really internalize it within myself. My mother knows some things, but nothing that's happened recently or the complete trigger of its occurrence.

Okay. I know. You're probably saying to yourself, "Sooo, who are you, Corin/Corey, and what happened, ALREADY?" Hahaha! All right, I guess I've stalled enough with sharing my family history and goin off on tangents in all. But, you know what? I needed that. Reminiscing is so therapeutic to me. Plus, some of it has reminded me of just how rich I am. And, honestly, a part of me doesn't really want to relive some of the details of why I'm here. I mean, Black, and me having herpes are mere aftershocks from the quake of experiences I endured years ago. But don't get me wrong. I know some aftershocks are just as traumatic as the actual earthquakes. Hence, my presence here now. I'm tired of the aftershocks being so traumatic. I need to rebuild my foundation to eliminate the onset of quakes altogether. It's more than apparent that the fault, (lack of self-worth), which lies south of the epicenter, the center of my heart, needs to be sealed and elevated via genuine, consistent self-care.

Contrary to my past actions, I know it's healing to talk to someone about it. Especially now since I'm dedicated to totally releasing the past and healing my wounds. So, I guess, for now, I'll accept you as my audience. So, relax, have an open mind, and please don't pass judgment upon me. Like you, I'm human. And during the majority of the moments in my life, I'm being the best me that I can be.

So that you can understand and visualize everything, I'm gonna give you a full, detailed description of who I am, what has happened, and what's goin on with me now. It's important for me to give you background so that you can fully understand the foreground of my life.

My name is Corin Rivers and I'm thirty four years old. I stand about five foot six with a medium build and wear thousands of micro, individually braided extensions in my hair that reach my mid back, which I conservatively wear up in a french roll at work and let down on the weekends. I've worn my hair this way since I was in college - low maintenance. One day, one of my cousins described my skin tone to be similar to milk chocolate. Being an advent runner has kept me in pretty good shape. So, men tend to be attracted to my long legs and high derrière, if I may. Haha! Sometimes I accent them with some fly jeans or a cute mini skirt or dress. But most often I understate my body by wearing long skirts and non-fitted jeans and tops.

Currently, I live in the Clinton Hill section of Brooklyn, New York in a brownstone I bought about a year ago on Washington Avenue. I'm an operation's manager in the Equity Linked Products Division at Computel Financial. You can say that I've learned to invest my money well in addition to earning a nicely stacked annual income. I was born in New Awlins, Louisiana, which is home for both of my parents and their siblings and was raised partially, there, and in San Fernando Valley which is located in southern California. My father, Stephen Rivers, is an engineer whose company offered him a V.P. position with their west coast office when I was thirteen years old. So, despite my disappointment of leaving my friends and family, especially Mama May, and fear of the unknown, we moved to Northridge, California, and lived in a beautiful home. My mother, Mary Rivers, still resides there with my father, and temporarily, my older sister, Shanice Gibbens, who's currently separated from her husband, and my two nieces – Diamond and Star.

After high school, I moved back home, to New Awlins, to attend Xavier University. I graduated, with honors, with a degree in Business Management. That was such a proud day for me - one of the happiest moments, ever, in my life. And to top it all off, I had plans to move to New York, within a month's time, to work for Computel Financial, a leader in the financial services industry. Get this, out of a pool of eight hundred candidates, I was one of twelve and the only African-American, selected and offered a position in their Global Operation's Management Training Program. At the time, everything was so surreal. I had never imagined living in New York, for one, or working on The Street a.k.a. Wall Street. I was offered my current management position seven years ago after working four years for the company and only three years after the training program. I guess you can say that I am an ambitious hard worker who is blessed with intellect, integrity, creativity, and a tenacious spirit. People say that I have a charismatic flare that encourages people to work hard and efficiently. I really do enjoy my work.

But, I know that I won't retire at Computel. You can say that me and Mama May are kindred spirits. Like her, I have the gift to heal among other things. And, actually, that's where my heart of hearts lies. For me, the concept of healing people through touch is like breathing air. On the weekends, I give massages to my friends and people they refer to me as well as work at a quaint day spa every other Sunday in Cobble Hill, Brooklyn. I received my massage license about six months ago after attending the Swedish Institute, Inc., as a part-time student in their night program.

The decision to become a massage therapist was an easy one to make. I adopted an interest in the power of touch and energy work when I was around twelve years old. I would spend lots of time in my aunt's library reading all the books she had regarding holistic healing modalities in addition to pickin her brain for hours on end about her experiences as a healer. I was so fascinated with the phenomenon of healing by touch and wanted it so much for myself that I think I willed myself into being a healer. It was, also then, that I was introduced to metaphysical thought, the power of affirmations, visualization, and meditation. I also became familiar with the seven major chakras and their purpose within the human body back then. But, it wasn't until I attended the Swedish Institute, that I discovered the gift of healing within my own hands.

Talk about an awesome, cool, miraculous day. It feels like just yesterday when my classmate, John Stevens, came to class barely able to move his shoulder. In fact, his shoulder was so inflamed that it prevented him from practicing massage that day. But knowing how John loved the art of massage, our teacher, allowed him to stay in class and observe the last lesson on deep tissue massage. During the break, John filled me in on what happened to his shoulder. Apparently, he'd strained a muscle during a tennis match the day before. The pained expression sketched on his face as he described his discomfort prompted me to console him with a gentle touch to his shoulder and a silent prayer of gratitude for its healing. When I removed my hand, John reflexively hugged me to say thank you. We both sort of stiffened during the middle of the embrace when we realized the positioning of his arm, especially his shoulder. Utterly surprised, I backed away as he began moving his shoulder and arm while looking at me in a strange distant way, not believing its mobility. It was like he was questioning 'what' I was as streams of tears ran down my face. Our amazement and bewilderment turned into five hours of deep conversation based upon various metaphysical concepts and the phenomenon of healing-by-touch at a twenty-four hour diner after class, as well as a comfortable *I get you* connected friendship since then.

Unh unh unh. Just thinking of that night always brings chills throughout my body. I didn't get home until 2:30 in the morning and probably slept for about five minutes, total, before I called in to work at 7:30 to let my assistant know that I wouldn't be in. My conscious self was unconsciously perplexed and exhilarated. I was on an unexplainable high that led to an impatient *me* waiting for a decent hour to call Mama May to share my news. She and I stayed on the phone for hours that day. She cautioned me into not sharing my gift, as of yet, with everyone until I'd totally grown into it – to focus the gift inwardly on myself for about a year before I shared it with others.

Remember earlier when I said that I had the gift to heal, among other things? Well, Mama May wanted me to become more comfortable with the latter. The, 'among other things' refers to my ability to sense and/or feel spirits. Ummm, yeah, you read that right – no need to go back and re-read it again. What that means is that, from time to time, I can feel the presence of spirits. It mostly happens when I enter old structures whether they are a person's home or business, while I'm trying to sleep at night, and/or during dreams. Sometimes it's really trying at night because I am not comfortable with it at all. In fact, it scares me. Yep, that's part of the fear me and Mama May was talkin about earlier. But, anyway, I can literally feel pressure on me while I'm laying down. It feels like they're, (the spirits), tapping me to wake me up. And, every now and then, if I open my eyes slowly instead of abruptly jumping out of bed, I'll see the comforter or sheet that's covering my body, move. And let me not forget to tell you about the dreams that I think I'm having until my subconscious suddenly realizes that a spirit is messing with me. During those episodes, I make this weird, horrifically authentic sound to make myself wake up. And sometimes when I wake up, I feel something, (that's not there according to the physical eyes), touching me. Humph. So, to say the least, and please excuse my French, that shit freaks me the fuck out. During those times, I find myself awake with my bedroom and/or living room light(s) on. For some reason I usually feel more comfortable sleeping on my couch than in my bed after those episodes happen. Go figure.

But, I give thanks that, for some reason, nothing ever bothers me while I'm visiting Mama May.

So, yeah, I'm definitely not your average type of woman. I enjoy the physical aspects of life, like running, giving massages, socializing with friends, family, and acquaintances in addition to using my analytical and leadership skills within the workforce. And I'm totally drawn to the unknown via metaphysical concepts and the spiritual realm via books and intriguing conversations. It's the up close and personal attention the spirits want to give me, at times, that identify my conflicting interests in the unknown – FEAR. Hence, I totally understood, then and now, Mama May's caution to heal myself, first, regarding my aforementioned fears, before I focus on healing others. Plus, I have a feeling that my *healing by touch* capabilities are not fully developed because I haven't had another episode like the one with John.

With all that being said, I feel like the character I play in my life's script is pretty cool – different. When I look at me from the outside in, I am genuinely captivated, even though the premise of me sharing my life with you is due to an inwardly, deep emotional pain. Humph. Well, thank goodness for my job at Computel. Though it may not be a good thing, all of the extra hours I've been spending there in the recent months have helped to numb the pain.

Oooh, wait! Please don't think that I'm only there to keep myself busy. My job definitely feeds me. I guess you can say that it quenches an unexplainable thirst I have right now within the intellectual *me*.

With that being said, don't think that I'm all work and no play. Though I enjoy workin and being in the comfort of my home most days, I have a pretty active social life. My best friend and roommate from college, Queenie, lives in Brooklyn, too. Her name is Simone The Queen Holmes. Everyone's been calling her Queenie since she was a little girl. Though she stands about five foot four, she has a tall spirit and a humongous personality and heart to go along with it. Her outward confidence exudes commanded respect whenever she walks into a room. Thus, her name is befitting to the outsider.

Well, anyway, she's a middle school math teacher and a talented West African dancer. Between her artsy friends and my alliances within black corporate America, there is always a play or musical, art showing, restaurant, lounge, coffee house, live band, party, etc., to experience and take in.

In fact, it's my social life that brings me to this state that I'm in right now - this sense of urgency that needs attention. I know that I have to get over this and heal myself NOW while I have the courage given that, in the past, I was too broken and connected to being the victim to focus my attention inward toward God's child, yours truly. Though I've been dealin with this for more than twelve years, this last episode with Black took me toward a place of despair that's incomprehensible. His accusations touched and pierced and punched and stabbed and jolted and hurt multiple selves. Hell, all of me. But, like I said, the background will help you understand the foreground. So, here it goes. How would you like to accompany me to my college days in New Awlins?

The Good
The Bad
The Ugly

sophomore year in college – early 1990's

During my sophomore year in college, I had the biggest crush on this guy named Deron Phillips. Talk about fine. Damn! I hope this isn't too much information, but the adult me just had to squeeze my legs together. Umph! I believe he created the word fine. And if he didn't, he damn sho contributed a minimum of three letters to that joint. Trust me when I say, as before, that you don't even understand. This brotha stood about six feet four inches tall, had a dark chocolate even tone, bald head, baby face, one-dimpled smile with the pearly whites, and a lean body that commanded your eyes to pay attention. He was a senior bio-med major who just happened to be in my speech class. That was the first sign of fate in the making because bio-med majors spent the majority of their time on the main campus where all of the science classes and labs were held. This speech class happened to be in my neck of the woods at a building formally called Xavier South. Though the entire student body, at one time or another, had to make their way to Xavier South to visit the Registrar's office, I spent most of my time there because I was a business major and the School Of Business and Career Development offices were housed there. Hence, my second home away from Katherine Drexel Hall, which was home to my dorm room. And so, to my gratification, some electives, like speech, were taught at Xavier South, as well, ergo the inner smile that warmed my tummy a many of Tuesdays and Thursdays that semester.

So any way, even though I made it a point to sit in the front row during all my classes, I made an exception in this particular one. Humph. See, he always sat in the second row near the windows. So I strategically sat in the fourth row at a diagonal to him so that he wouldn't see me paying attention to him so much. Ooooooo, I'm tellin YOU, I don't know how I managed an A in that class.

him

Miraculously, during the middle of the semester, the professor assigned a group assignment. And I just knew that fate was at play given the way the groups were selected. The professor had a hat with folded sheets of paper in it. And everyone had to select a sheet of paper. Once everyone had their sheet of paper, the professor explained that each piece of paper had a number on it, 1 through 5, and further explained where, in the class, each group-number should convene to discuss the assignment. So, yeah, you guessed it, we both were in the same group - group number three which displayed the second sign of fate. By our second group meeting, he asked me if he could walk me to my next destination whether it was my dorm, another class, or car. And let's just say, the rest was, ummm, dare I say pure fate.

Our courtship was easy and very sweet. We just fit. Whenever you saw him, I was somewhere close by, and vice versa. When we weren't studying or in class, we were engrossed in each other's worlds - touching, observing, and celebrating the intuitive rhythm between us. Many times, we unconsciously completed each other's sentences, or knew what the other was thinking from a simple glance. He was from Atlanta. Naw, wait. My bad. Decatur. Decatur, Georgia. I liked him cuz, not only was he southern, but he had a lil street in him in addition to being intelligent as hell. I've always appreciated a lil thug in guys, even to this day, because, well, I'm a lil green. And, to me, southern guys have a way of making me smile and becoming all mushy inside – a quality I've yet to observe in west or east coast guys. Any way, he was funny as hell. His sense of humor had me on the floor, laughing and in tears, a many of late nights, especially after he had smoked some herb and the silly bug took over him. Although I didn't partake in the recreation of smoking naturally grown herbs at the time, I enjoyed the aroma, like it was a stick of incense burnin, and just kickin it with my boo. So, when he became silly, I flowed with it. And when he developed the munchies, I easily rolled with him to wherever he wanted to go to get something to eat cuz, well, I loved and still do love to eat. If it was really late at night, we'd sometimes ride to the quarters to Café Dumonde and get some beignets. Or, if he was up for the drive, we'd hop on I10 and haul ass to We Never Close out in New Awlins East on Chef Menteur Highway for some ridiculously large po boys. They were known for piling your po boy with tons and tons of the meat of your choice which was hot sausage for Deron and shrimp for me. Shit, I felt like with all the excess shrimp I'd get, I could easily make a second po boy. Umph! And one thing my boo appreciated about me was that I wasn't afraid to eat in front of him. In fact, sometimes he was surprised about just how much I could put away – at times, more than him. Oh, the memories…

Ooooh, nanh let me not forget about those early evenings that we'd, or shall I say, he'd get the munchies, or we just wanted to go out for some good food. Then, we'd go uptown to Dunbar's on Freret Street. Humph, ya'll ain't had no comfort food until you ate at Dunbars. I used to tear their all-you-can eat red beans and rice up. What?! And their fried chicken wudn't nothin nice either, nanh. And though Deron loved the red beans and rice just as much as I did – always takin some off of my plate, he fell in loving admiration with their smothered turkey necks, which were the absolute truth. Ya heard me? Unh, unh, unh, I'm tellin you, those were the days.

When I think back to him, I imagine that people on the outside lookin in would assume that Deron was a 'bad boy' by, maybe, the way he dressed and the stand-offish and aloof demeanor he portrayed. But, everyone who took the time to get to know him found that he was an extremely sweet person who kept up with current events and loved to read philosophical oriented books. In fact, during that first time he walked me to my dorm, we somehow began talkin about deep books and authors and he mentioned that one of his favorite books was *Illusions* by

Richard Bach. And given that I was a fan of Bach, my favorite book being *One*, we easily joined each other's worlds by first seducing and marveling over each other's minds before we explored our physical selves with a simple kiss. There was never a dull moment between us. Some hot ones. But, no, never any dull ones.

There were times when we would go to Lake Pontchartrain (GOD bless my uncle's soul). I don't think I mentioned it earlier, but Lake Pontchartrain is commonly known to the locals as the Lake. While we were there, we enjoyed either walkin or sittin on the grass or a bench, or in his car talking about our lives - past, present, and future goals and accomplishments. He'd tell me how it was for him growin up in the hood versus suburbia, USA, where I grew up. But mostly, I'd say toward the end of our courtship, he joined my enjoyment of eatin crawfish out by the Lake. I'll never forget when he told me he had never eaten them before. I immediately persuaded him into goin to Dockside, this seafood spot close to the Lake at the corner of Downman and Haynes. The seafood was always so good there as well as reasonably priced. When I tell you that we went through six pounds of crawfish like it was only one pound, I'ma need you to imagine just how plump and well-seasoned that crawfish was - and I'm talkin all the time – during crawfish season that is.

Okay, so though I didn't participate in the smoking of naturally grown herbs at the time, I did join Deron and partook in an occasional machine manufactured daiquiri from this daiquiri shop that was located in the River Bend where St. Charles and Carrolton streets meet. Yes, there were definitely some advantages to datin a senior, ya'll, or shall I say someone who was over twenty-one years of age. (wink, wink) He'd get a half a gallon of a particular flavor, and with the paper cups we kept in the car, we'd go sit in the car by the river and jus chill. And sometimes after we'd get our drink on, he'd park the car on a street off of St. Charles and we'd ride the street car, (trolley), to Canal Street and back jus for the hell of it. We loved to take in the view that uptown had to offer, especially the picturesque huge oak and magnolia trees that outlined St. Charles Street. We both agreed that those trees looked like they'd been there since time began. Shooot, and still to this day, I wonder about the stories they'd share if they could talk – the trees that is. On a side note, I learned, a few years ago, that New Awlins is home to the largest collection of mature oak trees in the world. In the world, ya'll. I knew me and Deron were witnessin some naturalistic antiquity durin those rides.

Well any way, the Colonial, Victorian, and Antebellum styled mansions, which screamed big money (that old interest-bearing money) that lined St. Charles Street coupled with those parts of Loyola and Tulane Universities that were also situated along the route always provoked intrigue and wonderment within me of just how many slaves helped to build them, the homes and the schools that is, directly and/or indirectly.

It's so interesting how the layout of the city sort of recites the geographical story of its occupants once slavery was abolished. For instance, it's very common to see a mini mansion like this black and white one, I remember, that was situated on the corner of St. Charles and Fourth Streets. And then, not two to three blocks down on Fourth, moving toward South Claiborne, you find yourself in a poverty-stricken neighborhood. In other words, when slavery was abolished, the ex-slaves still needed to work. So, my assumption was it only made sense to build their homes close to where they worked.

That was the sort of stuff me and my sweetie paid attention to. Based upon the lay of the land, we quickly determined that it was a city of the 'Haves' and the 'Have Nots' – there wasn't much of a middle class.

Though Deron and I, both, loved and appreciated the old-timey-lazy-partying-mystical-sinfully-haunted-religious-hospitable feel of New Awlins, we mostly enjoyed admiring how the one and two story homes accented with stoops, large porches, cast iron balconies, and/or partitioned courtyards spread throughout the city, but mostly located in the Lower Garden District, French Quarter, and Faubourg Marigny neighborhoods together with the elaborate standing stone tombs within the various European-styled cemeteries. It all provided the perfect backdrops and sceneries to that multi-layered feel. Oh, how I love that feel still to this day.

Now that I'm talkin about Deron and that time period, conversations and ideas are coming to my mind that I haven't thought about in years. Like, for example, though he appreciated a lot of the architecture of New Awlins, Deron couldn't stand some of the plain-lookin narrow shotgun houses that occupied many poor neighborhoods. It was as if the site of their existence offended him. And I guess, I couldn't blame him in some instances because dependin upon where we were, some of the houses were literally leaning to the side they were so poorly built. And he also didn't like that there were so many highly populated housing projects in the city, too.

A lot of times, after our rides in the car, but mostly those on the St. Charles Street car, we'd find ourselves philosophizin about life, the south, slavery, and racism. Our favorite topic centered around the divisions within the New Orleanian black family. We could talk for hours on end about that whole light skinned versus dark skinned, creoles versus non-creoles, and good hair versus non-good hair idiosyncrasies. Hell, we used to trip off of the fact that both of us were actually attendin an historically black university where, according to our dark skinned tones, we wouldn't've been able to attend back in the day because we wouldn't've passed Xavier's paper bag test. Deep shit, ya'll. Deep shit.

Well, getting back to our outings, if we weren't too caught up into our societal/philosophical/historical debates or discussions, and it happened to be a Thursday night, we'd later find ourselves at Jimmy's in Pigeon Town, which was between the River Bend and uptown around Carrolton and Claiborne streets. Ya see, Thursday night was not only Ladies' Night, but it was reggae night, as well. And the fact that he liked reggae just as much as I did, and was a pretty good dancer, too, only added on to the many brownie points he easily accumulated jus bein him. The band that played was called One Love, and they used to easily put me in my windin mood - a groove Deron fell into with ease.

He even liked coming with me to Mama May's house from time to time. She and Uncle Charles really liked him. We'd all talk for hours about life, God, the unknown, etc. And Uncle Charles was always good at keepin us in stitches with his funny stories and exaggerated theatrics.

Funny, now that I think about it, Deron taught me one of my favorite past-time activities - shootin pool. That was our Sunday thing if we didn't have a lot of assignments or projects due that week. Initially, I liked the sexiness of the game. Especially, when he would come up behind me to show me how to hold and aim the pool stick. Oooh, I used to love the smell of him. His scent was sweet and spicy with a lil must (if that makes any sense). Umph. Oh so intoxicating. But, after a while, I decided to really pay attention to what he explained about the game, and eventually got into the mathematical angles associated with it. (Math was always my favorite subject.) I beat him, maybe, three times out of the hundred times we played. But, I learned a lot from him, and I must say that I'm excellent at pool, still, to this day.

I know it may seem like we did a lot for college students. But, you have to understand that I'm really only sharing the highlights. We were truly avid students. I like the fact that though school was top priority for Deron, he loved hangin out and tryin new stuff. And the cool thing was that money was never really an issue cuz one of his uncles, his favorite uncle in fact, always sent him money to make sure he never was without. And since he wasn't the type to spend it all at once, he always had money to take us out with when we wanted and needed to get away from our studies.

Damn. Nanh Deron was my boo fa real, ya'll. He was so gentle with me. We shared a lot of tender, intimate moments, that were, believe it or not, non-sexual. During that time, I was still a virgin. And though sometimes we both got hot and bothered, he knew not to press me cuz I was adamant from the start that I wasn't ready to have sex. Ooooh! To think, after all these years, I still get goose bumps at the thought of him. Well, that unforgettable courtship lasted a little over seven months. In fact, at that time, I was convinced that we'd get married. It just felt natural.

But, it turned out that marrying Deron was not my fate. One weekend, he had to go home to attend that favorite uncle's (the one I mentioned a moment ago) funeral. Apparently, his uncle found out that his wife was cheatin on him. And when he went to confront the other man, a fight broke out which ended with Deron's uncle being stabbed to death. Deron was devastated, to say the least. His pain was crazy deep because this uncle was more like a father to him who pretty much supported and encouraged his studies at Xavier and taught him how to be a man per se. Though he really wanted me to fly with him to Atlanta, I couldn't find anyone to cover my shifts at work. Humph, and between you and me, I really didn't want to go. I don't care for funerals. And I didn't want that to be the circumstance on how I met his family. So, my baby flew to Atlanta alone. I remember the details like they just happened a second ago. Though I wasn't happy about the circumstances of his trip, I was kinda giddy that he left me his car to use over the weekend while he was gone. We agreed to keep it parked on Palmetto, both, Friday and Monday so I'd know where it was on Friday when I got out of class and he'd know where it was on Monday after his last class. You're probably wonderin why I didn't take him to and from the airport. But, it just so happen that I had class when he was departin on Friday and arriving on Monday morning. And my baby never wanted me to miss class on his account. He was so sweet and thoughtful like that. He got one of his boys to give him rides to and from the airport.

Well, here it goes, ya'll. That Friday night after he left, when I returned to the dorms from work, my roommate, Queenie, was gettin ready for a party that her boyfriend's cousin was throwin in Gert Town, a not-so-desirable neighborhood directly across from Xavier. She made a big thing over how she and I wasn't hangin out as much since me and Deron started talkin - and why I should hang out with her that night with him gone and all. I reminded her that she was missin in action a lot with her boyfriend, Christopher, as well. But her comeback about how we always have an excuse when it comes to double dating with them or hangin out with their group of friends was so true cuz Deron didn't like Christopher or his boys. Apparently, he caught one of Christopher's friends, Anthony, starin at me the one time we all went to the movies together. Since then, we either rolled solo or with his peeps. Anyway, I was really missing Deron. And the only reason why I gave into pleas of me accompanying Queenie to the party was because she made a good point of me missing him less if I had something else to focus on. It made sense then. But oh, how I wish I'd stayed at the dorms, altogether.

Anyway, I decided to go and changed into a cute, denim straight skirt with a back split with my favorite white cotton blouse with soft ruffles at the collar and delicate lace at the capped sleeves with some white flats. No one couldn't tell me that I wasn't all that. But, as we were walking to Queenie's car, I instantly changed my mind and I decided to go by Mama May's. I'd just remembered that she told me that there was some gumbo waitin on me. Of course Queenie was disappointed, but I explained to her that I just didn't feel like partying. So, I went back to our dorm room, changed into an old jersey-knit mini-skirt, a t-shirt, some tennis shoes and packed a bag. I figured I might as well spend the night since it was almost 9:30 p.m.

On my way to Mama May's, I stopped at the drugstore, K&B, to get some cookies-n-cream ice cream. I figured that, together, the gumbo, ice cream and Mama May would numb me pretty good where, hopefully, I wouldn't miss Deron too much.

Well, to my surprise and later disdain, I ran into Lil Redd, an old friend from back in the day, (before I moved to Cali 'back in the day'), as I was coming out of K&B. He used to be my cousin, Kyle's, best friend. Lil Redd's real name is Anthony L. Carpenter, III. Both him and his dad are red skin toned and have sandy-brown hair. So everyone called them Big Redd and Lil Redd. At the time, I was so happy to see him that I gave him a big, long hug. The last time I'd seen him was during a visit, at Christmas, when I was sixteen years old. Well, before I knew it, forty minutes had passed as we played catch up and reminisced 'bout all sorts of things, including his crush on me back in the day. Lil Redd was the first guy I ever tongue kissed. And though we never were girlfriend and boyfriend, every boy at school and in the neighborhood knew not to look my way - that I was off limits. I thought it was cuz my cousin Kyle, who was a good fighter, had told everyone to lay off of me and my cousin, Mya. But no, that night, I found out that Lil Redd had put the threat out. Well, at least, that's what he said. Funny, I felt a little guilty for feeling flattered by the revelation.

After we soaked in the moments, he invited me back to his house - he said that even though his parents went to the 'country' for the weekend, that Patrice, his older sister who used to baby sit us when our parents went to card parties and cookouts, would love to see me. I knew that it was a little after 10:00 and I'd neglected to call Mama May, from the dorm, to let her know that I was coming over. So, as I accepted Lil Redd's offer, I decided to just stop by for a minute and head back to the dorms afterwards.

As I was parking my car in front of Lil Redd's childhood home, I noticed that only the light of the TV in the living room was on. The rest of the house was dark. I didn't think much of it cuz as long as I could remember, Patrice was always on the phone in the living room watching TV. When we walked into the house, into the living room, Lil Redd turned on a lamp and called out to Patrice. But there was no answer. He told me to have a seat while he went to see where Patrice was. I took a seat and began to look around at the familiar surroundings. It's almost like I stepped into a time capsule. There were old childhood school pictures of Lil Redd and Patrice all over the living room. And even though everything was neatly organized, there was dust everywhere - just like when we were kids. Right as I flashed back to this one time when Patrice got a whuppin, on the front porch in front of everybody, for lyin about cleanin up, Lil Redd returned with two glasses of Kool-Aid in his hands. As soon as we made eye contact, we busted out laughing cuz, as kids, we all loved Kool-Aid. And Lil Redd was forever gettin on punishments and catchin' whuppins for drinking all the Kool-Aid before dinner - especially after his mama told him to only drink water during the day due to him being a hyper child.

Any way, he nonchalantly said that Patrice must have stepped out, but that he didn't think she'd be gone long cuz she hadn't mentioned she was goin anywhere before he'd left the house earlier. I took my glass of Kool-Aid as we eased into a conversation about our present lives. He talked about him havin a hard time at Florida A&M and how he wanted to transfer to U.N.O., the University of New Orleans - said that he missed New Awlins and wanted to move back home. Afterwards, he got this weird look in his eyes and started askin me what I was up to and if I was seein anyone. That was my cue to blush and gush about Deron. So instead of getting up to leave after seeing that weird look in his eyes, I began telling him about Deron. But before I could really get into a good description he had swooped into my personal space sayin crazy stuff like, 'I bet he don't kiss like I do'; 'I bet he'd never love you like I always did', 'come on, Corin, forget that nigga'; 'get up with me.' So, of course I'm stunned. I immediately stood up and began backing away from him as he stood and tried to kiss me. I raised my hand to slap the shit out of him, but he grabbed it and bent it behind my back as he forcefully pulled me to him with his other hand. He began kissing my face like a mad man and tried to stick his tongue in my mouth.

I was so confused. I didn't know whether to keep my mouth shut to prevent his tongue's entry or call for help. Though my body felt paralyzed with fear, my mind told me to yell for help. So, I did. And, as soon as I did, he crossed one of his legs behind mine, causing my knee to buckle, which resulted in us crashing to the floor where I bumped the back of my head, badly. He raised both of my arms over and behind my head and held my wrists together with one of his hands. He maneuvered my legs opened with his legs, moved the crouch of my panties to the side with his free hand, and began fingering me. I was beggin and yelling for him to stop, tryin to get from up under him, and praying to God, it seems, all at once. And then that weird, scary look came as he told me that I better shut the fuck up or he'd hurt me. I was thinking, *So what are you doin now, makin me feel good?* And he started whining about how he didn't want to hurt me - that he always loved me. And I was like *Oh my God, this boy is crazy* - as if his actions moments before were that of a normal, respectable guy. Ignoring his warnings of him hurting me, I continuously tried to maneuver myself from up under him as well as free my hands from his one-handed grip. There was no way I was gonna go out like a chump. But his strength and body weight overpowered me. And before I knew it, I felt his penis near my vagina.

In that instance, I flashed back to a few years earlier when I lived in California - when I was always having disagreements with my father about going over my friends' houses in the neighborhood. Ya see, my dad was extremely strict. When he allowed me to go outside, I couldn't go beyond the front yard. Of course my friends either lived around the corner, at the opposite end of the block than me, or in a totally different neighborhood. And, it really didn't matter if my friends' parents were home or not, my father was very adamant about me only going as far as the front yard. Now, please keep in mind, we lived on a corner lot. The way the house was situated, along with our backyard, one side of the house took up half of a short block and the other side of the house was the first of about eight homes on the block it was perpendicular to.

Since I couldn't go over my friends' houses, they had to come to mine. The only problem was that their fathers had similar rules. But three of my closest friends, at the time, were so lucky cuz two of them lived next door to each other, while another one lived across the street from them. Anyway, I'll never forget the many nights of me overhearing my parents argue over me hanging out at my friends' houses. My mother was always the voice of reason, expressing that she trusted me to always do the right thing and leave a situation if I ever felt uncomfortable.

Well, one evening, my dad was going on and on about how I was talking to this guy outside on the corner - about how he wasn't sure how I'd carry myself in other people's homes since I didn't exhibit any class in front of my own. Ya see, earlier that particular evening, when he arrived home driving his BMW, I was leanin against his classic 1975, burgundy mustang as I was talking to a twelfth grader from my school. I was in the tenth grade at the time. It was getting close to dark, but the street lights hadn't come on yet, which were my signals of when to go inside. After my father pulled into the garage, he told me to come inside and waited until I said goodbye and walked toward the garage before he hit the button to close the garage door. He matter-of-factly told me to go in the front door and lock up. Once I shut the door behind me, after entering the house, he got in my face about standing on the corner talkin to some guy - insinuating hooker tendencies. When I reminded him that we lived on the corner and that he wouldn't allow me to leave from in front of the house, he became more irritated with me and ordered me to my room.

"Aw-ooouuuccchhh! Oh my God. Please help me!"

Just then, Lil Redd tried to enter me. The pain was excruciating. I tried to tell him to stop, but the words got lost somewhere in space as he lunged into me like a mad man. I must have blacked out for a while cuz the next thing I remembered was him standin over me, ordering me to get up. I tried to move, but was stifled by the pain. I remember wondering, so am I a whore now; maybe my dad was right after all - that I don't know how to act around boys. Some kind of way I managed to roll onto my side and brace myself up with my left hand. I remember that so clearly cuz through my teary-eyed blurred vision, I saw him handing me something pink and grabbed it, out of reflex, with my right hand. There was so much goin on in my head - so many thoughts, voices, cries, and moans. Somehow, it registered that he handed me a towel and was telling me to clean myself up. A part of me didn't want to put my hand anywhere near my vagina cuz of the pain and partly because I began to feel shameful and dirty, and I knew, through my mind's eye, that he was watching me. Humph! Ain't that something, of all the times my psychic abilities decide to kick in, it was then. I silently started talkin to my psyche, *so you couldn't've warned a sista in the parking lot at K&B, hunh?*

As I tried to get up, I felt a warm, wet sensation sliding down my legs. Of course when I looked down, I discovered that it was blood, and began sobbing as I forced myself to stand up. Through blurred vision, I saw him approaching me. I flinched when I felt his hand on my arm. You won't believe this, but that mothafucka had put his arm around me and was trying to comfort me by softly telling me not to cry - but at the same time accusing me of wanting to have sex with him. Sex! Sex?! He shattered my heart, compromised my physical strength, ripped up my dignity, scratched up my grace, took away my virginity, and bruised my body and soul. But in his ignorant, crazed, deranged mind, we had sex?! Disgusted and filled with an unexplainable bravery, I pulled from his embrace, wiped the blood as it dripped along my leg, and managed to grab my purse as I awkwardly limped-walked out of the house. As I was walking out of the door, he warned me that if I ever told a soul, he'd kill me. Feeling a chill pass through my bones, I began trembling as I searched my purse for my keys.

Waxing Gibbous

Dance to the music resounding within your soul.

The Blazing Numbing Effect

Once I was in the car, I prayed for comfort and sought out GOD's hands, feet, limbs, heart, and everything I could think of as I drove back to the dorms. I just needed to feel some kind of warmth, because my bones felt cold.

After I parked, I retrieved an old oversized sweatshirt of Deron's out of the trunk of the car, and tied it around my waist before I slowly walked into the dorm. Thankfully, I didn't run into anyone. I was able to walk directly to my room without having to interact with a soul. Once I was inside of my room, I began to cry and pray. I was so confused, y'all. I didn't know what to do. I felt so lonely, dirty, guilty, and full of shame. I kept beating myself up from not goin straight to Mama May's, to the party with Queenie, or stayin at the dorms, like I was gonna do in the first place, to wash my hair. Damn!

I was scared shitless and confused about reporting it to the police. I figured they'd say it was my fault for wearing that mini skirt, he'd get off, and come find and kill me. And I just knew that if I told any of my friends or family, they'd confront him which would propel his crazy ass to find and kill me. I couldn't believe my predicament or the thoughts I was having. I felt very small and helpless and couldn't keep my body from shakin. I smelled him all over me and just wanted him off me. So I stood up to start taking my clothes off so that I could shower. But as I slowly walked to my closet to get my robe, I discovered that the pain between my legs came from two different places, my vagina and a gash on my inner thigh. And that it was the gash that was causing the blood I kept having to wipe away. Eeeewww! Did he cut me with a knife or could the blood have come from the zipper from his jeans? Then, all of a sudden, before I could make sense of the gash, as if I heard someone abruptly whisper his name from some unknown place, I jumped at the thought of Deron. What would I tell him? How could I explain? Would he still want me? The volume of everything was so loud from the shame, ho-ish feelin, fear of death, confusing thoughts, his scent, disappointment, physical and emotional pain to my lost virginity, blood on my clothes, pierced heart, and the suspended explanations to everyone, that I collapsed to the floor shivering, crying, and blanking in and out of consciousness.

I guess I must have passed out, from exhaustion, because I was a little shocked and afraid when I opened my eyes to a panic-stricken Queenie calling my name. For a moment, I didn't know where I was. And because everything was so blurry (probably from me crying and just wakin up), I thought, for a moment, that I was in a dream. But, when I came to, and focused in on Queenie, I realized that not only was I not dreamin, but that she could see the shame bestowed upon me - dried up blood on my skirt and legs.

First, we just looked at each other, both of us confused and in shock for our own separate reasons. A part of me wanted to be cleaned up before Queenie got back. My mind and heart was so weighed with confusion that I hadn't even decided who'd I tell, if anyone. Not knowing how to begin, or really what to say, I sat up slowly and leaned my back against my bed as an effort to help me focus and pull one of those suspended explanations, I mentioned earlier, down into my thoughts and out through my mouth. But, before I could speak, everything vividly came back to me, and I started trembling and crying again. She sat on the floor beside me and held me as we gently rocked from side to side. She began repeating that everything was gonna be all right, that we'd get through this. Through my cluttered, confused mind, I felt her love and concern, and my tears eventually subsided somewhere in time. We sat in silence for what seemed like an eternity before she said, "Let's get you cleaned up."

I asked her to check if anyone was in the communal showers. She knowingly left the room without me needing to explain why. When she returned, she told me that no one was in there. And given that it was 2:00 a.m. on a Friday night, no one would probably be walkin in. So, we both went to shower in our favorite stalls that were about three stalls apart.

Normally, Queenie would have brought her radio, but I guess it slipped her mind. Once I was finished, I noticed Queenie had already left the shower. I thought it funny that I hadn't heard her water stop running. I guess I must have zoned out as I tried to wash the night away and get rid of his scent. But, that didn't help cuz I still remembered everything and I still smelled him on me. It's almost like his scent was embedded within all of my pores.

When I opened the bathroom door to step out into the hall, Queenie was standin there waitin on me. She took my towel and night-kit as we walked to our room. Once the door was shut, she asked me if I was ready to talk about it. I simply nodded and stared into space for about five minutes before I repeated the gory events of my evening. Once I was finished, she said she understood my hesitancy of telling the police, but told me it would be the best thing to do right now, especially since everything was so fresh in my mind. She kept repeating that he had to pay for this and that she was confident that between my family, friends, Deron, and a restraining order, that Lil Redd wouldn't be able to get near me. Well, to say the least, I wasn't convinced, and the mention of Deron's name crushed my spirit so much that I folded myself into a ball, on my bed, and cried some more. Queenie rubbed my back as she continued trying to persuade me to go to the police.

After about thirty minutes, she was able to persuade me into letting her take me to the hospital. Since she didn't have a car, she drove me in Deron's. I just wanted to make sure he hadn't damaged anything given the pain I was in. Cuz, since I was a little girl, I knew I wanted to be somebody's mama - that I wanted to experience childbirth. Plus, I knew he didn't wear a condom which prompted two continuous prayers on our way to the hospital. The first was that I wasn't pregnant by him, and the second was that he didn't give me a sexually transmitted disease. I couldn't believe that I, good-girl-by-the-book-yes-ma'am/sir-no-ma'am/sir-virgin, Corin Rivers, was going through any of this. I was hoping and praying that I was in someone else's nightmare and that I'd soon wake up, panting and sweating, to the sound of my alarm clock.

Well, once at the hospital, I was assigned a social worker/counselor who asked me a series of questions about the rape and explained to me that she and the healthcare providers of the state of Louisiana were mandated by the law to report sexual assault cases to the local authorities. Once I told her why I refused to report it, she simply held my hand and nodded that she understood. She told me that she still had to file the report. But, that she wouldn't submit it to the police department until the end of all of my examinations. That way, if, within the time I was at the hospital, I decided to report the rape to the police, I could wait for them to arrive or slip out of the doors before they entered. When I realized what she was saying, I began crying tears of joy. She matter-of-factly stated that one in six women is a victim of rape or attempted rape - and that it's a shame that most victims remain silent. She said she empathized with the silence though. After re-telling the gory details and answering her questions, she continuously emphasized to me that it was not my fault - that it did not matter, for example, even if I had all of my clothes off with my legs wide open. If I did not consent to having sex, then it is considered rape. Before rapping everything up, she gave me some psychological information designed to help rape victims' psyche. But she made sure that I understood the importance of seeking counseling and pointed out an extra sheet of paper detailing free counseling sessions for individuals and groups at the local 'Y'.

Once the social worker left, my nurse entered the room about ten minutes later. I'm telling you that she had to be the sweetest woman on earth, at that time. Her name was Lily Anne. She was a petite Creole woman with dark hair pulled up in a bun on the side. I'm guessing that she was probably in her thirties. She had a warm smile and a soothing southern drawl. Throughout the very embarrassing and uncomfortable examination, she tried her best to convince me to report the rape. Her soothing voice and gentle nature helped me to relax. She told me not to worry about being pregnant given the date of my last period. But, offered me the 'morning after' pill just in case. And since I didn't want to take any chances, I gladly accepted the prescription. I was relieved to have the option of not carrying his child. But, then I became hysterical with fear about contracting an STD (sexually transmitted disease). It was almost like she read my mind because she began explaining that I had two options on how to deal with the probability of being exposed to an STI (sexually transmitted infection), her term for STD. She explained that I could have contracted hepatitis B, chlamydia, gonorrhea, syphilis, herpes, genital warts, bacterial vaginosis, and trichamoniasis. As she was talkin, I was like damn, I had never heard of some of those diseases before. She went on to state that they could treat most of them right away via my consent, with a follow-up examination and testing within the next two weeks, or I could wait to see if I developed any signs and symptoms, and treat them accordingly with a follow-up visit in two weeks. I decided upon the former. Again, I didn't want to take any chances. She explained to me that unfortunately there wasn't a medication to offset herpes. I actually remembered that fact from my health class in high school. And although her reminder didn't sit easy with me, I did feel relieved that most of the others were treatable.

Then there was that whole HIV monster that created a series of chills throughout my body and queasiness within my stomach. Even though I took an HIV test, she encouraged me to come back within six months to take another one because, then, it was too soon to detect the virus. Though there was some torn tissue from his forcefulness and from me being a virgin, Nurse Lily Anne assured me that everything appeared to be fine and that I shouldn't have any problems having children in the future. She encouraged me to take warm soaks to alleviate some of the discomfort as well as explained that the physical pain would more than likely subside completely within four to five days with or without the soaks. Before I left, she gave me a packet of pamphlets encompassing information about the sexually transmitted diseases she spoke of earlier along with some condoms which I happily passed on about half of them to Queenie with the warning of her not always depending on Christopher to protect her.

That entire ordeal at the hospital took about three hours. Both Queenie and myself were spent by the time we got back in the car. On the way back to the dorms, I made up my mind that I was gonna call in sick to Popeye's, both, Saturday and Sunday. I needed to sleep in. I was emotionally, mentally, and physically exhausted from EVERYTHING.

Humph, but let me tell you, the shit got crazier the next morning. I woke up to someone bangin on the door and callin my name simultaneously. First, I looked around for Queenie, and was perplexed to find that she wasn't there. She hadn't mentioned she had to go anywhere this morning. After glancing at my digital alarm clock that glared 9:33

a.m., I forced myself out of bed, flinching as the pain between my legs reminded me of last night's events. I annoyingly swung the door open and found a jittery, impatient resident assistant named Diane, telling me that my aunt May was on the phone and that it was an emergency. First, I was thinkin why didn't Mama May call my room. But, after glancing at the phone, I saw that Queenie unplugged it probably so that it wouldn't disturb me if it rang.

After Diane gave me the message, she jetted to the bathroom down the hall, which explained her jitters. I quickly put on my robe and slippers and walked as fast as I could to the phone. I didn't know what to think. What kind of emergency could Mama May be callin about. I began to panic, thinking that either my parents or my sister were hurt, or worse, that they all were dead. I cursed Lil Redd for the pain that prevented me from getting to the phone faster than I did. Even though I hadn't run, I was out of breath, from panic once I said hello. Upon hearing my voice, Mama May quickly confirmed that I still had Deron's car this weekend and began telling me that she needed me to pick her up and bring her to the Carpenter's house because her car was in the shop. Apparently, Uncle Charles wasn't home and she needed to get there as soon as possible to console Rita, Mrs. Carpenter, cuz they found their son, Lil Redd, dead in their living room a few hours earlier. She said that it looked like he shot and killed himself cuz the gun was next to him on the floor and the police confirmed that there was only one set of fingerprints on it - his. She then began sayin how she didn't know how to break the news to Kyle and Mya.

Okay, so you know that I am stunned out of my mind and didn't know what to say or how to respond. The first thought was similar to good, I ain't gotta worry 'bout him tryin to kill me. But, was I supposed to feel sorry for him? Now, how would I look accusing a dead guy of rapin me just the night before? Who would believe me? Who would sympathize with me? What kind of person would I be if I ignored what my aunt had just shared and turned around and share some disturbing news of my own - MAMA MAY, THAT MOTHAFUCKA RAPED ME LAST NIGHT! But of course I would never speak that way to my aunt. In fact, I barely faked a surprised expression of concern. I told her that I wasn't feeling well and that I'd see if Queenie could take her over there when she came back to the dorm - that I'd been dealing with a stomach virus since the middle of the night. She told me not to worry myself or Queenie, that she'd ask her neighbor's son. She thought I'd want to be there since we were all so close growing up, but understood that I was feelin bad and would check on me later. As soon as I hung up the phone, I tried to briskly walk to the bathroom cuz I felt like everything that was in my stomach was about to come up. But right before I reached for the bathroom door, Diane came rushing out of it. We collided and I threw up all over her legs and shoes. Before I could apologize, I felt another episode, got to my feet, and ran to a toilet just in time to throw up more. I ended up staying in there for about 20 minutes, throwing up, it seems, every other minute. Obviously, after a while, only liquid was coming up and it was bitter as hell. Once everything began to subside, I heard Queenie talkin to Diane in the hallway. It sounded like Diane was telling her what happened, from her perspective, as Queenie offered to help her clean up the hallway. Diane told her that I probably needed more help - that I'd been in the bathroom for a while. Queenie, then, came into the bathroom and asked me if there was anything she could do for me. My voice was hoarse as I asked her to help me to my feet. As she helped me up, my eyes began to water. I couldn't believe that not only was I living inside of this real-life horror flick, but that I was the leading lady. Once we got to our dorm room, Queenie explained that she'd caught a ride with her mentor/big sister to get us some bagels and orange juice. I nodded my head in gratitude and said maybe later. She asked me if I thought I was having a reaction to the medication I took the night before. I thought I was answering her before she shook my shoulder a little and asked if I was all right - if I'd heard what she said. When I snapped out of my daze, I told her about Mama May's phone call. Once I finished, she heavily sat beside me and just hugged me. I cried some more until there were no more tears to cry. We sat there for at least an hour in silence.

At some point, Queenie encouraged me to lie down and get some rest. I did just that. I was in and out of consciousness the entire weekend. Everything was such a blur. Sunday, at around 6:00 p.m., Queenie suggested that I take a shower and ride with her to the store. In other words, she wanted to use the car. She said I could stay in the car if I wanted, but that I needed to get out of bed. I took her suggestion. I knew that I couldn't live in my depression forever - even though it felt safe, warm, and confusing, all at the same time.

Coincidentally, when we pulled up to the store, we ran into Patrice, Lil Redd's sister. Well, maybe I shouldn't say we ran into her cuz once I saw her, I pretended she was just a stranger walkin by. Thankfully, she didn't glance in the car. She wore a saddened expression that screamed desperation. I began to feel sorrow for her loss and cursed myself in the process, given the circumstances. But, then I decided not to be hard on myself. I mean who enjoys witnessing misery? Certainly not me. So, for a fleeting moment I felt compassion for her for grieving over her only brother - her only sibling. But, in the back of my mind, a part of me was glad he was gone. *GOD, please forgive me and help me to forgive him, as well. I never thought I could hate someone. I don't like this feeling. Please, help me, GOD!*

Once Monday arrived, I didn't have the energy nor the courage to go to any of my classes. Partly because I was afraid of runnin into Deron. I knew he was perplexed as to why I hadn't returned any of his three calls from Sunday night, and would be waiting for me either before or after one of my classes. So of course, I wasn't surprised when Candy, another R.A., came knockin at my door around 5 p.m. As soon as I opened the door, she informed me that I had a visitor and quickly turned and walked away. I knew it was Deron, but I asked who it was any way. She stopped in her tracks with annoyance, and sighed, "Deron" before she continued to the front desk. Ignoring her attitude and rudeness, I shut my door tryin to figure out what I'd tell him, if I'd tell him anything at all. After changing out of my pajamas and into some jeans and a t-shirt, I put my flip flops on and went to the lobby. Thankfully I was able to walk normal. The pain and discomfort had, just about, subsided completely.

As usual, my heart melted when I saw my baby. Damn, he looked so cute, especially with a concerned, questioning expression on his face. I soaked up his hug and bit back tears. I loved him so much. I wondered if our love was strong enough to withstand all the shit that just happened.

Well, the easy way out was for me to play the sick card - stomach virus. He quickly understood and didn't press me to leave with him. He stayed for about a half an hour, talkin bout his trip, the funeral, and his family. I could tell that he was sad, and tried to console him when I walked him outside. We hugged for a long time - both of us inwardly hurting.

He pecked me on the lips goodbye. I remember him lookin so vulnerable when he walked away.

Tuesday, I awakened with a sore throat and feelin achy all over. Luckily, I only had one class that day. By the time I made it back to the dorms, I was feelin horrible. At some point I had developed chills as well. Hoping to flush whatever I had out of my system, I drank a lot of the water, which I had stored in my closet, right before I took a nap. A few hours later, I woke up to Queenie entering the room with shopping bags. I quickly got up and ran to the bathroom. That water was beggin to come out of me. I remember feelin a weird sensation when I wiped myself after urinating. The area around my vagina felt itchy and a little irritated. Thinkin nothing of it, I blamed it on the cheap toilet tissue in the bathroom, and made a mental note to buy a softer brand the next time I was at the store. However, by the middle of Wednesday, it burned when I urinated. Anxiety and panic quickly filled me up. After my second class I ran to my dorm room to look for Queenie's schedule. I knew I needed to go back to the hospital, and prayed she'd go with me. As soon as I saw her and explained everything, she suggested that I go to the health center on campus. But, I didn't want to go there in case one of the student workers knew Deron or someone he knew. And I didn't want to explain my whereabouts to him 'til I was ready. She nodded her head, acknowledging that she understood, and accompanied me back to the hospital.

So, upon getting examined at the hospital, I was informed that the flu-like symptoms coupled with the cluster of opened sores near the opening of my vagina indicated that I might have gotten herpes. But, only a test would confirm it. Funny, I never thought to get a mirror to see what was causing the burning. I guess a part of me didn't want to know. I thought, shit. Opened blisters? Shit, shit, shit...

Unfortunately, when we returned the next day for the results, I was told that I did have herpes. Horrified, confused, and searchin for at least one answer to my repetitive question, 'why me', I burst into silent tears. My thoughts spiraled into multiple chaotic mental collisions followed by hysterical emotional wrecks. I couldn't believe that, I, Corin Stephanie Rivers, was actually the one going through all of this. This happened to other people. Bad girls. Fast girls. Not me. I mean, for real, are you fuckin kiddin me? All this time I've been stayin out of trouble. I'm the good girl.

I'm nineteen and still a virgin. Wait. Shit! I can't even say that any more. My friends and classmates from both high school and college have been wildin out for years – having sex like drinkin water. But, I'm the one being punished? What did I do wrong? I've carried myself like a young lady like I was told. *Why me, GOD? Please, help me understand. Why, me?*

Fortunately, it was Nurse Lily Anne who gave me the news. She sensed my despair and firmly held both of my hands in hers as she consoled me - trying to assure me that everything would be okay, that it wasn't the end of the world. Before I knew it, I looked at her as I said, "How do you know? Do you have herpes? Have you ever been raped?" I'll never forget her face when she answered no, she didn't have herpes, but, yes, she'd been raped. And further went on to explain the value in counseling, especially now that I've learned that I had herpes. She explained that, both, individual and group counseling will help me to heal mentally and emotionally by showing me that none of this was my fault and that I didn't do anything wrong. I listened intently because she just seemed so sincere, and I needed something to hold onto. Years later I realized that one of the hands of GOD I was searchin for came through one of his earth angels - Nurse Lily Anne. Once my tears subsided, she gave me some literature.

As I gathered my purse and jacket, Nurse Lily Anne told me that even though she didn't have herpes, she knew, through her work that I could still have a healthy sex life and children with an understanding man - that he could even be my current boyfriend. I thanked her and walked toward the door. Right before I opened it, she encouraged me that, in time, everything would be all right - to know in my heart that I did nothing wrong. She urged me never to blame myself.

When I left the hospital, Queenie went back to school and I caught a cab straight to Deron's apartment. I knew he'd be there studying and waiting for my call, especially since I hadn't spoken to him since Monday. I noticed his car keys in his hands when he entered the living room. I mustered up a smile from an unknown place within me and gave him a big hug. Though, we hugged a long time, I felt a heaviness from him I'd never felt before.

We drove out to the Lake, got out of his car, and walked hand-in-hand the length, back-and-forth, of one of the levees. It seemed like we walked silently for about thirty minutes. I wasn't sure what he was thinkin 'bout, probably missin his uncle. I know that I was simultaneously building up my courage to tell him everything, hold back tears, and preventing myself from running into the Lake and stayin. Finally, I opened my mouth and began telling him the whole story - from getting dressed for the party in Gert Town to the herpes test results today. Once I'd finished telling him everything, I noticed that we had stopped walkin. Initially when I looked up at him, I saw an expression I didn't recognize. Then I saw anger and hurt as tears ran down his face. Once he spoke, he kept asking why was I just now telling him all of this, that he thought we shared everything openly and honestly? I tried explaining that I didn't know how to share it cuz I couldn't believe that I had experienced it - that it felt like a bad movie I wished I could turn off. But, I guess that wasn't enough for him. Apparently he didn't want to talk any more. He looked at my hand in his as if he didn't know how it had gotten there, and just let it go - let me go. In that moment, I felt his spirit leave mine and my heart caved in. He turned and walked toward the car, and disgustedly said, "Let's go." Once we were in his car, I practically begged him to talk to me. But he never said a word. When we reached my dorm, he just said, "Goodbye Corin." Overwhelmed with grief, I got out of his car and watched him drive out of my life. I graduated from Xavier without ever seeing or speaking with him again.

A Much Needed Break

Now, that was some shit fo yo ass, right? Hell, wait. I mean fo my ass. Hahaha! I remember thinking that I'd never graduate - that I'd never get over the depression of the rape, having herpes, and Deron leaving me. Devastation lived within me for months. I kept askin myself and God, "Why me?" I'm the good girl. Why not Stacey, LaTronda, or Vanessa from high school? It's not that I wanted ill-will on them. But, they were the fast girls – always talkin bout the triple X-rated stuff they did with boys. And that was in high school mind you. Hell, I used to be appalled jus listenin to them sometimes. But, I wanted them to think that a good, studious girl like myself could be down, cool like that, with them - while all the while I was judging them in my head referring to them as the fast girls. Humph, karma is a motha.

Weeks after the rape, my life was such a fuzzy gray cloud, with a hint of a dot-sized blue sky. In other words, everything, everyone, and every experience felt lifeless, blurred, and blended into undefined colorless matter. I remember that I really had a hard time placing myself in a particular category. For instance, I couldn't look at myself as a good girl any more. Or, wait. Let me rephrase that. I didn't know how to look at myself as a good girl any more. I wondered if I was that ho that my daddy was implyin that I was for standing on the corner (in front of his house where I couldn't leave from in front of), a fast girl, or a I don't know what. It was like I became fixated on placin myself into a particular category. And what's worse, I couldn't imagine, visualize, or believe that anyone would ever want to be with me because I had herpes, an incurable disease, and hadn't yet been cleared of HIV, a fatal one. Humph. Nanh!

Oooh, oooh, oooh! That was some mo shit fo my ass. I don't know if ya'll feelin what I'm sayin to you. Shit! Hahaha! Please remember to ignore the laughter sometimes as, in some instances, it poses as nervous noise to fill uncomfortable moments.

But, I guess, the good news is that I obviously got through that initial turmoil all right cuz I'm sittin here tellin you my story, of which, demonstrates my courage to invite intimacy in my life again. Hence, Black and the few before him.

Yeah, some more good news disguised as that hint of a dot-sized blue sky, I mentioned earlier, is friendship. Let me jus say that it's really true about findin out who your true friends are when you're in need cuz my girl, Queenie, was and still is my Ace Boon Coon. Ya heard me? I don't know what I would've done without her. When Deron was missin in action, she was always there with a listening ear, thoughtful gesture, or a compassionate hug.

Humph. Sometimes when she thought I wasn't lookin, I could see the sadness in her eyes that she felt for me. And that, right there, hurt even more. Queenie never pressed hard about me not going to class during that first week after Deron left. Luckily, I didn't have any exams and she turned in the two papers I barely completed that were due in two different classes. Even though I resumed attending my classes the second week after Deron's departure, I, obviously, wasn't completely myself. In fact, one might have described me as a functioning zombie. I say functioning because the only things I forced myself to focus on were my classes. For weeks, I didn't go anywhere accept to class, my job at Popeye's, and back to my dorm. Thank God I was a cashier and not a cook cuz the way I was on automatic, not really conscious most of the time, I probably would have burned either a lot of chicken or the entire building down. Hahaha! Nanh that wouldn't have been cool at all.

Humph. I don't think I visited Mama May for two months straight. Luckily, in a dark kind of way, she was preoccupied keepin Mrs. Carpenter afloat after Lil Redd's death. By the time I did visit her, she was so worn out from maintaining her household and helping out at the Carpenters that we just sat on her porch in silence for a couple of hours speaking minimally. It was the most peace I had experienced in a long time.

A few weeks after that cool visit with my aunt, something within me clicked. I decided that I was tired of feeling sorry for myself. Though my feelings and wounds were still sorta organically raw at times, I knew that I had to push forward with my life. The most confusing and challenging concepts that I had to embrace was forgiveness of Lil Redd, Deron, and myself. I mean, I'd never been close to experiencing anything like what I went through. I knew that if and when I overcame the anger, hurt, shame, and guilt I felt toward myself, Lil Redd and Deron, that I'd be one hell of a woman. Who would've thought that forgiveness was so hard. Shoot, humph. You wanna know something? I'm honestly not sure I've forgiven them or myself, completely, to this day. But, I can say that I earnestly tried. I began journaling my thoughts, writing affirmations, and scheduling time to meditate when I knew Queenie would be away. I started praying more and crying less and felt better about myself. I think all of that helped me to move on with my day to day life with school and work. But, I know I built a wall around me when it came to guys and intimacy. I wasn't really interested in dating that year or the next. But I did, finally, contact the 'Y' and attended, both, individual and group counseling sessions.

It was, actually, during the time I was attending counseling at the 'Y' that Mama May recovered my lost voice I told you about earlier. I guess all the stuff started surfacing during the sessions, as I recounted the events of the rape and the fact that I couldn't bring Deron back into my life cuz he jus, sorta, disappeared. It was weird cuz I felt so completely powerless in one sense, but a little empowered in another - it sorta started clickin that the rape wasn't my fault.

I have to emphasize the sorta started clickin part cuz I was still confused about which category to place myself in. In fact, I remember, months after the rape, thinkin a lot about my fourth grade teacher, Mrs. Bordeaux. She used to say, "Y'all girls betta be mindful how y'all carry yourselves. Don't let these lil boys fill ya'll heads up with air cuz best believe that he'll take Sally down the alley. But he'll take Sal down the aisle." And, though that may be true in some cases, life, sometimes dictates the opposite outcome in others. Hence, me.

It was amazing, to me, how my friend Vanessa, who pretty much had sex with damn near half the football team in high school, got married the June after our freshman year in college to an electrical engineer major. And can you believe that they're still happily married after all these years?

I never would've thought that she, of all people, would be Sal, and me, Sally. Talk about a twist in my life's drama. Shit, Deron was a premed major. Remember?! Wasn't I supposed to be Sal?

Feelin a lil anxious, I sit upright at the edge of the chaise lounge and start fannin myself with my hand. *Oooh, shit! Why do I feel so hot? Why am I getting so upset? Damn, my heart feels like it's about to jump out of my body, it's beatin so fast. What's this about?* Thinkin back to that Sal versus Sally pondering, I realize that that's what got me all upset and that I need to get out of my head. Oooh, unh, unh. You know what ya'll, I's about to get my chill on. Enough of this story for tonight.

I wonder, aloud, of what I should do as I abruptly change gears. "Maybe a movie?" I say out loud to myself. "Hmmm." Leanin my head against the back of the chaise, I close my eyes in hopes to calm myself down. First, I try to focus on my breathing. But, my mind keeps takin me back to Vanessa, me being Sally, and then the rape. Instead of tryin to force myself not to think of anything, I decide to focus on my breathing as much as possible while I observe the different thoughts enterin my mind. Before long, my mind quiets down and I see a nondescript blue flower. *Hmmm.* I continue to breathe as I imagine a pale blue light all around me. After a while, I unconsciously open my eyes feeling much calmer. *Give thanks.*

Okay, so I know that the reaction I just had about Vanessa and me wasn't right or normal. Or, was it? I wonder why I got so angry. And, who exactly was I angry with? It couldn't have been with Vanessa or anyone from high school cuz, well, that just don't make no sense.

Jus rememberin that I said that I was gonna leave all that alone tonight, I decide to see what kind of movies Mama May and Uncle Charles have. Ohhh! Unh! Oooh! I guess I've been sittin for a long time cuz, shit, I'm feelin all stiff as I raise up off this chaise lounge. Hahaha! Damn, the image of a cat stretchin just entered my mind as I stretch my arms up in the air while my torso concaves forward with my legs in a half squat and my butt tootin out and up. Uh…uunnhhh! I chuckle to myself. I know I must've just looked a sight. But, damn, that felt good. I had to have released something with all of that stretchin, ooohin and uhhhin I had goin on. Shoot!

Once in the house, I lock the front door and engage the alarm. Before

I go to the family room to select a movie, I decide to see what Mama May left out for me to eat.

"Ohhh yeah!" I sing to the theme music from that Ferris Bueller movie. Once I open the refrigerator, my eyes automatically zoom in on a beautiful, healthy plate of food wrapped in some saran wrap. As I wink at the piece of healthily cut grilled salmon and blow a kiss at the seductive lookin green salad with carrots, tomatoes, garbanzo beans, and broccoli, my mouth begins to salivate – awaiting the upcoming party my taste buds will, no doubt, enjoy. Boi! Me and my aunt are kindred spirits I tell you. This is the perfect dinner for me tonight – not too heavy, not too light. Booyow!

Suddenly realizin that I only had a piece of watermelon today, I pass on heatin up my piece of salmon for two reasons. One, the oven and stove will take entirely too long. And two, I am not a fan of the modern contraption that produces *close to* instantaneous cooked results to food, a.k.a. the microwave, because it not only kills the nutrients within food, from the radiation used to heat the food up, but once the food enters the body, the radiation now embedded within the food, adds to the toxicity levels within our bodies. Thus, making all food and drink entering human bodies, by way of microwaves, mere non-substantiated matter that removes all hope of a balanced homeostatic environment. So, with that, I decide to eat my grilled piece of salmon cold and diced up on top of this awesome salad with some of Mama May's slammin homemade roasted garlic vinaigrette. Ohhh yeah! There's that theme music again. Hahaha! Now, it's movie time.

After I grab my plate of food, a fork, some napkins, and a bottle of water from the pantry, I turn the kitchen light off with my right elbow and head to the family room. Once there, I set my food and water down next to the lamp on the end table next to Uncle Charles' La-Z-Boy chair.

Lookin up at nothin in particular, I joke with my uncle as if he were here, "Yeah Unc, this La-Z-Boy's mine tonight, baby. Hahaha!" As I chuckle to myself, I damn near knock the lamp over tryin to turn it on. Damn, I swear I'm the clumsiest person I know. Once I steady the lamp, I clutch at my chest out of 'ohhh, how I don't wanna get in trouble' fear before I begin hearin my voice tremble from the relief of the outcome. "Ooooh, Lawd! Nanh, that was close. Shit, that's all I need is to scare

Mama May out of her sleep with the sudden shatter of one of her lamps hittin the floor. Humph, she needs to get some carpet or put a rug down in this joint. Hell, I don't care how gorgeous these hardwood floors are." Or maybe I jus need to be more careful. Hunhunhun! Smilin to myself over the sight of the little girl in me's reaction to the lamp scenario as well as my determination to keep my mood light, I ingest my last thought and cabbage patch over to the cabinet packed with damn near every movie ever made.

I really can't believe my eyes as I peruse over all of the DVDs and VHS tapes in front of me right now. Standing here makes me think that I need to extend my stay to a month, or hell, maybe even the whole summer. Lawd knows I got the vacation time at work.

Focusing back on the movies, I'm a little startled when my eyes fall upon my first, ever, favorite contemporary love story by an all black cast – *Love Jones*. Oooh, oooh, oooh, I'm feelin a happy dance comin on. This discovery deserves a drop it like it's hot (UUUNNHHH – hand slaps floor for affect) celebration. Happy, overjoyed, and tickled-pink over my movie, dinner, and good mood, I relax in my uncle's chair and commence to eatin my food and allowin Lorenz Tate, Nia Long, and Hollywood to enhance my outlook on happy endings. Black, who?

3 days later

Observin Mama May readin a book as she sits outside in the veranda, I revel at the peace and beauty radiating from her as I sit in the window seat from my guest room after just wakin up. I wonder for a moment about her love affairs – if she ever had any that went bad. You know, if any of them gave her any grief. Funny, she looked up right at that moment as if to answer my thought. Before she resumes reading, she looks at her cell phone and takes a sip from what appears to be a glass of water. Ever since I can remember, her and Uncle Charles have been like two peas in a pod. But, I can't help wondering what life was like before my uncle appeared.

Before I can continue with my wonderings, I notice Mama May lookin toward the driveway with a curious expression. Yesterday she mentioned that her landscaper, a young man named Tariq, would be coming this morning to do some work. But, Mama May's stiffened body language and curious expression tells me that she doesn't recognize the truck approachin even though she must've just buzzed the gate to open from her cell phone. Right before I turn to get my robe, I see my aunt's expression change into a warm smile. Expelling my breath that I didn't know I was holding, I relax back into the window seat.

Mama May places her book on the table and walks toward the truck which has a sign on it that reads 'Zyon's Landscaping'. Well, she obviously knows the extremely handsome man that exits the truck cuz she gives him a genuine, firm Mama May hug. Oh, how I love her hugs. But, back to him. What is he, thirty-somethin? Unh. De-li-cious. I'm glad to know that I'm not bitter – that I can still appreciate some good ole eye-candy. Hunhunhun!

Curious about her company, but not wanting to be seen, I get up and step out of view from the window. But, I remain close enough so that I can see and hear their exchange. After the hug, the man opens the passenger door to his truck and reaches in for a hot minute. At the moment he emerges, Mama May clasps her hands together and paints a smile so big on her face I feel like I can feel her cheek touchin mine all the way in this house.

When the man closes the truck's door, I can see that he has a beautiful bouquet of sunflowers in his hands. He presents them to her with a slow half bow of his torso. "For you, ma'am."

"Well, well, well…"

How funny. It looks as though Mama May is at a loss for words. How sweet.

"Good morning, Ms. May. How you doin today?"

"Just fine, son. Thank you so much for these beautiful sunflowers." Gazing at them joyfully, she adds, "Ooh, they're just brightening up my heart already."

Smiling and shyly looking away, the man says, "You're too kind."

After pulling away from admiring the flowers, Mama May says, "Ooh, let me get a vase. I'll be right back." Opening the screen door, she calls back, "You know, Zyon, you threw me for a moment cuz I was expectin to see Tariq's wild head of locs all over the place, not to mention his new pickup truck he was showin off to me last week."

Ooh, his name is Zyon. I like that name. So, he owns the landscaping business? Hmm, okay. Impressive.

Not sure of how deep into the house she went, he raises his voice a notch as he chuckles a little, "Hahaha! Aw, yes, the new truck. Oooh, wait! My apologies, Ms. May. I hope I didn't frighten you."

Umph, he's polite and handsome.

Mama May chuckles before replying. "You know, Charles is always on me about not checkin to see who's at the gate before I buzz them in regardless of whether I'm expectin someone or not."

"He's right, you know."

"Yeah, yeah, yeah, I know. I'll work on it for sure after this morning. Ha! So, what brings you here today? Tariq sick?"

"Naw. Well, wait." He chuckles. "Maybe lovesick. Got him a girlfriend down in Macon who he claims needed him to come down right away. Humph."

Shakin his head, he walks onto the porch, out of my view. By the squeaking sound I'm hearin, I determine that he's sittin in one of the rockin chairs on the porch.

Damn, now I can't see his fineness.

"And instead of calling another worker, I figured I'd come touch up things around here." He lowers his voice when he hears my aunt's footsteps approaching. "You know, see how my favorite client is doing."

Walking onto the porch with, what I imagine is her tall, clear, glass vase I saw on the kitchen counter yesterday, she laughs heartily. "Oh, you know me, Zyon. This here ole lady is always doing just fine. GOD is here to keep me company and my soul whole." She pauses for a moment before she adds, "And my sweetie pie keeps my heart blissfully light."

I can imagine she had a twinkle in her eye when she referenced my uncle. They're so in love. So that I can get a good look at Mama May's company, I quietly walk down the hall toward the front door and stand at an angle where neither of them can see me in the foyer – particularly the gentleman since I still have on my nightgown and a scarf on my head.

"You know, I'm so proud of Tariq." Pointing in no particular direction, Mama May admiringly says, "just look at what he's done with my landscape. Every day I discover a new angle of GOD's work through his hands. That child's come a long way. You've trained him better than well."

Squinting her eyes at Zyon, Mama May lowers her voice like she's about to tell a secret, "He isn't in any trouble with this here girl, is he?"

Shaking his head, he replies, "Naw, Ms. May. You know how young love is. They just wanted to spend time with each other. He's doin just fine."

It looks like Mama May's examining Zyon's words and face to see if he's being straight with her. I'm very familiar with that so-called examination. And it looks as though he probably genuinely respects my aunt given the way he's politely allowing her quiet scrutiny of him.

Gesturing toward the garage, Zyon asks, "You got company? A new car?"

"Hunh?" Mama May asks as she follows the direction of his eyes. "Oh, that's my niece's rental car. She's visiting me from New York. I'm hopin she stays the whole summer." With a sparkle in her eye, she says, "She's a nice girl. Beautiful. Smart."

Leave it to Mama May to big me up. But, shit, I'm sho not mad at her. Say more, say more!

Looking off in the distance, her voice trails off as she continues, "But something's troubling her right now. And it's troubling me, too, cuz she won't talk about it. And whatever it is has left her a bit haunted."

"Sounds serious, Ms. May."

"I know. I guess, in time, everything will be brought to the light."

Zyon sighs. "Yeah, I guess so."

Opening the screen door leading off of the porch and walking down the steps toward one of her gardens, Mama May yells back to Zyon, "So you helping me in my garden or not?"

Following her, Zyon smiles and shakes his head at her abruptness as he walks toward his truck. "Of course I am. Let me get some tools."

Jerk Chicken And A Glass Of Lemonade

Walking back to my room, I can't stop from smiling at the conversation I overheard between my aunt and the handsome landscaper whose super-fine presence commanded me to pay attention. Damn! He reminded me of someone - but I can't figure out who, for the life of me. Wait! Just then, Deron's face entered my mind's eye. "Deron." Talking to myself as I look in the mirror connected to the dresser, I wonder aloud, "Wow, I haven't thought of Deron so vividly in years the way I have since I've arrived here in Georgia." Damn, it was almost as if I could've touched his face jus now. "Is that who Mama May's friend reminds me of?" Shaking my head no, I turn around and begin making up my bed. Once I'm finished, I gather my toiletries and bath robe to bring with me to the bathroom so that I can take a shower. But right before I could leave the room, I hear my cell phone vibrating. So, I stop and stand still for a moment so that I can determine where it is, exactly. Following the sound, I retrieve it from under some clothes in the chair near the window. Upon looking at the display screen, I see Queenie's name.

Contemplating whether I wanna talk right now, I sigh before I answer, "Hey girl. Please don't be mad at me for not calling you back the other night. I just needed some time to myself."

"It's cool, sis. Trust me. Considering everything, I totally understand you needing your space. You know that I wouldn't have called again before you returned my call if it wasn't important."

"I know, girl. And of course you can stay at my place. You know that."

"I know. But I just needed to clear it with you, first, given your need to heal right now. And you never said, exactly, when you're planning to return to New York. I don't want to impede on your privacy."

Nodding my head, I agree. "You're right, I didn't say cuz I wasn't sure then. But, I've decided to stay the whole summer."

"Oh. Okay."

"So, anyway, what happened, girl? Oh boy's psychotic?"

"Girl, that's not even the half. But before we get into me, tell me what's goin on with you. How are you?"

Realizing that this will probably be an in-depth conversation based upon Queenie's sudden need to crash at my place and the inner shit goin on with me, I go ahead and set my things on the bed and sit back in my favorite place – the window seat I was watchin Mama May from earlier. I love it cuz it's an oversized, cushioned window ledge that's big enough for two people to comfortably sit on/in, and me to stretch out on/in and allow the sun to kiss my body with its rays as I look at all of the 'beautiful' of Mama May's landscape. Once situated, I pause for a moment, close my eyes, and wonder how much I wanna share about me right now.

"Hello? Corin?" Queenie slightly raises her voice, probably thinkin that one of our cell phones lost its signal. "Hello? Corin?"

Quickly answering to her second attempt, I respond, "I'm better than I was when I arrived here five days ago."

"Good, Corin! You know that time heals everything."

Sensing Queenie's thoughts, I sigh. "Don't I know it. I believe time and space heals. Sometimes, you not only have to let time pass, but you might have to distance yourself from the person and/or location of the event, as well, if you know what I mean."

"Yep. I feel you, ma." Softly giggling, Queenie shocks me with her memory of yesteryear, "Humph, I remember when you couldn't get out of the bed for a week straight after your break up with Deron. You have to admit that it's gotten waaayyy better."

Smiling inwardly as I reflect on the progression of my life since Deron, I admit, "You're right, Queenie. It has gotten a whole lot easier to deal with. Like I said, time and space…"

"I know it has, girl."

"Funny that you brought him up cuz his face just appeared in my mind's eye a few moments before you called me. It was so surreal. I felt like I could touch him."

"Knowing you, you're probably gonna run into him soon."

Smiling and looking at nothing in particular, I wonder aloud, "You think? Humph, now that would be a trip, hunh?"

"Uhhhh, ya think?"

"Okay, Queenie. What's the dealio with this Jamaican cat? I was hopin he was just the medicine you needed to get over Sule."

"I know, girl. Me, too. But, I only have myself to blame for this one. I mean, he told me that he was into voodoo. But, nooo, I didn't take heed. I ignored that bit of important..."

"Wait a minute!" I interrupted. "Did you just say voodoo?"

With a soft, embarrassed voice, Queenie answered, "Yep, that's what I said. And before you say anything further, I know that I have no one to blame but myself. I mean I strutted into this one with my eyes wide open, head held high, shoulders back, and a sway to my hips. Unfortunately common sense was nowhere to be found."

Sighing a pitiful chuckle, shaking my head, and rolling my eyes upward, I tell myself to listen to my friend and not to judge her cuz Lawd knows I've had my moments of forgettin who or what common sense was my damn self. Loneliness and lack of self-love are true motha fuckas. "Okay. Go ahead. I'm all ears." I have a feelin this story will take my mind off of my own story for a while. So, I welcome this distraction with the commitment of revisiting my reaction to that Sal versus Sally scenario very soon.

Queenie sensing my concern and tint of annoyance, plunges on with her story of how the crazy Jamaican dude was paranoid about everything from food to her havin any privacy while he was at her house. "Remember, the night you left was his birthday?"

Remembering, I nod. "Yes."

"Well, that night I had stopped to pick up some Jamaican food from Kadell's, complete with carrot cake and balloons to celebrate his birthday. I'm thinking that was the perfect way to celebrate someone's birthday you've only been datin for a month without goin overboard."

Nodding and attempting to lighten the mood a bit, I respond, "I agree. Pickin up the Jamaican food was thoughtful given your cookin skills."

Giggling in agreement, Queenie playfully snaps back with, "Shut up. Forget you. I can cook."

"Any way, you were sayin?"

"A-n-y waaayyy, his paranoid ass told me that he don't eat people's food who he don't know. So, I was like, are you kidding me? This is one of the best Jamaican restaurants in Brooklyn. It's always receiving rave reviews."

Reflecting upon the red snapper, rice and peas, plantains, and cabbage I had the last time I was there, I chime in, "Right, right. Kadell's food do be slammin. What?!"

"Ex-act-ly. I told him to trust me when I say that the food is better than good. But, he stood adamant about not eating the food. So, you know I'm pissed right now cuz I ordered jerk chicken for him which meant I couldn't save it for later for myself seeing that I don't eat chicken."

"Right."

"And you know, something had told me to get red snapper for him, too. Punk-ass nigga. Any way, you know I was beyond heated then."

I'm noddin my head as I visualize the scene. I know my friend was crazy upset by then seein as she don't like wastin food or money. "Yeah. I know you were. So, what did you do?"

"No, the question is what did that motha fucka do?"

"Oh Lord. What did he do?"

"That asshole proceeded to caress my breasts as he told me that he'd rather have me more than any food - thinkin that shit would turn me on."

"What? And what did you say?"

"I pulled back from him and looked at him like his ass was on his face. I went off on him for bein so ungrateful. I was like I went out of my way to stop at the restaurant, spent my hard earned money, got fuckin balloons and cake with candles, and all you gone say is that you don't eat other folks' food and you'd rather fuck any way. Shiiiit, can a sista get a thank you, motha fucka?"

Chucklin, I said, "Girl, you know you crazy. You better had told his ass somethin. So, what did he say after that?"

"Well, first he just looked at me stunned cuz I'd never cursed around him before. Then, I think he thought about everything I'd just said before he softly spoke his apology and gratitude. He pulled me close to him all fuckin tenderly and shit as he explained that he doesn't eat other people's food unless he watched them prepare it cuz you never know who's tryin to do voodoo on you."

"Hunh?"

"Exactly! Corin, girl, now it was my turn to be stunned. I realized that this man lives in constant fear thinkin that folks are tryin to do something to him."

"That shit is crazy, Queenie. Humph, spooky as hell."

"I know. Tell me about it. So, anyway, I stupidly went on to explain that the people at the restaurant didn't know that I'd ordered the food for him, and, that of course, I wouldn't add anything to the food. And do you know that when I looked at him he had a questioning look on his face."

"This is crazy, Queenie."

"So, me, BooBoo the motha fuckin fool proceeded to ask him if he thought I'd put something in his food. And that fool's response was, 'Let's drop it. You're getting upset, and I'd like to enjoy the rest of my birthday with you. I like you. Thank you for wanting to make my birthday special. I'm sorry for not saying it sooner.' He continued with how he didn't mean to make light of the situation - that all day he'd been thinking bout being inside of me. And I was thinking how I had been thinking the same until he arrived with this bullshit. And you know me, girl."

"Yep, I do. You fucked him, didn't you?

Silence.

"What is it with you in not wanting to hurt these guys' feelings? I mean, damn, Queenie, you should have made him leave. Not only had you wasted your money and time on him, but he practically told you that he didn't trust that you hadn't put anything in the food - that at the end of the day, you were only good for a good fuck."

"I know. But, I kept thinking of how it was his birthday, and how I didn't want to be the person to ruin it."

"You ruin it?! Do you know how crazy absurd that sounds? Wait, wait wait." Shaking my head and looking down while my right hand is raised partially, I apologize. "You know what? My bad. My apologies, sis. Hell, I for damn sho don't walk on nobody's water. I'm not tryin to judge you, jus want you to think more - honor you more."

"I know, Corin. You're right."

Thinkin about my own actions a lil more, I add, "Hell, I want us, women in general, to think more – honor us more. Shit. So, then what? I mean how did we get to you needing to stay at my place for a while?"

"Well, so, I masked my emotions, and thought of Sule while he kissed and caressed me. And to my surprised delight, the condom popped as he was tryin to put it on."

"Okay, and why was that delightful?"

"Cuz he didn't have another one, and I pretended like I didn't have any either."

"Wait, Queenie. He doesn't know about your color-coded stash?"

"Nope."

"Humph. So, then what happened?"

"He said he was gonna go and get some more condoms. And I told 'em that if he left I wasn't getting dressed to go downstairs to open the door again, that I wasn't in the mood anymore."

"Okay. Good."

"I know. He was pissed. But, he didn't leave. We both fell asleep pissed off at each other."

"Okaaay."

"So, then, the next morning I got up to wash up and get ready for work. I locked my bathroom door so he wouldn't just walk in on me unannounced, like he likes to do, while I took a dump and washed up. Well, I guess when he realized that I was doing more than peein, he tried opening the door.

"Wait. Did he knock first?"

Knowin my friend, I am imagining her frantically shakin her head no before she answers my question. "No! And it seemed like he started to panic when he found that it was locked. He kept demanding that I open the door. And I told him to just chill. I started thinking that I really needed some alone time – that his energy was draining me. I mean, there was this heaviness I felt that clouded over me. And I was hoping to come up with an idea of how to get him out of my apartment in the next ten minutes while I finished up in the bathroom. But, before the idea came to me, do you know that motherfucker used a damn bobby pin to open the door?"

"What?"

"You heard me. He rushed in on me so fast that I got scared for a minute. He was standing over me with this crazy/stupid look on his face cuz right as he was asking me what was I doing, he saw that I was brushing my teeth and I guess he felt as stupid as he looked. He clumsily recovered by asking me why I didn't open the door. And I explained to his psychotic ass that initially I was taking a shit followed by me washing up, and that I really didn't feel like sharing all of that with him."

"Girl, this is crazy."

"Tell me about it."

"Okay. So, continue."

"Well, first he just stared at me. I guess he was trying to figure out what he was gonna say next or maybe, after taking a breath, he realized it was a little funky up in there."

Cracking up laughing, I barely coherently say, "Girl, you know you stupid, right? Hahaha!"

Giggling as well, Queenie took a breath before continuing her story. "Finally, he just said 'Don't lock doors.' As he walked out of the bathroom, he said that I was cool and that he liked me a lot. But that was his rule. And of course I'm thinking, his rule? I closed the door behind him and turned toward the mirror to wash my face and rinse my mouth out. And do you know that psychotic ass checked the door knob to see if I had locked it again?"

"Shut up, Queenie. You are lyin!"

"Nope. So I was like ooh unh, unh. I gotta get out of this scenario. This motherfucker is crazy. Don't lock doors? Isn't this my place? Oh, hell no! What did I get myself into? Shit! So, when I came out of the bathroom he motioned for me to sit with him on my love seat. He started telling me that in order for this to work between us that he had to trust me, but I wasn't making it easy and maybe we should just be friends."

"Whew. Good, Queenie, your way out."

"Yeah, but wait. Somethin really weird happened."

"Aw shit. What happened?"

"Out of the blue, I started crying, telling him that I wanted it to work, and that he could trust me. But, it was like it wasn't me. A part of me was asking myself where the tears were coming from. How did they get here? And why was I saying those things."

"Wait a minute, Queenie. You're telling me that physically you were crying and saying those things, but you weren't? Hunh?"

"Yeah. It was like he had did something to me to make me cry and say those things. I mean, there was nothing in me that felt any emotion to cry. And I damn sure didn't want to work it out with him."

"Oooh, unh, unh. This shit is too crazy for me."

"I know. Apparently my reaction was what he wanted to see cuz then he pulled me close and told me that he could see in my eyes that I really wanted to be with him, and that we could make it work. So, I went on to say okay even though I didn't feel that way."

"Girl, you sho know how to pick 'em."

"I know. Loneliness is a motha. If I hadn'ta been missing Sule so much, I wouldn'tna gave this negro the time of day."

I think about what my friend just said and turn the words on myself. "Humph. Recognition and acknowledgement is half the battle my dawlin."

"Yeah. Well, anyway, a couple of days later, I got up the courage to not answer my phone when he called cuz I had an interesting experience that morning that felt like him all over it."

"Humph. I'm scared to ask."

"Humph. You should be girl cuz I woke up to a strange tingling, slight electric feeling at my feet."

"Hunh?"

"Wait, wait, wait. Listen to this, girl. When I removed my cover, I noticed that one of the leaves of my plant – you know the mother-in-law's tongue - was bent down and touching my foot, sending what felt like currents in my foot."

"Wait a minute, Queenie. What? The leaves on that plant stand straight up, they don't bend."

"Uuuuhhh, yeah! I know this."

"So, was it dyin?"

"No, Corin. That's what I'm tryna tell you - that bitch was healthy as fuck."

"Humph."

"So given the fact that I hadn't experienced that before, and didn't really wanna have that kind of touchy touchy feely feely relationship with any of my plants, I jumped up and put on some clothes, and carried that beautiful beast to the curb. When I looked out of the window an hour later, someone had scooped it up."

"So, do you think that Jamaican guy had anything to do with it?"

"I don't know. But, that shit was peculiar. And ain't nothing like that ever happened to me before he came into my life. That plant's always been right at the foot of my bed."

"Riiigghht."

"So, anyway, that's why I didn't answer my phone that day when he called me. I needed to figure him out of my life's script, as you would say, hahaha, as well as ponder why I wrote him in it in the first place."

"Okay."

"And when I finally did answer his call, the next day, I told 'em that I had to cool it with 'em for a while cuz I had some personal shit going on that had me consumed."

"Good."

"Yeah, that's what I thought until two nights ago – the night after we spoke."

"What happened?"

"I took the number four train to Utica and decided to catch the bus down to Halsey cuz I had heard that the A line had some delays. Though I didn't see his car..."

"Oh yeah. I forgot he was one of them taxi drivers."

"Yeah, girl. Well, even though I didn't see his car, I felt like he was watching me."

"What do you mean, Queenie?"

"I don't know. I jus had a crazy feeling that he was watching me. And it was confirmed shortly after I sat on the bus cuz my phone mysteriously rang just as I took my seat, and it was him asking me how I was doing. I played my voice down like I had a lot on my mind and things weren't cool. He got the message and let me off the phone."

"When the bus stopped at my stop, I was a lil hesitant to get off because I didn't know where he was. But, I got off, walked home, and got in my apartment safe and sound. I was really tired that night and literally took a shower moments after entering my apartment, and was in bed around 10:00 p.m."

"Hmmm. Yeah, that's really early for you. Shit, girl, you killin me cuz I feel like some creepy shit bout to come out of yo mouth."

"Humph. Well, before I knew it, I awakened to someone fondling my body."

"What the...?!?"

"Wait, wait, wait. Girl, you not gone believe this shit. No one was physically there."

"Oh, hell no, Queenie. Now, you lyin!"

"If I'm lyin, I'm flyin."

"Maybe you imagined it."

"Nope. I was lyin still in my bed, and someone was caressin my body. I even felt the cover move. When that happened, I jumped up and turned on the light. And I was the only one in my studio apartment."

Exasperated, I look at the phone before I respond. "Girl!"

"Well, sleep was nowhere near after that. I called and talked to my cousin, Patrice, for a while. I told her what had just happened - what I awakened to."

"Really? What did she say?"

"Once I finished telling her, she just began praying. I think she prayed for at least ten minutes straight. Then we talked for about an hour before I let her go to sleep."

"That was nice of her. My apologies sweetie for not bein there for you."

"No, Corin. Please don't apologize. You're dealing with your own stuff. I'm calling you this morning because I have to get out of this apartment. I need to find a new place. Hell, Patrice invited me to stay with her in Florida. I'm thinking, shit, maybe saying goodbye to New York is just what I need."

"Where in Florida does she live again?"

"Miami."

"Oh yeah? Well, Queenie, you know you can't run from anything. Wherever you go, you'll eventually just meet similar people and circumstances to help you learn the lessons you're running from, especially if you're destined to learn them, no matter where you are in the world. Scenarios will keep repeating themselves until you're ready to deal with them - with you."

"Humph. I know. I won't make any rash decisions. Plus, the weirdest thing happened when I got off the phone with Patrice."

"Damn, girl! There's more?"

"Yep. Sule called."

"What's so weird about his up and down ass?"

"Well, he said he was calling me back, that he saw that I just called, but I hadn't dialed his number in over a week."

"Oh. Yeah. Well, I guess that is strange."

"We talked for two hours straight."

"Wait a minute. You and Sule talked for two hours on the phone?"

"Exactly. Strange, right?"

"Yeah, well I guess the way you always jokin bout ya'll's five minute phone conversations, that is a lil..."

Just as I get caught up in the mystique of her story, she cuts me off. "I know, but it was right on time. By the time he and I got off of the phone, I was drunk-tired and immediately fell asleep. But my rest was short lived cuz I was awakened at a quarter to five in the morning by my doorbell. Startled and scared, I jumped up, breathin all hard, and ran to my window to see who it was. And whose car was right out front, but oh boy's. That crazy Jamaican stayed out there for about twenty minutes just ringing my doorbell."

"Oh, Queenie. This is serious."

"Uhhh, I know. That's why I'm calling now."

"Yes, yes, yes, a thousand times yes. Please stay at my place. Move in for heaven's sake." Hearing Queenie's whimpering, I stop talkin and allow my best friend the moment to cry before I reassure her that "This, too, shall pass."

"Thank you, Corin. Thank you so much for being my friend. I love you so much, girl."

"I know. I love you, too. And you're welcome even though you don't have to thank me for bein your friend. I kinda look at our friendship as being much more than friends, sisters, or any human relationship. It's more like air - always ever-present. It just is."

"Damn, girl. That's beautiful. Let me go before I never stop crying. Peace!"

"Peace, Queenie."

Silence.

Remaining at the window for a while longer, I pray for my friend as well as myself before I sit in quiet meditation for about twenty or so minutes.

As I come out of my meditation, I notice that my door is slightly closed, and I think I hear Mama May gently close the bathroom door. Smiling, I decide to greet her with a good morning hug as she comes out of the bathroom. Once I hear the toilet flush followed by running water from the sink, I decide to call out good morning before she opens the door as not to startle her. But, I hear her reply from the kitchen right as the bathroom door opens. Stunned, I momentarily stand in the middle of the hallway embarrassed as I look at the handsome face of Zyon. After about a second or two, I realize that I am inappropriately dressed and quickly back up into my room, apologizing and explaining that I assumed that he was my aunt. At the same time, Mama May appears, apologetically explaining that she didn't want to disrupt my meditation by explaining that Zyon was gonna use the restroom. So, she just closed my door a little to give me some privacy.

"Oh my goodness. I'm so embarrassed."

"Please, don't be" came out of Zyon's mouth as he watched me backtrack into the guestroom. Oh shit! This man is lookin at me with that 'you're so beautiful' look and it's throwin me so completely off balance. Humph, or maybe that's what I wanna see in his eyes and I'm throwin my damn self off balance. Ooooop! Did I just bump into the damn wall? Please tell me this is just a dream. Once in the room, I fall back on the bed hopin to wake up from the spastic-inclined dream, while at the same time, tryin to recapture just how fine that Zyon man is while I hope it's not a dream. Damn!

Whew, Mama May to the rescue. Once I'm securely in my room, I hear her apologize to Zyon for the little mishap and explain to him that I'm her niece, Corin, who's visitin from New York – the one she mentioned earlier. And I'm sure he's like, uhhh yeah, I figured that.

Then I hear him chuckle a lil and say, "No need to apologize, Ms. May. The pleasure was all mine."

I know my aunt detected that hint of flatter on my behalf, as did I. So, I wasn't imagining it. He was really checkin me out. With a smile in her voice, Mama May calls out to me, "Corey, girl, go on and put your robe on so that you can come out and meet a good friend of mine."

I raise up off of the bed at the sound of Mama May's voice. Wanting to jump up and down to celebrate the exquisite specimen of a man who just looked at me like he did, I instead bury my head in my lap after throwing myself into the chair by the window as to not draw any extra attention in my direction with any noise. And just cuz I know my aunt so very well, I cut my celebration short and yell out, "Okay, Mama May", before she comes into my room reiterating what she just said. I add, "Give me a moment please. I'll meet you guys in the kitchen."

"Good." I hear her engage Zyon. "Come on, Zyon. I just fixed you a tall glass of lemonade. Come on in here and rest yourself a little before you go to your next appointment."

"Oh, okay, Ms. May. Thanks. But, you shouldn't have cuz I'll have to leave shortly to get to Tariq's next client."

"Oh, well, a lil lemonade won't make you too late, son. Y'all youngsters have to learn how to slow down some."

Responding with a smile in his voice, I hear Zyon say, "You know what, Ms. May? You're absolutely right. I do have a few minutes I can spare. Which way to the lemonade?"

"Great," I hear Mama May exclaim before I hear their footsteps get lighter and lighter as they walk toward the kitchen.

Mama May thinks she's slick. But I ain't mad at her. Humph. Not at all. You go, auntie!

Once in the kitchen, I hear them ease into a lighthearted conversation about life's perfectly timed coincidences. Without speaking it out loud, I can tell that both were inferring the coincidence of Tariq going to Macon, Zyon helping Mama May this morning instead of calling another worker, and me visiting my aunt - all at the same time.

Not knowin when or how to make my entrance, I jus sort of casually stroll into the kitchen right as Zyon is about to give an example of a serendipitous moment he recently experienced. I could tell I caught him off guard cuz he jus sorta paused with an "oh" suspended in midair as he directed all of his attention toward me. After a few moments, he smiled and said, "Nice robe."

We all chuckle a little cuz instead of putting a robe on, I decided to put on a white t-shirt with a bright yellow butterfly on the front, an orange skirt that reached right above my knees, some white flip flops, and just let my braids hang free. I don't know, I jus wasn't feelin the whole robe concept.

Feeling a little bit uncomfortable from his stare, I try to think of something to say to divert his attention. So leave it to me to fill the space with a giggle. "Hahaha!" I turn toward Mama May. "My apologies for taking more than a minute. I thought it would be better for me to stop and brush my teeth."

Mama May joined my light laughter with, "Ooh thank you, girl. Good lookin out."

Caught off guard by Mama May's retort, I laughed louder as Zyon's head whipped toward her - surprised at her ebonic banter. As he chuckles, he asks, "What did you say, Ms. May?"

Grateful that the ice has broken with all of the laughter, I finally think to extend my hand to Zyon once it's died down, and introduce myself to him. "Hi, I'm Corin."

Not letting my hand hang in midair for even a fraction of a second, Zyon takes it in his own, which feels warm, rugged and manly (oooh, oooh, oooh, focus, Corin), and warmly tells me his name and how it's a pleasure meetin me. Shit, what is he, bout six foot two, three, sandy brown skin with a perfectly cut fade, lean and muscular (just how I like 'em), a lil bow to his legs, a two-dimple smile, pearly whites, and thick lips. Help me!

Thankfully, Mama May cuts into my dreamy state of mind, which diverts my eyes from his with, "Yeah, Corey, this is my landscaper. Or, I should say he's the owner of the company. His nephew, Tariq, actually does the work around here for me."

Exemplifying interests, I nod my head with a smile and an interjected "Oh" toward Zyon, first, and back to Mama May to encourage her to continue. All the while I'm thinkin how happy I am that I decided to come to visit my aunt for this moment alone. Talk about a sista itchin to do her happy dance. I guess doin it in my head will have to do for now. (Shiiit, bam! I just slapped the floor as I dropped it, ya'll. Tee hee hee. Ooop, dude just said something.) "I'm sorry, what did you say, Zyon?"

"How would you like to see Atlanta one day or evening?"

No he is not mackin me in front of my aunt?

"Sure. That would be nice." Oh yes I did return the mack in front of Mama May, and with a winked smile for that matter. Humph. Hell, I guess we ain't got much of a choice seein that she ain't budgin. I'M SAYIN!

Grabbin his cell phone, he says, "Please forgive me. I don't have any business cards with me right now. Do you mind if I program your phone number in my phone now?"

Still not believing that I'm in this moment, I willingly recite my cell phone to him with probably the same size grin/smile Mama May had when he gave her the flowers earlier.

Once he enters my number in his phone, he looks at me and says, "I just called your phone. Now, you have no excuse not to call me."

Lookin up at him, I smile as I reply, "Okay."

He gracefully thanks Mama May for the lemonade and starts walkin toward the entrance to the kitchen after glancing at his watch. Before he reaches the front door, he flashes both of us a smile and calls back to me, "I look forward to talkin to you soon, Corin." And to both of us, "Ya'll have a good day."

In unison, me and Mama May answer, "You, too, Zyon", and then look at each other with a smile.

Not able to hold her gaze, I turn away from Mama May and walk toward my room, partly embarrassed and thrilled. "I need to take my shower."

On my heels, Mama May, asks, "Cute hunh?"

"Yes, he is."

"You know you have to call him, right?"

"Uh, no, I didn't know that. Why do I HAVE to call him?"

Exasperated, she walks in front of me. "Because if you don't, it'll be weird between he and I the next time I see him."

"Oh, Mama May, I'm sure he'll get over it if I don't call. Humph, as handsome as he is, I'm sure he has a lot of admirers. AND knowing you, I know that little nuance, of me not callin wouldn't phase you a bit."

"You don't know that."

"Hahaha! Un hunh. Okay, Mama May. But, what makes you think I'm not gonna call? Hahaha!"

Zoomin in on the possibility I just threw out there, Mama May joins my laughter. "I may be old, but I ain't no fool. Any woman in her right mind will call that man as fine as he is."

"Mama May!"

"Humph. Don't sleep, my sweet dawlin. I may be married with some padded age on me, but I know a good catch when I see one. Plus, he has his own business, he's respectful, no kids, and not married. Puhleeeeze!"

Jokingly I add, "He could be gay. I mean, you do live right outside of Atlanta, the capitol for black gay men and the down low brother in the U.S., you know?"

"He was married, missy. Now he's happily divorced."

"Humph, that may be why he's divorced. The wife could have found out."

"You know what, you could be right, but I don't have time for all of that foolishness. Zyon's a nice young man. I'm not sayin to marry him."

"I know." I just don't want all of my stuff to get in the way. Need to release and let go of my past once and for all.

"Hell, you should let a southern man take you out, Corey. I think you'll notice a difference from what you're experiencing up in New York."

Thinkin back to Black and other men I've dated, I agree. "Yeah, I'm sure you're right." Lookin at my aunt with gratitude and askin myself why am I perpetrating with her when I know I'm gone call his fine ass, I finally give in a little. "I may not call right away, but I'll definitely call him before I go back to New York."

Shaking her head and walkin out of my room, she pauses midway down the hall, and matter-of-factly continues with, "All I'm sayin is sometimes a handsome distraction can do a world of good. Hell, if it was me, I'd call him this weekend if he doesn't call me before then. Shoot, I ain't never been one for games. If I like you, I like you. And, you'll know it. It's always worked for me. I know I'm not the norm. Do how you feel fit for you, Corey. He's a nice young man. I have a good feelin about 'em." Turning to walk toward her room, she mumbles, "Humph, now let me go get cleaned up so that I can get down to the battered women's shelter."

"Hunh? Wait! You're leavin? I thought you only volunteered there on some Saturday mornings."

"Yeah, I do. But, a volunteer called out sick, and they need help answering the phones."

"Oh, okay." Damn, I was hopin that she and I could hang out today, and that she'd come with me to my appointment.

"I'll say goodbye before I leave."

"Okay."

I know ya'll are like, "What appointment?" Well, Mama May knows the human resource manager of a popular chain of day spas in the southeast. And, the other day when I told her that I decided to stay the entire summer, she offered to call in a favor with this woman, who absolutely loved my interview and massage technique, so that I can get out and live and not mope around the house all day during my stay with her. And although I don't see myself as moping, but healing, I was excited about the idea of not only helping people through the art of massage, but also drivin around Atlanta to see if I can determine why it's called *the black mecca*.

But, I will say this, this state is backwards as all be damned when it comes to all of the ish (yeah, I said ish) a massage therapist has to go through just to work in this motha. Shiiit, it doesn't matter if you're certified and licensed by the state of New York, whose licensing exam is compatible to the national licensing exam for massage therapists. Unh, unh. There's a lot of unnecessary rigmarole imposed upon therapists here.

Basically, because of the antiquated negative connotations attached to massage parlors, i.e., places that give gentleman and lady callers *happy endings*, all massage therapists have to be cleared of being prostitutes before they can legally work at any establishment in Atlanta, whether its reputable or not. And for those of you who are confused about what a *happy ending* is, it's helping people reach sexual climaxes during their massages. **DISGUSTING.** If I am not anything else, I am a professional massage therapist.

But, even though all of that was a turn off, I figured, what the hell, $250.00 is not gonna hurt me to be cleared of prostitution. So, immediately after leaving the interview, yesterday, I went to City Hall East on Ponce De Leon to get fingerprinted. I completed and submitted the form for a background check, as well. Once I was finished there, I called one of the phone numbers, the Human Resources woman gave me in regards to healthcare facilities I could get a physical from if I didn't wanna go to

Mama May's doctor, to see if they had any available appointments. Instead of callin all of the numbers to see who had the first available appointment, I just called the one that was connected to a very popular hospital in Atlanta because of its name. And to my surprise and delight to get all of this over with, they scheduled me for a 3:00 appointment this afternoon.

I have to say that this has been quite a day so far with me. Humph, it's still early. I wonder what's next.

Full Moon

Expect good. Expect highness. Believe,
know, visualize, anticipate…

Stunned And Crazed

So, here I am. It's 12:30 p.m. now. I'll probably leave around 1:45 just in case I get turned around or can't find parking right away. But, my arrival time is really the least of my concerns. Right now I'm thinkin about the intake form that I'll have to complete at the doctor's office. Oh yeah, don't be surprised. It's always my concern when I have to go to a new doctor becuz you always have to complete one. You know, that form that gives the doctor an overview of your medical history. Yeah, that one. Well, best believe that on that form, there's always the statement, *Please Check Everything That Applies* which is ALWAYS followed by a small box or line next to that infamous word within a list that sends sharp knives between each vertebra of my spine when I see it - 'Herpes'. I always ponder whether I should check it or not especially in this case, for instance. You see, I figure that I won't hurt anyone, nor myself, if I don't check it cuz this isn't my actual doctor who needs to be aware of everything goin on with me in order to know how to care for me optimally. AND, I already found out, during my initial call, that aside from a TB test, they won't be doin any blood work, which is very fortunate on my behalf cuz if they did it, then it would prove that I have the 'H' word.

Yep. I know. I'm pretty pathetic sometimes. To say that it's a challenge for me to verbalize my situation, or just that word even, in every day conversation, or even to ya'll, is an UNDERSTATEMENT. So, you can only imagine the trials and tribulations I go through when I have to tell someone with whom I'd like to be intimate with that I have it. Ohhh, my sweet dawlins, trust me when I say it's an ugly well-rehearsed monologue, my un-triumphant moment in the spotlight. But, that's a whole notha story.

Well, let me get in the shower. Hey, if I'm lucky, I may be able to wash away my troubles.

Mama May knocks on the bathroom door as I'm dryin off. "Yes?"

"I'm gonna head on out. Call me if you need anything. Otherwise, I should be back here around 7 tonight."

"Oh? That's a long shift."

"Not really, I'm only covering from 2:30 til 5:00. But, I'm gonna stop by the farmer's market afterwards. Plus, I'm padding the time a little because it'll be in the middle of rush hour."

"Gotcha. Okay. I'll see you later."

"Okay. I'm gonna shut and lock the front door, okay?"

"Okay. Thanks!"

Dang, I hope I'm as youthful and active as she is when I'm seventy-five.

After I put on the same orange skirt and t-shirt I met Zyon in, I spruce it up a little with some bone-colored wedged sandals with matching purse and earrings. Then, I head for the kitchen to make me a smoothie so that I won't go to the appointment uncomfortably full. Plus, I figure it'll give me an excuse to grab something to eat in the city after I leave my appointment.

Once I'm downtown and determine which parking structure to park in, I come to the conclusion that enough is enough. It doesn't make sense thinkin about that intake form anymore cuz the moment of reckoning is upon me and I know exactly how I'm gonna complete it. As always, I will check the box. Sometimes I despise the fact that I don't know how to lie.

In the waiting room, I think about my integrity and how difficult it is for me to darken it. Oh, the joys of having to tell the truth. Sometimes I knock people's socks off with some of the things that come out of my mouth. But, it's like I cannot say or be anything that I'm not. So, yes, now that I'm actually in the moment and completing the intake form, I check all the appropriate boxes and pray not to be too hard on myself as I wonder what the doctor will think when he sees that particular box checked. I know. You're probably wondering why I care so much. And the thing is though, consciously I know that I shouldn't care, my subconscious keeps actin like it didn't get the damn memo. *Hmmm. Note to self, you gone have to overkill that message of unconditional self-love and self-acceptance so that you won't give a fuck of what others think about you.*

Well I have some great news. To my surprise, my visit is very pleasant. The nurse and doctor are very warm and communicative. They're both African American and young lookin like the majority of the staff. That's new for me. I'm not used to visiting a healthcare facility where the majority of the staff, including the doctors, are African American. But, hey, I'm all for new.

As the doctor checks my blood pressure and other vital signs, he explains to me that he's never conducted a physical for this reason before – a massage permit. I just smile even though my thoughts reflect more of a scowl for havin to go through all of this all in the name of being one of GOD's servants by helping people relax, release, and chill via the wonderful pastime of therapeutic-grade massage therapy. But, hey, I'm all for goin with the flow, right? Riiiggghhhttt. Many big ups to You, GOD, for blessing me with such a skillful gift to share with the masses.

As I prepare to leave, I sulk a lil at my empty hands that are supposed to be filled with an executed document indicating that I passed the physical. Not thinkin fully, I neglected to factor that it takes a couple of days to determine the results of TB tests. So, of course, it's now that I realize juussst how much I do not care for healthcare facilities no matter how kind the staff is to me cuz I really jus don't wanna come back. Shit, I wish I could take a picture of my arm where they took the TB test and have them fax over the executed form once they see that I'm okay. But I guess the deeper issue is do I really dislike healthcare facilities that much or am I just embarrassed that I have to see these people, who now know that I have herpes, again. GOD, please help me not to care so much. Wait, wait, wait. Let me go ahead and frame that note from earlier so that it's a fixed healthy thought in my mind that'll be consistently feeding my subconscious effectively. *Note to self, you gone have to overkill that message of unconditional self-love and self-acceptance so that you won't give a fuck of what others think about you.*

In my car, I decide to go to an Indian restaurant, one of two restaurants I found online yesterday when I decided that I'd eat in the city after my appointment. The second one's a Thai restaurant. Apparently, the Indian one is in an area of town called Little Five Points which isn't too far from where I am now. I feel my emotions growing more light and fluffy as I follow some easy MapQuest directions and discover that the restaurant's pretty close to the interstate which is perfect for when I am ready to head back to Mama May's.

Leave it to me to discover New York's West Village in Atlanta. Hahaha! It's complete with your all-natural, crown full of locs and nappy heads, dashiki wearin, all-black, skeleton-inspired paraphernalia, multi-pierced contemporary mix of individuals walking to, from, and in front of boutiques, restaurants, cafes and bars, and novelty shops. I'm actually laughing out loud as I walk in front of a store that sells crystals and incense and another, a few doors down, that sells vintage vinyl as I walk toward the restaurant after parking my rental. For a hot moment, I feel like I am back in New York for real, ya'll. The only major difference is that everything and everyone seem to be moving much, much slower here. And though I know that there are hustlers everywhere, I feel as if I don't have to walk completely guarded with that *don't fuck with me* attitude I've learned to paint on my face whenever I'm out and about in New York. Hmmm.

So, it looks like Little Five Points is full of surprises. You won't believe who I, literally, run into when at the last minute I decide to make a mad dash across Moreland Avenue so that I can be on the same side of the street as the restaurant that I'm goin to and to beat the street light and traffic. Nope, you won't believe it. Hell, I am buggin out yo! After it, DING, registers, I pinch myself a couple of times to make sure I'm not dreamin. And now I'm pinchin him so that I can hear his voice to make sure my eyes are not deceivin me.

"Ouch. Girl, you know you still crazy."

It's Deron, ya'll. "Deron Phillips."

"Wow. Corin Rivers. I thought that was you."

Everything about me is suddenly paralyzed.

"I'd been watchin you for a minute, tryin to determine if my memory and senses were serving me justly."

Am I smiling? Do something or say something, girl.

He keeps talkin as if I'm responding to him. "Yeah. It was the rhythm of your walk that made me look twice. And then your hair, the braids actually, that kept me lookin."

"Un hun hun." I give a dumb-founded half laugh as I grab a couple of my braids and look at them with a smile and a slight nod before I look at him again.

Talk about bein at a loss for words. I wonder if he can tell. Oooh, what to do, what to do? Do I hug him, smile, or continue to stand here with this Gumby-crazed surprised look on my face? Unh, unh, unh. The clock is tickin and my feet are still glued to this spot. Sooo, I guess I'm opting for the latter given that everything in me feels ridiculously heavy all of a sudden. It's as though a ton of bricks are dangling from each of my fingers preventing me from raising my arms and hands to give a handshake, a hug, or to fold them against my body. Damn mama! Get a grip! Calling on GOD, calling on GOD. Are you there, GOD? Do you read me?

Crickets.

"Oh my GOD, Corin." It seems like he's a little uncomfortable, too, but he finally pulls me in his arms kinda awkwardly as if he's unsure of how I'll react. "I can't believe that it's really you."

Do you read me GOD? Jesus? Buddha? Somebody HELP!

Pushin away from me, I hear him ask me, "What are you doing in Atlanta? Do you live here? Look at you. You're absolutely beautiful."

"Thank you." Oh shit, my voice. I can speak! I can speak! "Wow! Deron."

He steps a little further away from me and just looks at me for a moment as if he's trying to determine something. "How are you, Corin?"

I feel like his eyes are drilling into mine. Damn, he looks good. A little thicker and mature-looking, but damn he looks good. Say something, Corin. Tell 'em you're okay, girl.

"Do you live in Atlanta?"

Wait til I tell Queenie how motha fuckin good this negro looks. Though he's still lean, he's broader, and his body feels harder. And all of his dark chocolate and wet panties inspired one dimpled smile has me feelin flushed – embarrassed. Damn! I hope he can't tell. Come on Corin, find your voice again, say something. "Ummm, no. No, I'm just visiting. I live in New York."

"Wow! Really?"

Not really knowin what to say or how to stand, I look away for a moment.

I guess he picks up on my discomfort and awkwardness cuz he steps back from me more and glances away. "I guess this is kinda weird, hunh?"

"Yeah."

"Damn! This is crazy right here."

I look up at him for him to continue, hopin that he can erase the discomfort of the moment.

"I been thinkin bout you a lot lately. I even tried to look you up on the internet thinkin that you were either in Cali or New Orleans." Widening the smile on his face and in his voice, he thinks to himself for a minute. "I never would've imagined New York."

"Yeah, right? I got a job offer from a financial services firm during my senior year." I guess my shock is thawin out some cuz I'm able to look at him in his eyes for more than a moment.

As if just remembering something, Deron asks, "Hey. Ummm. Am I keepin you from something? I don't wanna hold you up."

Jokingly with a serious face, I say, "Yeah dude, as a matter of fact, you are."

I guess a little disappointed, he puts his head down briefly. "Oh. Well..."

"You're keepin me from some Indian food," I add with a smile.

"Oh, okay. You're on your way to Planet Bombay?"

"Yeah."

"Oh, may I walk you?"

Deja vu like a motha. This moment feels like the same moment he asked if he could walk me wherever I was goin after our group meeting all those years ago. The same tone and tilt of his head. Humph. Nanh, that's a trip. "Sure. You don't have to though."

"Cut it out, Corin. You know I'm dyin here."

"Yeah? Well, you should be."

"Hahaha!"

"Hahaha!"

We both laugh at the awkwardness of the moment, the years that have passed between us, the familiarity bouncing off of our words, and the congested hurt coupling our souls.

I wonder what he's really feeling. His demeanor tells me that he's let go of all of that anger he held against me all those years back. And though he seems genuinely happy to see me, he's definitely feelin a little uncomfortable as am I. Should I invite him to eat with me, exchange numbers, wait for his lead – what to do, what to do? Hmmm, I guess since he asked to walk me to the restaurant, the least I could do is extend an invitation for him to stay and eat with me. Who knows? He might have somewhere he has to be.

Once at the restaurant, he's elated at my invitation for him to join me, but explains that he's expecting an important call which may cause him to step away briefly. After we're seated, we're both quiet initially. Thankfully, I'm able to act distracted by checking out the menu. I don't know about him, but I'm kinda nervous. So, after I order, I sorta fiddle with my fingers and start lookin around and taking in the ambiance of the place while he goes back in forth with the waiter tryin to decide on what he wants to order. I'm glad they sat us at a booth instead of one of those little tables which scream intimacy. Not sure if I wanna be that close to him. It's an all right place I guess – it's clean. Nothing to scream about in regards to décor. The two televisions playing the Indian music videos are throwing me though. Hahaha! You can tell the choreographers and directors really get into telling stories in their music videos. All the dancing, acting, and props just seem so very extra. And that's all I'm gone say on that. Somewhat enthralled by the theatrics of the video, I jump at Deron touching my interlaced fingers resting on the table. Wow! I didn't even notice that the waiter had walked away. Okay, focus, Corin. Stop lookin at the TV.

"Thanks, again, for inviting me to dine with you, Corin."

I slowly pull my hands away as I nod at him, makin light of my invitation. "Oh, yeah. I'm glad that you had some time to spare." I look down for a moment and then look back at him jokingly raising my eyes. "I think."

"Hahaha!" First he laughs. Then I laugh, and before we know it, we just kinda settle into an ancient groove as we reacquaint one another with our surface selves before we attempt to decongest the hurt.

First I give him an abbreviated synopsis of my life in regards to work, my home, massage therapy, and how I'm visiting Mama May for the summer. I stay away from any personal information.

He gets all animated at my mention of Mama May. "Wow! How is your aunt? She's in Georgia now? I used to love our visits."

"She's great! Her and Uncle Charles are wonderful. They're both best-selling authors."

"Whhaaatt? Get outta here!"

"Yep! You wouldn't believe that they're seventy-five years old if you saw them."

"Yeah? I bet!" I can see his mind travellin back in time. "Damn, yo Uncle Charles used to have me on the flo tryin to catch my breath, I was laughin so hard at his crazy stories. Wow! It's good to hear that they're both doin so great."

Feelin more comfortable, I ask him about his life.

"Chana Saag?"

Startled a little cuz I didn't feel or hear the waiter approach our table, I raise my hand indicating that the Chana Saag is mine. And once he sets all the food on the table and refills our water glasses, we ease back into the moment.

I am so grateful for the arrival of our food cuz, now, I have an excuse to listen more and talk less. Well, that's my game plan, at least. I'm very aware that I'm still not quite in my body right now. So, please bear with me if I say or think something that doesn't make any sense. Thank you.

He tells me that since he had a 3.8 GPA and was finishing his last semester at Xavier with some general education courses, that his advisor, at the time, advocated upon his behalf that the University allow him to take incompletes in his classes, that horrific semester that he left, as to not hinder his GPA. He later completed the courses at Georgia Tech and transferred the classes and credits to Xavier. And, because of the extenuating circumstances of his uncle's murder, they allowed the transfer and mailed him his degree. He then attended Emory's School of Medicine in Atlanta, Georgia so that he could be close to his mom and family. Currently, he's a pediatrician at Children's Hospital – the Scottish Rite campus, wherever or whatever that is. He's never been married, but has a five-year-old son, whom, by the way he lights up when he speaks about him, he absolutely adores. He and the boy's mother are just friends now – he said that they weren't cut out for the long haul and that she's currently engaged to be married this December. They, apparently, have a good relationship and understanding. He told me that he has his son every Friday through Monday morning. And that the only reason why he isn't with him now is becuz he went with his grandmother, Deron's mother, to Gainesville to visit with some of his cousins for the weekend.

Ooo weee! Wait ya'll. I can't help but interrupt his story for a moment. I have to tell you that this food is off the chii-zain. My taste buds are so havin a party right now. "This food is so good. Are you enjoying yours."

"Oh yes! I love this place. I come here a lot."

"What is that?" I gesture with my head towards his plate. "What did you get?"

"It's Saag Panir."

"Oh, okay. I didn't recognize it. Theirs is much creamier than I'm used to."

He keeps lookin at me in that way that he used to that keeps sendin chills all over my body with extra emphasis at the top of my head. My thoughts are all over the place because I never thought I'd ever run into him ever again. And I'm hopin, as he finally initiates an explanation of his disappearance, that I'll finally get some form of closure in his regard. Ooooh, thanks, GOD.

"You know?"

Lookin up at him, I silently let him know that it's cool to bring it up, to keep talkin.

His keen ability to read me prompts him to smile, first, before he briefly looks away and then back into my eyes. "Corin, I'm sorry. I know you didn't deserve the way I ended it between us. But, I had so much goin through my mind, at the time, with the death of my Uncle Eddie, that I really didn't know how to be there for you or myself, for that matter. It was hard for me to wrap my mind around trustin you cuz you took so long to tell me about all that happened during that crazy weekend. And, plus, I was already developin a distrust toward women based upon how my aunt Mattie cheated on my uncle who, since I could remember, thought the world of her."

"But, Deron, really? You knew how crazy I was about you."

"Yeah. I know. And I felt the same way – if not more."

"Excuse me. You're suggestin that I didn't love you as much as you loved me."

"Naw. Maybe I used the wrong words. It's just that you were my angel. We were so good together. I was gonna ask you to marry me at the end of the semester."

"What?!" So, ya'll know I have a dumb-founded look on my face, right?

"Yeah. My mom had given me the ring that my grandfather had bought my grandmother on their twenty-fifth wedding anniversary. It was the only piece of jewelry he'd ever given her."

No this negro didn't just tell me that he was gonna ask me to marry him.

"But, instead of listening to my heart, I listened to the pain I was feelin from my uncle's death. And, in my mind, your story didn't make any sense. At the time I thought you had made all that up cuz you figured at some point, I'd find out that not only were you not a virgin all along, but you had a disease, too."

"That's crazy, Deron. So, you sayin that in that one moment, at the Lake, when I told you what had happened to me, that you determined that all of what we had, that I was, was a lie?"

"Pretty much."

"Nanh, that's some bullshit."

"Hunh?" Just before I respond, his phone rings. "Damn!" He looks at me with apologetic eyes. "This is the call I was talking about. Please excuse me." He answers the phone and mouthes 'I'm sorry' as he walks toward the door and steps outside.

But, I'm riled up now, and thus, proceed to continue the conversation in my head - practicing to make sure what I wanna say sounds right. This is sorta what I do before I present ideas at work – I even add what I think responses and gestures will be so that I'll know how to position my rebuttal. *"Oh, I know you're not surprised at my response. Oooh, unh, unh. You can't be. Not the way you just flipped my story. MY STORY."*

"I'm sorry."

"You have no idea what I've been through, what I'm still goin through."

He grabs my hand. "Wait, Corin. Please calm down."

"Calm down? Don't patronize me, Deron."

He lets my hands go – probably not knowing what to do or say next.

"I'm sorry, Corin. It was not my intention to patronize you. Please don't be

mad. It's just that this moment..." He looks away for a moment before he holds my eyes with his questioningly. "...us sittin here, it feels so..."

I know and feel that he wants to say that all this feels so familiar. But, I refuse to complete his sentence. Damn, I wish I could refuse the remembrance of the familiar and symbiotic pulse between us. Fuck!

"Well, I don't care about what your synopsis of my story was or is. The shit, the real shit, has yet to leave me completely alone. Unh, unh. In fact, the reason I'm here, in Georgia, is to get some retribution on the inward turmoil I've been goin through all these years."

Oh damn! I can't say that. He'll think I'm crazy for sure since I'm holdin on to shit from thirteen years ago. But, who gives a damn right now, right? It's just me. I'm goin in.

"My goal is to learn how to love and accept all of me all the time no matter who's around or where I'm at. And the crazy thing is, ya see, I get that you were hurtin. And really, I get your rational for leavin. I get it. I really do, Deron. You were hurt. A major part of your life had changed forever." *I nod my head for emphasis.* "Yep. And knowin how you felt about your uncle, the relationship that you conveyed that ya'll had, and how he provided guidance to you like a father, I totally get it. I mean, real talk? We were so young then. I guess I can get your reaction toward my news, too, if I place my feet in your shoes. But the only thing was that because of the shit I was goin through, I really didn't even think to put my feet in your shoes cuz they were so perfectly fitted in my own. You see, what you didn't realize was that your leavin was the first of a few episodes of rejection I experienced after the rape, after being told that I have an incurable sexually transmitted disease."

"Wait, Corin."

Yeah, wait, Corin. That seems a bit much given all the time that's passed. I turn to look at the blank wall beside me hoping to clear my head, but I can't seem to stop.

"No! You wait, Deron, becuz you don't seem to understand that I still hadn't been cleared of HIV at the time either. You know, that virus that can transform into, ummm, your deathbed. Can you even imagine the hell I was in?"

"No, I..."

Not letting him get more than two words in, I plunge more. "I don't think so. Shit, I didn't find out until about a year and a half later, indirectly from Mama May, who was repeatin the story of Lil Redd's suicide to one of my uncles on the* *phone, that his autopsy reported that he wasn't HIV positive. Who knows why they checked for that. Hell, I'm jus glad that they did."*

"Corin..."

"No! I ain't finish! This is thirteen years deep, Deron."

GOD, please stop me! Please stop these absurd thoughts now. Please help me stop.

"Okay." *I imagine he gestures with his right hand and gives a short nod of his head for me to keep talkin.* "I'm sorry."

"Uh, yeah. But gettin back to right after that shit happened. Do you know how it feels to think that you are completely powerless? For a long time, I didn't know, or maybe couldn't remember, how to conjure up hope. I mean, what the fuck was that?" *Ooooop, did I just curse?* "So, though, in your hurt, young mind, you thought that if all that I told you had really happened, I'd've told you when you first got back, or even while you were still away, I couldn't cuz, just like you were hurtin and beginning to distrust women, I was bewildered, scared shitless, lonely as fuck, in addition to hurtin and fightin, like hell, to still trust men – you. But, you..."

"You don't have to finish that."

Fuck! Why am I cryin? Where did all of that venom come from? Oh GOD, please help me get it together before he walks back into this restaurant. Shit, shit, shit, shit, shit! I can't go in on him like that. He'll think I'm a crazy woman. Hell, right now, I think I'm a crazy woman. I mean, his apology and explanation was cool I guess. A lot of this stuff is my shit - he didn't rape me. He obviously was going through his own hell while I was hoping he'd bail me out of mine. Humph! Shaking my head, I hurry and wipe my eyes, pull out my compact mirror hoping to fix my makeup before his return. And lucky for me the door opens right as I put my compact away.

I offer a half smile as he hesitantly sits down. We both speak at the same time.

"Look."

We chuckle and simultaneously encourage one another to speak. "Go ahead."

I nod at him, but he passes the moment to me. "No, you go, Corin."

"Look, I'm sorry about my outburst earlier. Thank you for your apology and explanation."

"Hey, I didn't mean to offend you."

I raise my right hand to stop him and shake my head. "Naw, that was your truth. Who am I to challenge it?"

"Don't dim your thoughts on my account." He looks at me with a crooked smile and winks. "Your fire, that passion to share your point of view…" He looks down for a moment – probably confused about all of the emotions swimming around us. "…I always respected it."

I smile, mouthe 'thank you' and gesture to the food. "It's cool. We're cool. Let's eat."

He complies by lifting his fork and grabbing a piece of nan bread. "I know this may feel crazy and awkward, Corin. But, damn, it sure is good to see you!"

I blush some, look at him, and wonder why I'm so drawn to him right now. Yeah, he's looking smack-yo-lips-make-you-wanna-slap-somebody good as all be damned, but it's really that magnifying pulse between us that has my nerve endings dancing a sassy marengue, sending me into non coherent fire-inflated twirls and dips, that has me bewildered and expressly throwed off. Plus, I'm trippin off my sanity or lack thereof given the way I went off on him in my head. Shoot, well, maybe that was just the release I needed. Or, maybe, I'm a lil touched. Haha!

As we complete our lunch with safe, small talk about how it's like living in our respective cities, I momentarily wonder how it would've been being Sal.

What, Exactly, Is Happening?

At my car, as he stumbles over all of the years that have passed since we were an us, I find myself just lookin at him. For some reason I feel light, like I can float. So, I hold onto the car for balance. I don't say anything. There aren't any thoughts in my mind. Well, if there are, I don't recognize them. I feel his sincerity in his stance. I hear his apology in his eyes. I can see genuine love in his aura. But, I can't move. I can't speak. I just let the moment massage my soul.

And, then, like magic, I feel an electric current run through my body when he takes one of my hands in his. It sends chills to the crown of my head. *Okay, so what is up with the chills at the top of my head – my crown chakra? You talkin to me, GOD?*

Hmmm, maybe You are. "Thank you."

Perplexed, he asks, "Thank you? For what?"

"This moment. Closure. I mean it just clicked in me that I forgive you, or better yet, that I forgive myself for all of the hurt and anger I held in your honor for so long."

"Oh." He briefly looks away before he holds my eyes with a look outlined with a momentous cool breeze on a hot summer day."

Oooh! Oooh! Oooh! An epiphany, ya'll. "Humph. How funny. I just realized that there doesn't have to be any bells and whistles goin off, nor do I need to draw psychological blood by overthinkin and/or goin off on you, or make you feel the hurt I felt back then, to release you from the resentment I've been, on the low, holding toward you for thirteen years.

It wasn't until you stepped out of the restaurant to take your call and I thought about what you said versus what I thought I wanted to say that I realized it's okay to let all of that go. Apparently, it was serving as a false armor that I don't need or want any more."

"Hmmmm, okay. You're welcome. I'm feelin this moment myself. I needed this. Closure is good. But, I'm hoping that it's just closure on that situation, not our friendship." He looks at me for a moment with what mirrors regret. It's hard to read him. We hug and I damn near melt in his arms, his body feels so good.

Before we pull apart, he asks me if we can keep in touch and if he can see me before I leave. So, I ask him for his phone number. And, as he gives it to me, I enter it into my phone, like Zyon did earlier with mine, and call him while he's holding my car door open as I get situated. "I'm looking forward to seeing you again, Ms. Rivers."

With a flirtatious smirk and bold head-to-toe once over, I reply, "I know this."

He throws his head back and laughs fully while backing away from the car. "You're something else, girl", he calls out. And just like that, the scene ends.

Whew! That was powerful. You go, Corin! I grab my MapQuest directions so that I don't waste any time headin back to Mama May's. "Nanh, let me look at these Map Quest directions real quick so I can get my bearings."

Comfortable with the directions, I start the car up.

Life is such a motha at times. Who woulda thought that I'd run into Deron, of all people. I mean, I know he's from Georgia and all. But, still, tho. I'm still shocked. It's like I never allowed the thought of maybe seein him, while I'm in Georgia, to enter my mind, even after seein his face so vividly this morning.

Oooh! Me, right now, ya'll, is so not a good look. I find myself in a hypnotic trance between the attraction that un-invitedly resurfaced about two hours ago amongst Deron and I, the healthy forgiving place that I'm in right now, and the unknown.

BONK! BONK! BONK!

Startled, I jump. Whew! Had this man in a Lexus SUV not startled me by honkin his horn and flippin me off, just now, as he rides the ass of my rental car, I wouldn't know that there's a trail of cars following behind me. And I can't even get mad at him cuz just as I pull over to the side of the road to let him and the others pass me up, I notice that my speedometer reads somewhere between thirty-five to forty miles per hour and the mileage sign on the side of the rode that I happen to stop next to reads fifty-five miles per hour. Hunhun. As the reality of five other drivers angrily pass me by, I mentally slap myself out of the trance so that I can make it back to Mama May's safe and sound and before nightfall or the next daybreak for that matter.

I am surprisingly happy to see that Mama May's home as I drive along the paved path toward the garages once inside the gate. At first, immediately after leaving Deron, I wished I was back in New York so that I could just go home and be alone with my thoughts. But, I am actually, abnormally, grateful that I'm not alone at this moment. I'd rather be amongst neutral human intelligence not intricately involved within my intimate life. Plus, if I was in New York, then there wouldn't be a possibility of me seein Deron, again, before I go back home. *Aw, damn. What was that? I really wanna see Deron again? For what? Okay, GOD, what's really goin on?*

It sounds like Mama May's havin a good ole time talkin on the phone. Dang, she's on the porch. I wanted to sit on the porch. I hope she doesn't stay on the phone long cuz I don't wanna have to go in the house out of respect for her conversation. Plus, I sorta wanna just vibe with her for a while before she turns in. Shit, I can't believe it's 8:30. Me and Deron must have talked for at least three hours straight. Damn! I grab my purse from the back seat right as I hear Mama May say my mama's name. Oh, okay. She's on the phone with my mother.

"Corey, ya mama says hi."

"Hi Ma! I love you!"

"You heard her, Mary? Un hunh. Okay then. Lookin forward to it."

Oooh, good, they gettin off the phone. "What you lookin forward to, Mama May?"

"Minding my bizness and staying out of yearn."

"Hahaha!" I raise both my palms at chest level to signal to her that I surrender. "You right. My bad."

"Un hunh. Your bad is right." She chuckles. "Nanh, where have you been? I had just told your mother that I was giving you another five minutes before I called the dogs after you."

I throw my head back as I laugh at her comment, facial expression, and the fact that I'm grown. But, I passively reply, "I'm sorry. I should've called. I hadn't noticed the time slippin by."

"Oh? Must have been having a good time."

"Hmmm. I guess I did. I ran into Deron in Little Five Points after my appointment."

"Deron. Deron."

"You remember Deron, auntie. We dated while I was at Xavier."

"Oh yeah. Wow! He lives here? How is he?"

"Yep. He's from here ya know."

"No, I don't know if I knew that. Humph, but then again, maybe I did, chile."

"Yeah, well, he's good. He's a pediatrician at one of the children's hospitals here."

"You don't say?"

"Yep. He looks good. More mature, obviously, and a lil broader. But, all in all, he looks good."

I can feel Mama May lookin at me, through me. But, I don't care. I'm tired of holdin so much in. "He has a five-year-old son."

"Oh yeah?"

"Yep."

"Is he married?"

"No. He hasn't married yet, and he and his son's mother aren't together. In fact, she's engaged to be married this December."

"Oh. Okay."

"What, Mama May?"

"I didn't say anything chile."

"I know. But it feels like you want to."

"Humph. No, you are feeling yourself right now, baby. I'm just listening."

"Yeah, you probably right. Hunhun. It was weird seein him, you know? It's been so long."

"Well, if I remember correctly, he hurt you pretty bad, hunh, Corey?"

"Yes ma'am. He just walked out of my life like what we had was nothing."

"Yeah, I remember being very shocked when you told me that y'all had broken up and that he dropped out of school. It just seemed so unlike him."

"Yeah. I know."

"Did you get closure today? Did y'all talk about what happened?"

"Yes and yes. We talked about it all and I do feel like I got closure."

"Well that's good, baby. Doesn't closure feel good?"

"Yeah, you can say that. But, it also feels confusing."

"How so?"

"Well, there's a part of me that's lookin forward to seein him again. We exchanged phone numbers."

"There isn't anything wrong with that, Corey. Just be sure to keep both of your eyes open."

"I will. I mean I'm not sayin we'll get back together or nothing."

"Un hun. Well, like I said, whatever y'all do, just be sure to keep both of your eyes open. And, hell, if you can, pry open that third one, too. Hahaha!"

"Ha! Ha! Ha! Auntie got jokes."

"Hey, like I said earlier, a handsome distraction can do a world of good. Humph! And some distractions help you think twice about others."

"Humph. I see that you're on a roll today, Auntie."

"Haaa! Yeah. Well, baby, I'ma go in here and take me a shower and meditate some before I lay my head down."

"Okay. Hey, I been meaning to ask you how Uncle Charles is doing."

"Oh, he's just fine, honey. He's havin him a good ole time in Europe. I may go up there before he comes back home. I don't know."

"Aw, that'll be nice. You should, Mama May."

"We'll see. Sometimes, though I miss him, I do enjoy my space as does he. Oh yeah, ya mama and Shanice will be here in two and a half weeks. I think it's the third Wednesday from today, if I'm not mistaken."

"Un hun. I knew you were gonna tell me. So that's what you're lookin forward to?"

"Any way, they'll be here from that Wednesday til that Monday. It'll be just them two. They're leaving the girls with your father."

"Good for Shanice! I'm sure she can use a break given the separation and all. Hey, do you think Mya will be able to come? That'll be cool, just us girls."

"You're right. That would be. But she's working on opening the doors to her health clinic in September. And they're still renovating the facility."

"Aw man. Well, maybe next time. I need to be better about keepin in touch with my cuz. I'm so proud of her."

"Yeah. Maybe next time. I'm very proud of her, too."

"I know you are."

Once the screen door closes behind Mama May, my mind immediately flips to Deron, our conversation, and that old feelin comin over me as if I was a sophomore at Xavier and we're at his apartment messin around. This shit is crazy. This is sorta how I ended up in bed with Black's ass. You know, instead of me focusing on moi, I was payin attention to his description. Remember?

Happy to pay me some attention, I shake off the memory of that night with Black with a forced shiver and place the thought of Deron behind my mind and take my journal out of my bag so that I can document the events of the day and all my emotions associated with them. I'm not surprised when I check my phone for the time and find that it's 10:15. Since I'm not even close to being sleepy, I decide to write some affirmations for a while to ensure that my self love is on automatic all of the time. Consistent repetition of anything turns into habit(s). And Lawd knows I need to learn how to love and honor me all of the time. After three and a half pages, front and back, are filled with actually only one affirmation (My body, mind, thoughts, words, and actions are Divinely healed now.), I decide to just sit back and zone out and just be with the stars. I go to bed once an hour or so passes, grateful for my *now*.

Peeling Away The Layers

Ididn't realize how quickly things would progress between me and Deron, my sweetie pie, after we ran into each other a few months ago. Shoot, no one could've told me that I'd quit Computel Financial, put my brownstone on the market, and move to Atlanta. But, here I am. I am truly the luckiest woman in the world to have found him again. As I twirl around in my wedding dress, I reminisce about our days at Xavier and how I always knew that he was my soul mate.

"You look stunning!"

"Ab-so-lute-ly beautiful!"

I stop twirlin for a moment to face my mom and sister. "Thanks, y'all!"

"Well, baby sis, this is it! The usher's about to walk Mom down the aisle."

My mom air kisses me so that she won't mess up my makeup. I don't know if I can smile any brighter. "Okay. I love you, Ma."

"I love you, too, baby. I'll see you on your way to the altar."

Ooop! By the mention of the altar and the immediate thought of Deron poppin in my mind, I do believe that smile got a little brighter. "Hahaha! Okay, Ma."

Wow! I'm really getting married. And to my baby. Time really does heal.

Queenie walks into the room with a big smile on her face, lookin as beautiful as ever in the burnt-orange-colored gown she chose to wear. I like the fact that her and my sister, Shanice, my two maids of honors and only bridesmaids, are wearing the dresses of their choice – Queenie in a long, seductive gown that gracefully falls on her curves in just the right places while Shanice opted for a short, sassy number that shows off her gorgeous legs and cleave.

"Okay, mamacita, you ready? Cuz it's time for me and Queenie to walk that walk?"

"Girl, I was ready thirteen years ago."

"I hear ya, sis. Dad's gonna knock on the door when they're ready for you to walk your walk."

"Okay. Thanks Shanice. I love you, girl. I love both of you. Now, please leave so I won't start cryin."

"Okay, baby. See you at the altar."

"Okay."

I squeeze Queenie's hand as we both voice a slight squeal before she turns and leaves with Shanice.

I close my eyes for a bit to take in the moment. And when I open them, my dad walks in, without knocking first, with a look in his eyes that I've never seen before, but I hope to repeatedly henceforth. Pure joy.

"Well, look at my baby girl."

"Hi Daddy."

"You look beautiful, baby."

"Thank you, Daddy."

"Now, you sho you wanna marry this young man?"

"Hahaha! Dad!"

"I'm jus sayin that it's not too late to change your mind."

"I'm absolutely super duper positive with a cherry on da top sure that I wanna marry him."

"Well, I guess you're ready to do this then, hunh?"

"Yep."

"Okay then, after you, sweet lady."

I feel like I'm floatin down the aisle as my family and friends oooh and ahhh at me. I start feelin a lil anxious when I can't see Deron clearly from everyone standin up and takin pictures. Right as I get to the second pew, my baby turns to me.

Lil Redd?! "AAAHHH!" My heart's about to jump out of my chest and I can't find my breath.

"Corey! Corey!"

I hear someone callin my name from far away.

"Corey! Corey!"

Someone is touchin me.

"What's wrong, baby? You're soak and wet."

"Hah, hah, hah, hah." I try to catch my breath before I answer. "Hah, hah, hah." Confused and a lil scared, I look at Mama May tryin to figure out who she is and where I am. I wipe my eyes and then my face out of reflex I guess. "Hah, hah, hah!" I close my eyes until my panted breaths calm down. I begin to remember where I am as I feel Mama May rubbing my back slowly in a circle. "I just had a nightmare."

"I know. I figured that. You look like you just saw a ghost."

I can feel and hear my heart beat. "Yeah, well…"

"You, okay? You want me to sit in here for a while til you fall back to sleep?"

"Haha!" Nervous laughter. What the fuck was that? Lil Redd? Deron? Me getting married? "No thanks, Auntie. I'll be okay. I think I'm gone just sit up for a while, maybe read or go out on the porch to get some fresh air." I avoid her eyes for no reason in particular. "What time is it?"

"Okay, baby. It's five fifty five in the morning."

"Oh. Okay. Thanks. I'm sorry for wakin you up, Auntie."

"That's okay, baby. Was it a spirit messing with you or a nightmare?"

"For the first time, I really don't know. Maybe a lil of both."

"Hmm. Well, I'ma go on ahead and lay back down for another hour before I practice my Zhan Zhuang. There is some sage in my meditation room if you'd like to burn some – just in case there's something negative lurking around."

"Okay. Thanks."

I silently attack my psyche once Mama May leaves the room. *What the fuck? Lil Redd? What was that all about? It felt so real. Are me and Deron getting married eventually? Do I want us to?* "Naaawww! Unh, unh!" *That has to be my mind playin tricks on me cuz he said that he was gone ask me to marry him when we were back at Xavier.*

Nanh, you have to admit that that was some mo shit fo my ass, right? You know, Deron confessing, so to speak, that I was, in fact, on the course of being Sal, not Sally. You heard him. Talk about a kick in the ass cuz Lil Redd sho put a stop to all of that shit. Or, do I do that with my negative attitude of how men will perceive me once they find out that I have herpes? Hell, I believe that we attract that which we think. And, you can say, to a certain extinct, that I am a lil obsessed with the concepts of rejection and/or not being the Sal girl, or woman. Shoot, if our dreams have any connection to our subconscious and conscious thoughts, then that nightmare I just had hit the frickin head on the nail. It's like I cannot visualize a happy outcome with a man in my own regard, hence, Lil Redd's ass at the altar.

Ever since I got raped, I feel like when I'm datin someone new, that somethin's gone come up or creep in and fuck everything up. Shit! I can't even have a happy outcome in my fuckin dreams. And where the hell did Lil Redd come from anyway? How he gone just pop up like that?

I know that rationally it makes sense that I'd dream Lil Redd up cuz of me seein Deron yesterday, our conversation, and my thoughts and emotions during and after our interaction. But right now is really not a good time for Lil Redd to be surfacing. Shit.

I determine that I need some fuckin air, so I put some shorts and flip flops on with my night shirt, disarm the alarm, and head toward the pool so that I can soak my feet and cool my body temperature down from my emotions.

I stop for a moment for no particular reason. I don't even know what thought I just had that propelled me to stop walkin. Hmm. After a few moments of standin still and thinkin about that dream, I start walkin toward the pool again. *I's got to cool down.*

Whew! Talk about a sista needin to get a grip. Humph. Plus… ooh, wait. *Ohhh yeah.* (That Ferriss Bueller theme song again.) This is good, ya'll. I'm always pleasantly surprised by the sweet aroma of all the lavender planted around the pool. I can't help stopping in my tracks and allowing its allure take over my nostrils. After more than a few moments, I decide not to put my feet in the water. Instead, I purposely sit in the chair closest to the largest amethyst crystal so I can just admire it for a moment. I'm always bedazzled by the deep purple that makes up the amethyst crystal because, to me, it's an enigma of royal adornment birthed directly from the earth just for my personal enjoyment. Aw, yes my dawlins, I am officially calming down now. *Thank You, GOD.* Yes!

My body temperature's miraculously coolin down and my heart beat is slowing, as well. This is just what I needed. *Lavender, take me away.*

Thankful for the meditative properties of the crystal and the calming effects of the lavender potted around the pool, I allow myself to zone out as I ask GOD for guidance regarding the anxiousness I felt after my dream in regards to Lil Redd and the outcome of my life. I must say that I'ma lil confused cuz I thought I'd let all of that go – that I wasn't affected from the rape or lost of Deron anymore – that it was more about me havin herpes that's been buggin me out throughout the recent years. But, then again, seein Deron yesterday brought back the organic nature of my yesteryear. And, real talk? Since I got herpes as a result of the rape, then that explains why I'm still affected by the rape. *Duh, Corin.* And I guess that even though I forgave Deron yesterday, and truly feel in my heart of hearts that I can move forward without any resentment towards him, that I need to communicate that to my subconsciousness.

Even though, in a physical factual sense, Deron and Lil Redd are part of the root of the cause, I need to put them to the side for right now, while I look at me today. Cuz, based upon how everyone looked in that dream, aside from Lil Redd, it was us today. And, the me today, well…I need some serious psychological assistance.

Like, for instance, look at what happened between me and Black. I allowed two months to go by before I told him about my situation becuz I was meticulously psychin myself out with all of my negative ready-made responses of what I thought he might say. And the ultimate conviction would be that him, and anyone else for that matter, would think that I was this bad girl out ho-in around – that I wasn't worthy of intimate love, a committed relationship, or kids. Yep, that's what lives in my head, ya'll – Doomsville to the nth degree.

It's crazy cuz part of what I told Black was true, though. I didn't tell him before that night cuz I didn't feel comfortable sharing something like that over the phone. Plus, I also had the grand idea to let him get to know me and see me as a person with ideas, goals, and a heart before we both focused on the lust we painted on one another. And though we did talk a lot on the phone, I just never got that feelin of *this is a safe moment* with him.

Humph, and shoot, now that I'm sharing all of this with ya'll, I'm seein that I really didn't feel all that *safe* when I told him in person that night either. I jus knew that he was lookin forward to comin to see me, to feel me and be inside of me, that I went along with everything so he wouldn't toss me to the side as the weird girl who shies away from intimate moments all the time. To me, in my low self-esteemed mind, I was caught between a rock and a hard place. I was tryin to please him, (acceptance from another), and fractionally being true to myself (non-acceptance of myself) with disclosure. I say fractionally because a part of me knew it was too soon for me to be intimate with him, that I still wanted to get to know him more. Hell, I believe that there's only so much you can learn about a person over the phone. You have to be around them during non-date moments to observe and take in how they observe and take in life. But, I didn't listen to that *common sense* part of me. No, I was in 'forget about me, it's all about him' mode – failingly hopin and wishin for Sal mode to be upon me.

So, I guess I have to say that timin isn't everything in regards to disclosure for me. I have to enhance my psychology to a more loving state.

We, meaning human beings, manifest our lives into existence every day by our thoughts. We are powerful beings. Please know this in the depth of everything that YOU ARE. There's so much power in our thoughts, feelings, beliefs, and emotions. I just need to alter my inner me and self-talk so that they're more persistently supportive of me so that I can help manifest positive and fulfilling outcomes by first believing in them and KNOWING that I'm worthy of them. I am physical, emotional, and mental proof that we can self-sabotage our lives by what we think just as much as we can appear as winners and successful achievers by the same method. Look at me! I am sitting very pretty in regards to my career, finances, and platonic friendships. But, me and romantic relationships haven't been harmonious in a long time – since before the rape, I guess.

Shiiittt! Life!

Now that I'm lookin back at that night with me and Black, I probably should've told 'em soon after he arrived. I knew, when he called to surprise me with the news that he was a couple of hours away from New York, that I was gonna have sex with him. I remember that he sounded so excited about seeing me that I couldn't bring myself to lettin him down. DING!

DING! DING! *I'm hearin You, GOD.* Maybe I shouldn't have waited until we were both all hot and bothered. But, I'm not gonna shoulda woulda coulda myself to death cuz, on that same note, he could have stopped himself. He didn't have to proceed forward.

Plus, on my behalf ya'll, from a personal perspective, I don't know how many of you have herpes or are in an intimate relationship with someone who does, but please know that it is a difficult concept to disclose, especially since there's no known cure. Sure, there are ways to prevent and lessen outbreaks via pharmaceuticals, diet, and management of stress levels. But, there is nothing on the market, today, that can kill this virus. Shoot. As I ponder nothing in particular, I realize that I have to give BIG Ups, again, to You, GOD. Yep, thank You! Cuz I'm realizin, the more and more I go on with *my story*, that I need to CONSISTENTLY focus more on me and practice honoring my thoughts, feelings, and beliefs in ALL situations in the moment of occurrence. I have to take care of me first, and others after I'm good with me. Ooooh, wait. Somethin just came to me. I have to stop concerning myself with being Sal or Sally, and lovingly focus on being Corin. Hmmm. *Now, that's profound GOD. Thank You. Thank You. Thank You for this peaceful environment, the revelations, helping me to heal myself, and the gift of meditation.*

Closing my eyes, I shift my posture to a more erect position with my back against the back of the chair, uncross my legs and place both feet flat on the ground, and point my palms upwards as they rest on my thighs uncrossed. First, I silently repeat, *Thank You, God* over and over again before I allow my mind to quiet as I focus on my breathing. I become aware of all of my inhalations and exhalations from the sound of my breath entering and exiting my nose, and my stomach expanding and contracting. Thoughts creep into my consciousness one by one. But, as I focus on the rhythm of my breathing, I don't notice them after a while. And, before long, *I just am* – in meditation.

After maybe thirty or forty-five minutes, who knows, I allow myself to focus in on my environment. When I open my eyes, I feel a thought enter between my ears. I recognize it for a second before it disappears. Damn, please come back. Havin a feelin that that thought was important, I make it a point to remain still. I begin watchin my stomach rise and fall through my periphery as I look at nothing in particular in front of me. After a few moments, I feel and hear the thought more clearly.

"Wow! Humph." I laugh at what jus gently landed in my mind. Hahaha! Wait a minute. I just had a mirror check, my dawlins. Gotta thank GOD for checkin me. Yep. *Thank You, GOD!* Okay, I'm not gonna leave y'all hangin. So, I know y'all already figured this out but it turns out that I'm still judging Vanessa, my so-called friend from high school, AFTER ALL THESE YEARS for something she had nothing to do with AFTER ALL THESE FUCKIN YEARS. Well, I be damned. So, why, you're probably askin, did I judge her so much? Wow! I shake my head at the truth of my thoughts. Becuz I haven't learned how to fully love and accept myself yet. Hence, the tightness in my chest that you witnessed the other day when I was tellin ya'll my story, and when I was massagin that Heidi chick back in New York. You know, when I was affirmin my self-love and acceptance. Hunhunhun! Damn. I'm gettin it, GOD. Whew! What a trip. When I think back, Vanessa, LaTronda, and Stacey ain't never did anything to me and they had nothing to do with me gettin raped or havin herpes. But, I spent a long time, back then and up to now, wondering why I got dealt a bad hand and not them. I guess it was easier to transfer my anger and confused emotions upon them instead of fully dealin with MY SHIT MYSELF.

How selfish and cruel of me. DING! DING! DING! Okay. So, this revelation trumps the one of me finally letting go of that whole Sal versus Sally fixation I'd been holdin on to since the fourth grade. Out loud, I verbalize my thoughts, "Oooh, oooh, oooh! Thank You! Thank You! Thank You, GOD! Thank You for pointing that out to me. Damn!" I'm definitely not happy with the reflection of myself that You've just shown me. But, I can't, and don't want to, deny it either.

OoohWeee! Are there enough apologies in the world that I can make upon myself in their regard? Hell, in my regard? Damn! Oh, how I hope so. They were my friends and I mentally betrayed them for years. Shit, and I guess by betrayin them through judging them, I was betrayin myself, as well, cuz I judged myself every time I judged them. *Oooh, double damn, damn, damn!*

Okay! So, I'm gone need Your help on this, too, GOD. Please show me how to forgive myself for those gross thoughts and sentiments I impressed upon them and myself, as well as, overcome all of this guilt I'm having now from that abominable revelation. Shaking my head, I absentmindedly whisper, "Shit! My issues are piling up. How many layers are there?"

Talk about a thousand-watt light bulb, on full blast, shinin through my thoughts and pre-thoughts. I am seeing that I NEVER really focused on me wholeheartedly after the rape. Sure, I went to counseling, wrote and recited countless affirmations, meditated continuously, and even forgave Lil Redd, Deron, and a portion of myself – so I thought. Hell, I'm thinkin NOT now. I mean, how could I have forgiven myself if I never accepted myself or my circumstances. For years, I judged three individuals, Vanessa, LaTronda, and Stacey, who probably think of me as a cool person and a good friend. But, all the while I was comparing myself and life experiences to theirs – I was judgin them. Wow! So much is comin to me at once. *So, I guess I was judging them and their life experiences because I was in constant judgment of my own? Shit! Hold on.*

Oooh, wait, ya'll. My apologies if it seems like I'm repeatin myself, but there are so many thoughts comin to me at once. And I'm tryin to discern them all. *Okay, okay, so if I'm judging others, I'm not acceptin myself?* Wanting to get up to walk around, I abruptly stand. But I find myself almost falling to the ground as I halfway miss the chair when I make myself sit back down from my sudden dizziness. Talk about a replay from when I'd just gotten off the phone with Black that infamous day at the spa.

Okay, wait GOD. Thank you so much for all of this insight. But, let me catch myself for a moment. While sitting down in the chair, I bend from the waist and hold my head between my legs to help the dizziness go away. Yep, this is a replay all right.

Once I get my composure, again, I slowly rise to an upright sitting position. Okay, so this shit is deep. I knew my self-love needed some workin on. And, now I'm seein that I never was really workin on it cuz I never fully accepted myself after that damn rape. Hell, maybe not even before that joint either since it supposedly inadvertently spawned such judgments of myself and others. *Shit!*

I allow my thoughts to play detective as I try to wrap my mind around all of this. *Okay! I was raped. Corin, you were raped. It happened. It's over. It wasn't your fault. You didn't ask for it. But, yet you never...* Wait! I never got over the fact that, I, Corin Rivers got raped. *Okay. I think I'm getting this.*

I have to forgive myself for being so hard on myself and others for all of those and these years, for getting raped and for havin herpes in spite of bein a good girl.

Humph. Okay. Sooo, when I take a deeper look into this shit, I see that I never ever forgave myself, or my elders, for that matter. I mean, if I had, I wouldn't have been so caught up on Mrs. Bordeaux's infamous reference to Sal versus Sally. And, keepin it real, ya'll, Mrs. Bordeaux wasn't my only elder. Others, like my parents, aunts, uncles, and their friends, instilled within me basic ladylike principles, like keep your dress down and your legs closed and guys will respect you, in addition to speak, walk, and conduct yourself like a lady, and guys will look at you in a higher regard than they do those fast girls.

And while I'm thinking about it, I've probably been subconsciously holdin resentment against, oooh, dare I say? I look up in the sky for a brief moment before I whisper the unmentionable. "You, as well, GOD."

My mind pauses for a few moments. I don't know if it's possible not to think, but I swear it feels like five minutes just passed and I was unconsciously conscious – whatever that means. And, now I'm afraid to think out of fear of betrayin *You, GOD,* further. *I feel like I've committed the abominable sin – feeling resentment toward You. Maybe I've always known that anger was there, but was too afraid to let the thought of it fully form in my mind. I guess I just admitted that I've been an undercover part-time enemy of Yours. Please! Please!* I cover my face with my hands as shameful tears flow out of my eyes. *Please, accept my humblest apologies. Oh, GOD. Shit, I now know that if I never got over Deron leaving me before yesterday, having herpes, being raped, or renaming myself as Sally, then I damn sho ain't over You letting all of that happen to me.* Hmmm, it makes me wonder if I'm really over Deron leavin like he did or if I'm just exhausted over holdin on to the hurt for so long. *Who knows?*

I grab at my chest to brace myself for a psychic blow, of some sort, and to verify, and hopefully calm down, the strong thumping from my heart. My accelerated heartbeat seems to activate my sweat glands in motion to cool the permeating heat envelopin my body. I simply sit still and observe my body react to the uncomfortable emotions relating to me and GOD.

When I admit myself back into detective mode, I notice that I must've calmed down a lot cuz I don't feel the sweat nor the heat that I just observed. And my face and eyes are clear of tears. "Okay. I said it." I look around me and up at the sky, playfully, to make sure a lightning bolt ain't sneakin up on me to strike me down. "So, okay, what do I do with that, GOD? How do I heal that? Me? Us? It's clear to me that you're helpin me uncover all of this about me. So, what and how now?"

I flip my thoughts over repeatedly in my mind. I notice that I'm neither happy nor sad about anything. And, I can't help but notice the hint of shame I keep tryin to sweep behind my heart as if to try to hide from GOD my accusations of ITS actions – my life. Then, I feel a comforting tingling sensation on my back and a light pressure at the top of my head. Likin the reassuring sensations upon my body, I silently observe my body's reception to it all.

It's not always easy lookin at yourself in the mirror. In fact, it's hard as fuck. But, I'm glad that I've finally braved the glance so that I can work on movin through all of this stuff. I didn't think I'd feel this way when I came outside, but I'm glad I had that nightmare. *And I'm glad it ended the way it did so that I could come out here and be open to You talkin to me GOD. I know it's You. And as always, I thank You.* I'm seein that I never forgave anyone or gotten over anything in a deep way. I guess that my prayers, meditations, and affirmations, all those years, were just tapping the surface of it all. I'm sure they helped me move on with my life so that I could get through Xavier. But, they never really touched upon the meat of everything.

This is so crazy interesting to me cuz I don't know how I feel about all of this. Of course, I am happy for the revelations. And I'm happy that I'm surrounded by all of this beauty and the stillness of the morning here at Mama May's. So, my synopsis is that a part of me is definitely very happy right now. With that, I join the stillness of the morning again, and fade the detective in me to black.

When I finally rise to go back into the house, I am clear that complete, consistent forgiveness of myself, others, and especially, GOD, are essential in order for me to move forward.

Loungin

Meditation or being still with GOD is so therapeutic to my peace of mind that I wish I'd have the right mind to do it daily as oppose to most of the time. Saturday passed with me being more at peace with myself than I've been in a long time. For a Georgian summer day, the weather was pretty mild. It must've gotten up to eighty degrees at high noon and the humidity was pretty low. The nice weather prompted Mama May and I to spend most of the day outside. We hung out by the pool for a few hours. We both read and put our feet in the water every now and then. Though I really wanted to swim, I didn't want to mess up the TB test for nothin.

That morning, after my meditation and revelations, I went to the store to pick up some viddles for us to eat during the weekend. I told Mama May that I wanted to wait on her like she's been doin with me. So, I picked up lots of fruit, vegetables, and some salmon. When I got back to the house, I made a huge fruit salad with watermelon, melon, cantaloupe, strawberries, plums, pineapple, red grapes, and blueberries. We pretty much ate on that and drank lots of water while we were chillin at the pool.

That evening I made her my signature curry spinach and chickpeas with brown rice for dinner. To say she enjoyed it is an understatement. In fact, I wanna say she went back for thirds, she liked it so much. Hun hun. Well, we topped our day off with the movie *Ray*, which, to me was so inspirational. Nanh, please don't think that I condone men cheatin on women or usin drugs or nothing like that. I was, actually, amazed at the success that Ray Charles carved out for himself, as an artist, being a blind man.

After the movie, we sat up and talked until both of us couldn't keep our eyes opened. We talked about everything under the sun and then some. She, actually, had me crackin up about the one time she went to a Ray Charles concert and how bad my grandmother talked about her for cutting all of her hair off for a popular hairstyle back then that they referred to as the 'poodle' hairstyle. The joke was that, at the time, the majority of the women would pin their hair up in, what they called, pin curls to attain the style. But, not Mama May. Unh, unh. She went ahead and cut her hair into the style, I guess to attain a more authentic look. And, apparently, my grandmother couldn't wrap her mind around why Mama May would take such measures just to go to a concert given by a man who couldn't see her even if she was picked to go up on stage and dance on his piano. And to top it all off, the latter wasn't even an option since her and her girlfriends' seats were up in the nosebleed section of the Municipal Auditorium – which is now a closed-down concert hall in New Awlins.

Mama May said that that was one of my grandmother's favorite stories to retell. Humph, I gotta give it to my grandmother cuz that shit was funny as hell – all of that for a blind man. But, according to Mama May, though, she definitely stood out with her black and red dress topped with her mama's black and red heals. She said that nobody couldn't tell her nothing and that she didn't pay my grandmother no never mind cuz she knew she was lookin sharp. It would've been nice if she had a picture of herself before she went to the concert. I can only imagine how pretty she looked.

Well any way, then she started tellin me about the days when she was a young woman, stories I had heard before, but was just as into them as if it were my first time hearing them. You remember what I told you, earlier, bout me and nostalgia, right? I was hangin on to her every word so much, in addition to puttin my imagination on blast, that I almost thought that I was one of her homegirls from back in the day who could throw in my own unprecedented memories. Ahunhunhun. Like, for instance, when she talked about her boyfriends and gentleman callers that didn't possess the savoir fair to carry the title of her boyfriend, I felt like we were old friends talkin bout the good ole days. And that was so cool cuz she went and got some old pictures, out of one of the closets, so that we could add backdrops to the stories. As I flipped through the photo albums, I couldn't help but admire, as I've done on so many occasions, how beautiful Mama May and my mother were and are. I don't know how any young man stood being in their presence, they were such knockouts back in the day. That might just be why my daddy and Uncle Charles never let either of them go.

Anyway, before going to sleep, we laughed and joked about the awkward way they used to slow drag (slow dance) back then. She said that the women would put one hand over their shoulder behind their back, and the other one behind their back closer to their waist while the men would press their bodies against theirs while they held the women's hands in place behind their backs. When she got up to demonstrate it, I couldn't help but think about how uncomfortable that looked and all the things, we, women go through to compromise our comfort, at times, for the sake of a man's comfort and enjoyment. Hey, but that's just me and my observations. She didn't seem bothered or annoyed by the compromised position they were in while she was demonstratin it for me. In fact, she was very playful and lighthearted about it. And that's so funny cuz her and my mama will hem and haw all day about how my generation and younger have lost all respect for one another based upon the way we dance and the music we listen to. Humph. But, nonetheless, yesterday was a cool day.

This morning I woke up chucklin bout my grandmother, Mama May, and the Ray Charles's concert at the Municipal Auditorium. I felt my smile linger from my own vague memory of the concert hall that used to be. All I remember is coming home from school, one day, and being told to put on a cute outfit that was laid out on my bed. My mom didn't tell me or Shanice until we were in the car that we were on our way to see the Jackson Five at the Municipal Auditorium. I don't even know if I can explain it in words, all the bliss I experienced that night. Right after she told us in the car, I suddenly couldn't keep still and couldn't seem to shut up as oppose to my sister who calmly sat in the car like my mother was takin us to school or somethin. But, all that was lost as soon as they announced The Jackson's as they walked and ran out on stage - Shanice ended up joining me and the rest of the auditorium with uncontrollable screams, cheers, and dancing as they started with a medley of all of their old hits. I wish I could remember the line-up of songs so I can give ya'll a more accurate picture, but a part of me was in so much shock, that I don't remember much about the performances, just mainly the happiness I felt and the fun I had.

Oh, but wait. I do remember this. Shanice had just bought Michael Jackson's album, *Off The Wall*, a few months before, and we both went ballistic when Michael transitioned from the Jackson Five's hits, to just his songs from the album. Shoot, I even remember my mama getting up and dancin to "Rock with You" and "Don't Stop 'Til You Get Enough." And don't even talk about when he cried during "She's Out of My Life." E-v-e-r-y-body went crazy wild then. Hell, I think I even shed a tear to add to the theatrics of the moment. Hahaha! Yep, my mama got us good that night. I was so elated, and still very surprised, even after we returned home because that was such an unlikely move from my mom – it bein a school night and all. It was like she gave us a free pass to scream, jump around, stomp our feet, and act like plum fools just for the night. Humph, and best believe that I still have the program book. Trust when I say that I ain't givin that thing up for nothin – I don't care how much money it may be worth right now.

So, anyway, I've been chillin most of the day in my room. It's been raining since early this morning which is cool with me cuz I happily don't have anywhere I need to be.

Me and Mama May talked for a while in the kitchen – me tellin her about my memory of The Jackson Five concert and more - as we sat and ate the phenomenal brunch I made earlier. Oh yeah, ya girl can get down. Please don't sleep. I hooked us up with some creamy yellow grits, perfectly seasoned baked salmon, home fries and a green salad. We ate so much that once we were all talked out, we both went and took a nap that felt mmm mmm good.

Now, I'm sittin in the window seat in my room takin a break from this book I've been readin, off and on, since I woke up this morning. It's called *Far from the Tree*. I've got to give it to the authors; they've successfully captured my full attention so much that I don't wanna put it down to meditate and journal, but I know I need to work on me. In fact, as of today, or really, since yesterday morning, I'm committed to consistent self-work every morning and evening via prayer, affirmations, gratitude, meditation, and/or exercise. Yep. It's all centered around forgiveness and…

"Corey!"

"Ma'am?"

"Your phone is ringin and it's in the den."

"Oh. Okay. Thanks."

As I walk to the den, I realize that I haven't missed my phone all day.

Right as I pick it up, it stops ringin. I see that it's a Georgia phone number and the only two people who have my number whose names aren't programmed in my phone are Deron and Zyon. I call it back out of reflex, and almost hang it up when I realize that I really don't wanna talk to Deron just yet. But, as I hear it ring, I realize that I'm frickin committed now. To my delight, I identify the voice as Zyon's.

"Beautiful?"

"Hi."

"Hey. I was just leaving you a message."

"Oh, okay. I hope it's sweet."

"Hahaha! Gotta be if it's for you."

Smiling from ear to ear, I walk back to my room and quietly shut the door for some privacy. "Okay. I like that."

"Un hun. Is this a good time?"

I pause for a moment cuz I really wanna meditate and journal, but the clock's illumination of 6:30 p.m. convinces me that since it's still pretty early, I can spare him a few moments of my time. "Well, I was about to get into something, but I can talk for a minute."

"Damn, all I get is a minute?"

"Well, maybe I'll spare a lil more."

"I guess a brother gotta take what he can get."

"Hey, every lil bit from me is platinum, baby."

"Hahaha! I think I like that."

"Ahun Ahun. Don't think about it. Be about it."

"Hahaha!"

"Hahaha!" I stop laughing. "Let me stop messin with you. What's up, Zyon? What gives me the pleasure of hearing your voice through my phone today?"

"Well, you been on my mind since Friday. Or, maybe I should say that beautiful smile of yours been on my mind since Friday."

"Hahaha! Okay. I like flattery nanh. Keep it comin."

"Hahaha. Hey, a brother's just speaking the truth."

"Un hunh. Brownie points already. This is good."

"Ahun hun. A funny lady, are you?"

"Humph, just speakin the truth."

"I hear you. Well, I wanted to call you all weekend, but today was the first time I got some time to myself since I've been covering for Tariq."

"Oh, when will he be back at work?"

"Tomorrow."

"Oh, well, that's good."

"Yeah, but even though I'm worn out, it was good getting my hands dirty. You know, reconnecting with the earth with such demanded intensity."

"What do you mean?"

"Well, since I've grown the business where I contract workers out to do the jobs I design, I manage more than I participate in the actual work."

"Oh, okay. I see."

"Now don't get me wrong, I like how it's evolved and everything, but I'm just saying that this weekend felt good vibing with the earth."

Hmmm. I didn't expect this from fineness. I like the way he talks, the way he puts things. "Well, do you think you'll have time to save a project, or, at least, a part of one for yourself every now and then?"

"Yeah. I was thinking that I'ma have to do that."

"Yeah."

"I have my own landscape at home that I redesign from time to time. But I think I'd like to challenge myself with another piece of land in addition to my own."

"Nice."

"Yeah. But enough of me, pretty lady, what are you takin a break from in New York?"

"Hmmm, besides me?"

"Hahaha! Yeah, I guess besides you."

"Well, I work in the financial services industry by day and I'm a massage therapist when I'm not doin that."

"Oooh, are you any good? Cuz I could sure use your hands right now."

"I'm better than good, my dawlin."

"Well, maybe I'm gonna have to find out for myself one day."

Oooh, I like how he didn't just volunteer my hands on his back as an option for us to link up soon. I just hate when guys do that. "Yeah. Maybe one day."

"Well, I know you said that you were about to get into something. So, I'm not gonna keep you too much longer. I just want to know when I can see you again."

"Ummm."

"Wait, let me ask you this. Do you like nature?"

I hesitate a little as I wonder where he's going with this. "Uhhhh, yeah, I'm all for nature. I think?"

"Hahaha! Don't worry, I'm not gonna ask you to join me on one of my jobs."

"Well, that's good cuz I can't say that I have much of a green thumb."

"Naw, naw, you're clear of all planting assignments."

"Okay, cool. Cuz I was about to say, is this brotha a workaholic or something? Gone take me out on one of his jobs and call it a date? Oooh, unh, unh. He ain't that fine." Ooop, did I just say that?

"Oh, okay. Hahaha! Embarrassed pajama girl got jokes."

"Oooh, no you didn't."

"Yeah I did. Besides, it wasn't like it was a bad look any way."

Briefly feeling my*self,* I put a big ole Gumby smile on my face. "We know this."

"I hope so."

Not knowin, really, how to respond, I allow my nervous laughter to save the moment and fill the space.

"Ummm." Zyon clears his throat as if he's stalling for time or hesitant about something. "Please don't take this the wrong way, but do you work out or are you naturally tone?"

"Hahaha! Zyon was checkin me out."

"Yeah. Well, a brother's not blind you know. You're a beautifully crafted creation."

"Well, thank you. And, to answer your question, both. I am a runner and I am naturally toned."

"Okay. Ahun. I like that. Well, I was wonderin if you'd like to climb Stone Mountain with me one morning this week. Tomorrow, if you're not busy."

"Oh." How different. I'm likin him so far. "Where is it? Is it far from here?"

"Not at all. No more than thirty minutes from your aunt's house, if that."

"Oh. Okay. And are we hiking the entire mountain? I mean are we goin to the top – is it a big mountain?"

"Yeah. That's the goal. It's usually a challenge, for some, during their first time. But, you'll see that it's not so bad. Especially, for you, since you're a runner."

"Okay. Well, yes, I'd love to. But, how is your Tuesday cuz I have an appointment tomorrow morning?" Yes, I gotta go back to the doctor so that he can sign off on my physical so that I can, hopefully, start massagin folks this week maybe. I miss touchin people.

"That works for me cuz I go every morning during the week. I'm an early bird. I like to get there around 6 so that I can walk up the mountain during sunrise."

"Oooh, see, now you pushin it."

"What? You're not a morning person?"

"I could be. But my preference is to sleep in while I'm on my vacation."

"Oh! Right. My bad."

"But, you know what? I think I can make an exception for the sake of gettin my work out on, especially, since I haven't done anything for over a week."

"Are you sure? Cuz we can do something else."

"Naw. This sounds cool. I wanna do this."

"Okay, well…"

Before I realize it, I'm cuttin him off. "I just hope you don't mind me being quiet at first."

"I don't mind at all. In fact, I prefer to hike in silence."

"Well, then, that's what's up. It's a date. I look forward to seeing you again."

"Yeah. Me too, Corin."

"Sooo, I'll be ready at, what, 5:30 on Tuesday?"

"Yep! That'll work."

"Okay. It was good talkin to you."

"Yeah? Well, after the hike, maybe during breakfast, coffee, tea, or whatever your thing is, I'll learn more about you."

"Yeah, maybe."

"Ahun hun. All right, then, pretty lady, I bid you a good evenin."

"Thanks. You, too."

If Gumby was here, he'd try to take his smile off my face for the gumbiness of it all. Hahaha! But, that was nice. Maybe Mama May is right. Maybe, sometimes, a handsome distraction can do a world of good. Humph, time will certainly tell.

Now, where was I? Do I want to meditate first or write in my journal? Hmmm, I guess I'll write first. I decide to start with gratitude. Thank You, GOD, for peace of mind. Thank you, GOD, for courage. Thank You, GOD, for my life. Thank You, GOD, for happiness. Thank You, GOD, for my family and friends. Thank You, GOD, for healing my mind, thoughts, words, and actions. Thank, You, GOD, for healing my physical, mental, emotional, and ethereal bodies completely so that they are experiencing Divine homeostasis NOW and ALWAYS. Thank You, GOD, for self-love, self-acceptance, and commitment to myself. Thank You, GOD, for my acceptance of myself. Thank You, GOD, for my forgiveness of myself. Thank You, GOD, for my forgiveness of others. Thank You, GOD, for my forgiveness of You, GOD. Thank You for removing resentment from my total being completely. Thank You, GOD, for harmony throughout every aspect of my life. I am Divine. I am powerful. I am important. I am respectful of myself and others. I am valued. I am worthy of happiness. I am worthy of a healthy romantic relationship. I am patient. I trust the process of life. I am normal and natural. I am normal and natural. I am normal and natural. Things always work out for me. I am captivating, charismatic, and graceful. I love and accept myself. I love and accept myself. I love and accept myself. I love and accept myself. I love and accept myself. I am kind. I am compassionate. I release the past easily and effortlessly. I release the past easily and effortlessly. Letting go is easy for me. I deserve love in my life. Thank You, GOD.

This is feeling good. Thank You, GOD. Now, I'm ready to meditate. So,

I sit back in the chair in my room and just breathe. I notice at first that I feel very calm. And then, I zone out for at least twenty or so minutes before I come out of it and just sit in the quiet of the room while I watch and listen to the rain outside my window.

Waning Gibbous Moon

Practice unconditional love upon yourself. Release everyone
and everything that is not in alignment with the Divine.

What Kind Of Doctor Are You?!?

Normally, I would have mentally told my body to wake me up this morning because I don't enjoy being jolted out of my sleep by an alarm clock. But, since I'm not at home in Brooklyn and semi out of my comfort zone, I didn't want to risk my internal clock and perception to deceive me by not waking me up. So, I'm panting like a wild woman, as if a lion just roared in my face to wake me up and is now lookin at me like it thinks I taste good, the alarm clock startled me so much. Ugh! Alarm clocks are sooo unnatural. No one should be scared out of their sleep, or out of anything for that matter.

It doesn't make sense to get upset about it. I'm up now. I purposely set my alarm for 6:00 so that I'll have enough time to meditate and journal before I leave for my appointment at 7:30. Since I don't know what rush hour traffic looks like in Georgia, I don't wanna take a chance on being late given that my appointment's at 9:00.

Thank God for affirmations. I love the way my mind obediently calms down when I begin to write them out. By the time I sit back in meditation, I find myself feelin better than good energetically.

I can't stop thinkin about Zyon as I drive into the city. Respectful, fine as fuck, got his own business, no kids, friendly, can put sentences together coherently. Did I say fine as fuck? Shit, peoples! There has to be something wrong with him. Wait! Stop it, Corin. Don't start, girl. Let it be. Be in the moment. Be in the moment. Don't self-sabotage with your thoughts. Okay, I just have to be in the moment. And while I'm here, I need to believe that good things can happen to me as far as romance is concerned. Wait. No. I need to know that. Okay, GOD, teach me how to love and accept me, unconditionally, in addition to teachin me how to know that I deserve good outcomes when it comes to love in my life. I deserve to be happy. Corin, you deserve to be happy. Now, stop overthinkin him and you and be in this moment right here. Shit, girl, you need to be easy and just go with the flow. There's no love or romance yet – only one phone call. One, Corin. And you're linkin up to hike a mountain. That's it. Be in the moment. Be easy, mama. Chill the fuck out.

As I switch my mindset to the here and now, I switch from I20 Westbound to I75/85 Northbound. I can't believe all of the traffic I'm driving in. Wow. I'm so glad that I left early cuz it looks like I'm gone be right on time with no time to spare. Whew. Good lookin out, Corin, the planner.

As soon as I walk in the doctor's office, I sense that something's very different. Unless layoffs were just announced, these folks are bipolar, off cuz it's Monday, or I'm over-sensitizing the situation.

Hmmm, my nurse from Friday just walked past me with no warmth in her body language or facial expression. I'm convinced that if I hadn't spoken to her, she wouldn't have spoken. Well, okay. I would assume that she had a bad weekend if my doctor, from Friday, hadn't just acted the same way when he passed me to go into his office. Confused by the cool tone in here, I decide not to let it get to me and relax back into my chair.

Well, all righty then. I look up at the clock on the wall and notice that it's 9:20. That small discovery has me a little annoyed at the lack of communication in my regard from everyone here, especially my nurse and doctor from the other day. All I need is for someone to look at my arm so that they can determine the results of my TB test and sign off on my physical so that I can be on my way.

Before I'm cognizant of it, my inner dialogue starts up. Corin, stop. You can be so impatient. Maybe they got started late. But, this man has clearly been in his office, with the door cracked where I can see him, for about fifteen minutes now. What's the hold up?

"Ms. Rivers?"

It's about time. I quickly paint a smile on my face, to hopefully, hide my annoyance. "Yes?"

"Let me see your arm."

As I extend my left arm so that the nurse can examine the area of the TB test, I wonder why she seems so abrupt this morning. She is definitely not the same woman who was all smiles on Friday.

"Okay. Good. Your TB test is fine."

"Wonderful. Thank you."

"You're welcome. The doctor will see you now."

"Great! Thanks!"

Even though her persona was apples and rocks different from Friday, I just brush it off cuz I know I'm gone be outta here soon comin. I hold my smile in place as she holds the door, to the doctor's office, open for me.

"Good morning Ms. Rivers."

"Good morning." Okay. He's definitely a different dude from Friday.

"I apologize for keepin you waiting. It's just that I wanted to consult with one of my colleagues about something before I signed off on your physical."

"Oh? Do I need to come back?" Please don't make me have to wait longer for this, GOD.

"Well, no. Let me just ask you a few questions. I've just been informed that my colleague is at an all-day seminar. And I don't want to inconvenience you any longer."

"Okay. Sure."

"How long have you had herpes?"

What? "Ummm, for about thirteen years."

"And what type of herpes do you have?"

"I don't know. I never had the blood test done to determine if it's type I or II." What is going on?

"Well, when you have an outbreak, where does it occur?"

"In my genital area."

"So, you have type II? You do know that type II occurs in the genital region, while type I occurs around the mouth."

Okay. I thought he was the doctor here. He should know this, shouldn't he? "Well, like I said, I don't know which one I have becuz I never had the blood test done. But, people, who have type I, can pass it on to someone through oral sex, if they have an outbreak around their mouth. Once that occurs, the person who just received the virus will have outbreaks in their genital area because that's where the virus was transmitted to them at. If they have sexual intercourse, during an outbreak, they risk the chance of passing it on to the person whom they're havin sex with." Wow, this man is lookin at me as if I'm really teachin him somethin. This feels weird. "So, I could have either one of them – type I or type II. But, please pardon my confusion, what does this have to do with you signing off on my physical? According to you, on Friday, you just needed to see my reaction to the TB test. And, the nurse just said it was fine."

"Yeah. Well, like I said on Friday, I've never completed one of these physicals, for someone wanting to be a massage therapist, before, and I just want to make sure that I'm comfortable either way, whether or not I agree that you're fit to give massages."

"What? That I'm fit? Wait a minute, sir, whether I have type I or type II herpes, I'd only get outbreaks around my mouth or in my genital area, not on my hands or arms. And, all of the thirteen years I've had it, I've only had outbreaks in my genital area."

"Yeah?"

"Yes." *Really, GOD. What is this? Test Corin for a lifetime here?*

"Well, I'm sorry Ms. Rivers, I don't feel comfortable signing my name in agreement to you being physically fit to do this type of work."

KISS MY MOTHA FUCKIN ASS! This is so not happening. I have to be in a dream. Hell! Fuck that, a continuous nightmare with sequels is what my life is becomin! But wait, Corin. Get it together, mama. Don't lower yourself by goin off on this ignorant doctor. "Okay, sir, please don't mistake this question as being sarcastic. But, have you ever gotten a massage before?"

"No."

Damn. Black people, when are y'all gone start takin care of you. I can't believe that this doctor has never received a massage before. "Okay. Well, during a massage, there's no kissing or any kind of sex goin on. Well, at least I don't do that. I always work at reputable establishments that provide therapeutic massage therapy to their clients. The only way I could give one of my clients herpes is to have sex with them. Herpes is a sexually transmitted disease."

"I'm aware of that."

"Okay, well, I don't have sex while I give massages, let alone take my clothes off, even. That's unethical."

"I hear what you're sayin, but I just don't feel comfortable. I'm sorry, Ms. Rivers. Here's your form."

I take the form from him and immediately see that he checked the box indicating that he doesn't feel that I'm physically fit to be a massage therapist. Damn. "Okay. Well, thank you for your time." Asshole!

I place the strap to my purse on my shoulder and I walk out of his office feeling very confused and a little sorry for him and his ignorance. I mean, clearly I wasn't expectin that one. I don't find it surprising that the nurse is so engrossed in whatever she's doin that she can't look up to say goodbye. And, so obviously, now I understand all of the weirdness, from the two of them, earlier.

Once I'm in my car, I wonder how I got here cuz I don't remember my journey to the parking lot. I can't say that I feel numb becuz my upper back, between my shoulder blades, feels tight and sore. And, that's not surprising cuz that's the backside of the heart chakra. And my heart fa damn sho feels broken to the nth degree times infinity right about now.

I turn on the ignition, and as soon as the car starts, quiet, hot tears begin to fall. Every time I wipe them away and try to force myself to stop crying, they persist more. Ooop, it's turnin into one of them ugly cries now with my mouth wide open. I'm developin this intense feelin in my throat where it's hard to take a swallow. Oh yeah, y'all, my quiet cry has transformed into a full-fledged ugly, hard one. It kinda feels like I have a lump in my throat - that I just ate two supersize orders of fries from McDonald's and I need water to push a clump of it down my throat. After a while of this discomfort, a thought finally enters my mind and tells me to focus on my breathing. Once I do, I have a few of what I call hiccup sniffles where, it's like, my body keeps inhaling through my nose in short multiple breaths while my head tilts up and back in a jerky movement as it follows the rhythm of the hiccup sniffles. Once it's over I'm rewarded with a regular exhale. The more I focus on my breathin, the less intense the hiccup sniffles. And, before I know it, I am calm. A little exhausted from the cry and the emotional hit to my psyche, but calm.

Comfortable with my emotions, I put the car in reverse so that I can get out of the parking lot and head back to Mama May's. Though I know that this is probably a good time to pray, I wallow in self-pity and slip into my *woe be unto me* mindset for a few moments before I speak out loud. "Why me, GOD? So what? Really? These are the cards laid out for me? This is how the stars are aligned for me? What is it that You want from me?" I mean, really, this is my career. I came to Georgia to heal. I'm makin an effort to heal and let go of the past. Is this your way of tellin me to focus on me and not work? If so, can a sista get a message in a dream or somethin? Like, what am I supposed to do with this? Feel less rejected? "Uhhh, not working. This shit has fucked up my love life, and now it's bleedin over into my career? Damn! What do you want me to do? Really! Help me, please! How do I get over this? Please, GOD!"

Desperate for peace, I commence to pray. "The Lord is my shepherd, I shall not want. It maketh me lie down in green pastures. It leadeth me beside the still waters. It restoreth my soul. It leadeth me in paths of righteousness for ITS name's sake. Yeh though I walk through the valley of the shadow of death, I will fear no evil. For thy rod and thy staff, they comfort me. Thou preparest a table before me in the presence of mine enemies. Thou anointest my head with oil. My cup runneth over. Surely goodness and mercy shall follow me all the days of my life, and I dwell in the house of the Lord forever and ever amen. The Lord is my shepherd..."

Okay, so the 23rd Psalm is helpin me some. I keep repeatin it over and over again cuz I don't have a clue of what else I can do at this moment. The sound of my voice coupled with me tunin in and out on the message is helpin me to keep out the noise of self-pity and doom and gloom.

Sometimes Disclosure Is Refreshing

Before I know it, I'm parked near Mama May's garages. Being on automatic is a scary thing cuz I swear I don't remember stopping to enter the code at Mama May's electronic gate let alone most of the ride to get here. Hmmm, it makes me wonder if all of this is really happening.

I yelp at the sharp pain I just inflected on my arm from pinchin myself to make sure I'm not dreamin. Okay, I guess I'm not dreamin. Damn!

I need to talk to my girl, Queenie, in the worst way. So I grab my cell phone out of my purse and call her before I get out of the car. "Damn! Voicemail! Where are you?!"

I grab my purse, get out of the car and walk towards the house. Right as I step on the top step of the porch, my cell phone rings and Mama May appears in the doorway with a warm smile on her face. "Good morning!"

I look at my phone and see that it's Queenie callin me back. I look back at Mama May as if to say I need to get this when something in her eyes penetrates my core. Before I know it, I start crying all over again and within moments I feel her arms around me. She walks me into the house toward the couch in the living room. She sits us down and just holds me.

"Go ahead, baby. Get it all out. That's a girl. It's gone be all right. Everything is gonna be okay, my baby. No matter what it is. It's gone be all right."

We sat there for a long time in silence after I finished cryin. Her house phone rang twice and she didn't budge. In her arms, I felt so safe, and eventually, at peace.

I'm tired of hidin and keepin secrets. Before I know it, I'm tellin Mama May everything – from Lil Redd, the rape and havin herpes, Deron leaving, all the way up until now, including Black, some others before him, and what just occurred at the doctor's office. I don't think I left anything out. *Talk about feeling refreshed and light.*

"I knew it was something heavy that was haunting you, girl. But, damn, Corey. I would have never guessed all of this. I am, oh, so very sorry."

"I know, Auntie."

"But, please know, within your heart, that we will get through this."

"Hunh? We?"

"Yes, you heard me right. I said we. I'm so glad you told me, Corey, so so glad." She stands up and starts pacing. I can see her mind travelling back in time. "This all makes so much sense now becuz I didn't understand your distance from the Carpenters when Lil Redd killed himself. I mean, I guess I figured that y'all hadn't kept in touch much after you moved to California. But knowing how you like helping people so much, I was shocked at your absence during that whole ordeal. I mean, you didn't even come to the funeral."

"Yeah, well…"

She stops me so that she can complete her thoughts. "Wait. And when you told me that you and your boyfriend had called it quits, I just assumed that it was your broken heart that distanced you from them cuz you made it seem like all that happened at the same time – the break up and Lil Redd's suicide."

"Yeah…"

"But damn. I guess it was your broken heart. Oh, you beautiful soul you. You're such a brave and strong young woman."

"I am?"

"Of course you are."

"I don't always feel so brave and strong."

"That's becuz you're the one goin through it."

"I guess."

"Look at all you've been through, baby. Sure, you just broke down about today's events. But hey, you're human. Who wouldn't have?"

"I don't know. I guess what you're sayin…"

"You guess? Corey, look at your life, your careers at Computel and as a massage therapist – soon to be a renowned healer. You own your own brownstone in Brooklyn, New York, for heaven's sake. You haven't allowed life to beat you down."

Listening to Mama May is liftin my spirits already. I guess it is better to look at some things from other people's point of view.

"And look at you, not only are you committed to overcoming all of this, you've never fully given up on men. Do you know how many women out there are bitter when it comes to men?"

"Hmmm. You're right."

"I know I am."

"Hahaha! Mama May!"

"Chile, it could've been so easy for you to have just given up on life. But, after all of that, you still had the tenacity to graduate with honors. Try and hone in on that awesome strength to shake off what just happened at the doctor's office and everything leading up to it. I know it don't seem like it now, but GOD is prepping you for something big. Shit, truth be told, he already has – you! You are a beacon of light and strength."

"Even though I'm feelin a little better after listenin to you, I don't feel like GOD's preppin me for anything. So, I can't say that I'm with you on that one, Mama May."

Her facial expressions tell me that she wishes that I could see things her way. And, maybe, one day I will. But right now, I'm where I am.

She sighs. "Corey, think about the revelations you had the other day at the pool. Think about the fact that you want to heal so much that you cancelled your original travel plans to travel throughout Europe in order to come here and pay attention to you. That's huge! Do you know how many people would've gone to Europe and shoved whatever they were going through into the depth of their minds and hearts?"

"And, later, they would've acted all sorry for themselves when they discovered that they developed cancer, heart problems, obesity, or some other challenging dis-ease becuz they didn't wanna deal with their problems. But, becuz you're choosin you, you know, choosin to heal you, is a huge feat. I can see you, one day, helping others by sharing your story with them." She points her forefinger into the cushion she's sitting on. "This story right here."

Hmmm. I never thought about that before. I wonder if I'd have the courage to share my story with strangers, and/or other people, besides Mama May that I know, for that matter. It's a thought though. "Okay. I'm hearin you, Mama May."

"Baby, I'm gone help you, as much as I can without getting in your way, to get through this."

"Thank you. I'd like that."

"Oh, baby, you don't have to thank me. It's a shame, though, as close as we are, that you didn't feel comfortable coming to me before now."

"I know. But, it was just so weird, especially after he killed himself. And, I really..." I stumble a little as I search for the right words as to not offend her in any way. "Auntie, I just couldn't see you not tellin my mother. And, with the way she talks, I didn't want the family all up in my business like that. Especially back then cuz I was so fragile."

"Yeah. And you know you are probably right. I would have told your mother."

I look at her out of appreciation for her honesty.

Right now she's lookin down at her hands which are folded in her lap. Her brow is wrinkled as if she's tryin to solve a math problem. "I can't even imagine what it's been like for you, baby girl. I'm so, so sorry."

"Please don't apologize and/or feel sorry for me, Mama May. I've been feelin sorry for me for thirteen years. Now, I jus wanna live. I really jus wanna finally forgive myself, GOD, and everyone I've held resentment toward ever. And, believe it or not, I wanna, even, forgive, Dr. No Good from this morning."

"Hahaha! Oh, now that's funny. That's his name, hunh?"

"Yep. Dr. No Good cuz he was wrong from a compassionate perspective and clueless from a healthcare perspective. Either way he's no good to anyone."

"Nanh, watch yourself. That's resentment talkin."

"I know. Can I have a few more hours on him though?"

"Of course you can, baby. Hehehehe! Of course you can. Get it out of your system."

We sit for a moment in silence before Mama Mays's curiosity starts talkin. "Corin?"

Oooh, she called me Corin. Must be serious. "Ma'am?"

"Do you mind if I ask you a few questions about what you just shared?"

"Not at all. I'm seein that, finally, releasing this story from my dark-inflicted mind feels freeing. Go for it. What do you wanna know?"

She takes a breath before she speaks. "Okay. Did you ever tell your mama?"

I look at her for a moment wondering about the motivation behind her question. But, then I decide to stop second-guessin, and just answer her honestly. "Yes. But not when it happened. And I never shared everything."

"Well when and what did you tell her?"

Thinkin back to when I told my mother, I sorta talk over Mama May. "In fact, I changed some of the facts."

"Oh yeah?"

"Yeah. So first of all, I didn't tell her until I moved to New York."

"Oh, okay."

"Yeah, it was when I first got there, when she helped me get settled in - before I started work at Computel."

"Oh. Okay."

"I dunno. At the time, I was wantin to feel close to her I guess, as well as, wantin to share a fear with her since I was too big-headed to admit that I was a little nervous movin to New York by myself and all."

"Unh hunh. I see."

"Well, I told her that I got raped by a guy from Xavier. I kept everything the same, from me runnin into him at K&B to me following him back to his place. But, obviously the reasoning of why I followed him back to his place changed. Instead of it bein me sayin hi to his sister, I switched it to me pickin up some old notes of his of a class that I was in that he'd already taken. And, instead of it bein a house, I said that we went back to his apartment."

"Hmmm. Interesting."

"What's interesting?"

"No, nothing a guess."

I look at her with a question mark all over my face. "Mama May."

"No! Okay, wait, I'm sorry, baby. It's jus interestin the lengths you went through to share it with her, but not to at the same time."

"Oh. Yeah, I really wanted to tell her everything, but I didn't want the family all up in my business, everybody putting their two cents into my life, especially since the Carpenters were involved. I just really didn't know how all of that would play out."

Chucklin a lil, she shifts her body weight. "Oh, yes. I guess we all can talk when we have some juicy information to direct our focus away from our own lives."

"And I figured, this way, me leavin out Lil Redd, she'd be less likely to be tempted to share it."

"Right. I see."

"And that's also why I never mentioned that I had herpes. I knew she'd come directly to you, and I just wasn't ready, I guess, to look in your eyes."

"Hmmm." Thinkin a lil on what I jus said, I guess she decided not to focus so much on why I didn't want her to know based upon her next question. "Okay, so what about Deron? How did you explain your break up?"

"I sorta was partially honest about that, too. I told her that he broke up with me cuz he said he didn't trust me since I didn't tell him what happened as soon as it occurred, and that he jus sorta left Xavier and New Awlins, for all I knew."

"I get your reasoning for keepin this to yourself, but you probably could've avoided all of the turmoil you endured the last thirteen years, or at least since you been in New York, if you'd just told the truth from the beginning."

"You're probably right. But, hey, we can't rewrite the past."

"Nope, sure can't. Well, what about HIV?"

"Oh, actually, I stopped worryin about that after about a year after the rape cuz…"

"What? Why?"

"Wait, Mama May. Let me tell you."

"Oh, I'm sorry baby. You go head on."

"Well, bout a year after everything had happened, I was visitin you and had overheard you tellin Uncle Thaddeus what had happened with the Carpenters and Lil Redd and I don't know if it was the grace of GOD, or pure serendipity that I was there, but you told him, that the autopsy showed that he was HIV negative."

"Oh yeah. I think I remember that conversation with Thaddeus."

"You do?"

"Yeah, he was fixed on tryin to figure out why the boy killed himself. And he came up with the idea that he probably was HIV positive or had full blown AIDS. And I told him about that autopsy. Funny, I'd completely forgotten all about it til now."

"Oh. Okay. Well, I'm forever grateful that my eaves droppin skills finally came in handy cuz that was one less thing I had to worry about since it supposedly takes ten years of consistent negative HIV tests to clear you of that monster altogether."

"Praise God! Does Mya know?"

"Nope. The only person who knows every, every, everything is Queenie."

"Well, thank GOD you have a friend like Queenie."

"Tell me about it."

"Baby?"

Oh Lord. What is she about to ask, now? "Ma'am?"

"I know that it's been hard for you havin this disease. And from what you've shared today from your experience at the doctor, I learned that it's not curable. But, what does that mean in terms of your sex life? Can you ever have a healthy one?

"Ye – ah."

"Why do you hesitate?"

"Well, I guess it's the question itself. I can have a healthy sex life once I release all of my shameful, dirty, fear of rejection, and *woe be unto me* feelings about the virus."

"Yeah. Well, with the affirmations, gratitude prayers, and meditation, it looks like you're off to a good start. Especially since you had the breakthrough about forgiving yourself, others, and GOD. I mean, that was huge, Corey."

"Yeah, I know."

"Do you mind explaining it to me, baby? You know, what you go through? We didn't have, or I should say I never heard of that disease in my day. And I definitely didn't know of anyone with a sex disease. Only prostitutes and, maybe fast girls and women, got those things."

First I, briefly, think about her reference to the fast girls. And not wantin to give it any energy, I silently forgive her and my elders, in general, for implying their casted judgments of others upon me in addition to forgiving myself for my own judgments that automatically surfaced when I heard her reference. Done, I allow my self-consciousness to stand to the side as I demand my courage to be in full effect as I answer my aunt's question. I know it's comin from love. And, now that I've put everything on the table, it doesn't make sense to back down now. Especially, since I feel so much lighter than I did when I first got here, over a week ago, when it felt like I had worlds upon worlds upon my shoulders.

"Sure, Mama May. Well, first, in the area that the outbreak occurs, it'll feel irritated and itchy. Then, after a day or so, a bump, or blister, or cluster of blisters forms where the irritation was. And then a day, or so, after that, the bump(s)/blister(s) open up and that's when the pain really commences. Cuz see, for me, it always happens around my vagina. So, GOD help me when I urinate and it runs over the broken skin, it burns like hell."

"Oh my sweet baby girl. That sounds painful."

"It is, Mama May, cuz it hurts to wipe or wash in the area when the skin is broken. And, dependin on the placement of them, it could be uncomfortable to sit down, as well."

"Wait a minute. They're not always in the same spot."

"No. unh, unh."

"So, how often do you have outbreaks?"

"It depends on my stress level. I used to have them every month around my period when I first got it. But, now, maybe one to three times a year, if that."

"If that?"

"Yeah, I think there was a year or two that I didn't have an outbreak at all."

"Oh. Okay. So, then, can you never have unprotected sex with someone? Does the man always have to wear a condom so that he won't get it? And what about babies? Can you have babies?"

"Whew! Okay. Okay, Mama May, be patient with me. This isn't the easiest topic for me."

"I'm sorry, baby. Do you wanna stop talkin?"

"No, I'm ready to talk about it. I'm tired of holdin so much in."

"Yeah, I bet you are."

"So, your first question is kinda complicated."

"Why?"

"Well, when I was first diagnosed, thirteen years ago, I was told, by the doctor and various pamphlets at health clinics, that as long as I wasn't havin an outbreak or experiencing any symptoms of an outbreak, that it was okay to engage in unprotected sex. However, if you were experiencing what I just described a minute ago, especially when the skin initially breaks, that you should either practice abstinence or make sure the guy wears a condom. And, that you should wait for, at least, seven to fourteen days after everything has dried up – until there's no evidence that anything was there before there's another opportunity to not infect someone durin unprotected sex."

This is a trip tellin all of this to Mama May. She's lookin at me with a hint of surprise and a large dose of empathy.

"Does it leave a scar?"

"Ahunhunhun. That part's a trip cuz after about five years of havin herpes, I had finally surpassed, I guess, a degree of shame from havin it, and would, every now and then, look down there, curious of the various stages of the virus. And I've always been amazed at how there's never a mark or a scar once the outbreak's over."

"Really?"

"Yeah."

"Okay. Well, that didn't sound complicated."

"Well, wait. I'm not finished. Ya see, the current literature on the market, is that you can still pass the virus on to your sex partner even if you're not havin an outbreak."

"Hunh? What, they've got studies or testimonials supporting that?"

"I don't know, Mama May. I..."

"Have you ever given it to anyone?"

"No, not to my knowledge."

"What do you mean not to your knowledge?"

"That no one I've had sex with has ever told me that I gave it to them."

"Have you ever had unprotected sex before?"

"Humph. You would think that this conversation would be semi easy for me to have with you becuz of our close relationship. But, as I'm talkin through all of this, I'm realizing that I've never shared this side of my life to anyone but Queenie. It's like I've kept my womanhood, so to speak, to myself."

"Yeah, I bet this can feel a lil weird. I'm pretty weirded out myself. I can only imagine what you're going through."

"Yeah. But, I'm cool. So, yes, I've had unprotected sex before, but only when I didn't have an outbreak. And, like I said, I've never passed it on to anyone. So, I really don't know how true the new literature is."

"Hmmm."

"And there's this pharmaceutical drug that's supposed to lessen the number of times you have outbreaks."

"Really?! Have you tried it?"

"Yeah, but you know how I don't really care for pharmaceuticals."

"Right."

"Plus, I started questioning the validity of the drug after really payin attention to the television and radio commercials promotin it."

"Why?"

"Cuz, like the new literature out, the commercials start off sayin that you can infect someone with the virus even when you don't have an outbreak. And, to take this drug to lessen the occurrence of outbreaks. Well, if you think about it, if you can infect someone when you don't have an outbreak, then what good will the drug do me?"

"Un hunh. I see what you're sayin, Corey."

"Thank you. The drug's only, supposedly, preventin me from havin outbreaks not from passin herpes on."

"Wait, Corey, but maybe the commercials are targeting people who wanna lessen the painful results of the outbreaks."

"Hmmm. I never thought about that before. But why even mention the thing about infectin folks when you're not havin an outbreak? I dunno. I just don't think that whoever came up with the concept thought it all the way through."

"I hear ya. So, then you don't take anything, then? You just hope and pray that you don't get one?"

"Not necessarily. Outbreaks usually surface when you're stressed out. I know you can't tell by my actions since I've been here, but that's why I run a lot."

"You're right, I can't tell."

My aunt can be very sarcastic if you haven't noticed. I laugh and push on her thigh. "Okay, Mama May got jokes."

"Haaaaaaaaaa!"

"Hunhun. So, anyway, I also make it a point to meditate and journal as much as possible, as well."

"Well, that's good."

"Yeah. When it's too hard for me to calm myself down to meditate, I either write affirmations or certain words over and over again, like I am at peace, I am Divinely protected, love, GOD."

"Yeah, that's good, Corey. That's real good. But, that's all you do to keep the outbreaks at bay?"

"No, watchin what you eat is essential, too. So, I also make it a point to only eat fresh food, no processed stuff."

"And all this time I thought you were just tryin to be health conscious like me."

"Hahaha! I know. But, I am kinda. In fact, I found out about the processed foods thing indirectly from you – from one of the books in your library."

"Really? What book?"

I get up and go to her library room and grab the book off the shelf. I hold it up so that she can see the title when I enter back into the living room. "This one."

"Oh yeah. *Prescription for Nutritional Healing*. That's a good book."

"I know. I bought one for myself. But, while I was at your house one day about seven years ago, I was thumbin through it." I begin thumbing through the book lookin for the information on herpes. Since I know this book so well, I pretty much find the section instantaneously. "See?" I point to a section that talks about foods and drinks to avoid. "Aside from the unhealthiness of processed foods, sugars, white flour, bread, and rice products, and sodas, I also stay away from them because of the negative effects they have on the virus."

Reading at her own pace, Mama May nods her head slowly, "Wow. This is good stuff, Corey."

"I know. I love this book. It also tells you things to consume in moderation durin outbreaks, as well, like dairy products, nuts and seeds, corn, and stuff."

"Yeah, this is a wealth of information. So, are you takin L-lysine, as well? It says here that it's an amino acid that retards the virus."

"Yeah. I take between 500 and 1000 mg every day in addition to eating lots of broccoli, cabbage, collard and turnip greens, kale and all sorts of other foods rich with it."

"Okay. Good. Well, I'm glad I was able to help even though I didn't know I was."

"Ahunhun. Yeah, I know. Right? I set the book down next to me and pause a moment before I continue. "Look, Mama May, I apologize for not sharin this earlier."

"No, no, no. I didn't mean that last statement in no way. You don't owe me an apology. This is your life. Shoot, I don't know what I would've done if the shoe was on my foot."

I embrace my aunt out of sheer relief of her not judgin me. "Thanks, Mama May."

"For what, baby?"

"For being beautiful you."

"Oh, well, you're quite welcome, my dawlin. I am kinda cute, hunh?"

"Auntie!"

"I know. I know. You're welcome, baby. But, wait."

"Hunh?"

"What's your personal verdict on non-protected sex given the new literature that's out?"

"Well." I look down for a moment. This conversation is a lil awkward. But, I'm feeling relief from holdin all this stuff in. Lookin up, I give my aunt a half smile, "If I'm feelin the guy and we've been together for a minute, I'll engage in it if he's comfortable, of course. But, I haven't done so recently cuz I haven't been able to attract a healthy relationship. Hence, the reason I came to visit you."

"Right. That Black fellow was the infamous trigger, hunh?"

"Yep."

"Well, what is it that they say? There's good in everything?"

"Humph. Yep. If it wasn't for him, I wouldn't've come here to heal."

"Unh hunh. And what about babies? Can you have them?"

"Yeah. But I have to have a C-section if I have an outbreak during labor. Otherwise the baby will become blind if it passes through my birth canal."

"Oh no!"

"Yeah. In fact, they recommend that women who have herpes schedule C-sections whether they're havin an outbreak or not cuz - well according to the original literature I received - sometimes a woman can have an outbreak on her cervix and not be aware of it becuz of the location."

"Hmmm. This is interesting stuff."

"Yeah. I know."

"Do you want kids, Corey?"

"Absolutely."

"Well, you know what? We're gonna work on getting rid of this virus, altogether."

"Hunh? Mama May, there is no..."

Not allowing me to finish, she politely shuts me up with her *don't even go there* look. "Baby, we will get rid of that virus."

First, I just look at her with a blank look on my face. And then I start to wonder if her healin powers can get rid of something like this and why have I allowed shame to encompass me so much that I neglected myself for thirteen years by not coming to my aunt who's proven time and time again, from her vast popularity, that she can heal just about anything.

She mistakes my silence for disbelief. "Come on now, Corey. You read *A Return to Love* by Marianne Wilson. You know that people have been cured of AIDS."

"No, no. I mean, yeah, I know. You're right. I was just wondering why did I opt to suffer all these years instead of comin to you from the start."

"Nanh, don't go second guessing yourself, baby. You've been dealing with a lot of stuff. Give yourself a break." I sit back as I watch Mama May's mind go to work. "Now, what we gone have to work on is your belief system. Baby, you have to believe and know that GOD will get rid of this virus for you. And, I'm gonna help you."

"Do you think your healing abilities will get rid of it?"

"Sweetheart, the reason I can help so many people with my healing capabilities is becuz I believe in myself and GOD, undoubtedly. I know myself, and GOD, like an eager student who's open to learning and witnessing the miraculous splendor of our CREATOR continuously. In other words, I easily let GOD step in as my ego steps out. I am completely open to the unknown and I sharpen my faith muscles by its acute angles of my life's manifestations presented to me through my thoughts, words, and actions. The key, my sweet dawlin, lies in believing and knowing INFINITE power within you. And, I'm gone work with you on this. Since we both know that you're a healer, too, we're gonna work this out together. Not just me alone."

"Okay. Thanks." I feel my stomach quiver a little at the thought of the task before me. "Thanks, Auntie! I'm feelin so much better than I did when I first got back from the doctor's."

"Well, good. But before you leave here, you will be feeling even better than you do now."

"I will?"

"Yeah, if you're serious about all of this. Thank you for coming here to heal. The healing plan you started yesterday with the prayer, meditation, and gratitude is real good. I'm gone help you take it up a notch with some other holistic healing modalities. But, before we start with all of that, I want you to go in my meditation room, get my massage table out of the closet, and set it up for me with the sheets and all cuz, when I wake up from the nap I'm about to take, I'm gone help you break up some of those toxins you're holding in your muscles from all of that toxic guilt, shame, and rejection you've been feeling."

I feel a smile on my face as I listen to my aunt love me. "Thank you, Auntie."

"You're welcome, baby. Nanh, you go on ahead and set my room up. I'm gonna go and rest myself for a lil while. If you gone eat, go on and do it nanh so your food will be digested by the time we get started. Matter of fact, let's see." She walks into the hallway so that she can look at the clock on the kitchen wall. "It's going on two o'clock now. So, be on the massage table at 6:30, okay?"

"Yes, ma'am."

I hear Mama May call my name just as I enter her meditation room. "Corey!"

"Ma'am?"

"Know that you are a Divine expression of ALL THAT IS, and that you are already healed."

I smile at her depth. "I know, Auntie. Thanks!"

She shakes her head vehemently with pursed lips before she speaks. "No. No, you don't know. But, you will, baby. You will."

The Labyrinth

Mama May's meditation room is so incredibly peaceful. Although her entire home feels warm and peaceful, there's definitely a different, indescribable delightful surge to the energy in here. She has lavender, pink, and white linen curtains at the windows, various crystals on the book shelves and scattered throughout the room. On one wall, the twenty-third Psalm is written in cursive in purple paint over and over again. She has an altar on the wall directly across from the entrance that has some candles, an ankh, a bible, and what looks like sage layin in an oversized seashell. And she has four very comfortable chairs that sit in each corner of the room. They feel like what I imagine white fluffy clouds would feel like if they had any solid consistency – they're so soft. She told me that she purposely selected them for this room so that she'll never get uncomfortable during her meditations. At the center of the room are three huge throw pillows sittin on an area rug with a beautiful butterfly in flight. When I asked her if the butterfly had any significance, she stated that it represents evolution to her given the stages of its life. She is so the bomb to me, ya'll.

Well, as instructed, I quickly set up the massage table. I move the pillows to the side and set it up in the center of the room complete with sheets and bolster to protect my back. Then I direct my attention to the emptiness residing in my stomach.

Once in the kitchen, I ponder on what I really want to eat. Though I'm really hungry and could probably eat everything in the refrigerator, I never like to eat so much food where it feels like I'm digestin it for hours on end, especially when I'm gonna get a massage in a few hours.

Woohoo! I'm gone get a massage, and from Mama May at that. Good lookin out, GOD.

I open up the refrigerator to peruse its contents. Hmmm, I know I didn't eat anything this morning, but why I am so hungry now. There are plenty of days that I don't eat until this hour. So, what's with all of this famishness goin on now? Today's events? Humph. Maybe.

I decide to make me a big salad and have some of those left over home fries, from yesterday's brunch, on the side, which I could totally do without. But, oh well, what's done is done. My mind is made up. Tee hee hee. Plus, the fries will probably add just enough substance to my belly to make me feel full. Oh yeah! There's that theme music again…dun dun nun nun, ohhh yeah!

Once I'm finished eating, I wash the dishes, and walk outside to Mama May's labyrinth. It seems to be finally callin my name. In fact, I'm actually a lil surprised that I've been here for a week now and haven't walked it yet given its one of my favorite things to do when I visit here.

At the starting point of the labyrinth, which I call *the doorway*, I close my eyes, hold my hands above my head with my palms facin outward as I tilt my head up toward the sky. "Thank You, GOD, for this moment, for Mama May. Thank You for lightening my load. I don't know the last time I've felt so refreshed. It felt great sharing all of that muck with Mama May. I know it was You, at times speakin through me, helpin me to push through the events like a champ. And I'm very happy that I, that we did it. Thank You. I know that I have a long ways to go in regards to healing myself, and I thank You for holdin my hands throughout the entire process while you enfold courage, patience, and committed consistency throughout my being. Amen."

I start walking the cleverly designed maze outlined with trees so tall and perfectly manicured and positioned, that you can't see pass them on either side of you. And though this is a very adult moment, I feel like a kid playin follow the leader as I follow the path the trees provide. It sorta feels like a mystery novel, as I suppose my life does at the moment, given that I really don't know what's before me with each turn of the maze. I can only hope that the path's culmination is fulfilling, ya know? And, I mean that more in regards to my life than the labyrinth cuz I know what's waiting for me at its center. It's the main reason I walk the labyrinth every time I visit Mama May.

Ya see, at the center of the labyrinth sits a two feet high, four feet wide clear quartz crystal that Mama May had carved into the shape of a lotus flower. I don't know if you can picture this, but try to imagine perfectly carved flower petals pointing out and upward. Right now the sun's rays are creating a colorful sparkling effect on some of the petals. Aw. It's so beautiful, y'all – so so beautiful. To top the picture off, imagine multiple golden-orange colored pieces of the crystal citrine, one of my favorite crystals, at its center. Together, their naturally jagged surfaces represent the seed case of the actual flower. Dope right? I don't know how she pulled such a beautiful piece of artwork off, but I'm so glad she did. It makes this moment, bein outside with nature like this, heavenly. Dr. who?

You know, I take back the comment I said earlier about me bein surprised that I'm jus now walkin the labyrinth cuz I know that everything happens in Divine timing. The fact that I just revealed my big black secret to Mama May and now, about an hour later, I'm sittin before a beautifully sculpted image of such a revered creation by GOD, the lotus flower, is full bloom evidence of the power of synchronicity. Shoot, it's not by accident that the early Egyptians looked at the lotus flower as a symbol of the sun, of creation and rebirth; and the Asian-Indians, long ago and now, look at it as a symbol for Divinity, fertility, wealth, knowledge, and enlightenment, and I'm in the midst of creating a new, empowered, enlightened me – a rebirth. No, this is not an accident at all. I'm exactly where I'm supposed to be right now.

I love the lotus flower cuz it wreaks mysticism. In case you don't know, it grows in muddy swamp-like water and is the only plant that fruits and flowers simultaneously, which to me, represents exact purity accompanying instantaneous abundance in the midst of turmoil.

- <u>Exact</u> for the precision of time and bejeweled adornment upon this earth
- <u>Purity</u> for the delicate white or pink petals that define its existence
- <u>Instantaneous</u> for the simultaneous timing of expressing itself through its flowers and fruit

- <u>Abundance</u> for the innate beauty its petals display and for the nourishment and healing properties they provide topically and inwardly
- <u>Turmoil</u> for the thick muddy water it must past through to share its beauty with the world
- <u>Mysticism</u> for its continuous rhythm of rebirth daily as it closes and sinks underwater at night and rises and opens again at daybreak

And do you know that every morning when it appears above water that there isn't a speck of mud or residue from the swamp on it? That's what I call precise timing. Aw, yes. Timing is everything, ya'll. Thank You, GOD.

Within moments my mind drifts back in time when I was a delicate flower amongst the muddy swamp-waters of New Awlins after the rape. In a way, when I think about it, it was like I was bein rebirthed every day that daylight surfaced cuz if it were up to me, I would've stayed in the cocoon of my dorm room. But, this unforeseen force, GOD, kept opening my eyes, *my pedals*, every day, amongst my inner turmoil, and helped me to place one foot in front of the other until I was able to do it on my own for myself.

Thankful for then and now, I take a bow in honor of GOD. Though I didn't feel like this earlier, I feel like today's been good, real good, thus far. I actually shared my big dark secret with Mama May and that freedom, alone, feels awesome. I'm seeing just how much stuff I've buried under cement, steel, and layers upon layers of anger, fear, and woefulness within the depths of me. Plus, I have a feelin that all of these unmemorable memories need to surface right now so that I can acknowledge their presence and release them gracefully – along with shame, guilt, and loneliness.

And, yep, I need to give thanks for Black's reaction, big ups really, for everything that occurred between us. If it wasn't for him playin such a compelling dramatic supporting role within my script, I wouldn't have come to my aunt's home lookin for peace, unconditional love, and self-healing to discover all of this stuff that I've been subconsciously and consciously holding on to.

In some ways, I feel so incredibly ashamed of the thoughts and beliefs I've held for so many years. But, in others, I'm glad that I've held them cuz when it's all said and done I can celebrate from whenst I've come. And I know, one day in the near future, I'll completely release the resentment I'm holding towards that doctor. One day I'll be able to forgive, let go, and move on instantaneously. I'm working on that day right now.

I feel like I'm piecing together the puzzle of my life. Right now the picture looks like a combination of cruddy-like brown structures, scattered seeds, and green plants. I have a feelin that when it's all said and done, it'll resemble a heavenly landscape painted with beautiful vibrant life.

Though I really want to get in the shower, somethin sits me down on the porch once I reach the house. I find myself truly baffled at all of the revelations I'm havin and I'm thinkin that either Mama May's home and grounds are anointed with highly evolved spiritual light beings whispering all of this into my thoughts, OR it sits on a portal to heaven's gates, OR I just needed to get away and focus on me, in this concentrated focused way. Humph. It could be all three of those. Who knows?

Last Quarter

Inward motivation is the starting point to success.

Let The Healing Begin

Sometimes a long hot soak is better than what the doctor ordered. At first, I'd decided to take a long shower before I meditated and journaled. But, now, as I feel today's events dissolve from my muscles, pores and mind, I can't help but lay back and visualize myself pattin me on the back for the last minute change to takin this soak. As soon as I saw that Mama May had some baking soda in her fridge and lavender oil in her massage room, it was on. I swear I don't know what property in baking soda that lightens the weight of the world off of your shoulders, but I'm a lifetime recruit.

I'm tellin you. If you ever feel weighted down by life or exhausted beyond comprehension, take a soak with some bakin soda. I kid you not, after about ten or fifteen minutes, you'll find yourself raisin up out of that bathtub so fast cuz you won't be used to how much lighter your body weight feels. Humph. Don't sleep, peoples. Recognize the pearls.

Well, I've been soakin for about a good twenty or so minutes and I'm now ready to get out of the tub. So, I unplug it and turn on the water to take a shower. I know. Don't trip. I'm weird like that. I don't bathe during soaks because I never really understood sittin in water filled with dirt, soap, and soap scum. So I always soak, first, to relax and melt away my stress. And, then shower to wash off the physical and nonphysical impurities no longer bonded to me via stress. Quirky, I know.

In my room, I notice that it's 5:30, an hour before my massage with Mama May. I grab my phone to make sure that it's silenced so that I'm not disturbed during my meditation, prayer work, etc. As I sit in the chair and close my eyes, I hear Mama May walkin around the house. I disregard the light noise outside of my room and meditate for about thirty minutes before I begin my prayers of gratitude in my journal. Once I'm finish, I sit with the quiet of my thoughts for the last fifteen minutes til my massage.

Inside of Mama May's meditation room, I notice that she's placed pieces of the crystal, citrine, probably for its healing properties, under and around the massage table, and is burnin, what smells like, frankincense essential oil. This is good cuz both of them have healing properties which I'll explain later. Right now my good people, I'm gonna relax myself and get on this massage table.

Oooh, I'm so excited. I'm about to get a massage from my auntie. She's in the room within moments of me getting on the table. Though she doesn't have to, she instructs me to relax.

"Nanh, you know you didn't have to tell me that, Auntie."

"Okay, chile. Now shush."

Clearly understanding her tone and sentiment, I instantly quiet myself down. As soon as she touches me I feel as though I'm being comforted by an angel. Her hands are warm – they feel like a burst of sunshine. The way she's manipulating my muscles is beyond skillful – more like instinctual. I try not to go to sleep so that I can consciously experience every part of this massage, but at some point I'm floating somewhere in la la land, completely knocked out. Before I know it, she's tappin me to turn onto my back. Nanh, don't get me wrong, I know she was massagin me cuz I was in and out of consciousness. But, I swear it feels like the time must've escalated cuz I feel like I just laid down. Damn she's good. My body feels light as a feather.

"Come on, baby, I know you're relaxed, but it's time for you to turn over."

Wow! I thought I did already. "Oh, okay, Auntie. I'm sorry. I could've sworn I turned on to my back."

"Hahaha. Yeah, you're good and relaxed. Touch detox is so magical."

I know the woman's sayin something, but I must be back in la la land cuz I coulda sworn I just saw Tinker Bell sittin on my left shoulder right before I started flyin next to a shootin star. At some point, I feel her hands massaging my neck. If her flow of work is similar to mine, then she's probably almost finished with the massage.

"Co-rey."

I hear Mama May singin my name, but I don't feel like answering.

"Co-rey."

I just heard my name again along with a soft bell near my right ear. I wonder if that's really Mama May or if I'm still dreamin.

"Corey."

"Hunh?"

"Baby, you're all set. I'm done."

I guess that is Mama May I'm hearin. I smile at my grogginess. "Okay. Thank you."

"You're welcome, baby. Hmmm, what are you smilin at?"

Gainin more awareness, my reply seeps through an exhalation. "Me. My thoughts."

"Oh, well okay then. Nanh, you take your time gettin up. You don't wanna bring a rush to your head, okay?"

"Okay."

"I'm gone go and wash my hands. When you get up, sit in one of the cushioned chairs."

"Okay. Thanks."

I take my time getting up – maybe five or ten minutes. I feel light and heavy all at the same time, if that's possible. Hun. Wait! Maybe it's my spirit that's feelin light and my limbs that are heavy cuz I'm so incredibly relaxed. Shit! I don't know. All I can say is, wow! That was the best massage ever.

Mama May walks into the room. "Oh, good. You're up."

Makin my way to one of the cushioned chairs, I respond with an air of cloudiness. "Yeah, I'm ummm. Ummm. I'm up."

Lookin at the clock, I notice that it's 8:45. No way. After determining I probably rested five or ten minutes when Mama May left the room, I realize that she gave me a two-hour massage. Damn! Now, that's what's up.

"How ya feelin?"

"Awesome! I feel like every muscle was meticulously manipulated."

"Wonderful, baby. You, so, deserved that massage."

I hear my aunt, but I begin to look around the room as if my scan will help me select the right words to further express how I'm feeling.

"Wow! It's like, even though I'm very relaxed, there's an excited energy flowin through me."

"Okay. Good. That's good, Corey."

"No, you're good. And two hours? That didn't feel like two hours. Hunhun. I know I keep sayin, wow. But, wow!"

"Hunhunhun! No baby, it's not me. It's GOD."

Thank you, GOD. "Give thanks."

"Well, I wanted to sit with you for a moment so that I can go over some ideas with you."

"Okay. Cool."

"But first, I want to share the dream I had when I took my nap this afternoon."

Perking up a bit, I try to force myself into being more aware cuz I know this is gone be pretty interesting. "Oh yeah? What was it about?"

"It actually wasn't about much."

"Hmmm. O-kay." *So, you brought it up, why?*

"Well, all I remember is seeing you in a room sittin on the floor lookin at some smoke comin out of a pot."

"Really?"

"Yeah, and some kind of way, maybe from a voice I don't remember hearing or from a thought placed in my head, I knew it was frankincense and I heard the you in my dream say that you need to burn this all the time - that it heightens you."

"No way! Really?"

"Yep, way."

"I knew that was frankincense essential oil. This is so crazy cuz..."

She politely interrupts me. "Wait, wait, wait, baby. Let me finish."

"Oh! My bad, Auntie. Go head."

"Yeah, well then the dream switched to me following you down an empty street. There was no foot traffic or cars in sight. When you got to the end of the block, you turned left. And by the time I got to the corner there was a bright red stone, about the size of a miniature refrigerator sittin there."

"Really? Red?"

"Yeah, even though it was red, I noticed it, in the dream, as the crystal, citrine."

"Hence, the citrine under and around the table."

"Yep."

"Oooh, I swear you're givin me chills, Auntie, cuz what I was about to say earlier is that I had a dream about a year ago that told me that I needed to burn frankincense often, and that I didn't have to burn it along with myrrh like I did from time to time."

"Mmm. Okay."

"And this year I've been over the top into citrine. I've purchased a bracelet, necklace, and ring with that stone in them. And, if you go in my room, here, and look under the head pillow on the right side of the bed, you'll find three small pieces of citrine there."

"Wow! Are you serious, Corey?"

"Yep."

"How interesting that the messages came to me, as well, in my dream."

"I know. Well, at least I know that I'm on the right track."

"How often do you burn frankincense?"

"I haven't burned any since I came here. But, I'll say, consistently, about five times a week for the last two months."

"Really? That's a lot."

"Un hunh. One day, about two months ago, while I was washing dishes and thinkin bout all that wasn't there between me and Black, the dream popped into my mind. And, the next day, I went out and got a whole bunch of frankincense incense – the super long ones, and started burnin it every evening that I didn't stay out late. Sometimes, if I'm up to it, I'll burn the actual resin on some charcoal that I bought a few years back."

I can tell that my aunt's getting excited about the connection we're makin now. "Okay. This is good, Corey."

"Yeah, I find that it relaxes me. But since I'm always pretty relaxed when I come here, I didn't bother bringin any."

"Okay. Well, from what you've shared with me, I think my dream is a definite confirmation that the frankincense and citrine are just what you need right now, especially, as you focus on healing yourself seein that frankincense promotes calm and present-moment awareness and citrine enhances the body's healing energy, amongst other things."

"Yep. I feel so, too."

"Wow! You're so protected."

"You think so?"

"I know so. And so will you – in time. Be patient."

"Okay."

"Humph, before long, such a question won't even come out of yo mouth."

"Okay. I guess."

Shaking her head, she looks at me as if I'm so close, yet eons away from knowin my*self* and it's kinda makin me feel a lil uncomfortable even though I know I've got a lot to learn about life. "Girl, GOD's prepping you for some good stuff. Look at how GOD, your angels and guides are talking to you."

"Hunnn. You know somethin that I don't know?"

As if I didn't just ask her a direct question, she clasps her hands and changes the subject altogether. "Okay. Well, on to some ideas I came up with to assist you in healing yourself."

I pretend not to be a little annoyed by her dismissal of my question and decide, for myself, that she does know somethin and that if I stop and think about everything, I know it, too. So, I'll take heed to her advice of being patient and move on like she has. "Okay! I'm all ears."

"Okay, so keep in mind that these are just ideas. I'm not saying that you'll be all better if you do them or even just one of them. Right now..." She hands me a notebook and a pen so I can write her ideas down. "...I want you to make a note of them and ponder on which ones, if any, resonate with you."

Because I know that my aunt consciously applies her anointment as a healer from GOD and is highly respected by the masses becuz of it, I'm hangin on to her every word as if there's no tomorrow. "Okay."

"Okay, so, from a physical perspective, I feel it'll be a good idea if you detox your kidneys and liver."

"Hmmm. Okay. Out of curiosity, why do you suggest that?"

"Well because, from what you shared with me, it sounds like you've been carrying a lot of anger and resentment with you since the rape. And we carry anger in our..."

I complete her statement with her. "Liver."

"Yes. You're familiar with the concept?"

"Yeah. I was taught that in my Shiatsu classes during massage therapy school."

"Oh, good. So, yeah if..."

I cut my aunt off out of the excitement building up in me. "So, I need to detox my kidneys becuz the kidneys hold fear. And I've been holdin on to fear of rejection."

"Yes, Corey! You've got it, babygirl!"

Maybe I do know some things. "Okay, this is good stuff. What else ya got?"

"Listen to you. Well, I want you to look at this womb meditation." She hands me a book entitled *Sacred Woman – A Guide to Healing the Feminine Body, Mind, and Spirit* by Queen Afua.

"You know? I think I heard of this woman through one of Queenie's African dance friends."

"You might have. She has a center in Brooklyn."

"Really?"

"Yes. I urge you to look through this book at your leisure. It has some awesome exercises, affirmations, prayers, and juice and food recipes that help women honor their bodies as sacred temples, with emphasis on the womb."

"Oh, okay. Sounds interesting."

"It is. I was thinking that while you're here, you can start off with a womb movement meditation." Mama May leans in to finger through the pages of the book. "See here? I marked the beginning with a Post-it note."

I nod my head yes as I begin to look at the various poses and read, silently, some of the affirmations associated with each pose.

I finally look up after a few moments of mentally takin in the sacred exercise. "I'm diggin this, Mama May. Wow!"

"Yeah, I was thinking that the exercises will help to heal and balance your sacral chakra, the chakra which is located in your womb."

"Riigghhht. This is good stuff."

"Oh yeah?"

"Yeah. Every now and then I focus on my sacral chakra, envisioning its color, orange, burning away the emotional, mental, and physical impurities I've placed there since the rape."

"Well, that's good Corey."

"Yeah, I know. Thanks. My thing is I'm never consistent with my practices. But, for some reason I can see me doing this movement meditation. Maybe this is the component that I've been missin. Thank you so much."

"You're welcome, chile. Just make a note of it for right now cuz I'm not finished yet."

Excited about healing me, I quickly close the book and give my aunt my undivided attention. "Oh, okay. I'm listening."

"Have you ever heard of fire breaths?"

"I think so. Are those the quick breaths through the nose?"

"Yep! Those are the ones."

"Ummm, yeah. What's her name? What is that girl's name?"

Hahaha! Mama May is looking at me perplexed.

"Who?"

"Umm, Queenie's dancer friend. Oooh, ummm, Trinity! Trinity was telling me about them. I tried doin them once."

"Oh, okay. Why just once?"

"I don't know. I did like the way I felt afterwards. But, I haven't a clue why I never did them again. You know? It's like I just said, my issue is definitely lack of consistency."

"Yeah, consistency is the key to changing negative thoughts, behaviors, and actions."

"Yeah, I know. I'd be good and on a roll for about two or three weeks, or maybe even a month. And then, for no substantial reason, I just fall off and start the pattern up in a few weeks or months later."

"Humph. I think most humans are guilty of not being consistent with acting out new, positive attitudes and behaviors. I don't think I became consistent with my practices until my late thirties on out. But, I can't lie. It wasn't easy. It definitely took more than a while."

I beam at how amazed I am by my aunt. "How long did it take you?"

She rests her head back on the back of her chair, and begin to file through her memory bank. "Oh, now let's see. You know how they say that if you do something consistently for twenty-one days, then it's a habit?"

"Yeah, I have heard that. I've also heard forty-four days, too."

"Well, let's just say that a good year, or so, passed before I noticed that my thoughts were less filled with self-doubt and replaced with overflowing, from my perspective, loving support of myself."

"Hmmm. That's interesting that you mentioned your thoughts and not your meditative and healing practices."

"Yeah, well, before you can meditate or heal anything, you have to think about it first, right?"

"Yeah. I never thought about it like that before."

"Yeah, so even though I was practicing habitual consistency with my prayer, meditation, and energy work rituals, I knew that I had to change the way I thought about myself more so than anything or anyone else. Then, I knew, my thoughts would constructively direct my actions."

"Dang, Auntie. That was deep."

"That's why I said, earlier, that you're off to a good start with the prayer, meditation, and gratitude. Because once your spirit is grounded through meditation and your mind is uplifted through prayer, affirmations, and gratitude, then your spoken word and, more importantly, your actions will automatically reflect the inner you – your thoughts."

"Hahaha! You're so my shero, Auntie."

"Aw, thank you baby girl. But, one day you'll be your own."

While I was thinking about bein my own shero, Mama May said something that sort of made me feel less intimidated about the self-work ahead of me. "I wanna clarify something I said a minute ago."

I look at her as if to say continue.

"Though I've been disciplined all of these years with meditating and all, life on earth is a continuous school, for all of us humans, which constantly tests our faculties of discernment. So by no means am I free of worry, self-doubt, or missing a day or two of meditation, energy work etc. I've jus learned to respond from a perspective of unconditional self-love other than self-destruction. Hence, less worry, self-doubt, etc."

"Hmmm. I like that. For some reason I feel less intimidated to heal myself knowing that ultimately, self-love, which is a feat in itself, is the ultimate objective. But wait, was that what you were wanting to convey."

"Yep! You got it, baby girl. Now, let's get back to you."

"Right. Me."

"Okay. So the reason I mentioned the fire breaths is because I noticed, from my brief research online when I woke up from my nap, that the herpes virus lives in the blood cells and..."

I absentmindedly cut my aunt off. "Yep. Hence, why I can't donate blood."

"What?" Mama May thinks for a moment. "Damn, you're right." She dismisses the revelation with a long blink of her eyes and a shake to her head. "But, we bout to change all of that."

"Yes we are. So, my bad for cutting you off. You were sayin?"

"I was saying that the virus takes up roots in the blood, so to speak, and when it's latent, it hangs out in the sacral ganglia."

"Right. Wow! You did do some reading on it."

"Yep."

"For a lil while, after I found out about the nerve endings, or sacral ganglia, I was applying therapeutic grade oregano essential oil to my sacrum area because I'd read somewhere that the oil, once it penetrates through the skin, could kill the virus."

"What happened? Why'd you stop?"

"I had an outbreak and figured it wasn't workin."

"Oh. Well how long had you been applyin the oil before the outbreak?"

"I don't know. Maybe a month."

"Hmmm. Now, I'm seeing what you're talking about. And I agree with you. I think lack of consistency is part of what's blocking your progress. It sounds like you have the knowledge, tools, and the desire to heal yourself minus the consistent drive."

"See? I told you."

"Yeah, well I'm not saying that the oregano would have been the cure. I'm just saying that it may take longer than a month before results are evident."

"Right. I hear you. But, tell me about the fire breaths."

"Oh yes. Fire breaths are a natural detox for the body because they oxygenate the blood. And the presence of oxygen means the absence of toxins."

"Right. Okay."

"So, since toxic thoughts, stress, and worry can produce chemical imbalances within the body resulting in a toxic inner environment, then

I'm sure that your system, from your fear of rejection alone, can use some natural cleansing."

"Oooh yeah. I'm likin this."

"Okay, good becuz what I like about fire breaths is that they balance and strengthen the nervous system as well."

"Oh, okay."

"Yeah, so I'm feeling very strongly about the possibility of the breaths shaking the virus up while it's active, or causing you to have an outbreak, or latent, in the sacral ganglia…"

"Unh hunh."

"…stimulating the nervous system in such a way, where it retards the virus altogether, from the abundance of oxygen derived from the breaths."

"Hmmm, okay."

"I'm not sayin that this will cure you of it. But, along with other practices, it will help your body to stop feeding its existence."

"Yeah. Okay. I think I'm getting it. Give me a minute so that I can write this down before I forget."

Mama May sits back in her chair and lightly clasps her hands together in her lap. "Take ya time."

Once I finish takin notes, I gesture for Mama May to continue.

"Okay. Do you have any questions so far?"

"Nope. Not yet. So far, in addition to my prayers, meditation, etc. work, I'm detoxin my liver and kidneys, doin the womb movement meditation, and fire breaths."

"Yep."

"It's a lot."

"Yeah, I know. But, these are things to choose from. You don't have to do them all."

"I know, but these are some great ideas and I know you're not done."

"Haaa! You're right. I'm not."

"Oooh, wait! I do have a question. How do I detox my liver and kidneys?"

"That book, *Sacred Woman*, has a recipe you can try."

"Oh, okay. I'll check it out."

"And if you're not comfortable with what she offers, we can research other liver and kidney detoxes online, as well."

"Right. Okay. Well, I don't have any other questions right now. What else you got?"

"Okay. You know, there are so many things that came to my mind, but I'm just gone mention these last two for now because there's a such thing as becoming so overwhelmed with options that sometimes you end up doing nothing."

"Hahaha! You're right."

"And especially since we have to work on your consistency, or better yet, your commitment to yourself."

"Oooh, I like that. My commitment to myself. Thanks for puttin it like that."

"Un hunh. Well, I think it may be a good idea for you to do Chi Kung."

"Hmmm, okay. I used to do it when I was in Massage Therapy School. It was part of our daily activities in one of my classes."

"That's good. Do you remember the type of Chi Kung you did?"

"Unh, unh."

"Well, what I do every morning is a form of Chi Kung."

"It is? I didn't know that. I didn't even know that there were different types. Hmmm, I just thought that what you practiced was an Asian exercise called Zhan Zhuang."

Mama May chuckles a little before she comments on my ignorance. "Yes, chile. Well, that's what it's called all right. But, yeah, there are different kinds that address different things. Like some forms focus just on the mind where others may focus solely on posture, breathing, or movement."

"Oh, okay."

"But Zhan Zhuang combines all of that together. People have reported that continued practice of Zhan Zhuang has helped to strengthen immunity, successfully treat chronic illnesses, produce high levels of daily energy, and cultivate the natural regeneration of the nervous center."

"Hence, how you're able to look and act so young."

"Hunhun, maybe it does contributes to my youthfulness. But, I always say that youthfulness is derived from doing what you love and being true to thine ownself."

I instinctively nod my head cuz I've heard her say that countless times throughout my life. "Yep, don't chase money. Do what you love and believe in yourself, and watch the money flow into your hands and overflow your bank accounts."

"What? You actually listen to me? Haaa!?"

"Hahaha! Of course. Notice that I'm not here cuz of money trouble."

"Humph, point taken."

She hands me another book. This one's entitled, "The Way of Energy – Mastering the Chinese Art of Internal Strength with Chi Kung Exercise."

"Well, okay. It looks like I've got my work cut out for me."

"Yes, you do baby girl. Just remember that these are just suggestions. You don't have to do any of it."

"I know. So, you said you had two more things."

She places a conspiratory grin on her face.

"Uh, oh. Look at that grin. What you got up your sleeve, Mama May?"

"Nothing out of the box."

"Unh hunh. I'm listening."

"Well, I was thinking that we could do something together as a family to help heal you. Maybe even heal others in the family."

"Humph. I don't know if I'm likin this idea cuz it sounds like I'll have to share my story with everyone in the family."

"Well, not everyone."

"Okay. Then, who?"

"Just the females."

"Well, the way my mama talks, then that'll be everyone – the guys included."

"No, not really. Not if we preface it right."

"Okay. Go head. I'm listening."

"Well, let me change it up a lil. I'm thinking that even if you never utter it to anyone else, that it'll be very healing for you to tell your mom the complete truth."

"What does she have to do with me healing me?"

"Well, you weren't being true to her or yourself when you told her all those years ago. Honesty represents the bricks that create the foundation of being true to thine ownself."

"I'm hearing you. I guess you have a point."

"Again, this is just an idea. You don't have to do it. It's just something to consider."

"Right."

"Well, my love, that's all I have for now. I wanna do some reading before I turn in."

Though I don't wanna be left alone with my thoughts jus yet, I don't say that to Mama May. "Oh, okay Auntie. Don't forget that I'm goin to Stone Mountain with Zyon in the morning?"

"Oh, you are?"

"Yeah."

"Hmmm, did I already know that?"

"You know? Now that I'm thinkin about it, I don't think I mentioned it to you before now. My bad."

"No worries. Have a great time, baby. He's a very nice fellow."

"Okay. Thanks, Auntie."

"You're welcome."

I watch her as she leaves the room and jus kinda stare into the hall for a while not thinkin about anything in particular. It's almost like I'm afraid to think. I liked all of Mama May's ideas except for the last one. But, I know the last one is the key to redemption. "Damn! Honesty is a motha."

After about twenty minutes, I get up, turn off the lights and make sure all the candles are out before I leave the room. With the books in my hand, I walk to my bedroom deep in contemplative thought about the tasks before me. Before I turn on the lamp beside my bed, I beeline to the blinking light from my cell phone on the dresser. I see that I have a text from Zyon. Instead of reading it right away, I walk over to the bed, cut on the lamp, and start changing into my nightgown. I grab my journal, stick my pen in it, and lightly toss it onto the bed. As you can see, I'm getting ready to shut it down ya'll. Now I just have to make a short trip to the lil girl's room, and grab a bottle of water out of the kitchen.

Back in my room, I arrange the pillows so that I can sit up and write my affirmations before I go to bed. Finally comfortable in bed, I take a look at Zyon's text.

Hey you! Jus confirmin tomorrow morning at 5:30. Was thinkin that you should meet me outside the gate so that I won't disturb Ms. May's sleep by ringin the buzzard on the gate.

Hmmm, thinkin ahead. Still likin him. I return his text with a single word, "confirmed."

Since the clock is tellin me that it's 10:30, I open my journal and begin writing my affirmations before I go to sleep. I figure that, tomorrow, I will look at the notes I took from Mama May's suggestions and determine, then, a plan of action.

I am optimally healthy. I am healed. My mind, thoughts, words, actions, and gestures are healed now. My ethereal, soul, physical, mental, emotional bodies are healed now. I am honest with myself and with others always. I believe in myself. I love and approve of myself. "Hmmm, no tightness in my chest. Thanks, GOD!" I am normal and natural. I accept me unconditionally. I am comfortable in my skin. I am compassionate. I am humble. I am forgiving of myself. I am forgiving of others. I am forgiving of You, GOD. I am forgiven by others and GOD. I am kind. I am a great friend. I am loved. I am love. I am loving. I am lovable. I am courageous. I am inwardly empowered and self-motivated. I trust the process of life. I am giving. I am supportive. I am Divinely guided, supported, directed, and protected. I am happy. Things always work out for me. I am a conduit of INFINITE healing for myself and others always. I am joyful. I know myself. I am a healer. I am intuitive. I am healing me now.

I place the journal on the nightstand, turn off the lamp, and lay down. Instead of setting the alarm, I mentally tell myself to wake me up at 5:00 a.m. before I transition into a very peaceful sleep.

Stone Mountain

As soon as I open my eyes, I know that it's 5:00 a.m. When I turn over to look at the clock on the nightstand, my knowing is confirmed and triggers a smile. "Good morning, GOD, angels, guides, and teachers. Thank you for waking me up." I turn on the lamp and grab my journal so that I can express my gratitude to the universe for my life.

About fifteen minutes later, I get out of bed, put some shorts, a t-shirt, and a sweatshirt on, and go and quickly wash up before I put on my socks and sneakers. As soon as I exit the side gate to Mama May's house, I see Zyon already waitin for me. He gets out of his car to open the door for me.

"Aw. How sweet. Thank you."

"I try to be and you're welcome. Good morning beautiful lady."

I blush a little before I return the greeting. "Good morning."

"You good? I saw that you text me after 10:30 last night."

"Ahunhun. Yeah, I'm good. Mama May gave me a two-hour massage yesterday. My sleep was peaceful aaand restful. I think I got a solid six hours in."

"Okay. Cool. Two-hour massage, hunh?"

"Unn hunh." I just smile, lean back, close my eyes and enjoy Bob Marley's "Three Little Birds" serenade me from his sound system. By the time I notice him parking, the intro to my favorite Bob Marley song kisses my ears and sends a curious chill through my body. But, he turns off his ignition before I hear the words.

"Okay, beautiful. You ready to do this?"

I briefly look around lookin for a mountain. When I don't see one, I look at him questioningly. "You tell me. Where's the mountain?"

"It's about two blocks from here. I like to park over here and walk to it. The walk warms me up before the hike."

I let out a breath - surprised that I was even holdin it in. *Girl, chill out. He's good people.* Convinced with my*self* encouragement, I allow my voice to come forth. "Oh, okay. Well then, yes, I am ready to do this."

The rhythm of our pace is even and smooth. I like that he's not boggin me down with conversation right now and honoring my request for silence. Go Zyon.

We walk through a gate at the end of the main street we were walkin on that leads to a large parking lot. I see the mountain clear as day ahead of me and slightly to the right. Given that I lived in San Fernando Valley, California, I definitely can't call this a mountain – it's more like two exaggerated hills sittin on top of each other, which explains why I didn't see it earlier. I was looking for elevated land that looks like it's literally touchin the sky. Silly me. I mentally wipe the sweat off of my brow, grateful for the fact that I won't keep Zyon out here all day waitin for me to get to the top.

Oh, but please don't get me wrong, nanh. It looks like a damn good work out and hike. I'm just thankful that it's not what I expected, especially since I haven't worked out, really, since I been here.

I have to say that I'm lovin all these people I'm seein out so early in the morning. Couples, small groups, and folks, on the solo tip, are gettin out of their cars, stretching, and preppin their minds and bodies for the hike before them, me, us. Okay, I'm ready to do this.

"Thanks for bringin me here, Zyon. I'm likin this already."

"Oh yeah? Ahun hun. Well, you're welcome. I jus hope you feel the same way during and after."

"Right! Hahaha! I think I will. Do you mind if I stretch a little?"

"Not at all, beautiful."

I like that he calls me beautiful. As I stretch into a forward lunge, I feel my muscles readying themselves for a good workout. Oooh, I so need this.

I can't help but admire Zyon's lean, muscular physique. So that it's not obvious that I'm checkin him out, I chat him up a little. "So, are we gonna jog up or walk?"

"Look at you. You sure you up for joggin up?"

"How steep is it?"

"Initially, the incline is gradual. But, the last quarter is pretty steep, though."

"Oh yeah? Do people go up that part? I mean the steep part."

"Yep. At one point, there's a rail that you can hold on to if it's too much for you."

"Hmmm, sounds serious."

"It can be for first timers. But I have a feelin that you'll be okay."

"Okay, cool."

He looks off toward the mountain like he's contemplating somethin. "Maybe start off with a fast-paced walk to see how you feel, at first, and then maybe ramp it up to an even trot if you feel inspired."

"Okay. Thanks. You ready?"

"Yep."

I can do this. I think this is gonna be fun. The mountain feels light and warm – kinda welcoming. I like the way most people are greeting one another. And those that aren't appear to be determined and focused. I'm likin this. I feel so encouraged. Thank You, GOD. This feels sooo good. I think I'm just gone walk up today, though. You know, gradually graduate to a trot.

Pushin my mind up the mountain helps me stay in the moment as I practice balance, strength, and agility on this crazy uneven terrain. Funny, I figured we would be hikin up a dirt trail. But, we're steppin on large rocks. The little dirt I do see makes you pay attention even more so that you won't slip and fall on one of these rocks. That would so not be a sexy look for me, or anyone else for that matter. Hey! I wonder if they call it Stone Mountain because it's made of stone. Duh, Corin. Please don't ask Zyon an obvious question like that, girl.

I guess we're at the last leg of the hike cuz I'm lookin at the railing he mentioned earlier. Ooooh, shit! I see exactly what he means about this steep part. Okay, mama. You got this. Push it, Corin. You got this.

Shocked, I think we're done once we reach the top of the railed section. "How ya doin, beautiful?"

I nod my head and give a thumb up as I catch my breath.

"Okay, good! We're almost there."

"Almost?!"

"Hahaha! Yeah, just follow me. You're doin great."

No this negro didn't say almost.

Watchin him and others ahead of him, I can see that he's right. The end is very near. It's steep. But it's doable. Oh yeah, I'm definitely comin back. This is a workout fo my ass. I'm gone graduate to a trot before I go back to New York. That's a bet.

It's so cool how some of the people at the top are cheerin folks, like me, on. It's obvious that Zyon's very acquainted with this mountain seein that he just eased up to the top of this bitch just as easy as takin a deep breath. I stop for a moment and look back at nothing in particular but, for some reason, am surprised at not only the awesome view, but my obvious progress. Damn. How beautiful is this?

I hurry up and turn back around to stay focused on my goal – the top of the mountain.

It sure does help havin Zyon's fine ass waitin for me up there. When I finally make it to him, he turns and slowly walks further towards the center of the top. He finally stops and starts stretchin. I follow suit, feelin fuckin exhilarated.

We stretch in silence for about five or so minutes before he speaks. "Do you wanna sit for a while?"

"Sure."

"Okay, cool. I was hopin you'd say that. I like to zone out on the view for a while before I head back down."

What I like most about the south is the plethora of greenery. And this view has me mesmerized on just how much underdeveloped land there is out here. It's so beautiful, y'all. I am lookin at a sea of greenery and a beautiful blue sky. Sure, you can see the city, but it's so incredibly minute in comparison to all of the trees. Wow! "This is so beautiful. Thank you for bringin me here."

"You're welcome. Did you like the hike?"

"Understatement, dude. Understatement."

"That's what's up, beautiful."

It feels like fifteen or twenty minutes passes before another word is spoken between us. And for the life of me, I can't tell you where my mind was. Maybe in captivated-ville. "This view is so awesome. What a wonderful treat after an awesome workout."

"I know."

"And you come here every day?"

"Yep. During the week. The only thing that'll stop me is the weather - rain, snow, and ice."

"Riiiight, right."

"Yeah, I usually double it up before I take in the view."

"Really?"

"Yep."

"You hike up, walk down, and hike up again?"

"Yep."

"Yeah. I can see that. You go, boy."

"Ahunhun."

I think I made him blush by the sexy boyish grin on his face. *Awe.* "I'm definitely comin back."

"Hey, well, any time you want some company, just let me know."

"Okay. The next time I may wanna follow you though so that I can know how to get here on my own."

"Dang. What I do?" He pretends to sniff under his arms. "Do I smell? Shit! Wait!" He, then, cups his hand over his mouth as if he's takin a breath test. "Don't tell me I forgot to brush my teeth. Huhuhu!"

"Hahaha! No. Not at all. Hahaha! It's just that, that, that, ummm…" It takes me a moment to finally stop laughing enough to speak a coherent sentence. "It's just that this seems like a peaceful place for me to…."

"You don't have to explain."

"I don't? Hahaha!"

"Naw. I'm glad you like it so much."

"Yeah, I do. Thanks. You're funny."

"Hey, enough with the thank you's. It's been my pleasure. And I'm glad you find me amusing."

He just kinda looks at me for a long moment. I try to hold his gaze, but I finally shy away from its intensity. "Oh. Okay." Okay, so where did this sudden nervousness come from?

"May I take you to breakfast?"

"Food is always good."

"Cool." He jumps up and reaches for my hand to help me up off of the rock we were sittin on and we start walkin down the mountain. "Don't sound like you're one of those chicks who's afraid to eat in front of guys."

"Nope. I'm not that chick at all. Trust."

"Oh no? Huhuhu! That's good then. Shoot, my motto is just be you."

"I feel you. But, hey, don't judge me if I end up eatin more than you, nanh. Cuz a sista can eat."

"Huhuhu! Maybe jokes. But no judgments."

"Ahun. That's cool. You know, there's something about this mountain that's so inviting to me."

He pauses and looks as if he's trying to remember something. "Maybe it's the giant crystal in it."

I turn toward him so fast, forgetting that we're walkin down a mountain, and temporarily lose my balance. He catches me before I hit the ground.

"Oooh, beautiful! You okay?"

Temporarily dazed from the close encounter with the ground, the feel of his body, and what he just said about a crystal in this mountain, I take a moment before I respond. "Ummm, yeah. Yeah, I'm okay. Thanks. You have fast reflexes. Ahunhunhun." Yeah, that's it. Feel the space with nervous laughter, Corin.

"Maybe. But, I also don't want any scratches or bruises to mar your beauty."

"You're so funny. Always quick with the flattery."

"I speak truth."

"Okay. Truth. But, you know sometimes those scratches and bruises we obtain from life enhance the beauty."

"I see you."

"Maybe. But wait, were you serious about there being a crystal in this mountain?"

"Oh. Yeah. That's where it got its name from – Stone Mountain."

Ohhh! Okay. I repeat the name as if I'd never heard it before. "Stone Mountain. Hmmm, that's deep. I was thinkin it was because the mountain is made of stones, like rocks."

"Yep, I bet a lot of folks think that, and they're right, too, I guess."

"But, how do they really know a crystal's in this mountain? I mean, have they done some sort of test or somethin?"

"I'll show you if you don't mind waitin on breakfast a lil bit."

Overjoyed with wonderment, I display all my teeth and gums. "Oooh, unh, unh! I don't mind at all."

"Okay, stay close to me cuz the part of the mountain I'm gonna take you to is pretty steep and there's no rail."

"Okay."

On the way down the mountain, he takes me to the right of the railed walking path. I find myself bracing my weight with my hands on the ground, behind me, as we go down further near some bushes and weeds. I'm delighted and thrilled to notice slabs of crystal poking through the mountain after travellin about thirty or so feet.

"Wow!"

"I know, right?"

I touch it to make sure it's real and then I pinch myself to make sure I'm not dreamin. "What an awesome moment! I've never seen crystal in its natural origins before. I've only purchased it from stores and vendors. For some reason, this moment makes their properties more real for me. Humph. Go figure."

"Would you like to sit here for a moment?"

"Yes, I would."

"Okay. I'll wait for your cue to leave. I'm in no rush."

"You sure? What about work?"

"Everybody know what to do. It's a routine day. No new jobs."

"Okay, cool."

I immediately begin thankin GOD for this moment, for ALL THAT IS, ALL THAT WAS AND ALL THAT WILL BE.

Though I don't wanna leave, I don't wanna keep Zyon hostage to my silence and wonderment. So, I motion to him, after about ten or fifteen minutes, to get his attention cuz it looks like his mind was far away from here.

"Hey, beautiful. You ready?"

"Not really. But I know I will return soon. Sooo, I guess we can go now."

"Okay. But only if you're sure."

"Yeah. I'm sure."

We walk down the remainder of the mountain laughin just about the whole way down. He's clowning me for almost fallin and my reaction to hearing about the crystal. Sayin stuff like, "Damn girl, how you gone forget how to walk at the mention of a crystal? You ain't into no hoodoo is ya? Like, a part of no crystal cult? Cuz that's information that a brotha needs to know right now. Shiiit, nanh don't worry. I'm still gone feed you to stay in yo good graces. Just promise to let me out and let me be - no questions asked." And his theatrics were on blast with his facial expressions and gestures totally magnifying everything. I'm so still likin him.

I explain to him that he's good, that I'm not a crystal worshipper or whisperer, but I respect their properties. Hence, the calm energy I felt from the mountain. Though I'd never been there before, I felt very welcomed, if that makes any sense. He seems satisfied with my explanation. Either that or he really thinks I'm weird. But it doesn't matter what he thinks – no matter how fine he is. Damn, this man is fine, too.

"You know? I always had a feelin that your aunt's giant crystals throughout her landscape were more than decoration."

"Yep."

"She's such a mystic to me."

"Oh yeah?"

"Yeah. I always enjoy being around her even if we're just working in her garden not sayin anything. There's a calm about her that I like."

"Yeah. Me too."

"I know I haven't known you long. But, I kinda get the same from you in regards to bein comfortable."

"Oh yeah?"

"Yeah. I'm really jus bein me with you. I'm not tryin to impress you or, wait, wait. I didn't mean…"

I look at him genuinely flattered. "I get it."

"You do?"

"Yep."

"Cool. You're definitely different from these Atlanta women. Not that anything's wrong with them. You're just different."

"So, you like different?"

"I do."

Okay, there's that intense look again. Hold it, hold it, held. You go mama. He opens the door for me and casually walks over to his side of the car once I'm in. As soon as he cranks his ignition in his car, my ears are kissed with Bob Marley's "Redemption Song." Without even thinkin that I barely know this brother, I break out into, I don't care if I need a voice coach, song for damn near the whole song.

"So, you're a fan?"

Ooh wait! Zyon's sayin somethin. "I'm sorry, what did you say?"

"Jus that I see that you're a fan."

"Of who? Bob Marley?"

"Yeah."

"Yeah, I like him. But, I can't say that I know all of his songs. This one, though, has always struck a positive cord with me."

"Oh?"

"Yeah. That part of relievin yourself from mental slavery is so deep to me cuz it's so true. But, yet, most of us fall victim to worry or negative thoughts and feelings about ourselves that populate our minds continuously."

"Yeah. I feel you on that."

"It's so funny when I hear people, that I refer to as the revolutionaries, preach about how we're still allowin the white man today to enslave us becuz they don't even realize that that statement, derived from a thought, their thought, is a product of their own mental enslavement that they're imparting on others."

"Welll." Actin like a member in a flavor-ful church's congregation, Zyon edges me on. "You betta preach, sista!"

"Hahaha!" He's so funny. "Quit it. You're so funny."

"Hun, I may be havin a lil fun right now, but I'm feelin you, beautiful."

"Cool. Cuz I'm serious that though you can hear Bob Marley's words over and over again, it's not until you make a conscious continuous effort to change your self-talk, that you'll always be enslaved to your mind which, to me, directs your actions and manifestations in this life or the lack thereof. So, if you go around thinkin and preachin that we're still livin in slavery, then your life will constantly reflect that."

More serious, he responds, "Hmmm. I like how you put that. I think that it's easier to be consistently negative or pessimistic because it's what most people know."

"Right."

"My mom passed a couple of years ago and..."

"I'm sorry."

"Yeah. Thanks. But, I used to get on her all the time cuz she used to be over-the-top filled with worry. It was like she didn't know how to relax."

"Really?"

"Yeah. Though I love to travel, I almost hated to tell her when I was goin on a trip cuz she wouldn't stop worryin until I was back in Georgia."

"Wow. That's deep."

"Maybe. But, it's so real for so many people."

"Yep. Me included." I tap my chest for emphasis.

"What? You worry a lot?"

"I have my moments. But, I've recently made a commitment to myself to change my inner dialogue in those moments so that it reflects a better, happier me."

"That's cool. At least you're workin on you." He parks the car. "All right, beautiful, you ready to eat?"

"Ummm yeah, but..." Lookin around, I don't see a restaurant in site. "Okay, so where's the restaurant – down the street, through a gate, across a parking lot?"

"Huhuhu! Naw! It's just around that corner. It's part of that building facing that street over there."

I follow his pointed finger as I get out of the car and notice the building he's pointing at. "Okay, so what part of town are we in? Looks kinda blah around here."

"Atlanta – the old Fourth Ward. We're not far from the King Center or, I dunno, have you heard of Little Five Points?"

"Yeah, I had lunch over there last week."

"Okay, well, we're not far from there, as well."

"Oh. Okay."

He holds the door open to a place called Thumbs Up. "Thumbs Up."

"Yep. You'll like the food here."

"I hope so cuz I'm uncharacteristically a lil hungry right now."

"Why uncharacteristically?"

"Cuz I never eat this early."

"Oh, okay. Well, I'm glad you're hungry cuz they feed you good in this joint."

"Cool! Lookin forward to it."

Catch Up Time

<u>two weeks later</u>

I mistakenly answer my phone when I reach toward the night stand to see who's callin. *Damn!* Wait. Okay cool. It's Queenie.

"Heyyy girrrrl." Oooh, my voice is draggin.

"Damn girl, did I wake you?"

"Naw. I just opened my eyes from a nap. My voice jus needs to warm up."

"I can call you back if you want."

"Oh no! I don't wanna start another two weeks of phone tag."

"Hahaha! Riiiggghhttt?! That was crazy. I was like, damn! What? My girl don't wanna talk to me?"

"Girl, you know that's not true. How've you been?"

"You know me. Busy as usual."

"Right, right. Well, contrary to what you been thinkin, I have been missin you. So catch me up."

"I know. I was jus playin with cho ass. I miss you, too, and I must say that I'm much better than the last time we spoke."

Sighing, I breathe, "Good!"

"Yeah, girl. Even though oh boy still calls me from time to time, I feel so much better now that I'm stayin at your house."

"Okay. Good. But, are you talkin to him when he calls?"

"Hell no? Girrrl, you crazy?"

"Naw trick. I mean, Queenie."

"Unh hunh. I heard that."

"Hahaha! I'm just makin sure you're not crazy."

"Naw, boo. I'm good. In fact, I wanted to tell you that I found a cute place not far from your place on Grand, near Gates."

"You lyin, Queenie!"

"Nope."

"That's what's up. We'll be walkin distance from each other?"

"Yep. I absolutely…"

"So, you…oops my bad what were you sayin?"

"No, just that I absolutely love it. It's a little more expensive, but it has way more room than I have now."

"Good, Queenie! I'm so happy for you."

"Thanks, girl! Me too. I'm happy for me too."

"Sooo, what's up with your lease at the other place? Are you breakin it?"

"Unh, unh. Remember it's a month to month deal?"

"That's right. Okay cool. So when's the big move?"

"Next Saturday."

"Okay. Good. I wish I was there to help."

"Me too. But not so much to help, but just to be here."

"I know mama. But, it seems like GOD has us separated for a reason."

"I guess so."

"So, have you started packin yet?"

"Not really. Trinity, Juanita, and Joy said they'll help me pack this weekend."

"Cool."

"You know? I don't know if it's your place, my motivation, or both, but I've been journaling every night for about five nights now before I go to sleep."

"Really, Queenie? That's good!"

"Yep. And I've been doin yoga in the morning before I go to work, too."

"That's what I'm talkin bout. Slow yo ass down some."

"Unh hunh. After this crazy shit I've been goin through with ole voodoo priest…"

"Hahaha! Voodoo priest! Hahaha!"

"Wait! For real though! I know that…"

Queenie's serious tone quiets my laughter.

"…some of my issues lie in that space between my ears, where I house a combination of that good and not so good self-talk, and others lie between my legs where I tend to support others' self-talk at times. And many of them stem from me always needin to be on the go – always needin to be doin something even if that means the person I'm doin it with is no good for me."

"Hmmmm, I hear ya." I nod my head as though she can see me in agreement.

"So, I decided to buy this yoga video for beginners to help slow me down. I figure at some point during, or between breaths, I'll actually make friends with myself and supportively honor and uplift my self-talk, spoken words and actions."

Again, I nod my head, but this time I think about how much her words and voice sound so much like my own. Interesting. "That's what's up, girl."

"Shoot. Who knows? Maybe, I'll gradually build up to complete stillness when I'm ready to meditate like you."

"Girl, yoga is a form of meditation. It's a movement meditation."

"Oh yeah?"

"Unh hunh. But any way, I think this is awesome, Queenie! "Jus please keep it up. I'm learnin that consistency is the key."

"Okay, sis. So, what's the dillio wit you?"

I catch my friend up on all my revelations, daily practices that I came up with together with Mama May, my infamous horrific experience at the doctor's office, Zyon, and runnin into and dreamin about Deron a couple of weeks ago.

"Damn, girl. No wonder you ain't been available to talk. I mean, after that shit with that doctor, shit." She pauses for a second. "Shiiit! That was some fucked up shit!"

I tilt my head back with a full belly laugh before I chime in. "Use your words Queenie. Hahaha!"

"How can you laugh about that shit?"

"Girl, cuz really, it's over and I'm not tryin to hold onto stuff like talkin about it any more."

"What? That don't make no sense. That asshole cost you a job."

"A job that I don't need. It woulda been somethin else takin me away from me workin on me – healin."

"Well, I'm still sorry, mama. Shit, you threw me with that one. How random."

"I know, right?"

"But wait, wait, wait. What kind of medical school did he go to anyway? And, shit, if he was a little confused about the virus, ummm, what about the frickin internet. Ever heard of research, mothafucka? Duh!"

"Hahaha! I thought the same thing, girl."

"Girl, you good cuz if that shit had happened to me, shiiit..." As silence fills the phone line, I imagine Queenie shaking her head *no* before she speaks again. "Humph, I honestly don't know what I'd do."

"Exactly. I could get depressed about it, write a letter to who knows who at the clinic, and then do who knows what. But, at the end of the day, I'd still have herpes and a low self-image of myself. Hell, if anything, it showed me that I have to strengthen my inner me even more since the shit has seeped into my professional life, as well."

"Hunh?"

"Queenie, I can't let this define me no matter the circumstance. I have to define me. And who ever don't like who I am innately, fuck 'em."

"Okay. So, who the fuck are you?"

"Hahaha! You funny, girl – real funny. But for your information, I'm actively workin on that new definition now. Hence, all my new found rituals."

"Okay. I hear ya."

"And what's up with all them shits miss Queenie?"

"I know. Hahaha! Girrrl! Shit, sometimes there's just not another word to express the perfect sentiment."

I laugh at the truthfulness of her reasoning. "Girl, you know you a trip."

"Okay, so changing the subject, you know you not slick, right? I mean I can't believe that you actually let weeks go by without filling me in on all the juiciness goin on wit you."

Kinda knowing that Queenie's either switchin to Zyon or Deron, I feign innocence. "Hunh, what chu talkin bout girrrrl?"

"Unh hunh. You know you ain't foolin nobody, Corin. I know you either likin this Zyon cat more than you're letting on, or you're hopin for a different ending to that dream you had about marrying Deron."

What I told you? "What? Girl…"

"Uhhh, yeah. This is me you talkin to, trick. Ooops, I mean, Corin."

"Hahaha! It's not like that."

"Unh hunh."

"As I grin from ear to ear, I explain to my dear friend that I'm good with jus bein friends with Zyon, and that he understands that I'm not ready for anything serious and respects that.

"Huhhh!"

But as I continue my monologue, I surprise myself with erratic giggles that just sorta resound out of nowhere as I hear my voice unconvincingly convince my friend that all of the time Zyon and I have been spending together mean nothing, especially as I recount that he and I had only gone hiking and to breakfast four, maybe six times. And my voice cracks as I half-way whisper and half-way sing-song that we went to dinner twice, maybe three times in the midst of remembering a penetrating stare he offered that made all of my future selves blush. For a moment I feel like I'm snitchin on myself when I realize that my story has turned into a pathetic plea for my friend to believe me. And the realization makes me burst out into a hysterical fit of laughter which causes a brief diversion from my plea to controllin more than a drop of saliva I have to scoop back into my mouth when I admit that we went to a poetry slam after one of those dinners. *Oops! I guess I got a lil excited there.*

"What?! Oooooh, unh, unh! See, I can't believe you, Corin. Dinner and a poetry slam? I knew you were holdin out on me! What's up with that?"

Talk about a guilt-on-steroids moment. "No, no, wait! I really jus don't want you to jump to any unnecessary conclusions cuz we really do just enjoy each other's company."

"Uhhh, excuse me miss thang but dinner and a poetry slam sounds like a frickin date to me."

Okay, so why am I feeling like I'm busted. "Hahaha! I promise you it's been real casual."

"Okay, Corin. You know what? I'm not here to condemn. Heaven only knows I can't wear those shoes. I actually think that it is okay to like him. Just pleeease take it slow."

"I'm good, Queenie."

"Okay. Well, enough of him, quickly fill me in on Deron. Don't mean to rush you, but I have somewhere I need to be in an hour."

I don't express it, but I'm disappointed that the conversation's about to end. I didn't realize it, until now, just how much I miss my best friend. "Oh, okay. Well, in a nutshell, we finally spoke last night and he asked me if I wanted to go to an open mic tomorrow night at a place called Apache in Atlanta. But, I told em that I can't cuz my mom and Shanice are comin to town in the morning and I wanted to jus hang with them."

"Oh really?! Your mom and Shanice are comin for real?"

"Oh, yeah, girl! Damn, I forgot to mention that, hunh?"

"Among other things."

"I'll take that. Ahunhun. But any way, yeah girl, they'll be here from tomorrow until Monday morning."

"Wow! That should be really nice."

"I know. I'm really lookin forward to it."

"Aw."

"I know. Hunhunhun. So, yeah, Deron asked if I'd wanna go the Wednesday after they leave cuz, apparently, the open mic is every Wednesday and I told 'em that I'd let him know by that Monday."

"Why Monday? Why you jus couldn't tell him yes yesterday?"

"I don't know, girl. I don't know if I really wanna hang out with him like that. Somethin tells me that I should keep him in the past."

"Hmmm. I don't know. Shit, I'm still in shock that you ran into him the way you did."

"I know, right?"

"Yeah. But, definitely listen to your gut with him. Don't do anything or go anywhere unless you really want to - not to just be nice."

"Yes, ma'am."

"Well, look, I don't mean to be abrupt, girl, but I'ma need to get off of this phone."

"Aw maaan. O-kay."

"It's been real good catchin up with you, mama. I love and miss yo lyin ass so much!"

"I didn't lie to you."

"What?!"

I clear my throat. "I just didn't share all of the truth all at once."

"Whateva, Corin."

"Hahaha! Well, I love and miss you, too! Sooo, what or who got you gettin off the phone so a-brupt-ly? I mean, I'm jus sayin!"

"Girl, well, one, Babacar's teachin a special two hour workshop out here in Brooklyn; and two, I'm tryin to catch some of Moshood's fashion show before I head to the workshop."

"That's what's up. I wish I was there to join you for the fashion show. But, you know you can keep your Sabar African dance all to yourself."

"Aw Corin, you have to try it again. Sabar is definitely a style of dance that gets better the more you try it and watch other people dance it."

"Yeah, well, like I jus said, I'ma leave the African dance to you, my dawlin. But, hey, if you see my friend, Fatima, at the fashion show, please tell her hello for me?"

"Fatima?"

"Fatima Jones, my friend in P.R. who got us tickets to that show at B.A.M. back in the spring."

"Ohhh! Right! She models for Moshood?"

"Yeah girl."

"Whew! Brave woman. There is no way I'd walk on a platform situated on the sidewalk on Fulton Street with just a beautiful wrapped skirt tied around my waist and nothing else." I think about the boldness of those female models sportin bald heads, cornrolls, afros, bantu knots, locs and twists as they strut to live drums along the platform, some with tribal paint adorning their faces, all with funky earrings, necklaces and bracelets crafted by Moshood out of leather, cowry shells, and much much more accentuating the raw beauty of Africa's daughters. And to top it all off, whenever one of the models wear one of his skirt wraps, also known as sarongs, whether it be long or short, they boldly grace the street with poise and confidence, keenly aware of the pedestrian onlookers and those riding by in cars, as if baring their breasts in public is a natural everyday occurrence.

"Yeah, girl, that's you and me both. I couldn't do it either. But, the last time I attended one of his shows and Fatima modeled, she covered her ta ta's with her hands."

"Oh yeah? See, nanh that's something I would do."

"Riiight?! Please take some pictures of some of the male models cuz all of them be fine as all be damned. Oh, and have fun. You deserve it."

"All right. Thanks ma. I'll be sure to do that. And enjoy your peeps, kay?"

"Okay, thanks! I will!"

That's my girl. I don't know what I'd do without her. Thank You, GOD, for our friendship. She knows me so, so very well. But, I really feel like I'm keepin a healthy perspective about me and Zyon. Hmmm.

The Eve Of The Unfoldment

I get up out of bed and go wash up and head to the kitchen so that I can wash the collard greens and chop up the seasoning for the brunch I'm preparing tomorrow for me, my mom, Shanice, and Mama May. I'm really lookin forward to seein my mama. Now that I've been consistently in a groove with healin me for the past two weeks, I feel different, lighter almost. Yeah, I feel lighter, like a weight's been lifted off of me. I don't know if it's from one thing, in particular, like the kidney/liver flush, or a combination of everything, from my affirmations, prayers of gratitude and meditations, to the Zhan Zhuang, womb, or breathing exercises. But I feel absolutely great and courageous enough to share the truth with my mom. And my sister, for that matter.

I am so glad that I'm finally getting over holdin on to all of this stuff. Constantly, I pray for consistent commitment to myself and it's been workin in such a way that I actually have to calm myself down to meditate at times becuz of my excitement about healin me. I am so loving this new found inner motivation.

It takes me about an hour and a half to prep the food for tomorrow's brunch. So, I go back into my room and do my womb meditation followed by some fire breaths. I feel so empowered. Thanks, GOD.

When I'm done, I hear Mama May movin around so I go and see if she wants to watch a movie with me tonight. As I approach her room, I hear her talkin to Uncle Charles so I quietly back up and go look through their collection of movies to see what I wanna look at tonight.

"Hey baby girl. What cha doin?"

Startled, I jump at the sound of her voice. "Oh, I'm in the mood to watch a movie tonight. So, I was just lookin through y'all's collection."

"Oh. I'm sorry baby. I didn't mean to startle you."

"Oh. No worries. I guess I was really into the summary of this movie." I hold it up for emphasis.

"Which one is that?"

"*Powder.*"

"Oh, yes! That's a good one, Corey. You'll enjoy it."

"You don't wanna watch it with me?"

"Well, hmmm…" She takes more than a moment before she concedes. "Okay. Why not?"

"Good! When was the last time you watched it?"

"Oooh, chile, nanh don't get me to lyin. Shoot. It's been at least five years I wanna say."

"Okay, good. It's not fresh, then."

"Oh, unh, unh. Your uncle Charles loves this movie."

"Okay, cool."

"Unnn hunh." She walks over to inspect a plant that has a couple of yellow leaves.

"I heard you talkin to 'em. How is he?"

"Oh, he's just fine." She gently removes the yellow leaves. "He may be home in two and a half to three weeks now. Getting a lil tired of bein away from home."

"Cool! I'll get to see him before I leave."

"Yep. If everything keeps movin accordin to schedule, you sure will."

I put the DVD in the player. "Can I get you anything from the kitchen, Auntie? I'ma bout to get me a bottle of water."

"Yeah. Bring me one, too."

"Okay."

Once I return, I start the movie, and get comfortable on the love seat as Mama May chills in Uncle Charles' chair.

About a half hour in, I start to make a comment to Mama May when I notice that she's knocked out – head back, mouth wide open. I decide to just let her be until the movie's over in case she wakes up periodically to watch it.

Damn, this movie is good. I wonder if Zyon's seen it.

Mama May stirs. "Baby girl, I'm gonna leave you be. Shoot, I can't keep my eyes open for the life of me."

I place the movie on pause so I won't miss anything. "Okay, Auntie. I'll see you in the morning."

"Okay, baby."

"Hey, what time should I be ready? I wanna go with you to the airport."

"Great! Ummm, I'm thinkin about leavin here around 8:30 in case there's some traffic."

"Okay, I'll be ready." I quickly go and get my phone out of the room so I can text Zyon.

> *Hi. Have you ever seen the movie, Powder?*
> *Beautiful!!! How are you? No, I've never seen that movie.*
> *I'm good. I'm watchin it now. Good stuff.*
> *Okay. Call me, if you're up to it, when it's over.*
> *You sure? It'll be after 10:30pm ish.*
> *Yep. Positive.*
> *Okay.*

Yeah. I'm glad I spoke with Queenie today cuz my conscience will keep me honest – help me keep Zyon in perspective. Cuz truth be told, I really really like him. But, what's even better is that I'm learning to like and accept all of me more and more every day. Kudos for me!

I unpause the movie and relax in my uncle Charles' chair. Hahaha! Everyone loves this chair.

About seventy minutes later, I am completely satisfied. So inspired from the movie, I'm more driven than ever to be and accept me always. "Now that was a powerful fuckin movie. What a message. Daaannng!?

With Zyon and me on my mind, I turn everything off, set the house alarm, take a shower, and get comfortable in my bed so that I can write out my affirmations and prayers of gratitude.

I am beautiful. I love and approve of myself. *Ooooh, I am so lovin the fact that my chest doesn't get tight any more when I affirm that I love and approve of myself.* I accept myself completely. I am worthy of happiness and a healthy committed relationship. I am inwardly empowered and self-motivated.

I trust the process of life. Things always work out for me. I am always in the right place at the right time. I am forgiving of myself, others, and You, GOD. I am compassionate. I am humble. I am kind. I am patient with myself, others, and life. I am joyful. I am honest with myself and others always. I respect myself and others now. I am trustworthy. I believe in myself. I know myself. I believe in You, GOD. I know you GOD. I am open and receptive to higher levels of You, GOD. I believe in the power of prayer. I am committed to myself. I love me. My mind, thoughts, words, actions, and gestures are healed now. My ethereal, soul, mental, physical, and emotional bodies are healed now. I am forgiving of myself, others, and You, GOD. I am forgiving of myself, others, and You, GOD.

Thank You, GOD, for forgiving me. Thank You for others forgiving me. Thank You for peace of mind, calm, and relaxation. Thank You for comforting and strengthening my family, friends, and acquaintances always. Thank You for my right mind. Thank You for Computel Financial. Thank You for massage therapy. Thank You for revelations, inner growth, and evolution. Thank You for my right mind, balance, all of my senses, and my motor skills. Thank You for optimum health. Thank You for helping me be comfortable in my own skin. Thank You for prayer, meditation, and affirmations. Thank You for crystals, medicinal herbs, and therapeutic grade essential oils. Thank You for flowers, trees, and plants. Thank You for air, water, my breath. Thank you for my family and friends. Thank You for fulfilling relationships. Thank You for harmonious relationships. Thank You for faith. Thank You for gratitude. Thank You for courage. Thank You for Infinite Wisdom. Thank You...

After I finished my prayers of gratitude, I sit in silence for about ten or fifteen minutes. Before I know it, it's 11:30. *Hmmm, should I call 'em?*

I hesitate pressing his name on my phone. And when he answers in a sleepy voice, I feel bad that I called at all.

"Hang up. We'll talk another time."

"No. Wait. Don't hang up."

"Uhhh, you sound like you were knocked out, though."

"I know. Wait. Hold on."

I guess he really wants to talk to me.

"Hello?"

"Yeah, I'm here."

"How are you, beautiful?"

"I'm good. What about yourself?" Damn, the sleep got him soundin crazy sexy. This is not good. Keep it light, Corin.

"I'm good. I just wanted to talk to you before your peeps came to town."

"Oh, okay." Hmmm, he's missin me already? I turn off the lamp next to my bed and get comfortable as I switch from sittin up to layin down.

"So, *Powder's* a good movie?"

"Oh yeah! That was an awesome movie! But I don't wanna go into any details cuz I want you to see it so we can talk about it."

"Hahaha! Oh, okay. Well, I guess I'll rent it this weekend."

"Okay."

"So, you ready for your mom and sister?"

"Yeah. I'm really lookin forward to hangin with them."

"That's cool. I hope you guys have a great visit."

"Thanks. We plan to."

"Cool, cool. You know, I know you said that you're here workin on you."

"Unh hunh. Yep."

"Well, I hope I'm not crossing any boundaries when I say that whatever you're doin seems to be workin."

"Humph. Oh yeah? What makes you say that?"

"You just seem different, but in a good way."

"O-kay. Well, thank you in a good way. Ahunhun. But, what makes you say that out of the blue?"

"I don't know. I can't quite put my finger on it. It's like you're lighter – not so weighed down by whatever you've been dealin with."

"Hmmm, okay. I'll take that." He's perceptive. I like.

"Yeah, you're more loose."

"Interesting. So, what you sayin is that I was a whore before, but now I'm more of a whore?"

"Hahaha! Stop it."

"Hahaha!"

"Look, I know we jus met and that…"

Oooh, oooh, oooh, and…

"…you're a private person in all. But, I jus want you to know that I see you, Corin, more and more and the view is captivating."

"Well, damn, I wasn't expectin that. Now I'm all throwed off and stuff."

"Hahaha! Good."

"Good?"

"Yep. It's good to shake things up, don't you think?"

"I guess."

"You guess?"

"Well, umm, I jus wanna make sure we're still on the same page."

"Uh, you lost me. In regards to what?

"You know, jus bein friends and all."

"Always, beautiful."

Could that have been any more awkward? I mean, damn Corin, why don't you open mouth and insert foot one mo gin. It sounds like the guy was jus givin you a compliment. "Cool."

"If ever I say or do something that you're uncomfortable with, jus let me know."

"Okay."

"Did I say something wrong a few minutes ago?"

"No. I was probably just readin into it."

"I don't think you were. You've been on my mind a lot lately in…"

"Hmmm…"

"…in a way that I wish you didn't live in New York."

"Okay. Ummm…"

"You don't have to say anything. I'll ease up."

"Okay."

"So, look, if I haven't scared you off, I'm grillin a week from Saturday. Havin some friends over and wanted to know if you can play spades."

"Hahaha, I ain't scared off!" Petrified is the operative word. "But, oooh, see, I like hangin out wit you and all. But, if you one of those mentally insane spade players whose life depends on winnin, I can't be yo partner."

"Good! I'm glad you warned me. But you're still invited to come through to eat, drink, and be merry."

"Damn! Just like that, I'm tossed to the side."

"Yep. Jus like that."

"Gee, thanks."

"Oh, there might be a dominoes table, too."

"Okay, see, nanh you talkin. I can get with some bones."

"What? So you think you got game?"

"I don't talk shit. I am the shit."

"Hahaha! I love it!"

"Hahaha! Nanh, don't forget I only do fish."

"I got you, beautiful."

"Okay, then. I'm lookin forward to it."

"Cool. Well, I better go if I'ma hit that mountain in the morning."

"Okay. But didn't you get the memo? It's supposed to be rainin in the morning."

"I never believe it until I see it."

"Hunhunhun. Okay. Good night, Zyon."

"Good night, beautiful."

He's likin me. And I'm likin that. GOD, I pray for guidance in keepin it slow and not allowin the negative circumstances of my past disrupt the thoughts, words, or actions of my now.

I lay in bed for a while, thinkin bout a lil bit of everything – my conversations with Zyon and Queenie, the movie, *Powder*, and how me and Mama May will be hangin out with my moms and big sis in less than twenty-four hours. Before I know it, I determine that my thoughts are not makin much sense and that I must be in a dream or something close to it. I'm in a building with bare white walls. It feels like I'm at a hospital. But wait! Oh, shit! I know that I'm sleep – that I'm in a dream. How do I know that? This feels crazy weird cuz I don't think I've ever been this conscious in a dream before. Hmmm. GOD, I know You got me wherever I am, so I'm jus gone walk down this hallway toward the two men up ahead to see if I can find anything out.

As I get closer to the men, I start to feel a heaviness in my chest – hurt, sadness.

Daddy? Uncle Thaddeus? What are they doin here and why are they lookin so sad? Are those tears in my daddy's eyes. Oh GOD!

As soon as I try to run to them to find out what's goin on, they disappear.

Waning Crescent

Tune in to your intuitive self and take heed.

I Didn't Know The Closet Door Was Opened So Wide

"I'm so glad you decided to come with me to the airport, Corey." Excited about seein my mother and sister, I smile at the moments yet to come of huggin them and feelin their warmth. "Yeah, me too, Mama May. I figure as long as the fruit salad's done and everything else is prepped, they can snack on the salad while I'm fixin the rest of the brunch."

"Oooh, I have a feelin we all gone have a good time."

I look over at my aunt for a moment so that I can witness the joy in her voice dance across her face and within her body. She's so cute. "You know, I have that same feelin, too." Hmmm, I jus realized that it's nice and sunny. I hope Zyon had a great hike. Oooh, wait! Where did that come from? Keep him in perspective, Corin.

We ride for a while in silence before my dream surfaces in my mind. "Oh, Mama May."

"Yes, chile?"

"I had a strange, sorta interestin dream last night."

"What was so strange about it?"

"Well, it was like I knew I was in a dream, like I was consciously aware of my thoughts."

She looks over at me with a look that I can't read. And for a brief moment, I swear her face seemed to have faded out a bit – like it became transparent.

"Wha the...?"

"Oh yeah?"

I don't know why I'ma push that transparency out of mind, but I am. Shit, maybe my eyes are playin tricks on me. But, I pinch myself for good measure to make sure I'm still not dreamin. OUCH! Hmmm. "Yeah. Well any way, I was at what I thought was a hospital and saw my dad and Uncle Thaddeus in a hallway lookin very sad. My dad, even had tears in his eyes."

"Hmmm, what do you make of it, baby?"

"I don't know. They disappeared as soon as I started to run toward them to find out what was goin on. And I don't remember anything after that."

"Hmmm. It could be a premonition about something or nothing at all. Only time will tell, baby girl."

"Oooh, I pray it's not a premonition cuz my mind immediately goes to thinkin that somethin's wrong with my mother, or will be in the near future given that they were lookin so sad."

"Well, what makes you think it was your mother?"

"I don't know. I guess I assumed it cuz it was my dad and uncle Thaddeus." I pause and try to put myself back into the dream to see if there were any more clues. "I don't think it was me cuz I was walkin down the hallway, remember?"

Mama May looks at me with a very strange look that feels haunting. "Yeah, I remember."

Again, I start thinkin about the dream and realize that it could have been someone aside from my mother. But, after a few 'what if' moments, I shake the dream off of me and focus on the reason why we're in the car in the first place.

Grateful for the sight of the airport, I shift my thoughts back to the excitement of hangin with my mom and sister. Once we pull up to arrivals and baggage, I see them immediately.

"Oh, look Mama May! There they are!"

"Hunh? Where are you looking, chile? I don't see them."

"Start makin yourself over to the curb. You will in a minute."

She puts on her right blinker and starts to maneuver the car over. "Oh, yes! I see them now."

My mama is such a beautiful lady. She and Mama May definitely look like they kin, but not sisters. For one, they have totally different body types. My mother is much shorter. She stands about five feet five and is a little thicker than her big sister, but not in an unhealthy way. She was always more curvier, and I guess, the weight just falls differently on her.

There's one thing about my mother, though, that I've never been able to wrap my head around. And that's, why, for the sake of livin, does she insists on hidin her natural beauty under tons and tons of makeup, red-tinted wigs, and costume jewelry. I mean, you can count on my mother to have a fully made up face and a wig on even if she's jus walkin at the local track for exercise. Thankfully, she leaves her big, clunky jewelry home on such outings. But, best believe that she'll have some monstrosity of a necklace restin on her voluptuous bosom and a forearm full of bracelets every other moment of her wakin day. Hahaha! And for the life of me, the wigs have always been like an out-of-place hat that perplexed me. I'm tellin you, if you saw the beautiful, thick, long gray hair that lives under those wigs, you'd be scratchin your head, too. But, all in all, she looks great! Oooh, I jus got the sudden urge to hug her – to touch her. Hmmm.

Nanh, me and Shanice could literally pass for the same exact person if we wore our hair alike, we look so much like one another. We take after my father so much that everybody used to joke with my mama – questionin if she was even in the bed when we were conceived. Funny, and so so so very true. We don't look anything like her. And what's so strange is that even though we look jus like our daddy, we favor Mama May a lot, who favors their daddy. But any way, Shanice looks good. She's picked up some weight since I saw her last, but she looks great!

Just as Mama May puts the car in park, I hop out the car to give my mama a big hug. "Hi Ma!"

"Aw, look at my baby." She hugs me tight. "Nanh, wait a minute, let me look at you." I step back so she can scan my body with her mother-inflated X-rated eyes. "Unh hunh. So, this is what a daughter looks like who doesn't call her mother in over three weeks."

"Oh, Ma. Leave her alone. You wouldn't've talked to her if she had called."

I nod my head in agreement to my sister. "Uh, thank you, Shanice."

"Excuse me ladies." We both look at my mother.

But, Shanice speaks up. "Ma, you're either always passin the phone to Daddy or tellin us to hurry up cuz you're in the middle of something. So, no one can ever get a real conversation from you."

"Well, I been talkin to yo ass for at least four weeks nanh, haven't I?"

"Oh, Mary, you know those girls are tellin the truth."

"Mama May, don't start with me. I just got here. Nanh, come on and give ya baby sister a hug."

I start to tear up as Mama May walks toward my mama with her arms open. As I watch them embrace, I think about how good they look for their ages. Sometimes it's hard to look at the years on them.

Shanice comes and side hugs me as we both take in the beautiful scene. "They look good, don't they?"

"I was just thinkin that. Yes, they do." I look over at my big sis. "As do you, beautiful. It's sooo good to see you." I turn to give my sister a big, proper hug.

"Well, thank you. But, you don't have to say that. I know I need to get some of this weight I've gained off of me."

"Ummm, please don't get all big sister on me by tellin me what to say when I speak." I chuckle to lighten the mood and the heaviness I feel from my sister. "So, like I said, you look good, sis."

"Ahunhunhun. Thank you. And, it's so good to see you, too, sweetie. You look divine as always."

"Thank you." I break away from her to grab my mother's suitcase. Shanice follows me with hers to Mama May's trunk while the other sisters go and get in the car.

On the interstate, my mama announces that she's hungry. "So, are we goin to get some breakfast? I don't know what's come over me. Hell, it's only six-thirty in the morning in California. I don't usually eat this early."

"Your body's probably thrown off from the flight and changing time zones. But don't you worry, your daughter is preparing a nice brunch for us."

"Yep, Mama. And you can start on the fruit salad I made last night until I finish everything else."

"Oh, wow! Well, ain't this something? My baby's cookin for me now? This, I gotta see."

"You know, Corin," Shanice says, "I don't think I've ever had any of your cookin. I better call my girls and tell them I love them now in case I don't ever see them again."

I look at Shanice with a 'oh no you didn't' look. "Oh, I see ya'll startin early with the jokes, hunh?"

"Corey can cook nanh."

"Oh, she's cooked for you, Auntie?"

"Yep. And, every meal has been a treat."

"Okay. Well, I guess since you're alive to tell us about it, I won't worry my girls."

Oh, I can tell that this is gonna be a fun visit. Thanks, GOD.

At the house, Shanice follows Mama May to the guest rooms so that she can put her and Mama's luggage away while me and Mama head straight for the kitchen. I get some bowls out of the cupboard and set them, along with forks, paper towels and the fruit salad on the kitchen table.

"Oooh, thank you, baby. You takin care of yo mama real good. Does May have any yogurt by any chance?"

Before I could answer, Mama May answers from the hallway as she and Shanice approach the kitchen. "No, I don't. I've stopped with the dairy years ago."

"Oh. Okay."

"How bout some mint tea instead?"

"Oh, that sounds good, May. Thank you."

"You're welcome. Can I fix you some, too, Shanice?"

"Sure. But, let me get it, Auntie. You sit down. Me and Corin can get this."

"You know what? Why don't all ya'll sit down and chill out." I shoo them toward the kitchen table. "I got this."

They all look at me with smirks on their faces before Mama May decides to respond, "Okay, baby girl. The floor is all yours. Humph. You ain't gotta tell me twice."

Shanice looks at me questioningly as she side-steps her way to the table. "You sure, sis?"

"Yep. This is your moment to chill, too, Shanice. See, this may be the only time I'll ever have an opportunity to host a meal for ya'll since all of you's be avoidin New York like the plague."

They all laugh in unison at the ridiculous truth I just spoke.

We settle into easy conversation, talkin bout everything from politics, celebrities, my mama's recent checkups at the hospital, the men in our family and their significant others, the latest and greatest on my cousins, Kyle and Mya, and my mother's favorite topic, everything that's wrong with her neighbor Ms. Darlene. I really don't think there was anything left unturned. By the time it was all said and done, I had completed fixin the brunch, we ate seconds and thirds, and moved the party on the front porch after I'd loaded and started the dish washer.

"Dang! Time flies when you're havin a good time." I switch from sittin in one of the rockin chairs to sittin on one of the steps. "I can't believe it's 2:00 already. It's so good to see ya'll."

"You, too, sis."

"You know, Shanice, I don't think I've ever seen you without the girls since before they were born."

"Hahaha! I know girl. Let's jus say that I needed a break."

"Unh hunh, to say the least," Mama says.

"I hear ya, Mama." You can't miss the annoyance in Shanice's voice.

"I hope so. I'm sittin right next to ya."

Shakin her head with a smile on her face, Shanice directs her attention to me and Mama May. "I know that me and Michael's separation has been hard on the girls. But I just needed to get away. You know, distance myself from it all."

"I can't believe you left those girls with Daddy."

"Hahaha! Believe it or not, he's really good with them. And they love him so much."

"Humph. You're a brave woman," Mama May says. "What are those children gonna eat?"

"Oh, that's easy."

I look at my mom for her to continue.

"He's gonna grill every day."

"Oh, right." Mama May smiles at no one in particular.

"Unh hunh." My mom always has to put her two cents in. "I just hope he makes them some kinda vegetables to go along with all the hotdogs, burgers, and chicken he's gonna grill."

Shanice looks over at me as if my mom's getting on her nerves. "Well, before we left, I showed him all the fruits and vegetables I separated in plastic containers and baggies for each day of the week."

"Yeah, right." My mom shifts her weight and waves a hand at Shanice like she doen't know what she's talkin bout. "Like your father's gonna follow that."

"Uh, yeah, Shanice, I gotta agree with mom on that one. You really think Daddy's gonna follow your little system?"

"Hey, with him, it's a toss up. But, I know they're in good hands."

"Of course they are. Ya'll betta stop talkin bout my brotha-in-law behind his back. Let him be with his grandbabies."

I nod my head at what Mama May just said. "Sooo, Shanice?"

"Yeah?"

"Just curious, but why didn't you leave them with Michael?"

"Cuz when I asked the girls who they wanted to stay with, Grandpa or Daddy, they both said Grandpa."

"Really?"

"Unh hunh. He lets them get away with so much more than Michael would. They ain't no fools, ya know?"

"Hahaha! Oh, okay."

"Plus, he's being served divorce papers tomorrow and I didn't think the girls should be there."

"What?!" Me and Mama May, both, look at her like how you gone say that all nonchalant-like.

"Yep. I've decided to divorce him."

I look over at my mom, who is curiously quiet, wondering what's goin through her mind.

"Baby, are you sure? Have you guys sought counseling?"

Shanice looks at Mama May with an exhausted smile. "I'm sure, Mama May. And no we haven't becuz I know it won't help."

"How can you be so sure, Shanice? You and Michael been together, for what, nine or ten years?"

"It's been ten years, Corin. And I'm positive becuz the problem isn't he and I, it's me."

My mom has to go to the bathroom all of a sudden.

"You can't run away from it, Mama. I am who I am."

"Nobody runnin away from nothin. I've been sittin here with ya'll since this morning waitin for you to finally say something, but now I gotta go." She looks back at Mama May, with wide eyes, before she leaves the porch.

"What, Shanice?"

"Say what, baby? What is yo mama talkin about?"

"I'm gay."

"Hunh?" Mama May clasps at her chest.

Tears begin to fall down Shanice's cheeks. I instinctively go over to console her. "Why are you cryin?"

"Becuz I hate that I'm hurting Michael and the girls and, and…"

"And what baby?" For some reason Mama May's voice is unrecognizable. And before I can remember how to turn my head in her direction, I hear my mother's footsteps comin toward the porch. Nanh I know that woman ain't pee that fast. She jus didn't wanna be here when Shanice told us. This must be killin her fa sho since she always caught up in what folks think.

"The woman she's been having an affair with died in a car accident a month ago." Me and Mama May both look at my mom with mouths wide open as she steps back into the scene reciting consequential evidence to Shanice's confession.

"Well, all-righ-ty then." I sit back in the wicker loveseat next to Shanice. "Wow. You are dealing with a lot, sis."

Overwhelmed with tears, she just nods.

I look over at my mom with wide eyes; she's sat back down in one of the rockin chairs. She returns the look, throws her hands in the air, and shakes her head. We, all, just sit quietly for who knows how long. I don't know what anyone else was thinkin, but I was tryin to wait until Shanice's tears subsided before I began a soft interrogation. My sister's gay? I begin to zone out on that question and many others like: How long has she known? Oooh, how long was she seein that woman? Does Michael know? How is she gonna explain that to the girls? Or shit, has she done that already? Damn, my sister jus told me that she's gay. Interesting. Talk about an interesting summer.

Shanice looks at me and then at Mama May. "I know ya'll have questions. Go ahead. I'm ready."

Mama May immediately jumps in. "Well, how long have you been gay? I mean, I mean…"

"How long have I known?"

"Uh, yeah. How long have you known?"

"Well, I think I knew for sure when I was in junior high."

"In junior high?" Surprised at her answer, I, first look at her, and then at my mother. My mother just turns her head forcing me to leave her out of it.

"Why have you waited so long to come out, baby?"

"I don't know, Mama May. Shame, maybe. I was so caught up in what I thought people would think, not wantin to disappoint Mom, and especially our family, that I decided to suppress myself around ya'll as to not embarrass anyone." She looks at my mother who remains quiet.

"Mary, did you ever suspect anything like this?"

Forced to join the conversation, my mother looks at Mama May with a *how dare you* look. "Ummm, well, I thought it odd that she never brought a boy home until college."

Mama May whispers Michael's name as though she had forgotten all about him and suddenly remembered that he exists. "Michael."

"Yes, Michael. I jus thought she was a bookworm. You know Shanice was always bringin home awards and scholastic achievements."

"Yeah. I remember that."

Finally discovering my voice again, I ask my sister if Michael ever suspected anything.

"To my knowledge, he's only suspected something within the last two years and that's because I fell in love. I started wanting to be with her more than I wanted to be with him and it became harder and harder to pretend."

"Hmmm, okay."

"But, let me clarify, when he did suspect something, he thought I was havin an affair with a man. He was just as shocked as all of ya'll when I told him that it was a woman and that I'd been gay since my teenage years."

"Wow. Poor Mike." I look at my sister briefly, afraid to look in her eyes becuz I'm truly at a loss for words and don't wanna come across as if I'm judgin her cuz I'm not. I'm jus shocked.

"What are you thinkin, Corin?"

"Honestly?"

Shanice cocks her head to the side and widens her eyes with sarcastic emphasis. "Uh, yeah."

"Okay, drop the sarcasm, girlie." I widen my eyes back at her. "Shoot, you the one flyin out here tellin us that you like women."

"Whew! Ain't that something?" Mama May slaps a thigh and starts shaking her head.

I look at Mama May noddin as I smile and sarcastically raise my eyebrows. "I'm jus sayin."

"You right. My bad. Yeah, please be honest with me."

"Well, I was thinkin about how I'm at a loss for words and how my heart goes out to you for you not bein able to be *you* all these years. And that it may take a while for you, the girls, and Michael to heal from this secret double life you've been living."

"Humph. Tell me about it."

"The good thing is that you're, at least, honoring who you are now which is a huge step toward healing."

"Humph. Thanks, but I don't feel like I'm honoring me too much right about now."

"No?"

"Unh, unh. Feels more like shaming me."

"Hmmm, but at least you're defining you and not allowing what you think others will think of you, define you."

Both Mama May and my mom agree with me. "Unh hunh."

"She's got a strong point, Shanice." I'm a little caught off guard at my mother's sudden participation in this conversation.

"Yep. I liked the way you put that, Corey."

"Thanks Mama May."

"Well, I love you, sis. And I'm proud of you, too."

She reaches out to hug me and I welcome the embrace. "Thanks, sis. I needed to hear that."

"You're welcome. This, too, shall pass."

My mother and Mama May chime in. "Amen to that."

Shanice gets up and faintly smiles to herself. "Well, I wanted to get that out in the open and out of the way. If you wanna ask me more questions, feel free to ask me later." She yawns a long, wide yawn. "I'ma go and take a nap. Couldn't get into a good position on the plane." She looks at me with a question mark in her eyes. "Are we still gonna watch a movie later, Corin?"

That doesn't feel like the question she wants to ask me. And I'm such a trip cuz I'm caught up in Shanice's question and laughin at how nosy I can be at times. Ya see, Mama May and my mama are talkin amongst themselves about somethin and I can't hear what they're sayin. And it's killin me. "Oh, yes! I'm still down."

"Okay, cool."

"How's eight or nine o'clock?"

"Whichever is good with me cuz I'm on California time."

Mama May turns toward us. "Can ya'll make it eight o'clock cuz I'm game for a movie?"

My mother adds her vote. "Me too."

"Okay, party people, eight o'clock it will be. I'll give you all a fifteen-minute warning, okay."

Everyone says, "Okay."

"Oh, are ya'll gone leave the selection up to me?"

Shanice lazily tells me to go for it. Just to wake her up. My mom pleads for me not to select a scary movie – "anything but a scary movie."

"Okay, Ma. Mama May?"

"You know me."

"Yep. I think I do." Her and my mother walk outside off of the screen porch. "What are ya'll bout to get into?"

"Mindin our business," Ma replies. "And you?"

"Ahunhunhun. Okay, Ma. I hears ya."

"Well I hope so seein as I didn't stutter or whisper."

Me and Shanice respond at the same time. "Dang!"

"Okay, Mama."

"Look. I know ya'll grown, but dang is still too close to damn. Choose your words cautiously."

Me and Shanice look at each other with a knowing smile and respond in unison. "Yes, ma'am."

Shanice goes to her room to take a nap, Mama May and my mother walk toward the labyrinth, and I decide to go to my room to journal, meditate, and get my womb movement meditation on.

Damn! Shanice is gay, hunh? Shit! This makes me wanna keep my news to myself for right now. Hell, I wouldn't wanna send my mama into a cardiac arrest or anything. Ahunhunhun. I can hear it now on the morning news, "Woman falls into coma following a heart attack after learning that her only two children have been lying to her all of their lives."

Yeah, no. That wouldn't be a good look.

Hmmm, I just realized that no one mentioned dinner. Maybe becuz they were stuffed from brunch? Well, I guess I should get started on me so that, afterwards, I can go and make a stir fry, finish cookin the rest of those greens, and make some potato salad. Shoot, I don't know why I didn't make any potato salad earlier cuz I sho gotta taste for it.

What?! Mama, No!

the next day

"What?! That cannot be the time. Ten-thirty?! Shoot. Well at least I slept good." I sit up in my bed and grab my journal. I only hear one pair of feet walkin around the house. So, it might be Mama May. I don't wanna risk leavin my room yet cuz I really wanna get my Zhan Zhuang and journaling in before I engage in any conversation. Consistency, Corin. You got it, mama!

When I first started doing Zhan Zhuang about a week and a half ago, it was so easy to unconsciously straighten my legs, turn my head, or even absentmindedly scratch my earlobe or scalp if either of them started itching. But, thankfully, I'm much better now. In fact, I love how I'm forced to quiet down my reflexes cuz it's like, to me, this exercise is a metaphoric lesson on how to observe life and proactively plan as oppose to react unclearly to everything.

Once I finish the poses, I slowly lower my arms and place my hands on my knees, place my feet and knees close together and begin to move my knees around in a circular motion ten times clockwise and ten times counter-clockwise. And then I swing my arms back in big circular motions – all to add oxygen back to my limbs. Afterwards, I'm compelled to sit on the bed quietly as I observe a cool tingling sensation move throughout my body invigorating my senses. I'm so glad that Mama May suggested this exercise. It's very calming.

At some point I decide to become aware of my surroundings and begin to focus in on the voices I hear outside of my room. Determining that it's Mama and Mama May in the kitchen talkin, I lazily get up, and gather my toiletries so that I can wash up before I join them.

"Well, look at sleepy head finally makin an appearance today."

My mom never fails with the sarcasm. "Good morning, ya'll." I look pointedly at my mother with a forced smile. "Mother."

"Good morning. You do realize that it's after eleven o'clock?"

I flop down in one of the chairs at the kitchen table. "Yes, I do. Don't you jus love vacations?"

Mama May starts chuckling. "Leave that girl be, Mary. Ta tell you the truth, I'm surprised you're up right now. It's not like you had to get up and cook Stephen breakfast. You're on vacation, too, ya know."

"Uh, May, I'm talkin to my daughter. Thank you very much."

"I was jus sayin."

"Unh hunh. I heard you."

It's so funny to watch them clown each other. This is such a priceless moment for me.

"Good morning, fam."

Everyone looks toward Shanice. "Good morning."

"I fixed some oatmeal if ya'll hungry."

"Oooh, thanks Mama May. I am famished."

We all look back at Shanice like she crazy cuz we damn near had to draw blood over the greens last night the way she was downin all the food. "Nanh, chile, I don't want you to take this the wrong way becuz you are more than welcome to all the food you want in this house. But, do you have a tape worm livin up in ya? I mean, damn!"

My mother spit out the tea she was drinkin from laughin at Mama May. "Now that was funny, May."

Mama May ain't finish. "Ahunhunhun. Well, you know, I watches people and, Shanice, you been eatin, girl. And please believe me when I say that I mean this with all the love in the world. It's showin big time."

"Hahaha!" My mama can't stop laughin. I'm tryna hold mine in cuz it's hard to read Shanice even though she's laughin, too. But, I eventually bust out laughin my damn self. "May, girl, I'm so glad you said something cuz I knew she'd think I was pickin on her if I said anything."

"You know what? Forget ya'll. Shoot, I'm goin through some things right now." Shanice playfully pokes her lips out like her feelings are hurt.

Cool. By the way she's jokin and gesturing, I figure she's cool with the jokes.

"Yeah, you goin through the refrigerator, freezer, pantry, cabinets..." Oh no she didn't. My mama's on a roll now. "Hahaha! May, please tell this chile right nanh that there's no food in the drawers."

Mama May's laughter turns into a cough before she responds. "Nanh, Mary, you know you need to quit."

Funny, funny, funny. Damn, this is funny.

"What? Look who's talkin."

Mama May does a lousy job at actin surprised. "What?"

"You know you wrong, May. Shoot, you the one who started it."

"Ha!" Mama May slaps her thigh one time before she endearingly looks over at Shanice. "I guess I did, didn't I? I'm sorry, baby."

"It's okay, Auntie. Ahunhunhun. Truth be told, I needed to hear it from somebody else's voice other than the one in my head."

"Hey, I have an idea Shanice."

"What's that sis?"

"You and I should go to Stone Mountain one day. Shoot, we could go today, if you'd like, once the sun starts to go down."

"Okay. And what're we gonna do at Stone Mountain?"

"Climb it."

"Uh, yeah, no, I'm good."

Mama May and my mama burst into another fit of laughter.

"Why not?"

"Look, I'm on vacation. I came here to chill out."

"Okay. But, if you change your mind, just let me know. I'm planning to go tomorrow morning."

. "Okay. Thanks." Shanice's words are mere formality. I know she won't take me up on my offer.

"You know? It would have been great if Mya were here." We all look at Mama May.

"I know, Mama May. I know. I miss her, too." Life is so funny. I just knew that me and my cousin would be inseparable forever. I mean, even after I moved to Cali when I was thirteen, she and I still managed to be best friends – both of us alternating holidays to visit each other all the way up into our senior years. But, though we love each other to pieces, our close bond became more of a loose one during our freshman year in college. She didn't wanna stay in New Awlins and go to Xavier with me. Naw, she wanted to go to Howard. And we've never been able to tighten back up since.

"Yeah. But, everything's in Divine timing. Don't ya'll think it's interesting that the three of ya'll ended up at my house in Georgia at the same time?"

"You know, May, I was thinkin about that this morning when I woke up. Cuz it's not like we planned these trips."

"Right."

Mama May looks at me amusingly. "So, miss thang, are you gonna finally tell your mother why you cancelled your trip to Europe?"

I playfully pretend like I didn't hear her as I add a little maple syrup and butter to my oatmeal.

"I know you heard me, lil girl."

Now I'm caught between eating a spoonful of oatmeal and trying to determine where to begin. Shit, I know that my mom is hurt that, in her eyes, Shanice is pretty much a stranger to her. And I don't know how to confess, admit, or share that I've been keepin a large part of me from her, as well.

I smile and eat a spoonful of oatmeal.

"Ummm, yeah Corin," Shanice said. "I'm curious, too. Why did you cancel your trip?"

Oh no she didn't. I look at my sister with a 'you wrong fa that' look. And she just smirks at me. I swear her look is tellin me 'oh you laughed at me? Well, enough of me, now it's your turn'. And my silent response to her is 'Beeeeyaatch!'

She laughs. So, I laugh.

My mother looks at both of us incredulously. "What's so funny?"

I look at Mama May and she gives me a warm smile and nod of her head which tells me it's time.

"Nothin Ma. Jus trippin out."

"Unh, hunh. So I'm waiting."

"Well, it's kind of a long story."

"Unh, hunh. I ain't got nowhere to go. But wait, you ain't gay, is you?"

We all laugh at the perfectly planted joke.

"Ummm..."

"Ummm, my ass! Don't play wit me lil girl. This is not the time."

"Hahaha! No, Ma. No, I'm not gay. Hahaha! And, I'm sayin! What's with all the hostility?"

"Shit, cuz I was about to say." She looks over at Shanice. "No offense, baby, but that woulda been a bit much for me to handle –both of my daughters lyin to me most of their lives."

Shanice raises her hands, palms facing outward, to her chest and leans back into a defenseless position. "No offense takin, Ma."

I look at Mama May who just smiles the warmest smile ever at me. So, I decide to get a little serious. "Ma, if you don't mind, could we discuss this after breakfast cuz I'd like to enjoy the taste of this oatmeal."

"What?" She looks as though she wants to say something flip, but then changes her mind in mid-thought. "Okay. But, when are you talkin? I mean, how soon after breakfast?"

"Immediately."

"Okay. That's fine."

Mama May's voice seems to calm the sudden fast beat of my heart. "How bout we all go and sit by the pool?"

"That sounds like a great idea." I look at Mama May with gratitude for putting her two cents in. She probably senses that I need the aroma of the lavender to calm me when I disclose my everything to my mom and Shanice.

"Oh yes!" Shanice is lighting up. "That sounds real cool. I'ma put my bathin suit on just in case I decide to put more than my feet in."

"Did you buy one for the trip?"

Everybody looks over at my mom with 'please don't start with the fat jokes again' looks.

She feigns innocence. "What?"

Mama May smiles and shakes her head at my mom. "So, do you miss Stephen? You guys rarely travel solo."

"You know what? Not really."

Me and Shanice look at her surprisingly before Shanice speaks up first. "Really, Ma? Wow!"

"What? Y'all act like we're always glued together."

"Not glued. More like pasted."

"Hahaha!" I fake high five Shanice. "Good one Shanice."

"They have a point, Mary."

"What? So, you're tellin me that you're missin Charles?"

"Of course I miss him. The man's been gone for damn near a month now. What's wrong with missin your husband?"

"Nothin. It jus hasn't hit me yet."

"Okay. It was just a question, Mary. You know you try to play stuff off like you jokin a lot, but you really can be an uptight person."

"Whateva."

Mama May throws my mom a look I can't discern. Then she goes and whispers something in her ear. Hmmm. I wonder what's that about.

Thankfully, Shanice changes the subject. "I can't believe that this is my first time visiting you since you've moved to Georgia, Auntie."

"I know. You have to come more often."

"I will. I love it here."

"Good. And, next time, bring the girls, too."

"Oh yes. They'll love your landscape, the pool, the labyrinth. Oh! And your statuesque crystals are absolutely beautiful."

Feelin my sister, I throw my two cents in. "Aren't they though? My favorite one is the lotus flower at the center of the labyrinth."

"Riiiggghht?! You saw how I was just starin at it."

Mama May interjects. "But, wait. When did you get a chance to…"

I look between Mama May and Shanice. "She had me out there walkin with her in the middle of the night. My bad, Auntie. I didn't mean to cut you off."

"Hey, I'm still on California time."

Mama May looks at Shanice comprehensively. "That's okay, baby girl."

I acknowledge Mama May with a smile before I respond to Shanice. "Yeah, I know. And, truth be told, I really enjoyed our walk."

"Me too."

My mom is sitting quietly with a smile on her face. "What are you smiling at, Ma?"

"Oh, I don't know. Just enjoyin the moment, I guess."

"Good for you, Mary." There goes that unrecognizable look again from Mama May right as she gets up and clears the table. "Ya'll ready to go to the pool?"

Oh no she didn't. Why is everybody so quick to put me on blast?

"Well, I know that I am, May. What about you two?"

Even though my mom's addressing me and Shanice, she's only lookin at me. So, I hold her eyes with my response. "Now is cool."

"Okay, then. I'll meet ya'll there in about five minutes. I'ma go and put my bathing suit on."

No one acknowledges Shanice's announcement about changin into her bathing suit while in the house. But, now we're all just sittin around the pool waitin for her to come and join us so that I can get this story outta the way. Always enthralled by the lavender planted by the pool, I lean my head back, close my eyes, and recline my chair so that I can relax into its aroma. I wish all of the world knew about the relaxation effects of lavender. Cuz then, I don't know, I think the world might be a nicer place to live in.

"Oh, Mama May, this is the bomb!"

"What is, baby girl?"

"Everything. But, especially, the lavender."

"Oh yeah. I know you love this lavender."

"You know? I have to agree with Corin, May. This lavender is the bomb."

I just smile at my mother's comment.

Mama May looks at my mom in an exaggerated way. "What did you say, Mary?"

"She said this lavender is the bomb."

"Yeah. That's what I thought she said, Corey."

Ever since Mama May whispered into my mother's ear in the kitchen, she's toned her personality down. I wonder what she whispered to her.

"Michael's been served the divorce papers."

We all just sorta look at Shanice, tryin to read her mind. My mom finally speaks. "How are you, baby? You okay?"

"Ummm, I guess so. Well, at least I am now."

Me and Mama May exchange looks. I don't know what Mama May's thinkin, but I'm thinkin that maybe this isn't a good time for me to share what's been goin on with me. "Hey y'all, I have a great idea."

Everyone turns to me for me to continue.

"Let's go to the mall. I haven't been to a mall yet since I been here, and maybe that'll lighten things up."

Mama May shoots me a disapproving look.

"You know, baby, that sounds like a good idea. But, maybe tomorrow. Right now, I wanna hear about you."

Oookay. I guess my mom isn't gonna let me out of this one.

"Yeah, Corin, Mom's right. We can go tomorrow or even Saturday. I'm really, okay. Yesterday was all about me. Today is your turn, sis."

"Ummm, okay." Corin, you got this mama. Jus be you, do you. I am normal and natural. I love and approve of myself. I accept myself. I am Divinely guided, supported, directed and protected.

"Corin?"

I look at my mother and nod my head yes. "Okay, so Shanice I've never shared this with you, or really anyone except for Queenie. I mean, until I came out here, Queenie's the only one who knew the entire story."

My mother has a knowing look on her face. But, I feel positive that Mama May hasn't told her anything. "Anyway, Ma, you only know a partial truth. The majority of what I told you was a lie."

"What are you talkin about, Corin?"

"I'm getting to it, Ma." I take a deep breath in and sigh as I exhale. "Okay, so I got raped my sophomore year of college."

"Nooo!" I notice Shanice's eyes quickly dart in my mother's direction. That can either mean that she faked her reaction cuz my mother told her or she's checkin to see if my mother's okay, checkin to see her reaction.

"And Lil Redd was the one who raped me."

"Who?!"

Startled at the intensity of my mother's inquiry, I jump a lil before I answer.

"Lil Redd."

"Are we supposed to know who this person is, Corin!?"

GOD, please embrace my mother with calm energy right now. Thank You.

"Lil Anthony Carpenter, Mary. Rita Carpenter's son." Ooooh, good. Thanks Mama May.

My mother looks at her sister as if she's speakin a foreign language. "Rita Carpenter's son? But, didn't he kill himself?"

Right now Shanice is crying silent tears. I wonder if they're for me, her, my mother, or all of us.

"Yes, Ma. Apparently, he shot and killed himself after he raped me."

"Oh my dear GOD." My mother gets up and pulls her chair next to mine. Shanice follows suit while Mama May sits back and observe. "Baby, why didn't you tell me? Oh my dear Lord!" She grabs my hands and I notice that she's shaking.

"Mom, it was such a traumatic experience for me, you know with him killin himself and all, that I jus didn't know how to tell you, or anyone who was close to the Carpenters, for that matter. It was such an incomprehensible nightmare that I didn't feel like reliving it every time someone called to check on me cuz you had told them what happened."

She gasps a little once she realizes what I actually said. Shanice gets up and lightly rubs her shoulders. I cry at the sight of my mother's tears. But, my tears aren't from sadness. They're from me feeling relieved, free, and light. I guess I did need to tell my mom the truth.

Always thinkin ahead, I pull out a compact pack of tissues out of my pocket and give a few to my mother and Shanice. Not knowin what to say, I sit still and wait for my mom or Shanice to speak. Thank You GOD for forgiveness of myself, others, and You, GOD. And, thank You for forgiving me and encouraging others, like my mom, to forgive me, too.

"Okay. So let me be clear about this. You were only raped once, right?"

Shanice's expression reads perplexity and annoyance. "Hunh?"

"Oh. Yes Ma, I was only raped once." I look at my sister and explain that I told her a totally different story initially. And she nods her head to let me know she understands. But, her pierced lips and wrinkled brow tells me that she's still annoyed. I wonder if she's upset that I never shared this with her, that I went through this, that my mom's upset, or all of the above. I know that right now I feel bad that I'm hurting my mom. But, I must say that I am sorta enjoyin these organic moments of truth between all of us. Shit, tiptoe-ing around shit is so stressful.

"Well, Corin, why did you tell me at all? I mean, you kept it to yourself for about, what, three years. And then, when you did tell me, it was a lie?"

"Ma, I don't know. It was so impromptu. I was feelin a little anxious about livin in New York all by myself with no family near. Everything was so new, big, and different."

She nods her head like she's understandin me.

"And I guess I was feelin very vulnerable, but wanted to put up a good front to you in regards to bein excited and comfortable about livin in New York and bein out of school and all. I don't know..."

She looks at me with sad eyes that tug at my heart and my tear ducts.

"I don't know. I guess the vulnerable side of me wanted to feel close to you in some kinda way – I wanted to be held. I guess babied, in a sense. So, I fabricated that story."

"I see. And the reason why you didn't tell me the truth initially was becuz you'd figured I'd tell people?"

"Well, yeah, like the family and all. Given that we were so close to the Carpenters, I couldn't imagine you not tellin anyone. And I jus don't think I could deal with re-telling the story every time someone called to check on me. Or, worse, endure folks' 'look at poor lil Corin' looks every time I was in their presence. The experience was hell enough."

"You know, I remember once durin one of your visits home durin your junior year, your father had mentioned that he noticed something different in you – that you were sorta distant."

"Oh, GOD, don't even mention Daddy to me right now. I know at some point, probably sooner than later, I'll tell him. But, when it happened, I kept thinkin that he was right, that I didn't know how to carry myself like a lady."

"Oh my GOD!" My mother covers her mouth with one hand and jus looks at me for about thirty seconds before she gets up and shares my chair with me. She gives me a hug. "Baby, I don't know the particulars of what happened with you and Lil Redd, but I know it was not your fault. You do know that, don't you?"

"Now I do. But it took me a long time to get here."

"Oh my GOD." She pulls back from me and it's almost like I can see her mind travelling. "Your father loves you, Corin." She looks over at Shanice who's sat down in her chair. "He loves both of you girls. And sometimes out of his love for you and fear of y'all gettin into any trouble, he might have said some things..." She stops to wipe her tears.

Shanice reaches out to touch my mom. "We know, Mom."

I instinctively embrace her and notice that she's trembling again. "Yeah, Mom, we know." She's remembering those arguments they used to have about me, my friends, and stayin in front of the house. Yep, I can feel it. "We know."

She nods her head as I hand her some more tissue. "Baby, I can't even begin to imagine what all of that was like for you. I'm so sorry that you had to endure such a thing."

"Things."

She snaps. "Well, things, Corin."

I annoyed her. "No, see, what I mean by things is that it didn't just stop at the rape and suicide." I went on to explain the entire story – my visits at the hospital following the rape, Nurse Lily, the herpes, Deron leaving me, counseling sessions at the 'Y', strained intimate relationships, psychological turmoil, hell, self-imposed imprisonment from everything, Black, that doctor here in Georgia, all of my revelations, and what I'm doin now to heal. I purposely leave out Zyon becuz it's way too early to determine anything about he and I.

By now both Shanice and my mom have sat back in their original chairs. There focus was so acutely on me, I felt like they were watching a real good movie filled with action, suspense, and drama – my life, my life, my life, my life in the sunshine. Ooops. My bad, ya'll. I had a brief Roy Ayers' moment.

Mama May appears with a tray filled with peanut butter and jelly sandwiches, sliced fuji apples, bottles of water, paper plates and napkins. I've been so enthralled with my story and my mom and Shanice that I hadn't realized that Mama May had left and gone to the house. Humph, I wonder how long she was gone.

"Whew! Girl! GOD bless your beautiful heart."

I look at my mom, both of us with dry eyes now, and feel, what I imagine, a feather feels like. It feels like tons of thoughts, words, conversations, secrets, discretions and much more packed within in dozens upon dozens of big rig trucks are now lifting off of my shoulders and dispersing into the abyss of love. Maybe it's that unconditional self-love, that ultimate goal I'm workin toward. "Thanks Ma!"

"Wow, Corin. I had no idea. It's like I don't know you at all."

I look at my sister, again, with that 'oh no you didn't' look. "Ahunhun. Uhhhh, likewise."

"Hahaha! Touché."

"Yeah, exactly." *Trick.*

Shanice laughs as though she actually heard me say 'trick'.

"So, May, how long have you known about this?"

Mama May continues to prep the table for us to eat at while she addresses my mother. "Hmmm. Was it the day you came home from that doctor's office?" She looks at me for confirmation.

"Yep. That was the day."

"Oh yes, that doctor. Somebody needs to speak to him. Now did you write a letter to somebody on his behalf?"

Mom mode is in full effect. "No, I didn't. I still don't feel like it's a battle worth fightin. I'm more important. And it's not like I needed or need a job for the money."

"Yeah, but what if he does the same thing to someone else?"

"I hear you, Ma. But, right now, I can't concern myself with that. I'm healin me."

"Unh hunh. Well, I'm glad that you did come here. Thank you so much May for lookin after my baby."

"Our baby."

"Yes, our baby." The two sisters exchange an endearing look.

"But, you know somethin, I feel a world of better since I've finally told you, Mom. I mean, y'all, it's so crazy but I feel so light."

"Well, I hope so with all of that muck you'd been carryin around."

Muck? Did I get that word from my mom?

"Ahunhunhun."

"You know, Corin, for a minute there I thought that you were gay."

"Hunh?" Me and Shanice laugh a little becuz we both responded at the same time.

"Yep. Me and your father even had a conversation about it once."

Oh no they didn't. "Ummm. Hunh? Why? When?"

She looks so childlike as she explains their rational. "Well, you never once brought anyone home or spoke about having a boyfriend except for that Deron fellow back in college. "And…" She briefly looks down as she giggles a little. "Um, yeah, we wondered."

"Well, when did you stop wonderin?"

"Hahaha! I guess I can say about, what, maybe an hour ago. She throws her head back and laughs a full, hearty laugh.

"What?!"

Mama May and Shanice join my mother with the laughter. "Oh, this is funny to y'all?"

Wipin the newly formed tears from her eyes, my mother tries to contain her laughter. "Well, baby, think about it, whenever I asked if you were seein anyone, you always told me that you were workin on you."

"Yeah! And?!"

"And, you're about to be thirty-four years-old and you haven't mentioned anyone since college. I was thinkin, well damn, how much workin she need? I mean, now that I have the whole story, I get it. You're a strong woman, baby."

"Thank you?" So, I guess that was a compliment?

"Yeah. You've been dealin with a lot. So, yes, I get it now." I guess her smile acted as the period in her statement given its out of place glow.

I think about what she just said and realize that I guess I could see her point. But damn. "Okay. Well, let's be clear." I look at all of them to emphasize my point. "I like men!"

"Unh hunh. Okay." My mom playfully looks at Shanice and Mama May as if she doesn't completely believe me.

Dumbfounded by her animated antics, I address her with disbelief of my own. "Oooh Mama. No you didn't."

"Hahaha! That was a good one, Mary."

My disbelief points toward my aunt. "Mama May? Say it ain't so – not you too?"

"Good one or not, May, it was a real thought."

"Mama!" I feel like my thoughts are playing ping pong in this conversation just as my sister starts laughin.

"Hahaha!"

"Shanice?!"

Hell, this entire concept is so absurd and out of place that I might as well lighten up and join them. So, in one leap, I jump off of my high horse and join the laughter that feels like it's shaking the pool, the eruption is so profound. And finally, after moments of contagious, sporadic giggles from all of us, I make one last stance. "Okay, well, please let it be known that although I've had some unpleasant experiences with the opposite sex, to say the least, I am still very much attracted to that particular species of existence."

They all nod their heads in agreement without any sarcastic looks, grunts, or words. Then Mama May encourages us to eat up before anyone else makes another comment.

"Corin, all jokes aside."

I hone in to my mother's serious tone. "Okay."

"Now, you mentioned that this herpes is not life threatening. But, can you have babies?"

Hmmm. I look forward to the day when I can hear or say the word, herpes, without inwardly cringing. "Yes." I give her a more thorough explanation of the virus than I did when I initially disclosed it to her and Shanice earlier, but not as detailed as I gave Mama May.

"Okay. Well, I'm glad that you're workin on yourself, baby. I suppose I have some self-work I need to do as well. You girls have shown me levels of courage and honesty that I've ignored so much within myself, I never realized they existed within anyone. And I wanna thank you both for that."

Me and Shanice both reply, "You're welcome."

"Okay, so it's Thursday and we're leavin on Monday morning. Nanh May, you ain't got nothing you wanna drop on me tomorrow, do you?"

We all get in another good, long laugh before Mama May answers.

"No. No, I can't say that I do."

"Whew. Thank GOD!"

"Oooh, umph. Mama May this peanut butter and jelly sandwich is hittin the spot."

We all look at Shanice as if to say 'what hasn't hit the spot for you?'

She looks at us questioningly, "What? Shoot, I don't know the last time I ate a peanut butter and jelly sandwich." She looks at the sandwich in her hand for a moment before continuing. "I really feel like a kid again. And these sliced apples are divine. What kinda apples are these?"

I answer for Mama May. "They're called fuji."

"Oh, okay. I've seen them in the store, but been stuck on Granny Smith's for so long that..."

"I know. Me, too. But, now every time I go and get groceries, since I been here, I get the fuji apples. Girl, they are the bomb."

My mom reaches in for a slice and immediately nods her approval. This moment feels sooo good. Thanks, GOD.

"I was raped once. I was the same age you were, Corin. Nineteen."

Me and Shanice look at each other first before we look at my mama. Mama May has a knowing grin on her face that speaks 'you go girl'. Everyone has stopped. No one is speaking, eating or drinking anything. We allow time and the stillness of the moment to seduce my mother out of her story. I think all of us are pretty aware of the fragility wrapped vulnerability that took a chance and spoke out just now. So, this is our way of expressing our respect. "Me and one of my girlfriends, hmmm, what was her name?"

She takes a long moment before she speaks her friend's name. "Janice. Janice Cook. Yeah, one night we went to a party in the lower ninth ward and met these two nice lookin guys who told us about another party uptown. Me nor Janice drove at the time. We caught the bus just about everywhere we went back then. And because we felt comfortable with the guys, we didn't think nothing of it by getting in the car with them to go to the other party. Plus, I think what helped was that one of them knew the guy, Tyrone, who we knew from around the way, who threw the first party. "Well, when we got to their car, I got in the back with the guy I had been talkin to and Janice got in the front with the driver."

She pauses and looks off. I'm so proud of my mother. I know this is a huge step for her and she's doin great. I feel like a psychologist reading her body language and the lack thereof. She hasn't attempted to make eye contact with any of us yet. She's holdin on to her peanut butter and jelly sandwich as if she's gonna take a bite at any moment. But, I think all of us know that she's already taken her last bite, at least for a while now. "Well, me and Janice instantly knew that they weren't going uptown because of the direction we were driving in. Janice spoke up first and asked where they were taking us. And the one that I was paired up with told her to shut the fuck up and just ride. She and I quickly exchanged looks. That was such a chilling moment – to see all the fright in my girlfriend's eyes. Or, hell, maybe it was the reflection of my own."

She shrugs nonchalantly. Me and Shanice look up at each other just as my mother sets her sandwich down. "They ended up turnin off into a semi-wooded area. And as soon as the car stopped, both me and Janice made an unsuccessful attempt to jump outta the car. Both of the guys immediately pulled us toward them. The one with Janice rough-handled her the entire time. He pulled her out of the car through the driver side. She was kicking and screaming the whole time he dragged her away. It was eerie hearing her screams in between my own. Well, anyway, once they were gone, I tussled with the monster left with me. I was scared to death. I think my entire body was shaking. No. I know my entire body was shaking 'cause I can still hear the rattle of my teeth clanking together from all of the fright I was holding. But I will say that that fright dressed up like adrenaline too cuz I knew that I wasn't gonna make it easy for him – for whateva he was planning to do. By the time he pulled me outta the car, my blouse and stockings were ripped and my wig was hanging on to my head, like I felt like I was hanging onto my life – desperately."

I guess she's relivin the moment becuz I swear I jus saw fear dressed in a run down black dress pass through my mama's eyes. "He pushed me forcefully on the ground. My knees and my right palm bled from the gravel that pierced through my skin. I didn't have time to run or turn around before he jumped on me from behind. I wasn't prepared for his body weight, so I fell heavily forward. I heard Janice screaming and struggling while I was being raped. I remember feeling a lil gratitude that I didn't have to look at his face while he dehumanized me."

Damn, this is some deep shit. GOD, I wish she had told me. I can't believe my mother survived this. Revelation occurring. Oh shit, this whole experience is swimmin around in my DNA, in Shanice's DNA. Danyum!

"I swear that either my guardian angel or Janice's whispered in her ear with the perfect idea."

My heart can't take much more of this story. "Oh my GOD, Ma. What happened? How did it end?" She doesn't allow my urgency to distract or prompt her to look in anyone's direction. She just continues the story at the same pace, tone, and pitch she'd already been in.

"Well, Janice pretended like she was having a heart attack. And luckily she was so convincible that the man stopped what he was doing and called out to the man who was raping me. I later found out that Janice didn't get raped – that he just beat her up. The guy got off of me and half ran and dragged me to where they were. At first they panicked before they decided to take her to the hospital. As soon as we were out of the car, at the hospital, Janice straightened up and we both ran to some cops who were coming out of the emergency exit. We told them what had happened and they just sort of looked at us all funny at first. I don't know, maybe they were in shock. But, then, I told them that I had a wig on and that the wig is still at the location. With that, they decided to check it out. Me and Janice rode with one cop while the men rode with the other. As soon as we pulled up to the place they took us to, we all saw my wig lyin in the middle of the pathway. And they arrested those guys on the spot."

Hmmm, maybe that's where her attachment to wigs came from. Humph, sometimes, you never know the lifelong imprints a traumatic experience paints on the canvas of our daily lives.

Shanice speaks first. "Ma, I'm so sorry that you went through that. Please excuse me when I say, Damn!"

"Is this the first time you've told somebody about this?" I ask.

"No, I told May about, what, ten years ago?" She looks at my aunt for confirmation. When I follow her eyes, I witness the sweetest moment I've observed between my mom and my aunt.

"Yes, Mary. It was about ten years ago."

"So, you never told Daddy?"

I look over at my sister. "Okay Shanice."

"No. I never told your father. Sometimes a woman's secrets are deeper and more vast than the universe."

Shanice looks at her quizzically for a brief moment before she just nods as if something just clicked.

My mother looks back at my aunt. Mama May walks over to her and motions for her to stand up. As soon as my mother does, the two of them embrace for a long while. "You did it, Mary. I'm so proud of you."

My mother just nods her head as quiet tears fall. Shanice and I are observin the preciousness of the moment. I want to make a comment about the police needing to go to the scene. I mean, my mom did say that her stockings and blouse was all ripped up. But, I leave it alone with the notion that there's probably something she left out. Either that or we just witnessed an example of police insensitivity.

When they break away, my mother announces that she's going to go and lay down for a while and would like to treat everyone to dinner tonight. "Hey, May, do you know of any good Ethiopian restaurants?"

"As a matter of fact, I do. But, you don't have to treat me for dinner, Mary."

"Uh, I know what I don't have to do thank you very much."

She turns and walks toward the house and Mama May waves her off and smiles to herself. "Well, girls, I know you didn't expect any of this."

We both shake our heads no.

"But, you know what, Auntie?" I say. "It feels good, though. You know, refreshing."

"I don't know if I can say all of that," Shanice says. "I guess, now, for me, I wanna know y'all more. I realize that, in a way, we've been havin surface relationships."

Mama May nods in agreement. "Yeah, baby. I think a lot of people think they have close, personal relationships with others. But a large fraction of us only share a small fraction of who we are with most people. I betcha that very few people know all there is to know about another. It's more like a group of three to eight people may collectively know all there is to know about one person."

"I never thought about that, Auntie. Why do you think that is?"

"Well, Shanice, I think most people are afraid to reveal their total selves to certain people out of fear of scaring a person off."

I nod. "Yep. Fear of rejection."

"That's the phrase I was thinking of, Corey. Thank you."

"You're welcome, Auntie."

"Okay ladies, like your mother, I'ma go and lay down, too."

"Let me help you bring this leftover food and stuff in, Mama May." I grab the tray she's holdin and call back to Shanice. "Do you wanna stay and swim with me? I'ma go and change into my swimsuit."

"Sure. I'm about to get in right now."

"Okay, cool. I'll bring the Backgammon set just in case you're in the mood for a lil Acey Deucey."

"Oh no you didn't jus go old school on me."

I have a flashback moment of us havin this same conversation about twenty-three years ago. "Oh, yes I did."

"So, you really think that you want some a dis?"

Sure that Mama May's out of hearing distance, I let the shit-talkin begin. "Hahaha! Oooh, unh unh. You must be ready to get yo ass kicked, hunh?"

"Hahaha. N-E way, Corin! It's always good to dream, baby girl."

"Hey, first you gotta dream it to achieve it. And, personally, I see the ass-kickin goin in my favor. Sooo..."

"Yeah. That's it. Pump yo-self up. You gone need that confidence to pick you up while I'm sayin Acey Deucey, sucka!"

"Hahaha! Girl, I'll be back. Let me put this stuff up."

By the time I return, Shanice is chillin on an inflatable chaise-lounge-sized floatation device at the deep-end of the pool with her shades on. I ease into the water one step at a time at the shallow end. As soon as I enter the pool, dialogue commences.

"Well, this trip is sho full of surprises."

I wait until I'm wadin in the water beside her before I respond. "Humph. Girl, tell me about it. Hell, I was trippin off of all of my stuff. No one in the world could've prepared me for what you and Mama have added, as supporting casts, to my life's script."

"Humph. I bet. The funny thing is it's almost like GOD is makin us look at ourselves in a 3-D mirror. Cuz, neither one of us can get mad at the other since we all was hidin stuff from everybody."

I toss Shanice's comment around in my head. "Hmmm, I like that - 3-D mirror analogy. But, shiiit, I feel like my 3-D mirror is embedded in a x-ray machine that's capturing all the tears and punctures of my soul."

"I love talkin to you cuz you always elevate concepts to deeper levels, like Mama May. You're a lot like her, you know?"

"Yeah."

"Ahunhun. I used to envy y'all's relationship when we were younger until one day I set a date to hang out with her during my spring break when I was a sophomore in college. And, although I love her like breathing, sometimes I just don't get everything she's about."

"Hmmm, okay."

"Yeah."

I look at my sister and, for some reason it strikes me that, like everyone else, she and I are all doin the best that we can do at any given moment with the knowledge and tools we're equipped with. "Well, I'm glad you let that envy go."

"Oooh, yeah girl. That's been gone."

"Cuz, it'll do nobody no good."

"Yep. So, what do you think all this means for us?"

I sigh a long sigh before I answer. "Honestly, I think it means that we're healing. For you and I, we'll probably accept others more, the more we accept ourselves more. And for Mom, I think the more she sees us accepting ourselves more, sharing our lives with her more, then she'll be more propelled to accept and share herself more consistently."

"I like that, Corin."

"Me too.

I smile at the moment, at my sister, at my comfort of sharing my experiences with her, my mom and Mama May, at the lightness of my shoulders that used to feel so weighted down, at peace.

Fufu And Sage

"**H**as either one of you spoken to your mother yet this morning?" Shanice and I look at each other to check if the other has spoken to our mother and then both shake our heads no.

"Hmmm, it's almost noon and..."

"And I'm all right."

We all look toward the kitchen door at my mom.

"Oh, okay. I was gone make one of them go in and check on you if you didn't come out by noon."

"Well, I appreciate your concern. But, I'm jus fine. I decided to sleep in some. You know, it's only 8:45 a.m. in California?"

Mama May playfully rolls her eyes. "Yeah, I know. I'm jus glad you finally realized that."

"Ahunhunhun. Yeah, I guess you can say I did. It's weird when you don't have to do anything for anyone but yourself."

"Unh hunh."

"I'm so used to getting up and making coffee and breakfast for Stephen every morning that I forgot how to not do that, it's been so long."

Shanice and I are just sittin back enjoyin the banter – lookin from one sister to the next as if we're watchin a tennis match. We turn toward Mama May.

"I know exactly what you're talkin about. It took some getting used to when Charles started travelling with his books."

"Okay. Hmmm."

Shanice gets up from the table. "Can I get you something, Mama? I just made some pancakes. May I make you some?"

"Oooh, what kind did you make?"

Shanice smiles a big smile. "Blueberry?"

"Humph, like you had to ask. You know I want some." She looks over at me and Mama May. "How did ya'll like the pancakes?"

Mama May speaks up first. "Ab-so-lute-ly loved them."

"Yeah, they were better than delicious." I pretend like I'm licking my fingers.

"I know. And she won't tell nobody her secret." My mom rolls her eyes.

"Nope. If I tell ya then I'ma have ta kill ya. Hahaha!"

Mama May shifts in her chair. "Well, I'm glad we're altogether cuz…"

"Oh, hell no, May. What's this about, hunh?"

We, all, sorta look at my mom blankly before it registers what she's getting at.

"You a spy for the government? Shit, what is on yo mind, now?"

"Uhhh, if you'd let me finish, smart-ass, you'd know by now."

"Ahunhunhun. I got yo smart-ass." My mom gestures for Mama May to continue.

"Unh, hunh. Well, anyway, I got to thinking about what Corin was talking about last night at dinner."

I look at my aunt blankly. "Hunh? What was I talkin bout?"

"About how you, we, us, are the product of all of our ancestors and how their thoughts, fears, traumas, triumphs, etc. are flowing through our blood - within our DNA. And, just how much of our actions, reactions and proactions, are ours versus theirs, or a combination of everyone."

I nod my head recalling the conversation and gesture for her to continue.

"Well, I was thinkin that we can create a ritual, or an exercise, where we bless our lineage."

"I don't think I'm following you, May."

Mama May first looks at my mother and then at me and Shanice and explains how we can write down the names of all of our ancestors, gather all the pictures we have of them, and create a prayer of some sort that addresses fears, rapes, shame, lack of self-love, self-love, confidence, triumphs, etc. for all of our ancestors who came before us, us, and those that will come from us. She says that we have the power to heal, forgive, and plant self-love in place of all that negative stuff.

"Oooh, Mama May." I shiver from a chill that leaves my body. "I just gotta chill. I absolutely love that idea."

"I figured you would, Corey. Part of the idea came to me that night I gave you the massage. Remember?"

I search my mind a little and shake my head no. "Sorry, Auntie."

"No worries, baby girl."

"I like your idea, Auntie," Shanice says.

Ma looks hesitant. "Hmmm, I'm not really sure about it, but I'm game for trying somethin new. When do you wanna do this exercise?"

"How about before you and Shanice leave?"

"O-kay. That soon, hunh?"

"Yep. I figure, there's no time like the present."

"Well, I'ma need to understand this better, then. So, explain why we're doin this again."

"Ma, it's like we're healing the lineage."

"I get that, I think. I jus wanna know how."

"Okay. Well, like take MonMon, your mom, for instance. You said she was fifteen years old when she gave birth to Uncle Thaddeus, right?"

"Yes."

"Well, you also said that Uncle Thaddeus' father was married at that time and didn't want anything to do with him or MonMon."

"Right."

"Well, I'm totally speculating now, but for all we know he raped her – molested her. I mean, wasn't he a grown man with kids of his own?"

"I'm not sure of his age back then. You May?"

"No, I can't say that I remember that. But, from eavesdropping every now and then, I know her being pregnant at that age wasn't nothing she was proud of. It was like she brought shame to Papa."

"Hmmm. Yeah, I guess you're right. Plus, after that, all the men she met, up until Daddy, used to beat and take advantage of her."

I squirm at the thought of my grandmother bein so young with a baby and men beatin on her.

"Yep, remember when Thaddeus told us that he used to feel so helpless when they used to beat her up in front of him?"

My mom nods her head slowly with a distressed look on her face.

"See, Ma, to a certain extinct, those experiences are within you because they lived within the cellular memory of Grandma who birthed you. And then, you birthed me and Shanice. And our kids will have those cellular memories within them, too."

"Okay, I guess I'm gettin that part. But how can we heal it?"

"Prayer, Mary. We can pray to reprogram all of that through forgiveness, acceptance, and releasing it in love so that only the love is passed on, not the tragedies. Shiiit, the more I think about it, I feel like we should start empowerment rituals with each generation of women."

My mom looks at her. "So, we all create individual prayers or what?"

"We can. What do y'all wanna do?"

"Well, since you're the oldest woman in the family..."

"Watch yo-self Corey."

"Hahaha! No, seriously, since you're the eldest and are a world renowned healer and all, I vote that you create and recite the prayer. What do ya'll think?" I look at my mama and Shanice for their input.

"Sounds good to me. Shoot I wouldn't know what to say."

"I agree with Mom," Shanice said.

"Okay, so Mama May, you're the woman."

"Yes, I know this."

"Hahaha!"

Shanice, who's been pretty quiet, finally speaks. "This is sooo awesome. I'm lovin this like a warm piece of granny smith apple pie with a scoop of vanilla ice cream."

Everyone looks at Shanice, but Mama May is the only one who decides to comment. "You funny."

"What Auntie?"

"Only you would compare this moment to some food."

"Hey, it's my way of saying that I'm enjoying this moment."

"Yeah, well, okay."

I run into my bedroom and grab my journal so that I can start writing down all of the ancestors that we know of so that we can include them in our prayer.

"Corin, Corin! Girl, what are you up to?"

Pantin from the excitement and my quick dash, I smile big when I answer my mother. "Nothin Ma. Jus wanted to get some paper so we can list all of our ancestors." I hold up my journal as my proof.

"Oh, okay."

Mama May smiles and Shanice nods her head.

Now, my mama seems to be getting into it. "Okay, so let's get it started."

Oh, oh, oh, oh. Oh, oh, oh, oh, let's get it started. Oh, oh, oh, oh. Oh, oh, oh, oh. Ooops, my bad, ya'll. I had a Hammer moment. Hahaha!

Mama May starts callin out names while I write them down.

When I called our Grandma Cresie, Ma screeches, "Grandma Cresie?!" Ooops, don't look like my mama wanna add Grandma Cresie.

"What's wrong, Mary? You have a problem with Grandma Cresie?"

"Ummm, it's jus that I don't remember her havin a hard life."

"Yeah, but remember, who knows what she went through when Pops' drinkin habit broke up their marriage."

"Umph."

"And, she was so caught up in making sure we did everything all proper and stuff..."

My mom looks at Mama May questioningly. "Yeah. And?"

"And, it was like she was afraid that we'd mess up and just be us – who we were, or better yet, become too much like Mama."

"Hunh?"

"Well, you know how she undermined Mama all the time?"

"Yeah, I guess. But, it just seemed like she only wanted the best for us."

"But, who's to say that we wasn't already getting it?"

"Humph. I guess I see..."

"Remember how caught up she was in what people thought about our manners."

"Yeah. Well, what's wrong with that? She was teaching us proper etiquette, right?"

"Yes, I agree. Proper etiquette." Mama May looks down as she nods. "She did want the best for us. But, I don't know about you, Mary, but I detected a level of insecurity, too."

"Really?"

"Think about it, Mary, at what point do you just live and be you without wondering what the other person thinks about your house, the clothes on your back, the way you act in public, your husband's profession, your son's lack of education, and the shame he brought to the family by marrying our mother? Humph, I think we should pray for her. Shoot her blood is running through our veins, too."

"Well, okay, then."

I wonder what my mom's really thinkin about right now.

"Go ahead and write her name down, Corin."

"Yes ma'am." I do as my mom tells me. I write down her name.

Mama May continues naming relatives.

I look at Mama May for clarification. "Were you serious about doin empowerment rituals with each generation? Cuz I think that's an excellent idea."

"Yeah. Why not? It's something different, altogether, from what we're planning, tho."

"Yeah. I get that. But I think it sounds cool – like we can have a rite of passage or something."

"Yes, Corey! That's what I had in mind."

Getting excited, I almost drool on myself. "Ooops, pardon me, y'all."

"Corin!"

"Okay, Ma. I said excuse me, pardon me."

She shakes her head like I should know better than that.

An-y-way! "So, Mama May, what do you think about all of the women coming together when each of the young girls in the family turn eleven or twelve years old and we each tell them our stories – the good and the bad."

"Well, look at you. One day you don't tell anyone but your best friend, and now you wanna tell all the females in the family."

"Hahaha! I know, right? I jus think it may help them to know the good, the bad, and above all, self-love."

Shanice cuts in with a joke. "I thought you were gonna say and the ugly. Hahaha!"

"Oh Shanice."

Shanice continues. "But seriously, hopefully while they're getting all of that, they'll also realize that they don't have to be ashamed of who they are or any of their experiences – that if they don't feel comfortable with tellin their mommas, that they have cousins, aunts, and great aunts that'll listen to them out of love."

Mama May exclaims, "Yes, Shanice!"

"You know, Corin…"

Uh, ohhh, what's my mom about to say now?

"I'm glad that Shanice just said that cuz I've been meaning to tell you since our talk yesterday, that you could've told me about your rape and all."

I look at my mother so she'll know to continue.

"I wouldn't have told a soul."

"But, Ma, you tell Mama May pretty much everything."

I nod my head in agreement to Shanice. "Yeah."

"Maybe I do. Maybe I do keep May and my brothers abreast of all the goings on in my life. But, I'm telling you, Corin, I wouldn't have told anyone that. I can't say that I know all about the inner turmoil you endured all those years. And I know I can't comment on what it feels like having herpes, either. But I do know that sense of emptiness, shame, and dirty feeling that you feel after you've been sexually violated. That shit takes time to go away."

"Hmmm, okay."

"That's why I agree with Shanice so much. I see that my silence hasn't helped anyone, especially myself. And I don't think that our stories will prevent our future generations from enduring pain, but they can sure help prep them, warn them, and let them know that they're never alone and always loved."

"That was beautiful, Mary."

My mom looks at her sister sincerely. "I mean what I say." And then she looks at Shanice. "And, Shanice, I want you to know that it don't matter what your sexual orientation is, you are my baby girl – the first human, aside from ya father that taught me unconditional love. I love you so, so, so much. And we will get through this triumphantly."

"Thanks, Ma. I love you, too."

Finally, she addresses both me and Shanice. "Ya know, I guess I never thought about it until your auntie just spelled it out, but I have a lot of my Grandma Cresie in me in regards to caring about what others think. But this trip has shown me that all of my nitpickin on you girls, throughout the years, drove you away from me and I don't like this feeling at all."

"Aw, Ma, you don't have to..."

"Don't interrupt me, Corin."

"Yes ma'am."

"And I just wanna say that I'm not perfect, I don't know how long it'll take me to change my ways, but I am open and committed to this change. Just, please, be patient with me."

"Of course, Mama." First Shanice gets up to hug her, and then I follow suit. All of us, including Mama May are moved to tears. This is such an emotional visit.

"Praise GOD!" Mama May's the first to speak.

I give thanks, too. I can't stop smiling cuz I think I'm finally understanding that concept of it not ever being about my plan, but Yours, GOD. This summer had nothing to do with my plan. Your plan has triple trumped mine in the most delightful way. "This is awesome, y'all."

We finally pull apart after enjoyin the vibes of a feel-good hug. Still wiping at our eyes, my mom leaves the kitchen and returns with a box of tissue. We all thank her for thinkin of the obvious.

"Okay, Mama, let me get you those blueberry pancakes." Shanice gets up and turns the pilot on under the skillet and starts mixin up a new batch of pancakes for my mother. "Would ya'll like any more pancakes? Corin? Auntie?"

"No baby. I'm plenty full."

"Unh hunh, I'm plenty full, too, but, shoot go ahead and hook me up with two mo, girl."

Mama May looks at me like she's never seen me before.

"What?"

"Well, didn't you have a large stack of four already?"

"Hey, I'm on vacation. Hahaha!" I turn toward Shanice. "Hook me up, please, sis."

"Hahaha! You got it!"

"Damn, you girls know y'all can eat."

"Okay, so let's get down to business." Everyone turns to my mother. "Come on over here and sit down, May. We have to iron out the details of this prayer ceremony we gone have before me and Shanice leave."

I can tell that Mama May is debating between sayin something flip or obligin my mother. Her silent walk to join us at the kitchen table tells me that she opted for the latter.

"Now, what day would y'all like to do it?"

We all respond, "tomorrow", as if we'd already spoke about it.

"Go ahead and write that down, Corey. We should record all of this. This will be part of our family history."

"Okay, Auntie." I open my journal and write down tomorrow's date. "What do y'all wanna call it?"

We sit in silence, while Shanice is cooking, and ponder the name of our ceremony.

I can't help but exclaim, "This is so exciting."

"I know, sis. I know." Shanice winks at me. I can tell that, like me, she's feelin the fullness of the love that's in the room.

"You know, y'all, if I didn't know better, I'd suspect that we're not alone."

"Oooh, May, I think you're right." My mother shifts in her chair. "I just got a chill cuz I was thinking the same thing. Oooh."

"Unh hunh, they're here."

"Who Mama May?" Shanice flips a pancake before she turns the fire down some. "What ya'll talkin bout?"

"You know what they talkin bout, girl. And I'm sensing it, too? Our ancestors are all around us."

Shanice's eyes get big. "You think?"

I look at my mama and Mama May, and just nod.

"But, wait, Ma." She places a plate of pancakes in front of my mama who immediately pours maple syrup over her pancakes. "I didn't know you was into any of that stuff."

"Well, I'm not. I am a church going woman. But, I can't help what I'm feeling now. May, I wonder if Mama's here."

"I think she is, Mary. I think she is."

A single tear travels to my mother's cheek before she wipes it away. She closes her eyes and starts movin her mouth. I guess she's prayin. "Hahaha!"

"What's so funny, Mary?"

Me and Shanice look at my mother curiously. "Yeah Ma, what's so funny?" She looks at us and keeps laughin.

"Oh my goodness. Well, either cousin Lily, cousin Alma, or both of them are here cuz I just saw a flash of cousin Lily walking down the street, on her way to church, with her dress tucked in her girdle."

Mama May busts out laughin and now the two of them are in tears and can't seem to stop laughin. Me and Shanice jus sorta look at them – amused at their animation.

"Oh, girls, wait a minute, wait, May." Just when we thought we were about to get the full explanation, they both fall out laughin again.

Now, after a good minute has passed, Mama May attempts to fill us in. "See, cousin Lily used to always get on yo uncle Terrell about not putting the trash out in the evening. And this particular Sunday morning she woke him out of his sleep whuppin his ass becuz he didn't put the trash out the night before. And after whuppin him, she went to the bathroom before leaving out to go to church. Well, when she was finished, she told 'em that he was on punishment for a week.

"She, then, slammed the door when she went outside. And him and his crazy self came and got us all sneaky-like, laughing and stuff. And we was like, why you laughing after you just got put on punishment? He just opened the front and screen doors, told us to step outside, and look at Cousin Lily. So we did as he said, and hahaha."

Oh oh. Here we go again.

"Hahaha! She was walking down the street with her ass all out cuz part of her dress was caught in her girdle and it had a big run in it across the right cheek. All you saw was a big ass, white drawers, and a high yella to near white/pink leg with a big ole green vein peeking through, saying hi to the world."

Now me and Shanice are laughin. And Mama May and my mama have joined in, too.

"Oh my goodness, that's terrible." I barely get out, I'm so tickled.

Mama May waves at me to stop talkin. "Wait, wait, wait. Me and your mama was going to church, too, but we used to leave after her cuz she always went early to talk to her friends. So, we wasn't completely dressed yet. Ya mama only had on one shoe, but still dashed outside to tell Cousin Lily, discretely, about her dress. But, some kind a way she slipped and fell forward and her dress went up. Her ass was out, too. She yelled out on her way down to the ground which made Cousin Lily turn around to see what had happened. As soon as she did, old man Turner, a neighbor who lived two houses down who was sweet on Cousin Lily, was standing on his porch and said "unh, unh, unh, the Lord sho is good. Mornin Ms. Lily." Now, my mama has pushed away from the table, legs all spread, head back, tears runnin down her face she's laughin so loud.

"Stop it, May. Please stop. Hahaha!"

"Hahaha!" Even though it's a funny story, I think me and Shanice are getting more of a kick out of watchin them.

"So, so…" Mama May's tryin to catch her breath and talk at the same time.

"There's more?"

Mama May shushes Shanice so she can continue. "So, then, cousin Lily quickly responds to Mr. Turner by saying, 'Amen to that, brotha Turner. Ain't GOD good?' And Mr. Turner said, "Shooot, He just answered my prayers." And by then Terrell, Terrance, ya mama, and me are all outside and just bust out laughing cuz Cousin Lily had no clue. GOD bless her heart. So, then, Terrence goes to help ya mama up and I run up to Cousin Lily and fix her dress for her. By the time Cousin Alma makes it to the door to see what's going on, everything's ova and she's tryna figure out why we're all laughing and her mama is walking back toward the house pissed and embarrassed."

"Whew! Hahaha! I needed that, May. Thank you."

"No, thank Cousin Lily. Hahaha!"

Shanice starts to pay closer attention to the stove, I guess to make my pancakes now. "Hahaha! Yeah, I needed that, too Mama May, cuz y'all was freakin me out earlier."

"Well, baby, we didn't mean to. We was jus saying what we was feeling. Maybe that was yo cousin Lily…"

I interject with, "Great Great Aunt Lily."

Mama May corrects herself with, "Yes, ummm, your Great Great Aunt Lily, I mean, probably lightening the mood for ya."

"So, you really think they're here?" Shanice looks around hesitantly.

"Oh yes, baby. But it's nothing to fear. They won't harm you – they love you."

Shanice looks at my mother as she nods in agreement with Mama May. "Yes, baby, all these women that we've named won't harm you none, especially sense they can see that you're not comfortable with the concept."

"Unh hunh. But, Mama, I'm still not clear as to when you became comfortable with all of this."

My mama looks at Shanice and motions to her to let her finish chewing the pancakes that are in her mouth. "I don't know if I'm comfortable with it or jus used to May talkin like this. But, I do have to admit that I feel like they're here, too." She hunches her shoulders and adds, "I can't explain it."

I guess Shanice is okay with her explanation cuz she goes back to finishin up my pancakes. As I hand her my plate for her to put them on, I direct everyone back to the ceremony. "So, what are we gonna call it?"

Oooh, an idea is reentering my mind. Hmmm. "Oooh wait, ya'll. Give me a moment. Right before y'all..." I motion at Mama May and my mother. "...started laughin, a thought came to me about what we should call it." Everyone looks at me for me to continue. "How about *Sacrednicity*?"

Mama May looks at me quizzically. "*Sacrednicity*? Is that a word?"

"No. I made it up."

My mom simply tells me to explain and Shanice finally takes a seat as she starts eatin some extra mini pancakes she made for herself.

"Well, in my mind, it's actually the combination of three words – Sacred, Ethnicity, and Synchronicity."

Mama May smiles and nods her head at me, Shanice looks like she's thinkin about what I just said, and my mother tells me to explain further.

"Okay. Mama May, where can I find a dictionary?"

"Ummm. Oh. There's actually one on the small bookcase in my bedroom."

"Okay. Thanks." I hurry to her bedroom to get the dictionary so that I can formally define each word. "Okay, so listen to this. Sacred, regarded with reverence; ethnicity, traits, background, allegiance, or association; and synchronicity, an apparently meaningful coincident in time of two or more similar or identical events that are causally unrelated.

"To me, and correct me if I'm wrong, the reasoning behind this ceremony is to not only heal our lineage, but to celebrate unconditional self-love, acceptance of others, and supportive communication between and among generations – fundamentals that we hold dear, that we hold in high regard. The fact that we're choosing, first, to address the experiences and lives of our ancestors by reprogramming the cellular memory flowing through us addresses traits, background, etc. from ethnicity. And, finally, the mere coincidence of us unloading our deep secrets here at this point in time and then coming up with a plan of action to heal the entire family as we heal our individual selves displays synchronatic bliss."

Everyone seems to be digestin what I just said. Shanice starts to say something, but then stops.

"What?"

"Nothin. I really like it. Wow, it's so clever how you came up with that in such a short time."

Mama May and my mother tell me that they like it, too.

"But, just one thing."

"What's that, Shanice?"

"Ma, will you please tell Corin to stop makin up words." She frowns up her face. "Synchronatic, Corin?"

"Hahaha! You know, I was just about to say that synchronatic is not a word." My mom gives me a comical stern look.

"It may not be a word..." Mama May takes a sip from the glass of water she just poured for herself. "...but y'all felt its sentiment."

My mom nods. "True, true, true."

Shanice rolls her eyes and then smiles. "Yeah, well, I guess so. But, in all seriousness, I love it. I think you should write it down, sis."

"Okay. I will." After I write the name of the ceremony under the date, another idea pops into my mind. "Oooh, ya'll, I don't wanna monopolize this whole thing, so jus stop me if you think I'm doin too much, but I have another idea."

Mama May urges me to share. "Go on and tell us the idea, Corey."

"Yeah, baby, what else do ya have?"

I look at Shanice for her approval. "Girl, none of this is anywhere near my farthest idea of ideas. Share on."

"Ahunhunhun. You funny, girl. Okay, I was thinkin that we can make some waist beads that we bless during the ceremony."

"Some waist beads? What for?" My mother squinches up her face.

"Ummm, okay, I'll explain what I mean, Mama. But can you please stop makin that face though?"

"Lil girl, don't play with me."

"Ahunhunhun. Okay, Ma. Well, even though they're called waist beads, they typically hang near the sacral chakra…"

"The what?"

"Hold up, Mary. Corey, you may wanna keep it simple."

"Okay, well, they typically hang near the womb, something that we, as women need to regard, more, with reverence. It puts the 'wo' in woman."

"Okay, I was with you until the last part."

I turn to my sister and pray that what comes out of my mouth makes sense. "Woman is derived from wombman. Of the two sexes, we're the only ones with wombs, which gives us the ability to birth life. While that life is developin in the womb, it is taking on all of the experiences, emotions, thoughts, words, and actions, past and present, of its mother, as well as those of its mother's mother, and so on."

"Okay. Now, that makes sense to me."

Whew. Good. Thanks for speakin through me, GOD, cuz I know sometimes things sound and feel right in my mind, but it's hard for me to articulate it verbally.

Since I'm making sense, I continue on. "The waist beads can be a bejeweled dazzlement of healing crystals and colors that symbolize the healing of our lineage as we revere the portals, or wombs, through which our family thrives."

"Corey, I like how you're thinkin."

"Thanks, Auntie."

My mom looks at me. "Yeah, I think that's a unique idea – sacred."

"Yeah, Ma. I like that. Sacred." I let the concept marinate in my mind.

"You know, a thought came to me while you were talkin."

"What was that, Ma?"

"Let's acknowledge our ancestors in more ways than jus with the prayer and waist beads."

"Hmmm, what cha thinkin, Mary?"

She looks at Mama May and then at me and Shanice as if she's tryin to read what our reactions will be to what she's about to say. "Well, why don't we have different foods, in raw or cooked form, in honor of our ancestors, present while we're having the ceremony?"

"Okay, Mary, I think you're on to something."

I nod in agreement to Mama May.

"Oh, wait y'all. Finally, I think I have an idea, too. Shoot I was feelin a little left out." We all smile at Shanice and edge her on to continue. "Mama, remember when you had that research done on our ancestry and it told us that we are descendants of the Hausa, Fulani, and Tikar people from Cameroon today?"

"Oh, yes, baby!"

"Well, why don't we look up certain foods that they eat, and maybe try and make a dish in honor of them."

"I love that, sis!" Oooh, I jus gotta chill. "I jus gotta chill, ya'll."

"Me too, Corey. Oooh, me too." Mama May rubs her arms as if she's cold.

My mom gets back into mom/organizer mode. "Corin, are you writing all of this down?"

I was so caught up in the moment that I forgot my role. "Oh, no. Let me get all of this down – waist beads, foods of our ancestors."

Shanice pushes away from the table. "Mama May, may I use your computer so that I can look up those foods, or dishes?"

"Absolutely, baby. It should be on already. Just press any key for the screen to light up."

"Okay, Auntie. Thanks!

"Well, whether we're going to the grocery store or to the arts and crafts store, we have some shopping to do. So, I better get a head start on getting ready."

"Good idea, Mary. I'ma go ahead and start getting ready, too."

I smile as I watch my mom and Mama May slowly walk toward the kitchen door. "Now, y'all do know that me and Shanice can pick everything up."

"Yeah, but I wanna get out."

"Okay, Mama."

"Yeah, and I wanna spend all the time I can with y'all while you're here."

"Cool, then." My mom walks to her room and Mama May turns

around and starts putting dishes in the sink. "No, no, no. You go on ahead and start getting ready. I'll rinse all of these dishes and place them in the dishwasher."

"Okay, baby. Thank you."

"No problem."

On the way to get myself ready, after I finish cleanin the kitchen, I bump into Shanice who tells me about a meal we can prepare for tomorrow's ceremony. "Hmmm, fufu and stewed fish and vegetables in red gravy? Sounds yummy."

"I know right. I was thinkin that we can make our rendition of it."

"I agree, Shanice."

"What are you about to do?"

"We're all gettin dressed so that we can go shopping for the food and the arts and crafts for the waist beads."

"Okay, cool. See ya in a minute."

After about thirty or forty minutes, I hear Mama May and Mama talkin all animated-like in the kitchen. So, I hurry up and slip on my sundress and sandals, put my braids in a single pony tail off to the side, and go check out what they're talkin about.

Me and Shanice get to the kitchen at about the same time with the same amused look on our face. Shanice's curiosity shines on. With laughter in her voice, she asks, "What are y'all so excited about?"

They both look at us. "Oh, good." My mom motions for us to come and sit down. "Oh, wait, Corin, where's your notebook?"

"Right here." I take it out of my purse. "I wanted to bring it jus in case we came up with some more ideas while we're out."

"Okay, good. Well, May has an idea. Go head, May. Tell 'em."

"Okay, so it's still the concept of honoring our ancestors during the ceremony."

Me and Shanice both nod.

"But, I was thinking that we should have something present that represents all of our ancestors. For instance, Cousin Li, oops, I mean Aunt Lily, Mama, Clementine Parker, well all of them are from New Awlins. So, we was thinkin of makin some good ole bread puddin."

"Ohhh! Thank you, Jesus." Shanice dramatically looks upward and then acts like she's bowin down to Mama May cuz our auntie makes the best bread puddin on this planet. "Thank you, thank you, and thank you, again."

"Girl, you know you are crazy. Now, wait, I'm not finished."

Shanice and her crazy self straightens up like she's a kid getting ready to receive a big bowl of ice cream and cake from Mama May.

"Relax yo-self chile. The rest ain't got nothing to do with food."

Now she slumps all over, playfully, lookin disappointed.

"Girl, you know you's a clown. A-ny-way, I was thinkin that we can burn some sage and sweet grass in honor of our Native American ancestors, Grandma Cresie and em."

"This is good stuff, Mama May." I get my pen out of my purse to write down the bread puddin and sage and sweet grass.

My mom gets up to look over my shoulder – I guess to see what I'm writing.

"Hmmm, I don't see any other food." She looks at Shanice. "You didn't find anything."

"Yeah, I did..."

"Ooops. My bad, Mama, I didn't write it down."

Shanice starts explainin what she found. "It looks like all three groups of people eat a stewed red-gravy dish with fufu."

"Fu what?"

"Mama! Hahaha! It's called fufu. It's made out of starchy root vegetables, but people in Cameroon refer to couscous as fufu, too."

"Oh, okay. I've had couscous before."

"Well, we gone have to make a side of rice for me cuz couscous give me gas."

"Really Mama May? That's too bad cuz it's so good."

"Trust me, Corey, I know. I used to eat it a lot. That's how I know it gives me gas."

"Okay then. We'll make some rice, too. Me and Shanice was thinkin of substituting the beef and goat for fish in the stew and add some cut up yam and corn since those are two vegetables they're known to eat."

"Ummm..." Everyone looks at Shanice curiously cuz she has this confused look on her face. "Can we back up a lil?"

"What's up, sis?"

"What's sage and sweet grass and how is burning them a good idea?"

Even though I can answer her question, I look at Mama May to explain it since it was her great idea.

"Well, typically, baby, some cultures, like Native Americans, burn sage to clear away all negativity from a space – for instance, thoughts, words, attitudes, energies, spirits, etc. And the concept is whenever you clear out the old or bad, then you burn something to attract the good. And some people burn sweet grass, cedar, frankincense and myrrh, etc. as substances that help to add positive, higher elevated vibrations to a space."

"Okay. So, does that mean the house is gonna be smoky durin the ceremony?"

"Not necessarily the house, but maybe the actual room we'll be in may have a light hint of smoke."

"Hmmm. Okay."

"See, what I have in mind is to get up tomorrow morning to sage the house, not just the living room where we're gonna have the ceremony. And I'm only doing the whole house because this is my ritual once a month. But, I'm gonna leave the windows opened so that the smoke isn't too heavy, okay."

"Okay."

"And, then, during the ceremony, while we're reprogramming our cellular memory to higher elevations, I'll burn a little sweetgrass to enhance the effect of the prayer."

"I guess. This is all pretty foreign to me, but I'm gain."

My mom gets up out of her chair, grabs her purse off the table, and briefly rubs Shanice's shoulders. "It is to me too, baby. But, for some reason, it feels right."

Shanice puts her hand on top of my mother's and just nods.

"Well, nanh, girls. It sounds like we have a ceremony to prepare for."

"I'm so glad you're into this, Ma. You and Shanice have made this trip such a treat for me. It all feels so right." I side hug my mama as we walk out of the kitchen to go shoppin.

Fear Is Stifling; Self Love Is Liberating...

The Ceremony

I set my journal on the nightstand and jus let my mind wonder. It's a little after midnight and I'm still wired. Since it was kinda hard for me to calm my mind when I came in my room about an hour ago, I wrote extra affirmations to make up for it.

Today was so much fun. Full, but fun. I enjoyed planning and shopping, and makin my waistbeads with my mom and 'em. In fact, the jewelry makin class that me and Queenie went to back in January paid off cuz I was able to put the clasps on everyone's waistbeads so that we can put them on during the ceremony.

When I tell you that nothing could have prepared me for this summer, I really need you to feel me on it. I mean, the emotion I'm feeling is beyond elation. It will forever go down into the history books as the turning point within my life and my journey here on earth as Corin Rivers. I feel like the ceremony we're doin tomorrow and all the subsequent rights of passages are bigger and more profound than I'm presently recognizing them to be though my conceptualization seems pretty vast right now.

I know that my self-work is helping me tremendously, as well. All of my daily prayers, affirmations, energy exercises and womb stretches combined with all of the honesty and healing taking place amongst me and my family have me feeling energetically on fire, emotionally calm, and spiritually at peace. My thoughts are becoming more mindful and less destructive becuz I'm now recognizing and cancelling out the worry, self-doubt, and fear in the moment they occur.

I wonder what Zyon's doin.

Livin in the moment is so freeing. The old me would have mentally married me and Zyon off as well as worried myself to death by now over what I think his reaction would be toward me havin herpes. But, now, as I acknowledge that I would like to talk to him, that I sorta miss him, I realize that I jus really wanna say hi, see how he's doin. This is so contrary to my past actions of tryin to think of ways to appear clever, exciting, and unique to a man I'm interested in so that he's so enthralled with me bein so different from other chicks he's dated. And, right now, my mind is totally jus where he and I are, at a friendship level as oppose to thinkin about sex, the talk, or the possible rejection of me. Gotta give thanks for that. Thank You, GOD.

I pause for a moment and wonder if I should call him or not. I reach in my purse for my phone and feel it vibrating. Oh, who's callin me? When I look at my phone, I smile all Gumby-like cuz I see that Zyon jus sent me a text.

> *Hi Beautiful!*
> *Hi. I was jus thnkn bout you.*
> *That's good to hear.*
> *Can u tlk?*
> *Not really. I'm outside of 1 of my boys house waitin 4 him 2 come out n-e min. We bought 2 go chow dwn.*
> *Wow! This late?*
> *I know, rite? Bad habits of a bachelor. Lol. U njoyn ur folks?*
> *Understatement.*
> *Cool. Look, bout 2 drive now. Jus wantd 2 holla at u 4 a min.*
> *Sweet dreams beautiful. Ttyl.*
> *Ok. Hv a good nite. J*
> *Thanks! Cll me 2mrw if u can.*
> *Ok.*

That was a nice surprise. He was thinkin of me. Hmmm. Ooop. Someone's knockin at my door. I glance at the digital clock at the same time I tell who ever it is to come in.

"Hey girl," Shanice says.

"Hey sis, what's up? You wanna go for another midnight stroll?"

"Naw, not really. I was thinking of watching a movie and wanted to know if you felt like laughing with me."

"Oh Lord. What movie you talkin bout?"

"Friday."

"Hahaha! Sure. I love that movie." I cut out my lamp and follow her down the hall toward the family room. "Hey, you want some popcorn?"

"Already covered."

"Booyow! Good lookin out. Wait! Microwave popped or stove popped?"

"I didn't see any microwaveable popcorn."

"Cool."

"And knowing you like I do, I made sure I brought some bottled water in there, too."

"My dawg. Let me go to the bathroom real quick."

"Kay."

<u>the next day</u>

Hmmm. I wake up to the smell of sage. Mama May's at it already? I look at the clock and see that it's five minutes til ten. Shit, she might be finished. I yawn a yawn that turns into an elongated stretch and convoluted pose, that for a second, I wondered how to get out of. Hahaha! It looks like I'm gone have to reprogram my body before I go back to New York since I can't seem to open my eyes before eight o'clock any more. Shoot, as much as me and Queenie have hung out late, I still always managed to open my eyes by seven at the latest.

I sit up in bed, grab my journal, and write my affirmations and prayers of gratitude. When I finish, I hesitate to get up and go in the kitchen cuz I hear people movin around. *No, Corin, stay focused.* My own thought of encouragement persuades me to be still and meditate which I'm glad I do since I didn't last night.

Afterwards, I take some more time to jus chill out in my room. I love my me time. I decide to show my face around noon.

"Hi."

"Well, good afternoon to you, sleepy head."

"Good afternoon, Mom. How did you sleep?"

"Oh, I guess I slept pretty good. And you?"

"Great. Thanks!"

"Hey Mama May, how are you?"

"Jus fine, baby girl."

"Cool. It smells good in here." I close my eyes and take a long sniff into the air to over-emphasize my sentiment. "Ahhh. Bread pudding. Mama May."

"Yes…"

"Oh yes it is!" I spin around at the sound of Shanice walkin toward the kitchen. "Good morning, everyone!"

"Good afternoon, Shanice."

Man, sometimes I swear, all you can do is laugh at my mother.

And it looks like Shanice has a similar thought as she brightens her smile on her face. "Good afternoon, Mama! How are you?"

Hahaha! I love it. "Did I just hear the front door open, Shanice?"

"Yep, I been out chillin by the pool."

"Cool."

Mama May takes a big pan of bread puddin out of the oven.

Shanice looks at Mama May with wide eyes. "Oooh, Mama May, can your favorite niece get a piece of that while it's still hot?"

"Oooh, that's okay, Mama May, I'm not hungry for that right now. I jus want me some fruit." I jokingly nod my head toward Shanice and add, "but maybe Shanice might want some."

"Whateva, Corin."

"Hahaha!"

"Well, nobody's eating any of this until after the ceremony." She goes back to the oven and takes out a small loaf pan filled with bread pudding. "But once this settles after ten minutes everybody can share some of this one."

Shanice walks over to Mama May and lays a hand on her left shoulder. "You know you my favorite aunt, right?"

"Probably because I'm your only aunt that makes bread puddin."

"Nanh, you know that's not true, Auntie. How many of the small ones did you make?"

"Jus the one."

"Now that's funny." Shanice's expression changes drastically when she realizes jus how little there is to share.

Reactin to her disappointment, my mom and Mama May look at each other and start laughin with me.

"Oh, so all y'all gone jus laugh at me like that? Humph. That's okay, jus as long as I don't have to wait until later today for a taste, I'm good."

"Hey. Did we ever decide on a time to have the ceremony?"

"You know, Corey, I thought about that while I was sagin this morning. I don't think we did."

I look at Mom and Shanice to include them in the decision. "Any ideas?"

Mom shakes her head. "It don't matter to me. What about five?"

We all either nod our heads or speak our agreement to five o'clock. Then Mama May stops wiping down the stove and gestures for us to follow her.

. "Oooh, I know what she gone show us."

I playfully nudge at my sister. "Know what? What you know?"

Mama May stops at the living room and extends her hand. "After you."

I'm the last to walk in. I know it's something good cuz of the expression on my mom's face. And when I finally walk in, I slowly look around and take in the peace. "This feels like a sanctuary, Mama May."

"Yes, this is absolutely beautiful," Mom says. "Girl, when did you do this?"

Mama May answers, "This morning."

"I helped."

Me and my mama look at Shanice, shocked.

"I couldn't sleep and I heard someone at the door around seven this morning. When I got up to answer it, Mama May was already letting them in."

I turn to Mama May to ask who even though I knew the answer based upon all the beautiful roses placed in vases throughout the room.

"Zyon and Tariq."

"Zyon was here?" I wonder why he didn't mention that last night.

Double oh Mama detects something. "Who is Zyon?"

"He's my landscaper." Mama May winks at me and then fills us in on everything. "I called him yesterday after we got back from shoppin to see if he could get his hands on these roses. And…" She opens up both of her hands. "Voila!"

"This is beautiful, Mama May." I walk over to what I presume to be an altar. "This is awesome." Mama May has pictures of my grandmother, Ruth Hayes, my grandmother's mother, Mary, who my mother's named after. No one knows anything about her becuz she died givin birth to my grandmother and, apparently, Papa, didn't talk about her much to my grandmother. There are also pictures of Aunt Lily, Cousin Alma, Grandma Cresie, Aunt Lucinda, and three name cards in Mama May's beautiful calligraphy. One says 'Clementine Parker', another, 'Mother of Grandma Cresie and Aunt Lucinda', and the last one, 'all of our ancestors that we're not aware of'. Also, on the altar is a beautiful piece of rose quartz crystal, I guess to invoke love, especially self-love; all of our waist beads coiled up on different parts of the altar; a beautiful bronze ankh, a white-feather, and a sage smudge stick layin next to some sweet grass. And there's beautiful, white chiffon fabric that's draping the couch, chairs, and the altar/table and three tall, thick white cylinder-shaped candles on the altar set behind everything. This feels very sacred.

Mom walks over to the altar and starts to look at the pictures. "I wonder what Clementine looked like."

"Ha! I was wondering the same thing when I wrote her name out on the card."

"Okay, so what's this for, May?" Mom holds up the ankh briefly.

"Oooh, can I tell her what everything stands for, Auntie?"

I don't know what's come over Shanice, but I like it. My mom looks at her as if to ask, 'how does she know what any of this means'. But, Shanice doesn't disappoint. She stands next to my mom and picks up the ankh. "Ma, this is an ankh and it represents the key to life."

"Hmmm, o-kay."

"Mama May's philosophy is that the key to life is self-love. Which is also why she placed this beautiful…" She lays a few fingers on the crystal. "rose quartz crystal here. It's property energetically enhances self-love."

"Energetically, hunh?"

"Yeah, it has been passed down through the ages that gem stones and crystals carry different properties that may help with healing, meditating, blocking negative energy, and self-love, just to name of few."

"Unh hunh." My mom is lookin at her with disbelief.

"The three candles represent, the past, present and future."

"Hmmm, okay. I like that."

"Yeah, and the feather represents lightheartedness."

"Lightheartedness?"

"Unh hunh. When you practice lightheartedness with yourself and others, you're more prone to accept yourself and others without judgment. It's mostly experienced when you practice present-moment awareness."

"Humph." My mom simply nods her head.

I look at Mama May. "I love all of this, Auntie. Wow!"

"Good. What about you, Mary?"

"Girl, you know all of this symbolism is different for me. But I trust you."

"Yeah, I know that this is a lot for you, Mary."

"No, no. Well, yeah it is, but, somethin feels right about all of this. And I love what you've done with the room. It's lovely. Now, have you finished the prayer yet?"

"Yes. Let's go back to the kitchen so we can talk about our ceremony."

We all walk back to the kitchen. As soon as we get there, Shanice grabs a spoon and a small plate and puts some bread puddin on it. She eats a spoonful before she sits down. "Oooh, Mama May, this bread pudding is slammin."

"Thank you, baby."

She starts to sit down, but straightens back up abruptly. "Umph. Do you have any rice milk by any chance?"

I grab an unopened carton out of the pantry. "Here, Shanice. I saw this in here the other day when I was grabbin a bottle of water."

"Cool. Thanks."

I grab a spoon and taste a lil of the bread pudding on Shanice's plate while she's pourin herself a glass of rice milk. "Oh yes, Mama May, you did yo thang."

"Excuse you! Don't be eatin none of my bread pudding. Get some of your own."

"Girl, relax. That's all I'ma eat til later. So, bon appetit."

"Unh, hunh. Cuz I will hurt you ova some bread pudding. Don't think I won't."

I open my eyes wide and wiggle my fingers in an exaggerated spooked out way. "Oooh, I'm scared."

"All right, girls. Settle down. Let's finish ironing out this ceremony so we can start prepping the food."

We both answer Mom in unison. "Yes ma'am." But, I quickly raise my left hand as if I'm in grade school, or something. Ahunhunhun. I crack myself up sometimes. "Ummm, jus so we're all clear, me and Shanice are cookin the meal. You and Mama May are relaxin."

"Well, thank you. You don't have to tell me twice."

Mama May speaks up. "I second that."

I lower my hand. "Okay, good, then."

I go to my room to get my journal so that I can keep recordin everything. When I return, everyone's sittin at the table and lookin at me like I'm holdin them up. "All right. I'm comin."

As soon as I'm ready, Mama May starts tellin us what she came up with.

"Well, I was thinkin that today's ceremony could be a blueprint for all future rights of passages for our family."

We all either nod our head or utter our agreement.

"So, Shanice, once we're all gathered in the room, I want you to welcome everybody to Sacrednicity, state your full name and who your mother is. Then, I want you to light all of the candles, pausing after each one to state what they represent – the first for the past to represent our ancestors, the second for the present to represent all the females in our lineage that are alive, and lastly the future, all of the offsprings."

Shanice is nodding the whole time Mama May tells her of her responsibility. Her demeanor mimics a child's happiness and honor for personally bein selected by the classroom teacher to bring a note to the office in addition to an adult feeling connected to somethin of high value.

"Nanh, once you're done explaining the candles, you'll introduce Corey."

She continues to nod her head. "Okay, Auntie."

"Nanh, Corey."

I pause briefly from writing to look up at my aunt in acknowledgement. "Yes, ma'am?"

"I want you to reintroduce yourself, tell us who your mother is. And then I want you to define Sacrednicity to all of us and briefly talk about the items on the altar. But leave the sage and sweet grass for me. And as long as you're livin, this will be your role. Both of you." She looks over at Shanice to make sure she's clear about what she's sayin.

Ooooh, ya'll, I'm feelin all excited. "Okay, Mama May. I love this. You've been busy."

"I know, Auntie, wow. This sounds great already."

My mom is jus sittin back smiling at first. "Ever since we were little, she was always good at planning and takin lead of things. A natural leader."

"Okay, ya'll. Nanh stop it. Let me finish." We all shut up so she can continue. "Nanh, Mary, when Corey's finished, I want you to go up, introduce yourself and state who your mama is."

"Okay. I can do that."

"And then I want you to introduce everyone to the ancestors starting off by letting us know that we're acknowledging all those ancestors who's names we don't know. Then, on Mama side, follow through with Clementine Parker and her descendants, and then do the same by starting off with Grandma Cresie and Aunt Lucinda's mama and her descendants."

"Yep. Okay. I can do that, too."

"Okay. Then, we'll close the ceremony with my prayer. While I'm sayin the prayer, each of us will be holding our individual waist beads in our hands. Once I'm finished we'll place them on, around our waists, and the end. We eat."

"Love it! I jus got goose bumps, y'all."

"Me, too, girl. Look!" Shanice shows me the raised bumps on her right forearm.

"Yeah, May, this brings it all together. So, you say this is what we're gonna do when each female in our family turns twelve?"

"Yes. I feel like the more we say the prayer, the stronger the energy to reprogram our DNA. The only difference is after the prayer, maybe about four or five of us will tell our individual stories, like you all did this weekend, but I'd like to balance the stories out with positive experiences as well."

We all nod our head in agreement.

"Yes. Absolutely, May. That makes a lot of sense."

"Unh, hunh. We can talk about the rights of passages more in detail later, but I was thinking that the mother of the young girl, the initiate, should first sit down with her and explain the reasoning behind the ceremony, informally, and help the child with their waist beads prior to everyone arriving in town. So that by the time all of us arrive, the waist beads are already completed and the child has an idea of what's about to occur and its importance."

"Yeah." I raise a finger to interject a thought. "So, since none of us live in the same city, let's always make a weekend out of it where we have the opening ceremony, you know, what you jus described. And then the next day we could close it out with general questions and individual blessings from the elders that are presented orally and in greeting cards."

"That sounds great, Corey. Shanice, get ready, cuz Diamond will be the first to experience this."

"I was jus thinkin that same thing, Auntie."

My mom looks over at me and my journal. "You stopped writing, Corin."

"Oh, shoot. My bad. Let me finish writin all of this down. Thanks Ma."

"Unh, hunh. You're welcome."

Mama May pushes away from the table. "Well, like I said, we can discuss the rights of passages more in detail at a later date. Right now, let's jus focus on our ceremony in a couple of hours."

"Absolutely, Auntie."

"I'm gonna go and take me a nap."

I close my journal and look at my sister. "So, you ready to cook? I don't wanna wait until the last minute. Sorta wanna relax a little before the ceremony and it's two o'clock now."

"Sounds good to me."

"And I need to go and call ya father back," Mom says.

"Tell Daddy I said hi and that I'll be out to visit soon."

"Will do."

5:00 p.m.

We all laugh at one another when we show up wearin all white to the ceremony. What a funny, yet somewhat eerie moment given that we never discussed what we were gonna wear.

The ceremony is goin along as planned. *Sacrednicity* is and feels like its name. Though, all of our roles and parts are obvious to us becuz we know each other, our history, and the layout of the ceremony, each of us is takin our role seriously. The depth of emotion flowin in this room is nice and humid – meaning that its warmth is stickin to my heart with acuteness. My mom just finished talkin about our ancestors. Now it's Mama May's turn. This is the only part that isn't obvious to any of us except Mama May seein that this is the first time she's sharin the prayer with us.

I look at both Mom and Shanice when Mama May gracefully walks to the altar. And their facial expressions, though still, are dancing with anticipation. Hmmm. Maybe it's their eyes that are dancing. Nonetheless, it's obvious that this is the momentous moment of the ceremony.

"Good evening. My name is May Richmond. And I am the daughter of Ruth Hayes. First, let me say that I love each of you, ancestors and absent family members, included, like my Mya. I am so happy that we are releasing all that is not of the light from our lives. In that theme, I saged this room and most of this house this morning to clear out any negative, dark, non-enlightened thoughts, words, actions, energies, and entities. And now, I am going to burn this sweet grass." She lights the sweet grass and slowly walks around the room allowin its essence to reach each corner, crack and crevice. "I'm burning this sweet grass to help embellish the prayer that I'm about to express." She sets the sweet grass down, stands in front of the altar, close her eyes and smiles.

"Thank You, GOD, for comforting, strengthening, and uplifting our family. Thank you for the lives, the personal life scripts of our ancestors. Thank you for their lessons, experiences, triumphs, defeats, strengths, revelations, evolutions, lies, hurts, love, peace, healing or lack thereof. Thank you for their blood, their DNA, their feelings, emotions, and thoughts flowing through our veins interweaving with our own makeup in a dynamic whirlwind of choreographic collisions and sweet kisses. Thank you for reprogramming their contribution to our lives, henceforth, and our comprehension of their ancient energy within us so that we pull solely from unconditional self-love infinitely. Thank you for continuous self-acceptance, acceptance of others, and evolutionary thoughts, words, and actions in our daily lives. Thank you for *Sacrednicity* – for always bridging the gaps amongst family members, past and present, so that we, always, keep an open flow of communication intended for us to learn from, and uplift, one another. Thank you for the gift of forgiveness – forgiveness of ourselves, others, past and present, and You GOD. Thank You, GOD."

She opens her eyes and asks us to hold up our waistbeads. We not only hold them out in front of us, but we all stand as well. "Thank You GOD for this unique, beautiful symbol to adorn our bodies and to serve as a reminder, if we forget, of jus how precious we are, jus how sacred our temple, our womb is, and that we must honor, protect, and respect the bejeweled gift of all gifts given by You, the ability to birth life, to birth dreams, and to manifest self-love through deliberate conscientious attitudes. Thank You." She looks at each us for a moment. "Go ahead and adorn your wombs, wombmen."

I smile at her reference to wombmen.

Unabashed, we all either lift our tops, and me, my dress, and put our beautiful waistbeads on. Mama May takes a seat and we follow suit. And we jus sit in silence for a while. I think, each of us are receiving the moment independent of the other. For me, I feel more connected to myself than I've ever felt in my entire life. I definitely feel connected to my family, too. But I feel like all of the self-work I've been doin in addition to this ceremony has gifted me an over-the-top excited feelin of bein me. And, wow, this feels so good. I am actually excited about bein me. Not, jus me the massage therapist, or me the runner, or me the manager, but me a wombman. Thank You, GOD. Thank You, thank You, thank You. Thank You for Sacrednicity. Thank you, ancestors. I feel you. Thank you for loving me the way you do.

Maybe fifteen or twenty minutes pass before my mother finally says something. "I thoroughly enjoyed our ceremony, ladies. We all did wonderful. And, May, that was a beautiful prayer. Thank you."

"You're welcome."

"Yeah, Auntie, that was an awesome prayer. Shoot, I don't know if it's from the time I've spent with all of you over the past few days or Sacrednicity, but I feel like I can return to California with my head held high and accomplish anything. Right now I feel so comfortable bein me."

"Oooh, Shanice, I was thinkin the same thing – that it feels good to be me. I don't feel ashamed of my past. Shit, it makes up me. I'm sorry, Mama and Mama May. I didn't mean to curse. It's jus that…"

"Chile, you don't have to apologize. We know you respect us."

"Unh hunh." My mama nods her head in agreement to Mama May.

"Thanks ya'll. So yeah, in a nutshell, I was jus sayin that I feel you, Shanice."

"You know, I was a lil sad that Mya couldn't experience this with us. But, I do know that everything happens for a reason and that the four of us were supposed to experience the first *Sacrednicity* together like this."

"Yeah, I wished my niece was here, too. But we'll all travel to Jamaica and have an irie time when her daughter makes her rite of passage."

"Yes indeed." Mama May gets up, clasps her hands together, and look toward the kitchen. "Well, who'd like to join me for some salad, fufu or rice, fish stew, and bread pudding."

"Whew! I thought you'd never ask." Shanice gets up, starts walkin toward the kitchen and then doubles back and almost collides into me.

"What girl? You forgot something."

"I jus wanna blow these candles out before we get in there and forget all about them."

"Good thinkin, girl."

In the kitchen, I cut the burners on so that we can warm the food up.

Before I Let Go

The way I been day dreamin lately, you'd assume that I'm love-struck over some man as oppose to with myself and the memory of the great time I had while Shanice and my mom were here. I can't believe they're gone. I miss them so much. I'm definitely gonna have to get out to California soon – fa sho before the holidays. So needless to say, the past week felt a little melancholy. But, I must say that since *Sacrednicity*, I've been more amped and motivated to continue with my self-work. In fact, I couldn't calm myself down enough to sit still in meditation Monday or Tuesday. So, I'm glad that I have the Zhan Zhuang to make me, at least, stand still.

Right now, I'm sittin in the window wonderin how today is gonna play out at Zyon's. We've been talkin, pretty much every night since my mom and Shanice left. Thursday was the one time we made plans to meet up, before today, at the mountain, and I overslept. I was so mad at myself when I finally did open my eyes cuz I jumped up and out of bed and grabbed my phone to find five missed calls and a text sayin that he figured I'd overslept and would call me when he's back in his car. Right as I finished readin his text, my phone lit up alertin me that I had an incoming call – him. And that's when I realized that my ringer was off. So, even though I'd prefer to show up fashionably late to reduce the time I have to interact with folks that I don't know, I feel like I should jus go a lil early, be me, and make the best out of the day. Hey, what's the worst that could happen? His friends hate me, I fall on my ass, or oooh, oooh, better yet, his best friend turns out to be Deron. Umph, nanh that wouldn't be a good look at all. Not at all.

To make Thursday up to myself, I woke up early today and climbed the mountain on my own. I felt so rejuvenated after writin out my affirmations when I returned that I decided to start readin another novel that I brought with me from New York that I purchased a while ago – *The River Where Blood Is Born*. It's startin off slow. But, I'm likin it so far.

I jump at the sound of my phone ringin. I look at it first to see who's callin. Ooooh, Queenie. "Hey Ma! How are you?"

"Fabulicious!"

"Oooh, I like that. You sound so upbeat and happy."

"I know. I'm jus in a good mood, girl. Nothing and everything, in particular."

I throw my head back and allow my laughter to fill the room. It feels good to hear my friend's good-mood voice. And then a thought pops into my head. "Wait a minute. Today's Saturday. What are you doin callin me? Ain't you supposed to be movin?"

"Girrrll!"

"Oh Lawd! What nanh?"

"I ended up moving on Thursday during school hours."

"Really? Why? What happened?"

"Well, remember I told you that Trinity, Juanita, and Joy was coming over last weekend to help me pack?"

I think about our last conversation for a minute. "Umm, yeah."

"Well, I don't know. I guess I started feeling all brave and stuff cuz I ended up deciding to stay at my apartment Sunday and Monday. You know, I wanted to make sure I was more than ready for my move."

"Okay."

"So, Trinity came back over on Monday to help a lil but mostly to keep me company."

"Un hunh."

"Well, I swear he must've been doing a stake out cuz not five minutes after Trinity left, if sooner, that motha fucka was ringing my doorbell."

"What?! What did you do? Call the police?"

"Unh, unh. I just ignored him until…"

"What? How long was he out there?"

"I don't know. I jus remember hearing my neighbor on the ground floor opening the main door and asking him if he could help him with something."

"Oh, okay. Good."

"Unh hunh."

"So, what did crazy say?"

"That my neighbor couldn't help him, that he came to see me. And my neighbor said something like, maybe she not home since she not answering the bell."

"Oooh, girl. I swear this sound like a movie."

"I know right. Talk about the repercussions of acting out of loneliness."

"Shiiittt! Okay, so keep goin. Damn!"

"So, crazy said that he knew I was home cuz he saw me moving around. And my neighbor was like, 'well as loud as this bell is, she know you here and it don't seem like she wanna see you. So I suggest you leave before I call the police. Hell, you disturbing my fucking peace."

"Whaaat?"

"Yeah girl."

"So, did he leave?"

"Yep. And then my neighbor and his wife came up to see if I was all right, and I told them that I was and I thanked him for speaking to him – that he didn't have to do that."

"Girrrl!"

"I know, girl. You know how private I am. I hated to involve them."

"Shiiit, good thing they were home though. It let him know that you wasn't in that brownstone by yo-self waitin for his crazy ass to find a way in."

"Yeah. So, I apologized for inconveniencing them and told them that I would be moving by Saturday."

"Right, right. Wait, but Sat…"

"I know, I know. I'm getting to it. So, when I thought Trinity was home, I called to let her know what happened. I didn't wanna text or call her while it was going on cuz I didn't want her to come back and he try and hurt her or something. You know, with his crazy ass and shit."

"Right. That was smart."

"So while we were talking, Trinity asked me why was I waitin til Saturday?"

"I told her cuz Friday was payday and I needed that check to pay the movers since I was strapped from paying four months' rent upfront – first month's rent and three months for a deposit."

"Damn, girl! Four months up front?"

"You know I got credit issues and these New York brokers ain't no joke."

"I know. But damn!"

"So, …"

"Wait! You know you could've come to me, right?"

"Yeah. But who knew that I had to, that he woulda showed up again?"

"True."

"To me, I was cool til I got paid. So, anyway, she told me she'd loan me the money, to call to see if the movers could move me on Thursday."

"Oh, okay."

"Yeah. She convinced me that if they could move me during school hours, to just call in sick and move then. That way, I had a better chance of crazy not showing up looking for me cuz he'd assume I was at work."

"Smart. Hmmm, okay."

"Unh hunh. So, now I'm all moved in and just feeling silly groovy, enjoying my new space, boxes and all."

"I heard that, ma. Take a deep breath."

"Think I'm not. I might unpack some more, or I might just chill until Babacar's class tonight."

"I vote for the latter."

"Hahaha! Me too. Girl, you know I'm loving my new neighborhood. I'm right by the 'C' train, a bookstore, a dentist, two Chinese takeout spots, Golden Krust for my spinach patties and coco bread, a bodega for my incidentals when I'm not able to go to the grocery store, and most of all, my Joloff's."

"Uh, excuse me my dawlin. I know this. It's my neighborhood, too."

"Oh yeah, I forgot to mention you. You shoulda been the 'most of all'. Hahaha!"

"Unh hunh. Yeah right! Now that you have to pass Joloff's on your way home every day, they don't ever have to worry about goin outta business wit yo greedy ass."

Knowing my friend like I do, I picture nodding her head, yes, as she laughs. "Hahaha! Girl, you know you probably right…"

"I know I am."

"…cuz I haven't cooked a meal yet. I feel like, all at once, I'ma turn into some cabbage, carrots, yam, cassava, fish, and joloff rice before the summer's over, I been eating so much Tiebuu Jeun."

Knowin how my friend loves Joloff restaurant, I can't help but laugh at her corny joke as I silently send up a prayer that she doesn't go into debt eatin there every day.

"Hell, since I moved over here, I feel like I'm gone start talking Woloff fluently any day now."

"Hahaha! Now that was funny!"

"And come fall, my students gone be looking around and asking each other what's goin on with Ms. Holmes when I start pulling out a mat and commence to praying five times a day."

"Hahaha! So what? Now you a Muslim?"

"Unh, unh. I actually just thought of that one – it'll be a good excuse for me not to completely lose my mind and flip the fuck out in the classroom."

"Ahunhunhun. I hear ya. But, wait a minute now, aren't two of those prayers supposed to be done at home - one early in the morning and the other in the evening?"

"Leave it to yo ass to get all technical and shit. Can't I just get some kudos for praying to GOD, I mean ALLAH, instead of screaming on one of my students? I mean dang – I'm jus sayin."

"Hahaha! You's a plum fool, girl."

"Unh hunh. Wait, wait. All jokes aside. Check this out." She pauses briefly. "Damn, I knew there was something I wanted to tell you."

"What girl?"

"Last week at Sabar class, after the warm up, I caught myself literally blushing to the drumming intro."

"The drumming intro?"

"Yeah. There's this rhythm that the drummers play before the start of every class. And for some reason, when I heard it last week, I started blushing."

"Dang, that sounds interesting as hell. You were blushing at the music?"

"Yeah."

"You sure you didn't catch one of the drummers makin sweet eyes at you, Queenie?"

"Ahunhunhun. I'm telling you, Corin, it was the music. I felt so embarrassed that I started nonchalantly looking around to make sure no one saw me."

"Well?"

"Well what?"

"Did anyone see you?"

"I don't know. Not from what I can tell."

"That's deep, girl."

"Yeah, ya think? But, anyway. Enough of me. What's up with you? How was last weekend, ya mom, Shanice?"

"Great, great, and great!"

"Oooh, do tell."

I fill her in on all the bombshells disclosed, the bonding, and of course, *Sacrednicity.*

"Ha! Well, damn. Ya'll had a full weekend to say the least."

"Ya think?"

"Oooh, and, your aunt is so the bomb. Both of ya'll. Shit, all of ya'll."

"Ahunhunhun. Yes, yes, we know this. Thanks, but what made you jus say that?"

"Uhhh, *Sacrednicity*! That shit sounds sweet as hell."

"I know, right?"

"Unh hunh. Shoot, my family wouldn't've been able to do no shit like that."

"You don't know that, Queenie."

"Humph, but I know ghetto."

"Hahaha! You stupid."

"Girl, you know my sisters are as ghetto as they come which is so mind boggling to me cuz we weren't raised like that."

"Girl, after last weekend, I realized that you can be living with strangers, that you call family, all your life. Remember I said Shanice is gay."

"Ahunhunhun. Right, right. I remember."

"Ooh, ooh, ooh. So did you go out with Deron?"

"Girl, no."

"Nooo? Why not? What happened?"

"I don't know, Queenie. When he called me on Monday to see if we were on for that open mic on Wednesday night, somethin jus clicked in me. It was like I was over it, over the past."

"And you sure that wasn't your small way of getting him back for leaving you hanging back in college?"

"Yep. I'm sure. It wasn't until that conversation that I was completely sure that that was genuine forgiveness I felt and expressed to him that day I ran into him."

"Okay. So, was it awkward after you told him you didn't wanna go, and I presume, see him before you leave."

"Yeah. Big time. But, I did it."

"Okay." She pauses. "Okay, good for you, mama. Congratulations!"

"Thanks! Yeah, I jus let the awkward silence ride."

"Okay, so, any new developments with Zyon?"

"Ahunhunhun."

"Oh no you not giggling. What you holding out on now?"

"Nothin. I swear. It's jus that I've finally admitted to myself that I like him."

"Unh hunh. I'm sure that helped with your decision about going not out with Deron."

"Maybe. Maybe not. I am gonna see him today, tho."

"Oh really?"

"Yep. He's havin some friends over."

"Friends?"

"Yes, friends. He's grillin and I guess havin a spades party. But he said there might be a game of dominoes goin on, too."

"Oh, nanh that's yo thang, right?"

"Yep, I loves me some bones."

"Okay. So, you know what, Corin?"

Oh Lawd, I can hear it in her voice. Here comes mother Queenie. "What?"

"Don't second guess yourself or anyone else for that matter. I know how self-conscious you can get in those types of scenarios when you only know the host."

"I won't. I feel good about it."

"Good, girl. Yeah, just relax and enjoy yourself."

"I am. I mean, I plan to."

"Know that he has to socialize with everyone else, too."

"Queenie!"

"What? Corin, you know you and so do I."

I back down some. "You right. Ahunhunhun."

"And so, do we detect that he might be liking you like you liking him?"

"Oh yeah. Unh hunh." I nod my head, as if she can see me, for emphasis.

"So know that there may be some people there scoping you out on his behalf."

"Yes, Mother. I know this."

"And we're always over-the-top nice to the females even if they're stank, right?"

"Most times."

"Corin!"

"Girl, calm down. I'm good. I'm actually lookin forward to it – ta seein him."

"Cool. Well good then. What time are you going over there?"

"Ummm, around three."

"Okay. Cool. What are you wearin?"

"Damn, Queenie!?"

"What? Are you not used to this?"

"Ugh!" This is our ritual. She knows I'm not mad. "Well, I'ma keep it simple and cute."

"Okay. Details please."

"It's hot as hell out here. So, I'm gonna where those cute linen pants that wrap into a tie at the small of my back and hang right below the waist, with my "#7" one-shoulder tank top."

"Uhhh, yeah, how about simple and sexy?"

"Ahunhunhun. Okay, so it's simple and sexy."

"What shoes, sandals I mean?"

"Probably my strappy brown ones."

"Oooh, yeah. I love those. And you always hook yo-self up with the accessories."

"You know this."

"Well, okay, it sounds like you're ready."

"Yep."

"Cool. Well, girl, let me get back to gettin my chill on."

"Okay."

"And you betta call me with the details in the morning. Shit, right now my love life is livin vicariously through you."

"Ahunhunhun. Okay. Love ya sis."

"Love you, too, Corin. Have fun!"

"Thanks! I will."

After we hang up, I pick my book back up. I'm glad Queenie's safe in her new space. Thanks for lookin out for her, GOD.

<u>Zyon's house</u>

Zyon lives in an area of town called Buckhead off of Paran Road. Though most of the homes are grand in stature, Zyon's brick medium-sized cottage is more unassuming and quaint in comparison. But, I have to say that his landscape is beyond beautiful. Wow! He's good. So creative.

As soon as I put my car in park, a champagne-colored Escalade pulls in behind me. Damn! Why did they park behind me? They got all that room over there to the right next to those other cars. Humph. I be likin a clear path out in case I need to suddenly dip. Both the passenger and driver doors open at the same time. Zyon gets out of the passenger side. Damn, he looks good.

"Beautiful!"

I grab my purse and get out of the car with a huge smile that I can't seem to make smaller. "Hi." Though I know the driver's waitin for me to look his way, I can't seem to pull away from Zyon's eyes as he walks up to me and gives me a huge hug.

"Beautiful is an understatement."

I can't ignore a compliment. So, I direct my attention toward his friend and smile. "Hi."

Zyon slowly pulls away from me, but holds on to my left hand. "Corin, this is my boy, Malik. Malik, this is beautiful."

I giggle at his introduction and extend my right hand toward his friend. "Nice to meet you."

"Likewise." He slowly bows his head and attempts to kiss my hand, but Zyon playfully pulls me back toward him.

"Hey, hey, hey. You tryna get cut, bra?"

Oh, this is gone be fun – observin Zyon among his peeps.

"Come on, beautiful. You hungry?"

"I could eat."

"Cool. Everybody's out back." He slows his pace a bit so Malik can walk in front of us and looks at me with somewhat hungry eyes. "You look really nice."

I look back at him with confident, sassy sex appeal. "Thank you."

"Dare I say sexy?"

"I double dog dare you."

"What ch'all whisperin about back there?"

Oooh, damn, I forgot about Malik just that quick.

Zyon responds to him without takin his eyes off of me. "Keep walking, bra." And then he grabs one of my braids. "You look really sexy."

Damn, this brotha is fine. GOD, please help a sista keep everything in perspective. "You think?"

"Unh hun. Very much so."

"Well, thank you." Damn, I can't stop smiling. And why is Malik walkin backwards, toward the house, in front of us all up in my grill? Can a sista not be on display please?

"Dang, she all cheezin and shit."

Oooh, no Malik is not putting me on blast like that. I'm so embarrassed cuz he's frickin right. I got this big ass Gumby ass grin on my face. I pleafully look at him to give me a break.

Zyon puts an arm around my shoulders, and I can't help but notice the comfortable fit. "Man, leave my friend alone."

I guess he's either answerin my plea or listenin to Zyon cuz he backs off of me. First, he jus looks at us in a strange way that I can't read. And then he waves us off, turns around, and walks through the front door. He enters the house a few steps ahead of us.

Before walkin into Zyon's home, I notice a beautiful jade bush to the left of the walkway positioned right below a large picture window. Oooh, I absolutely love jade. I just can't seem to ever keep the jokers alive. Hmmm, maybe they're outdoor plants.

Inside of Zyon's home, I immediately look to the left to see what's near the picture window and find myself looking into a study furnished with a tasteful mahogany-colored desk with a comfortable-lookin burgundy leather swivel chair that's perfectly positioned so that he can turn around and look outside the window if he chooses. Sitting in the middle of the room is an exactly matched burgundy leather loveseat with brown and beige swede and leather throw pillows on it which happens to offset an area rug very nicely, filled with different shades of browns, burgundy, lots of tan, and a splash of green. Oh boy has some good taste. I'm impressed. He has mahogany lookin bookshelves built into the wall housing a plethora of books, and a few potted plants dispersed throughout the room. Though it's a very masculine look, it doesn't appear to be overbearing. His beige walls with off-white trim help to lighten the room up. As we continue to walk straight ahead, we enter his living room which feels very homey and comfortable. I see he likes greens, browns, and burgundy. The furniture in here is brown. Hmmm, all dark colors. Such a guy. I turn to him slightly. "I'm impressed. Your home is beautiful."

"What? Shocked are you?"

"No. Just impressed." I begin to look around admiring a sculpture here and a painting there when a thought crosses my mind. "Uh, so wait a minute. I just thought of something."

Zyon drops his arm from around my shoulder, grabs my hand, and slightly squeezes it as he gives me his undivided attention. "What? What's up?"

"What's up with you knowin I was on the way, but leavin your party before I arrived." I look at him amused so that he knows I'm jokin. "I mean, I'm jus sayin." Damn, his smile is sendin my insides into all kinds of eruptions. Can a sista get some help, please?

"Look, I really didn't wanna leave." He looks at his boy for help, but Malik playfully looks away. "But, he wanted me to take a spin in his new ride."

"He lyin to you, beautiful. He didn't have to leave then. He coulda waited."

Everything about Malik, his stance, tone, facial expression, tells me he's lyin. But, I play along any way and turn toward Zyon. "Oh really?"

"Oh, it's like that?" Zyon stares at his boy. "Really?"

I guess his look reminded Malik of something cuz he changed his story real quick. "Naw, I'm jus playing, sis. I'ma have to leave in about an hour, and I knew he wouldn't leave if he was in the middle of a spades game."

"Smart man." Zyon turns to me. "Trust me when I say that you woulda been in good hands if I wasn't here, though."

"Oh yeah?"

"Yep. My sister's been looking out for you."

"Sure have." I turn around toward a female's voice. "Hi Corin. I'm Sheila." She playfully punches Zyon on the shoulder - "this knucklehead's sister."

"Oh, hi." Oooop. Totally caught off guard. Where did she come from? Wow, she's gorgeous.

She takes me from Zyon. "Come on, let me show you, now, where the restrooms are, girl. Cuz once these fools, myself included, start talkin shit at the card table, you gone be on yo own."

"Ahunhunhun! Okay. Thanks." I like her.

She pauses and looks me up and down before snappin a finger in the air. "You are workin that outfit. I'm lovin those pants, girl." With the black girl poke-out of her lips, she swings one of her hips out to the side before we start walkin again. "Unh hunh. Those are tight."

I look down at my pants cuz I temporarily forgot what I was wearin. "Oh thanks! They're my favorite."

"Do you mind if I ask where'd you get em?"

"Not at all. I got em at this boutique in SOHO, in Manhattan."

She stops and looks at me as if she forgot something. "Oh yeah, you're not from here, are you?"

I shake my head no. "Nope."

"Well, good for you ma cuz I sho was gone bite."

"Hahaha!"

"Okay, so this is a restroom." She stops walkin and opens a door to our right.

"Oh, okay. Cool."

"Now, let me show you the one that's off of the deck, outside, where we'll all be. Jus so you'll have a backup in case one is occupied."

"Okay, thanks." Dang, she's so friendly.

"Girl, you welcome." She leans in a little like she bout to tell me a secret. "Let me jus warn you not to take none of the shit talkin that you bout to witness to heart, especially if it's toward you."

"Ahunhunhun." Damn, how bad do they get? "Okay. Thanks for the heads up."

"Unh hunh. Jus know that it's all in good fun."

"I hear ya." We go through some French doors that lead to a picturesque backyard filled with about twenty or so people, some standin around while others are sittin at a cluster of card tables yappin it up and eatin. And everybody's bobbin their heads to the old school hip hop the DJ's spinnin. "Let Me Clear My Throat." Awe shiiit, that's my joint. "Ooooh, nanh he's takin us back for real, what? That used to be my joint."

Sheila looks over at three women who start playfully wildin out to the song. "Humph, and apparently theirs, too. I can tell, already we gone have some stories to tell after this." She quickly looks at me as if to explain herself. "But, don't get me wrong. It's all in good fun."

I respond to her with a smile, a nod, and a light giggle. "I hear ya." As I take everything in, I realize that I'm not even a lil nervous. I think I'ma like this. Everybody seem to be enjoyin themselves. Why did I assume I'd see kids?

At the sound of Zyon's laugh, I whip my body around to look behind me jus in time to see him dappin up a handsome man at the grill.

Sheila watches me watch them. "Girrrl, that's our cousin PJ who's a nut."

I nod my head. "Oh, okay."

"Yeah, let him tell it, he's the cook at all the barbecues."

I don't hide my confusion as I watch him maneuver the meat on the grill and wipe excess sauce from his hand on an apron. "What? He's not the cook?"

"Girl, please. That nut just got here five minutes before you. He always wearing that dirty ass apron thinkin that the late comers, specifically the ladies, will think he barbecued and that it's his special sauce, as oppose to Zyon's, that he'd be willing to share over drinks."

Before I know it, I'm laughin out loud. "Nanh, that's funny." I look at Zyon and PJ for a moment determining that they damn near look like brothers before I look out over the entire backyard.

The lawn is perfectly manicured with a big pecan tree creating a lot of shade towards the back end of the yard, or shall I say grounds – it's so grand-like. All of his bushes seemed to be showin off their freshly cut hedges. However, I must say that I am a little surprised that I don't see many flowers. But, wait! Damn, now that I look at the yard more, it resembles a frickin golf course complete with a few slight mounds creating uneven terrain. Wait a minute. "Sheila, is this a golf course?"

"Ahunhunhun…"

"Yes, beautiful, it is. Sorta like a miniature one."

I turn around and smile at Zyon. "Hey!"

"Hey, back." He looks at his sister amusingly. "So, Sheila, can you like, uhhh, I don't know, walk away."

I nudge Zyon on his shoulder playfully. "Oooh, Zyon, that was so mean."

Though Sheila's playing, too, her punch to his shoulder looks like it hurt. "Girl, he just showing out in front of you. See, he trying to play it off like he ain't in pain."

I look at Zyon and start to laugh at the pained/amused/shocked expression on his face. "Hahaha! Oooh, are you all right?" I rub his shoulder consolingly.

"Unh hunh." He looks at his sister. "You know that was dirty, right?"

"What? Oooh, was that the shoulder you hurt yesterday?"

"What you think?"

"I'm sorry, Zyon, I forgot." His sister hugs him as she continues to apologize and look at me with wide eyes. "Girl, him and my son, Tariq, were wrestling yesterday, and well, they just so rough, ya know?"

I nod my head to let her know that I get what she's sayin.

Sheila breaks away from Zyon and looks at him apologetically. "All right. So, I'm gone leave ya'll be." She walks away.

Zyon doesn't acknowledge her though. He jus looks at me with this smile on his face. "Come on. Let's go get you some food."

He grabs my hand.

"Okay."

"I barbecued you some salmon."

"Hmmm, you did?"

"Unh hunh." He stops walkin. "Wait! Please don't tell me that you don't eat salmon."

"No, no. I mean, yes I do. I jus never had it barbecued before."

We start back walkin. "Oh, okay. Well, baby girl, you in for a treat."

"Oh, it's like that?"

"You'll see."

When we reach the food, he shows me that my fish is on a smaller grill off to the side. "I can put it in the oven in the kitchen if you'd like. You know, to make sure no one touches it."

"No, no, this is fine. Shoot, you made so much, I can share."

"Cool." We walk over to a table that has a lot of food spread out – potato salad, baked beans, macaroni and cheese, corn on the cob, a tossed salad with an array of salad dressings to choose from, a fruit salad, cake, Jell-O, and hot dog and burger buns.

"Wow! Don't tell me you cooked all of this."

"What you tryna say? You don't think a brotha can pull this off?"

"I didn't say that."

"Hahaha! I'm messin wit you. I did all the grillin and my sister and her friends did the rest."

"Oh, okay. Hey, do you know if there's any meat in the baked beans."

"Unh, unh. There's no meat in them."

"Cool."

He points toward the card tables, where all the folks I mentioned earlier are eatin at. "All of the drinks are in coolers over there – sodas, beer, wine coolers, water, you name it."

"Okay. Thanks."

"So, go ahead and fix you a plate, and come on ova. We bout to start playing cards in a minute."

"All right." Oooh, I'm so hungry. But, I betta be cool. Don't want folks thinkin that I'm greedy or haven't eaten in a while. Bein mindful of where I am, yet bein true to me, I fix me a healthy plate and walk over toward everyone.

"Hey, don't forget your napkins and fork."

First I look down at my hands and notice that I did forget my napkins and fork. Then I look behind me to say thank you. "Thanks."

"You're welcome."

What a cute couple. By the wild head of locs, I'm guessin this must be Mama May's landscaper. "Hey, are you Tariq?"

Both him and the young lady at his side look surprised. "Yeah. Who are you?"

"My name is Corin. May Richmond is my aunt."

The surprised look melts into a warm smile. "Oh, you're Miss May's niece?"

"Yeah."

"Okay."

The young woman at his side speaks up. "Hi, I'm Dajaunna."

"Hi Dajaunna. I'm Corin."

"Here. Since your hands are full, we'll bring your napkins and fork with us. We bout to grab some more food."

"Ahunhunhun. Thanks, Tariq. Preciate ya." Now, where did they jus come from? It seems like they appeared out of nowhere just like Sheila did earlier when I first saw her in the house.

5 hours later

Wow. I can't believe how fun today's been. And I especially can't believe that I'm still here helpin Zyon and his sister clean up.

"Well ya'll, I'm about to go." Sheila tosses the dish rag she was usin to wipe down the countertops with into the sink.

Zyon walks toward her. "Thanks for all of your help, Sheila."

"No prob, dude." She looks over at me and then decides to walk my way. "It was nice meeting you, Corin."

"Likewise." She gives me a hug and a wink and whispers, "He really likes you."

I jus smile as she picks up two bags full of wrapped leftovers.

"Wait, Sheila. Let me help you with that." Zyon grabs the bags from her.

"Thanks."

Grabbin the goodies that I wrapped up for myself, I figure I should be makin my way back to Mama May's. "You know what? I'ma walk out with ya'll."

Zyon quickly turns toward me with this puppy dog look on his face. "You leaving?"

Behind him his sista is shakin her head no and mouthin don't leave.

Feelin a lil uncomfortable, I shift my weight over to my left leg. I guess he really wants me to stay. "Well, I don't wanna over stay my welcome."

"As far as I'm concerned, you just got here. Don't go yet. It's still early."

His sister is still smiling and shakin her head no.

Oooh, he betta not try nothin or he gone see anotha side of me. I shift my weight over to my right side and wonder why I keep shiftin my weight. "Well, okay. I guess I can hang out some more."

"Cool. I'll be right back."

I set my leftovers down and walk toward the living room with them as his sista quickly nods her head yes and then pretends like she wasn't doin anything when he turns back toward her.

Alone in his livin room, I pray for the strength to keep it light when he returns cuz the sexual tension has been so strong between us sense I arrived earlier.

He locks the door behind him when he returns. "You wanna watch a movie?"

"Sure."

"Come on. Let's go to the den."

I get up off the couch and follow him. I can't help but think just how well his business is doin cuz everything in his house screams quality, money, V.I.P.

In the den, I start walkin toward a comfortable lookin chair, but quickly rethink the message I'd be sendin. *Corin, girl, you got control. You ain't gone do nothin you ain't ready to do.* So, I sit in the love seat instead so that he can join me.

"What are you in the mood for?"

"Ummm, it don't matter. Jus as long as it's not scary."

"Hey, what's wrong with scary? I'm here to protect you."

"Yeah, but it's jus lil ole me when I close my eyes."

"Hahaha! True, true. Hey, why don't you come over and select a movie while I go and get us something to drink and snack on."

"Okay, cool. But, I'll jus take some wine. I don't think I can eat anything else, I'm so full." I rub and kinda hold my tummy as I think about jus how much food I devoured in the last five hours.

"Bet."

He leaves the room and I peruse through his enormous collection of movies. Shit, he could open up a DVD rental shop with all these movies. Uncle Charles and Mama May ain't got nothing on him. I take off my sandals to get comfortable and try to determine what movie I wanna see. Oooh *Devil In A Blue Dress*. I love me some Don Cheadle. But, he probably wouldn't wanna see this. I put it to the side just in case he's open to it. Ooooh, *Brown Sugar*. Nanh, I could watch this movie over and over and over again. Right as I set it to the side, Zyon enters the room, sets some wine and chips on a table, eases up behind me and wraps his arms around me.

Oooh, damn, I hope he can't feel my heart poundin. Shit, or hear it for that matter.

"Damn, baby." He backs up a lil. "Did I scare you? I could feel your heart beatin fast."

Damn! I turn to face him. "Ummm, ahunhunhun." Shit, what do I say?

He grabs both my hands and damn near stimulates my g-spot with his eyes. "Look, I jus wanted to hang with you alone for a minute. I ain't got no ulterior motives, okay?"

Feelin crazy silly and beyond embarrassed, I tentatively nod my head. "Okay."

"But, on that same note, I do want it to be clear that I like you and I wanna get to know you betta."

Findin my voice on the seventh floor of happyville, I manage a coherent reply. "And you don't mind that I live in New York?"

He moves his head slowly from side to side. "Unh unh. The way I see it, Beautiful, distance is just space between two points. There are many ways to bypass it."

Hmmm, what does he mean by that. "Like how?"

"Planes, trains, cars, phones, letters, emails, texts, conversations, thoughts."

"Right. Okay."

He steps into my personal space. I can feel his internal sun warmin my everything.

"Like I said earlier, I don't have any ulterior motives. But a brotha been wanting to feel your lips and two-step with yo tongue since I met you."

Oh damn! "Oh yeah?"

He kisses me full, slow, melodic. His sun's rays are forcefully piercin through and openin up my pores one by one which propels me to grab the back of his neck, and he, the fullness of my ass. *Back up, Corin. Back up girl. Corin!*

I slowly pull away somewhat afraid to look him in his eyes for fear that he'll see how wide open I am right now. So, instead of lookin at him, I turn toward the movies I picked. But, before I make it to them, he grabs me and turns me toward him and kisses me more intensely. He slowly walks me back until my back is against a wall, holds my hands up pressed against the wall at head level, and just kisses me. Our torsos are not touchin. He's purposely positionin the lower half of his body away from me which makes me give into the kiss even more. I like the way he kisses. This moment sorta feels like a teenage moment – hot, new, innocent.

He eventually transforms our tongue dance to small peck kisses where I can feel the soft plushness of his full lips. He pulls away from me after lightly kissin my forehead. "Beautiful?"

I breathe my reply more than I speak it. "Yes."

"You ready to watch the movie you selected?"

I swallow as an attempt to settle myself down. "Yeah, sure."

"Okay, cool." He steps from in front of me, but grabs my hand to pull me toward where I laid the DVDs down. "So, what did you decide on? *Brown Sugar*? Hahaha!"

"What?"

"Nothin. I guess I could take one for the team. Ahunhun."

Still tinglin, I try to get in movie mode. "Well, what about *Devil in a Blue Dress*?"

"Oh, what? You a Denzel fan, too?"

"Yeah, but not like most. You lookin at a Don Cheadle chick."

"Don Cheadle?"

"Uh, yeah. That's baby daddy material."

"Oh, you funny, hunh."

"Hahaha!"

"Well, I'ma take one for the team tonight. Let's go with *Brown Sugar*."

"You sure?"

"Yep. Baby daddy material can wait."

"Hahaha! Okay." I sit on the love seat and pour me a glass of wine while Zyon starts the movie. Once I drink about half of my wine, I'm comfortably relaxed, restin my head on Zyon's chest as he rests his arm along my shoulder. Without even thinkin, I fall asleep halfway into the movie.

Wait! What Happened?!

Wow, that wine must've put me out cuz I feel like I been sleepin for a month of Sundays. But, wait. Where's Zyon. Clearly I'm layin on my back in a bed. But, I can't seem to focus my eyes on anything. Everything looks crazy blurry. I blink my eyes to try and refocus, but everything remains blurry.

"Praise, God, my baby's wakin up."

Hunh? Nooo. Was that my mother?

"Oh Mary! It looks like she's tryin to focus her eyes. Press the button for help."

And is that Auntie Joyce? Press what button for help? My vision slowly starts to clear up. Wait, nooo! Why is my daddy lookin at me like that with tears in his eyes?

"Welcome back, baby girl." My daddy kisses me on my forehead and a soft hand squeezes my hand while a calloused one squeezes the other.

What? Welcome back from where? Ohhh shit! Where am I? What did Zyon do to me?

"Okay, we're gonna need everyone to clear the room."

Clear what room? Who's that talkin?

"Oh dear. She looks afraid."

Uhhh, ya think, Ma? What's goin on? Wait, I just realized that I'm not talkin. Why can't I talk? What's this in my mouth? And why does everyone, especially my parents, look so young? Am I dreamin?

"We'll be right back, baby. Jus hold tight."

Hold tight? Was that Uncle Terrell? Only Uncle Terrell says hold tight. He's alive? Wait, did I die?

"Excuse me nurse, may I stay please? She's obviously wondering what's going on."

Nurse? I'm in the hospital? Whew! Good. I didn't die. But, how's Uncle Terrell alive? I know that wasn't Uncle Terrence. Was it? Naw, I don't remember him saying hold tight.

"Ummm, sure, ma'am. But will you please stand over to the side?"

"Yes! Yes! Thank you so much." My mom leans in so I can see her face. "I'll be right over here, baby."

Okay, Mama.

"Well, hello there. Welcome back."

Back from where?

"I am your nurse. My name is Lily."

Okay. Hi Nurse Lily.

"You gave everyone a big scare you know?"

Uh, no, I don't know. And why you shinin that light in my eyes? Who's messin with my knee? Why am I feelin a tingling sensation at the bottom of my right foot?

"Well, hello there."

Hmmm, he must be the doctor.

Nurse Lily puts that thing around my arm like she takin my blood pressure. I feel it squeeze my arm as she pumps whateva this jig-a-ma-jig with air. "All of her vital signs and reflexes check out, Doctor Davis."

Doctor Davis?

"Okay, wonderful." He looks at me. "I knew you'd come through."

Uhhhh, through what?!

"Has she made any audible noises yet?"

"No, doctor. Not yet. But, she appears to be cognizant of sound by the way her eyes are responding."

"Excellent."

"Doctor, will my baby be all right?"

Yeah Mama. Please get clarification.

"So far things are looking good."

"Okay. Good."

"Let's give her some time to get used to being conscious again."

"How much time? How long will it take." My mother's voice sounds panicked.

"I'm sorry, ma'am, but that's hard to say because everyone's different. But, give me a moment so that I can explain to her what's happened in case she doesn't remember."

"Oh, okay."

Yeah, please give me a clue.

The doctor leans in so that he and I make eye contact. I feel as though he wants to make sure, from lookin at me, if I'm understandin him. "Okay, Corin. You've been unconscious for almost three weeks."

Unconscious? Three weeks?

He turns toward the nurse. "Okay, Nurse Lily, I see what you're talking about. She clearly understood that."

Nurse Lily responds to the obvious. "Right, doctor."

"Corin, can you blink your eyes for me?"

Yes. I blink my eyes.

"Good, girl."

"Praise GOD."

Yes! Praise Him, Mama, and keep talkin so I can hear yo voice.

"Okay, Corin, I want you to blink once for yes, and twice for no."

Okay.

"Excuse me, doctor."

Thanks, ma. Keep talkin.

"May my husband come in please? He's right outside."

"Sure, ma'am."

I hear my mother walk away and call for my daddy. Within moments I see them both on my right side and the doctor and the nurse are on the left.

"Corin."

Yes, doctor. My mom quietly explains to my dad about me blinkin my eyes while the doctor continues to talk to me.

"By the semen we found from your vaginal examination and the…"

Oh, damn! Don't tell me Zyon raped me. Please, GOD, nooo.

"Corin, Corin." The doctor's callin my name calmly.

Oh shit, focus Corin. The doctor's talkin to you. I must've shut my eyes becuz when I opened them again, my mom and dad look relieved.

"Corin, can you hear me?"

Yes doctor! What?

"Blink once if you can hear me."

Oh yeah. Okay. I forgot to blink.

My mom and dad both let out big sighs after I blink once.

"Okay. We found residue of Anthony Carpenter's semen inside of you when we examined you when you first got here."

Anthony Carpenter? Was that a friend of Zyon's?

"Do you remember being brutally attacked and raped by Mr. Carpenter?"

My mom covers her mouth with one hand, in shock, after I blink twice.

"Baby?"

Yes Daddy? I look at my daddy.

"Lil Redd. Do you remember being attacked and raped by Lil Redd?"

Yeah, but who told you? I blink once. *Ohhh, that Anthony Carpenter.* I look back at the doctor hopin he'd ask me again.

He looks at me. "Okay, do you know Lil Redd as Anthony Carpenter?"

I blink once.

"Yes. Praise GOD."

I look at my mother wonderin why she's praisin GOD about that and tryin to figure out why they askin me about a rape from about fifteen, or so, years ago. Shit, I'm tryna determine how I ended up here and where Zyon is. This all feels so weird and confusing. And I still can't get over how young my parents look. I mean, if I'm not mistaken, they look like they did when I was in high school and college.

Ugh! Every time I move, I feel a pain in my chest.

"Corin, try not to move. We will remove the tube in a few moments. We're waiting for a tech to get here from another ward of the hospital so that we can conduct some tests."

I blink once.

The doctor and the nurse are lookin at me peculiarly and then the doctor looks over at my parents. "Mr. and Mrs. Rivers, may I speak with you outside for a moment?"

No, ya'll! Please don't leave me.

"Don't worry none, sweetie, they'll be right back."

Okay. So, why does this nurse seem to know what I'm thinkin?

"I wish we knew what was goin on in yo pretty lil head, Corin. But, time will tell. As we run tests, we're gonna slowly disconnect all of these tubes and wires from you – the first one being the one in your mouth. Just try and lay still, baby. It's just protocol that we make sure that you're okay before we disengage everything. I can tell that you're not sure how you got here. Things may get better in time once you're able to talk and ask questions."

She keeps on talkin like we havin a conversation. She seems really nice. I feel like I met her before. But, what she mean by 'may get better'?

"That Anthony fellow really did a number on you. In addition to you suffering a traumatic blow to your head, you also have a couple of rib fractures – hence, the ventilator, or tube, in your mouth."

Why is everybody talkin about Anthony? Don't she mean Zyon?

She keeps on talkin as if I'm talkin back to her. "Yeah, sweetie, you were pretty bad off when you first got here. But, I could tell that all of the prayers your family and myself was sendin up to the heavens were working because you were healing so steadily each week that I jus knew you were gonna open your eyes any day. And now look at you lookin back at me. You sho have some pretty eyes. Dem GOD's eyes for sure. Oh yes my precious dawlin, I do believe that you're gonna be jus fine."

Ooooh, I just felt something sting me? I wonder what that was. Wait, why am I feelin so sleepy?

I hear my parents talkin as they come back into the room along with some other familiar voices. But, I can't seem to keep my eyes open. Guess I'm fallin asleep.

When I wake up, my room is quiet and mostly dark. I attempt to get up, but my limbs feel so heavy that I quickly give up. Hmmm, it looks like I still have a tube goin down my throat. What the hell has happened to me?

I guess I must've gone back to sleep because the next thing I remember is wakin up to my mother's beautiful smile. "Oh, Stephen." She quickly glances behind her. "Baby, she's up." Then she looks back at me. "Good morning, sunshine."

Good morning, Ma. I blink once.

"Aw well, looka here. Hi Beautiful."

Hi Daddy. I blink once.

Mom walks to the other side of my bed so that each of them can hold my hand. "Baby, the doctor said it looks like they'll be able to take the tube outta ya mouth today. They didn't want to take a chance yesterday with you jus wakin up out of the coma. So, they gave you a mild sedative so that they could monitor the strength of your lungs. And, you, my baby girl passed the test."

Cool. I blink once.

"They said that each time they came in to check on you, last night, and to check your vitals, that you were doin great – gainin unexplainable strength within hours."

I blink once. *That's interestin. I don't remember them checkin on me. Wasn't I asleep most of the time?*

"I know you must be very confused, Puddin'."

Puddin'. I love it when my daddy calls me Puddin'. I blink once at my daddy.

"Well, let me explain everything to you."

I blink once.

"We don't know how you ended up at the Carpenter's house, but Lil Redd beat you up pretty badly and raped you."

Hunh? How bad did he beat me up?

My dad keeps talkin, keeps fillin in some of the gaps for me. "From the condition of the livin room, it looks like you put up a good fight, though. But, some kinda way he hit you in the back of your head with a lamp."

He did? I must be in somebody's dream. Whose dream am I in? I don't remember any of that.

I look at my dad questioningly.

"Yeah, ya see, Puddin', they found some pieces of the base of the lamp in your hair. But they don't think that caused your unconscious state, but perhaps another blow to the head."

What? This is crazy.

"It doesn't look like she remembers any of this, dear."

Uh, ya think, Ma?

"I know. I'm lookin at her, too, Mary. But, I gotta tell her the truth."

"I know baby. Go on."

"Well, Corin." My daddy never takes his eyes off of mine as if he's afraid he won't see them again. "When the police and paramedics found you, you were barely breathin, layin on your back half way between the living room and the front porch with your head on the front porch. So, we're thinkin that's where the unconsciousness occurred, when the back of your head hit the cemented porch.

This is some crazy shit. That's not how it happened. I left the Carpenter's house and drove to the dorms. Queenie found me and, eventually, took me to the hospital. How did I end up back at the Carpenter's unconscious? Who's dream is this that I'm in?

I hear a door open. "Well good morning, Mr. and Mrs. Rivers. How y'all doing this morning?"

Okay, that's that nurse's voice. I hear my parents greet her.

"Excuse me, Miss Lily?"

"Yes sir?" The nurse is shinin that light in my eyes again.

"Well, I jus told Corin what happened and it looks as though she doesn't remember any of it. How soon before we can talk to her to get her side of the story?"

"Maybe, as soon as a matter of a few hours. Right now I'm goin to give her a pain reliever which, like yesterday, might cause her to fall asleep for a couple of hours. While she's sleep, we'll remove the tubes and everything. The pain reliever will be in place just in case she raises her head or speaks too quickly when she comes to. You know she had more than a bump on her head."

"Yes, Nurse."

"Your daughter's a trooper though."

"Yes, she is. Praise GOD." *Thanks, Ma.*

"Yes, ma'am." Nurse Lily smiles at my mother, and I hear the door open again.

"Well, good morning, again, folks."

Dr. Davis. Again?

"Good morning doctor." My mom and dad respond in unison.

"I'm glad you folks are here. Now when she wakes up in a few hours, we're gonna do a couple of tests and take some x-rays. But we won't do the CT scan that I mentioned to you yesterday until tomorrow morning. It's scheduled for 9:30. So, with that being said, we won't give her any medication or food or drink after 5:00 p.m. today. We want her body to be as neutral as possible."

My dad nods. "Okay."

"And, I ask that in the next few days that you do not encourage her to speak too much."

Both of my parents look at Nurse Lily questioningly. But, she just widens her eyes and slightly shrugs as the doctor continues talking. "Be mindful that her throat will be sore from the tube being in there for almost three weeks now, and that there will be times when she may feel like she's about to gag. So, let's give her some time to heal. You might wanna get her a small chalkboard of some sort, or pad and pencil to keep it simple."

The pensive look painted on my dad's face dissolves a little. "Okay, doctor. Nanh, this CT scan is not gonna hurt our baby, is it? *Yes, Daddy! Find out everything you can. Oooh, Lawd, I'm feelin sleepy again.*

"No sir. I assure you that our staff are more than capable of performin the test. She'll be just fine. The important thing is that she doesn't move during the test because movement obstructs clarity. And given that her muscles are weak from non-movement over the past couple of weeks, I'm sure we won't get an argument out of her about being still."

My dad just nods while he glares at the doctor with that pensive look again.

My mom reads my dad's mood. "Okay, doctor. Thank you."

"You're welcome, Mrs. Rivers."

I guess I'm off to sleep again cuz even though they standin right next to me talkin, I can barely understand anything right now. I wonder if Lil Redd killed himself in this version.

Okay, I must be dreamin cuz if I'm not mistaken I'm in my bed at Mama May's house now. Well, alright-y then. I am sooo trippin out off of all of this.

"Corey."

"Yes! Finally, normalcy. Hi Auntie."

"Hi baby girl."

"I don't know what's happenin to me. One moment I'm at Zyon's watchin a movie and the next I've travelled through time to right after the rape and wake up in a hospital from a coma. And my dad was there, and…"

"Hush, baby. We may not have a lot of time."

"Don't scare me, Auntie. A lot of time for what?"

"For me to explain. Ya see…"

"Oh Lawd, nooo!"

"Come on, baby. Let me explain." She waits for me to nod before she continues. "Ya see, there was never any Zyon or any house in Conyers, Georgia, that you visited or a reality in New York…ummm, how do I say this?"

"Hunh? What are you talkin bout?"

"Hear me out, baby."

"Okay."

"You were sleepin. You've actually been in a coma for almost three weeks."

"Oh, nooo. Not you, too, Mama May."

"Listen, Corey. The life you think you experienced for fifteen years, I shouldn't say it didn't happened, ummm, cuz it did. It's just that it happened in another dimension. Right now, you're still a sophomore at Xavier University."

"What? But I own a brownstone in Brooklyn and work at Computel Financial. My best friend is Queenie."

"Well, yes, I suppose Queenie may be your best friend – she's your roommate at Xavier."

"Hunh? What about Black? Havin herpes? My visit to you?"

"Another dimension."

"Hunh? No. So, you sayin that *Sacrednicity* never happened?"

"No, I'm not sayin that. All of it happened – just in another dimension – another realm."

"Well, where am I now? In another dimension?"

"Not really – more like between worlds."

I attempt to get out of bed, but I can't seem to move.

"Be still, chile. Life will get better for you, baby. Be patient."

"How?"

"It'll come to ya, Corey. You'll see."

I'm unable to grasp what she's tellin me or even that she's real cuz her body keeps fadin in and out it seems. "It will?"

"Yes, baby. Nanh, listen to me, nanh. When you first woke up, didn't you notice some faces that surprised you?"

"Yes! Uncle Terrell is alive!?"

"Yes, baby! That's cuz he never died."

"But we were all at the funeral. He drowned in Lake Ponchartrain, remember?"

"I know. But, it was another realm."

"Okay! Will you please stop sayin that."

"I'm jus tryin to help you figure all this out."

"Okay. Well, tell me this. Where is Deron? Was he real? Is Lil Redd dead? Did he kill himself or not?"

"They'll answer your questions when you wake up."

Exasperated, I close my eyes. I don't feel like talkin to Mama May any more. When I decide to open them again, I'm back to my real life, I guess, lookin in my auntie Joyce's eyes. Auntie Joyce. Now where has she been? It feels like I haven't seen her in a while.

"Hey dere, baby girl."

I smile. Oh my goodness, I can smile. I open and close my mouth to check if I can feel my lips press together. Hot damn, I can feel my lips again.

Aunt Joyce is watchin me feel for my lips. "Hmmm, I guess they do feel a lil funny, hunh baby?"

I blink once instead of tryna talk.

"Yes, good thinkin, Corey. I was told to tell you to try not to talk cuz we have to let ya throat heal from that tube."

I blink once.

"Good girl. You don't know how happy I am to see them beautiful eyes of yours. I knew with all the fight and spunk up in you that you was gone pull outta that coma."

As she's talkin to me, our relationship is startin to come back to me. Auntie Joyce is my mother's only sister. Hmmm, so who was Mama May? Oooh, GOD, angels, guides, somebody please clue me in on some things.

"Uncle Buddy told me to give you his love. You know he was pullin for you."

Uncle Buddy? Oh, he's her husband. A memory of me playin cards with Uncle Buddy flash in my mind. *Oh right.* I see us laughin hard at something. *Uncle Buddy and Auntie Joyce.*

"Joyce, is she awake?"

Mama!

Auntie looks briefly over her shoulder. "Yes, dawlin. Our baby is awake."

I hear some shuffling and then footsteps before I see my mother's face. I smile.

"Oh yes. Our baby is back. Look at that beautiful smile. How ya doin, Corin?"

I blink once toward my mother. *Oooh, let me ask them about Lil Redd.* As soon as I attempt to speak, both of them immediately stop me.

"Nanh, Corey, what did I jus tell you?"

I look at my auntie cuz I jus noticed that she called me Corey like Mama May did. And now that I think about it, Auntie Joyce always called me Corey. Hmmm, so maybe Mama May was or is Auntie Joyce. Ugh! I'm so confused.

"Yeah, baby, you listen to ya auntie." I look over at my mother. "They'll be plenty of time for talkin. Shoot, now that I think about it, you have no choice but to do what I been tellin you all yo life, to be quiet and listen." She smiles the most beautiful smile at me. I love my mother so much.

"Hahaha! Good one Mary." They give each other a high five. Oh yeah, the high fives. They always give each other high fives. Wow, I guess this life is comin back to me. Hmmm.

My mama continues talkin in the middle of their high five. "Besides, your father's bringin a lil chalkboard for you to write on a lil later."

I reflect my mother's smile to her and Auntie Joyce and attempt to raise my hand for a high five, but I could only seem to manage to lift a finger. They both recognize my gesture and cover my hand with theirs as instantaneous tears begin to flow from both of their eyes.

After our heartfelt moment, a nurse comes in and takes me to some lab to take some tests and x-rays. When I return, my mom and Auntie Joyce start updating me on everybody and who's called and wished me well wishes and prayin for me. Apparently, from Auntie Joyce's stories, I do have twin cousins named Kyle and Mya and they're her kids. Shiiit, I'm tellin you that even though this shit is crazy as fuck, I'm glad to learn that I do have a sister named Shanice cuz it felt good bonding with her, I guess, in the other dimension. Humph, go fuckin figure. And, accordin to my mother, she just brought a guy named Michael over for Sunday dinner before all this happened with me. Hmmm, I wonder if it's the same Michael she's gonna marry and get a divorce from. Oh shit, wait! I wonder if she's gay. Oooh, nanh this is getting interestin.

A nurse walks in rollin a cart. I wonder where Nurse Lily is. "Well, hello gorgeous."

I blink once.

"Oh, good. Y'all keepin her from talkin."

My mother chimes in, "Jus makin sho we do what ya'll say so our baby can get on outta here."

The nurse chuckles a little as she adjusts my bed into a more upright position. "Yes, ma'am. Thank you."

She situates the rollin cart on the side of my bed. I see that it's some sort of mushy cereal like oatmeal or cream of wheat and a bowl of red Jell-O. She looks over at my mom and aunt.

"Now, I don't wanna intrude. I could tell that ya'll was talkin to her in all. I can feed her myself like I came to do, or I can let one of you ladies do it. Either way..."

My mom cuts her off before she could finish her sentence. "Oh, thank you Nurse Brenda, but we can feed her. Shoot it'll be like old times..." She looks over at me and holds my eyes. "...me feedin my baby girl." Then she starts talkin like she talkin to an infant. "Yes it will. Yes it will." She finishes with an endearing kiss to my forehead and a light pinch to my left cheek. *Umm, so really Mom. You really gone be over-the-top like this? Hahaha! But, honestly, I'ma ham when it comes to attention.*

"Well, okay then. I figured y'all would opt for the latter. Just ring my bell if she starts gagging. Make sure the portions are no bigger than this." She shows them the amount of cereal and Jell-O to put on a spoon at a time.

Before my mother starts feedin me, Auntie Joyce stops her, grabs one of her hands and one of mine, closes her eyes and starts prayin. When she's finished, she looks at me and encourages me to visualize the food tastin good and goin down my throat with no complications.

I blink once.

Dinner was uneventful. I guess the visualizing either worked or my throat's not as bad off as they think.

It's now about an hour after dinner and I have a room full of folks - Uncle Terrell, Uncle Buddy, my dad, and Queenie, all have joined my mom and auntie Joyce. Apparently my uncle Terrell knows one of the nurses here at the hospital who told the lead nurse to turn a blind eye to all of my visitors. It feels so good bein surrounded by so much love. All the jokes and warmth I'm feelin are beautifully fillin my heart up to the rim. My family know they can act a fool when they want to, especially the men folks when they get together. My daddy keep tryna keep people from encouraging me to talk, but he da main one crackin jokes on everybody makin me laugh. Aside from the circumstances of why we're all together, I wouldn't change a thing about this evening. And then, again, you know what? I take that back. Everything happens for a reason, and if I hadn't've been raped and beat up into a coma, then this beautiful day wouldn't have happened. So, like Mama May said, who eva or what eva she is, there's good in everything.

"Hey Puddin'."

I smile at my daddy.

"Well, baby, the doctor has reassured me that you're on the path to a full recovery." He looks up at the ceiling. "All praises."

I blink once. *Give thanks.*

"So, I want you to know that I'ma head back to California day after tomorrow. But, ya mama is gonna stay here until you're completely healed."

Aw Daddy. I know you have to get back to work. But, oooh, it's been so good seein you. I blink once. And before I know it, tears stream down my face.

"Oh baby don't cry."

Everybody chimes in. "Corin, don't cry."

My dad grabs one of my hands. "How about I come back when they discharge you?"

I blink once. But, I really wanna let him know that he doesn't have to, that I'm jus feelin so full with emotions right now that I can't stop the tears. And I know that if I blink twice, he may take it the wrong way. So, I jus squeeze his hand. And without any warning, he folds over me weepin.

"Oh, baby girl, I'm so sorry about all of this."

My mother rubs my father's back and grabs one of my hands. "That's right, baby. Let it out." She's encouragin him to talk and cry. Well, this feels odd. I don't think I've ever witnessed my father cry. Shoot, it wasn't until I left the house for college that all his strictness sorta melted away. But tears? Hmmm.

"Baby…"

I blink once.

"I know you never understood why I was so hard on you when you became a teenager and why I hadn't been so hard on your sister when she was comin up. But, you see, I didn't know how to tell you how a father, or shall I say, a man can read a female before she open her mouth – jus from her stance, posture, and walk. And, baby, you jus had so much vulnerability written all over you. He starts cryin again.

Wow, the tears are really sorta weirdin me out right now cuz my dad's always been this strong, solid piece of concrete substance that not much of anything penetrated through. Well, at least, that's always been my perception of him.

"Oooh, but GOD saved me cuz I swear if that motha fucka hadn't've killed himself, I would've killed him with my bare hands."

I shiver at the truth of that statement piercing through my father's eyes. Well, at least I know Lil Redd is dead.

I guess Uncle Buddy saw the fear that surfaced in my eyes at what my dad just said cuz he's pullin him off of me right now. "Come on, man. Let's go. Visitin hours are over any way."

My dad looks over at my mom who returns his look with a plea. "Ya'll go on. I think I wanna stay here tonight with my baby."

My dad comes over and kisses me on the forehead. And then, one by one, everyone comes over to say goodbye. It feels strange sayin goodbye to Queenie given that we didn't have a one on one conversation. But, I know that there will be plenty of time for that.

"Girl, we gone catch up soon." Queenie gives me a look like there's so much she wants to say.

I blink once and smile.

My mama pats my hand a few times. "Baby, give me a minute. I'ma go and make sure your father's all right."

I blink once. Uh, yeah, I was wonderin when she was gone say that. Shoot, he need a hug for real.

When my mother returns, she tries her best to prepare me as she informs me that per Queenie, Deron never came back to school.

Apparently, he was too grief-stricken over his uncle's murder. And he supposedly hung up on Queenie, after she thought she heard him whimper, upon hearing about what Lil Redd did to me. I listen to her for as long as I can before I can't keep my eyes open any more.

"Oh, okay, baby. I see you sleepy. You go on ahead and go to sleep."

I hope she don't think I'm bein disrespectful, but I'm jus so sleepy. Hmmm, what I'd do to wake up at Zyon's in the middle of *Brown Sugar*.

"Yeah, but that's not gonna happen, baby."

"Oh, GOD. Please don't tell me…"

"Yes, Corey. You're back with me."

I open my eyes to a faded silhouette of Mama May. "Okay, so who are you anyway? It's almost as if you hijacked my auntie Joyce's life."

"You know who I am, Corey."

Oh, Lawd. Here we go.

"Listen, Corey. All of this will begin to make sense as you mature and come into total awareness of who you really are."

"Dududdu. So what, is this another episode of the *Twilight Zone* starring yours truly?"

"You'll see, baby girl. You'll come to see that you have some special gifts."

Sort of interested in what she's sayin, I perk up a lil bit. "Like what kind of gifts? I mean, obviously you keep showin up in my dreams or other worlds for a reason. Is there something you wanna tell me?"

"Baby, you are a highly-evolved soul. You're extremely psychic."

"I am?"

"Yes, and you're a healer."

"Like you are in whatever dimension you live in?"

"Yeah, something like that."

Mama May's silhouette vanishes. But some kinda way I know she's still sittin on the edge of my bed. It's like I can sense her.

"Very good, Corey. I'm glad that you know that I'm still with you. As time passes and you mature, you're gonna be able to sense spirits around you instantly even when your physical eyes won't see them."

"Without gettin scared? Or, wait, that was in the other dimension, right? Me getting scared when I sensed spirits." Shit, I guess I'm just gone flow with this other dimension talk. This is all so very weird.

"Right. But, you have that gift here, too. And you need to learn how to not fear them. When you get your strength back, I want you to write down everything you remember about the dimension you just left when you were visitin Conyers and living in Brooklyn."

"Why?"

"Because all of the lessons and revelations you learned will help you, your friends and family, and tons of people you don't know."

"You know, all the stuff you're tellin me about me is how I remember you."

Mama May materializes and smiles at me in a conspiratorial way. In fact, in this moment, time is showcasing flashes of my entire life to me. But, it's movin so fast that it's hard for me to grasp anything fully. I jus feel a lot of love, happiness, and gratitude. Oh, shit! Now, I'm movin or flyin really fast. It's like I'm sittin upright in a chair, but there's no chair. Oooh, this feels like a ride gone bad at an amusement park. It's as if something's pushing me through space at astronomical speeds surpassing all levels of my immediate comprehension even though I'm able to recount it as it's happening. And now I'm hearing voices, only a few recognizable to my ear, though. As I fly through time, space, realms, or who knows what, I begin to hear what sounds like a radio in between stations before I hear a heavenly compilation of music that reverberates throughout each cell within my body, or maybe my soul. Silence? Complete stillness. Thank You, GOD.

"Corey."

"Mama May?"

"Corey, always pay attention to your life. To thine ownself be true within every instance."

Wait, that's not Mama May's voice. "Who's speakin?"

"Know that you are loved, Divinely guided, supported, protected, and directed. Open yourself to INFINITE TRUTH and bask in the keys to healing – forgiveness, present moment awareness, nonjudgment of yourself and others, GOD."

"Who are you? Who's talkin to me right now?"

"I am you, baby girl."

"Hunh? What happened to Mama May?"

Mama May appears before me. And then some other women stand side by side to the left of her. "Look closely, baby girl."

"What am I lookin at Mama May and why does your voice sound so different, so melodic?"

"Look at me. Look at us. Look at you."

I begin to really look at Mama May and all of the women standing to the left of her, and I jump at the obvious recognition.

"That's right, babygirl, I am your future self." She gestures to all of the women beside her. "We all are. And we're always with you. Seek us out often. We're just a thought away amongst your angels, guides and teachers while you're on the earth's plane."

Wow! Mama May is me? I mean, I'm Mama May?

"That's right, baby girl. Everything you remember about me and my life is actually your own. Well, at least it could be based upon your decisions and actions in your current lifetime."

I feel like I'm listening to her with all of my senses. My awareness seems to be extremely clear. It's like every cell in my body, including the spaces in between, are takin in her words crisply.

"You're feelin the way that you do because, Corey, the person isn't just listenin. You see baby, your, or shall I say, our soul is listenin, too."

I look at her, at all of me, in awe. "So, I'm gonna be you?"

She nods her head and disappears along with all of my other selves. But I can still feel them. "Yes, baby. Know that you can be anything you choose to be. Always believe that within the depths of your heart."

"Okay."

"Since human beings have free will, the opportunity to make different choices, things may appear off course at times, but I'm here to tell you that you were born to be a healer. And before long, the masses will acknowledge, seek out, and respect your gifts and mission on earth."

Now, I'm seein four, maybe five lights. "Okay, so what are these lights that you're showin me?"

"I'm not showin them. They're showing themselves to you."

"Hunh?"

"They're your ancestors, baby. They're letting you know that they're always with you, as well."

"What? Which ones? Clementine? My grandmother? My great great aunt Lily?" I can't seem to think straight. I have so many questions for them.

"Be patient chile. You will get your answers – all of them."

A thought comes into my mind. "Kyle and Mya are my cousins in both dimensions. Auntie Joyce wasn't in the dimension with you and neither was Uncle Buddy."

Mama May materializes again with a smile on her face. "Go on."

"You were married to Uncle Charles in the other dimension."

"That's right."

"But now that I think about it, he was away in London during my entire visit to Conyers. And I can't, for the life of me, remember how he looks."

"Unh hunh."

"So, if he was your husband, does that mean he will be mine?"

She smiles at me and begins to walk away.

"Will I have twins and name them after my cousins Mya and Kyle?"

She's fading out.

"How was it that I was myself and you, all at the same time, in the other dimension? Please don't go. Wait, I have one more question. Who was Zyon?"

She's totally gone now and I don't sense her. But, I feel, what I can only imagine love feels like as the scenery abruptly changes and I find myself standing in Zyon's backyard observing the beautiful greenery and golf course he carved out. It almost feels like I'm in a picture frame. As I begin to contemplate on how I got here, I hear her voice faintly pass by my left ear.

"Redemption."

Redemption?

Oh Lawd, I'm moving again. Damn, can a sista get a warning. As I travel through space, time, dimensions, or maybe even jus my mind, I begin to hear a radio stuck between stations again. And once my body stops shooting through the ethers, I hear what sounds like a lullaby at first, because the words and music feel like they're wrappin me up in a baby's blanket and rockin me to peace. But, as the song progresses, I recognize it as Bob Marley's *Redemption Song*. I guess this song is special to me in both dimensions. The truth it tells is unyielding – my Redemption's Lullaby.

I wonder if Mama May, or my future self I should say, was tryin to tell me that Zyon represented redemption to me. The only thing about that is I never got a chance to tell him everything. How do I know that he was redemption?

"Baby girl, redemption doesn't come from anyone or anything outside of you." Wow, her voice is so melodic. Where is she? Everything's black. I can't even see my own hand that I'm outstretchin in front of me. "Your redemption blossomed through your continued actions of self-healing. Since you're not fully aware of all of your gifts just yet, let along how to use them, the only way you were able to tap into your gift of healing, to overcome that horrific assault you endured, was to travel to another dimension to be touched by your future self. Everyone else that accompanied you from your actual reality, like your mother, Shanice, Queenie, and Deron needed to be there to validate your consciousness, so to speak. And unbeknownst to them, they will prosper from it, as well. As you mature, astral travelling won't be necessary – healing will occur upon your will. And, well, Zyon…well, he assisted with illuminating the inner light that surfaced when you decided to commit to yourself."

I feel my eyes open. "Huh, huh, huh…" Ooooo, I'm tryin to catch my breath.

"I'm here, baby girl. It's all right."

I scan my environment to determine if I'm dreamin, in another dimension, in space or in the hospital. Though, the light in the room is very dim and I can't make out my mother's face, initially, her voice and touch are unmistakable. Oooh, Lawd. I'm back in the hospital in New Awlins. Nanh, that was pretty intense, GOD. Wow!

"It was jus a dream, baby."

I blink once.

"Was it a nightmare?"

I blink twice.

"You sho? Cuz you looked spooked a moment ago."

I nod my head.

My mother clasps her hands together. "Look at my baby gainin her strength back. You nodded your head."

I smile.

"You know baby, I have more to share with you. I stayed tonight becuz I wanted some moments with jus the two of us."

I curiously look at my mom.

"Well, baby, the doctor wanted us to tell you this bit of news after they disconnected you from all the machines and after a full day of monitoring your vital signs without them. Given the nature of the crime and the fact that they didn't know when you'd wake up from the coma, they told me and your father the results of all of the tests they gave you upon arrival and some they conducted a week or so after you arrived."

I continue to look at my mother curiously.

"Well, it seems as though we won't know for sure, for about ten years, if you're completely safe from HIV. However, we found out from Lil Redd's autopsy that he tested negative. And given that we don't know his sexual history, we can't completely rule it out."

I close my eyes to the fear tip toe-in under my skin. Plus, I have a feelin that I know what's next.

My mom pauses for a moment and looks down at my bed before she continues.

I must have herpes in this dimension, too.

"Baby, one of the tests, a blood tests that is, did show that you have herpes."

I close my eyes at the nightmare before me. But, when I do, I see Mama May shakin her head no. And then thoughts begin to claim my attention in my mind. *You have nothing to worry about. You are healed.*

I am healed? I don't have herpes nor am I HIV positive?

I can tell that Mama May's plantin thoughts in my mind. *Take another test on your own, after you leave the hospital. Remember, you were born to be a healer.*

I think about the thoughts swimming around in my mind for a few moments before something inside of me decides to trust them. Unknown courage propels me to hold my mother's hand and squeeze it as I erase the hurt and fear from her eyes with hope within my own. I wonder if my mother had been raped when she was younger in this dimension like she was in the other one. And if she was, I wonder if she'll tell me, or me and Shanice for that matter.

"Hmmm, you took that better than I expected you to."

I smile at my mother as I wonder just how much of that other dimension I will share with her - that she'll understand and believe like I do.

"I always knew, from the moment I laid eyes on you, that you're a special person, Corin. I have a feelin, that in time, the world will know, too."

I mouth 'thank you' to my mother.

"You're welcome, my baby. I want you to know that I am always here for you, no matter what, okay."

I blink once. Partly to acknowledge what my mom just said and partly to blink back tears. Aw hell, might as well let 'em flow.

My mother joins me with drops of her own.

a month later

Oh when the Saints (BOMP BOMP BOMP)
Go marchin in (BOMP BOMP BOMP)
Oh when the Saints go marchin in (bomp bomp bomp)
Oh I want to be in dat numba
Oh when the Saints go marchin in...

Nanh, ya'll remember that I love my New Awlins, right? Can you say crawfish boil (or affectionately called burl)?! Aw yes my good people – pounds upon pounds of all you can eat crawfish is pure-dee-heaven for me. Nanh, jus so you, the virgins, can absorb the entire experience of a crawfish boil, I have to explain that you're not just feastin on crawfish alone. Oooh no, unh, unh. You also get to munch on corn on the cob and red potatoes that were boiled in the same pot with the crawfish, soakin up the same seasonings, causing a throw-down, foot stompin, raise the motha f'in roof party in yo mouth no matter what you put in it. And Uncle Buddy added some turkey necks, too. "What?! Slttttttt. Unh, unh, unh." I can't stop lickin my fingers this food is sooo good.

"Well, well, well! Look at my pretty niece."

I look up for a moment from my food that's laid out on a big paper plate on top of a whole bunch of newspaper spread out on the floor in the living room to acknowledge my uncle. "Hey Uncle Terrell."

"How are you, beautiful?"

"Much, much better."

"That's good baby girl – real good. It's so good to see you up and walkin around like a wide-eyed cat ready to take on the world."

"A wide-eyed cat, hunh?" Grateful for the ability to laugh, I throw my head back slightly and allow the joy that's been filling up my heart since I arrived at Aunt Joyce and Uncle Buddy's an hour ago, drown my senses with giggles.

Everybody's here, Mya, Kyle, Shanice, my mom and dad, Uncle Thaddeus and Aunt June, Uncle Terrell and Uncle Terrence, and my girl, Queenie is here, too. They're all here celebrating my life with me. No ya'll, it's not my birthday. They jus celebratin that I survived that crazy ordeal. Thank You, God, for my life, my family, my gifts...

Mya and Queenie enter the living room, with Shanice two steps behind them, and lay out their newspaper near me, as everybody else trickle in one by one. What started out as a backyard crawfish boil is now an inside gatherin due to the storm pouncing and roaring outside. Umph, I know I'm repeatin myself, but I love me some New Awlins – tropical storms and all. And I guess since I'm the guest of honor, folks are comin by me to show me their love. Did I mention just how much I love my family? Well, I do. I notice that the grownups didn't bring any food with them, though. The men will probably end up at the dining room table while the women conjugate at the one in the kitchen. I'm guessin they wanna talk to me before the beer and liquor take over their minds.

"So, Corin."

I look at my uncle Thaddeus who's standin at the French doors that lead to the dinin room.

"When you was in that coma, you really dreamed that I won the lottery?"

"Hahaha!" And the games begin. "Hahaha! Yes, Uncle Thaddeus. You won about three million dollars before taxes."

He slaps his left thigh and reflexively lifts his leg up. "See what I told ya?" He looks over at my uncle Terrell, who's sat down on the couch, as if to prove a point and then looks back at me. "Do you remember what year that was, what numbers I played? Shit, did I have on my lucky shirt when I played?"

Aunt June, who just walked up behind Uncle Thaddeus, chimes in. "Oh Lawd, please don't say he had on that shirt. That thing needs to be buried twenty feet under."

"Hey, woman, mind ya business." He playfully winks at her. "Shoot, you betta look like stayin in my good graces from here on out if you want any part of my winnings."

Aunt June waves him off with a pointedly rolling of her eyes.

I shake my head at my uncle. I kinda wish I hadn't shared bits and pieces of the other dimension cuz who knows if any of those experiences will come to pass. I mean, in a way I hope they don't cuz my life was filled with turmoil and anxiety with me dealing with havin herpes in all. I look over at my uncle Terrell briefly cuz I could tell that he's a lil deep in thought. Why did Uncle Thaddeus have to bring up that other dimension? Between my auntie Joyce and my mama, everybody knows about my experiences there – including Uncle Terrell dyin in Lake Ponchartrain.

My mama, who's probably been listenin from the dinin room, walks in and picks up on Uncle Terrell's mood like me. "Terrell, don't go getting in no deep thought over something that ain't even come to pass."

He just looks at my mother with the saddest eyes I've ever seen in my life. Damn! Why did I have to go and open my big ole mouth? Hunh! Mama May, I mean my future self told me that the other dimension will help me and others, not hurt them. Shit, I can't even look at my uncle right now.

To lighten the mood, my auntie Joyce tries to nonchalantly offer some words of encouragement toward my uncle as she sets a miniature cooler filled with soda, water, and wine coolers in the middle of the floor next to Kyle who's strategically positioned himself in Queenie's path so she's forced to pass by him every time she enters and leaves the room. I can't believe that Kyle is smitten on Queenie. How cute. "Yeah, Terrell, you need to let that go like yesterday. Shoot, for all we know, Corin was jus dreamin." I guess auntie Joyce was listenin, too.

"Like hell she was!" Everyone looks over at my uncle Thaddeus. "Shiiit, I'm keepin hope alive til I get my money."

My cousins crack up at the absurd insensitivity that just floated into the room while Queenie looks at me with wide eyes. And on cue, everyone turns their back on my uncle Thaddeus, and give one another an exasperated look before filling the room with replacement chatter. I notice my uncle Terrell observe and listen for a while before he leaves the room followed by my mother who had sat next to him.

As soon as they leave, I notice, for the first time, that the TV is on – maybe cuz it's on mute. But, what holds my attention is watchin Jamie Fox actin silly on the Jamie Fox show. For a millisecond, a part of me wants to tell everyone that he's gonna win an academy award in 2005 for portraying Ray Charles in a movie. And, that Ray Charles will breathe his last breath in June of 2004. But, I decide to keep the thoughts to myself for now since I don't really know if any of that'll come to pass. So instead, I make a mental note to add that thought to my journal filled with other thoughts, revelations, exercises, and experiences of the other dimension. I tell ya, time seems to hold a lot of weight right now – wonderin what will or won't make the cut from the other dimension. GOD, I pray that you embed present moment awareness within my every waking and sleeping moments. Thank you. Cuz Lawd knows I have my hands full with dealin with the realities of this dimension alone.

Shiiit, ya'll, I got something to share with you that spooked the living daylights out of me durin the ride over here. Ya see, I was ridin in the backseat of my parents' rent-a-car while they were in the front. I was a little tired from my sleepless night last night so I laid across the seat on my back with my knees bent. And I kid you not, while I was layin there my body jus started trembling, out of nowhere, involuntarily. It was crazy. I wasn't cold or afraid of anything, but my entire body just started shakin. A little fearful and confused about what was happening, I sat up to show and tell my parents what was goin on with me and was confronted with a live and in-color view of the Carpenter's house for about two seconds as we drove by. And I don't know why, but I decided to keep the experience and revelation of the obvious reaction of my cellular memory of the location of the rape to myself. Shoot, you have to admit that that was a trip, right? I mean, though I know the Carpenters live close by Auntie Joyce and Uncle Buddy's, there weren't any anxious or leery thoughts that crossed my mind about being in the vicinity of their home. So take note, ya'll, cellular memory is for real.

Funny, I've noticed that no one brings up the Carpenters. I wonder if that's a friendship of the past now or if, I in time, can help heal it by showing everyone that I don't hold anything against them. I guess time will tell. I know my mom and aunt Joyce are missin Mrs. Carpenter. They were such good friends. This is all so weird. Ugh!

Triumph Is Your Birth Right...

Epilogue

two and a half years later

"**G**irl, I can't believe you're actually finished."

I look at my girl Queenie as I ponder on the fact that I'm actually a massage therapist now. "Yep, who woulda thought that I'd drop out of Xavier and move to New York to attend the Swedish Institute, right?"

"Humph. Who woulda thought?" Queenie smiles at me for a long moment before she continues. "So now, you're gonna look into the Reiki thing, right?"

"Ahunhunhun. Yep, now it's the Reiki thing. Ahunhun."

"What?"

"Nothin girl. I'm jus havin fun with you."

"I'm so proud of you, Corin."

"Thanks! Me too. I'm proud of me, too."

"And, I'm so happy that you decided to join me here, in Miami for a couple of days."

"You happy?" I look at Queenie like an eye is missin off of her face. "Shoot, I'm ecstatic. Chillin on the beach, not doin anything but eatin, lookin pretty, and getting my drink on was jus what a sista needed."

"What? Corin needed to get her drink on?"

"Hey, even us spirituals like to get down and dirty some of the time."

Queenie's laugh is full and playful. "Girl, you know you a fool. Shooot, if this is how you get down and dirty, then remind me not to invite you to Jamaica next year."

"Hahaha! Wait! Why not? You goin to Jamaica next year?"

Queenie pokes her lips out and nods her head. "Unh hunh. And what goes on in Jamaica, stays in Jamaica."

I shake my head at how serious I know Queenie is. "Girl, you's crazy for real. You jus bet not forget about the good sense yo mama gave you."

"Humph, ain't nobody gone be thinking about my mama in Jamaica."

I laugh at the realness of that statement. "I heard that." Lookin around and takin in the scene, I switch up the conversation. "So, who told you about this spot? I like the vibe – the ambiance."

We're at a little café somewhere off the beaten path in Miami. Though it's pretty dim in here, the walls appear to be painted a goldish orange with a reddish trim. Very funky. But, I have to say that the art on the walls along with the velvet lookin couches and chairs perfectly positioned around the stage along with miniature tables set for two really add to the funkiness of it all. Queenie and I are sittin at a table somewhat in the middle of everything soakin it all in.

"The concierge at the hotel mentioned it to me. But, she didn't know if it would have live music tonight or poetry. And you know me and my live entertainment."

"Yes, I do." I finish my drink off and grab a couple of french fries off of my plate. "Either one is a winner."

"Yep, especially poetry. And to think, we lucked up with both tonight." Queenie follows my lead and starts in on the fries, too. "You know it's killin me that we can't stay for the whole show cuz of my flight." She looks at the empty stage. "I'm really feelin the poets."

"Yeah, me too. I hope we get to see at least three more acts. How much longer we got?"

Queenie looks at her watch. "Ummm, about an hour. You know what I just thought of?"

I look up from my plate before I fill my mouth with another helping of french fries. "What's that?"

"That in about five years or so we're gonna be checkin our cell phones for the time and typin messages on them to one another."

Oh my Queenie. I wonder about that other dimension sometimes. "Yep. Maybe. Time will tell."

"Yes it will. Oooh oooh oooh, I had another thought."

"O-kay. What's that, Queenie?"

"That if the second half of the show is as good as the first half, that you should totally stay."

Caught off guard by that thought, I stumble over my words a little. "Ummm, uhhh, why would I stay here, at a lounge in Miami, by myself?"

"What's the difference between being by yourself here or at the hotel? You gone be by yourself til midnight tomorrow night any way, when your flight leaves."

"So, what, you don't want me to come to the airport with you?"

"It's not that. I just want you to live a lil, get outta yo shell."

I grab my halter top for emphasis. "Uhhh, single black woman, here, livin on her own in New York."

"I know. And I'm so proud of you. But, from your conversations, I can tell that you haven't been getting out, like talking about it. All you do is go to school and to your counseling sessions. I want you to let loose, girl." She throws her hands in the air and starts swayin and snapping her fingers to the sound of the music in her head given she's not on beat with what the dejay's playin.

"Well, for your information, that's not all I do. And, as a matter of fact I was just about to tell you about this place in Fort Green, Brooklyn called The Brooklyn Moon Café that I wanna…"

"Oooh, I know exactly what you're talkin bout. It's on Fulton Street, right?"

"Unh hunh."

"And by the way, you don't have to say Brooklyn after Fort Green. Everyone knows that Fort Green is in Brooklyn."

Ignoring her annoying correction, I continue with a slight roll of my eyes upward. "Any way, I heard that they have poetry there sometimes."

"Unh hunh. They do! You should go!" Queenie always gets a little excited when I can relate to a part of her home town.

"Yeah, uhhh, that's what I was gonna say if you'd let me talk. That after comin here, I decided that I'ma have to check that spot out cuz one day, when I was walkin by, I happened to look in as someone was comin out and it looked like it had a lotta flava ya know – a cool vibe. See, that'll be getting out."

Ignoring me, Queenie travels somewhere in time to New York.

"Oooh, I can't wait until this last semester is over for me so I can move back to New York. Lawd knows I like me some NOLA, but I'm missin the adrenalin of the NY."

Joinin her trip, I find myself hangin out with her there. "I can't wait either. In fact, I've been meanin to ask you how you felt about livin with ya mama for a couple of months until my lease is up. Then, we could get a place together."

I'm startled at Queenie slammin her hand on the table. "Damn it, Corin! I was thinking the same thing."

We both raise our glasses in unison to toast the idea and bust out laughin when we find them empty.

Once we calm down, Queenie zeroes in on me for either clarification or confirmation. "So, you really feelin New York like that, Corin?"

I look at my friend directly in the eyes so that she can feel my seriousness. "You know what? At first I didn't have any feelings either way if I'd stay there for a while or not." I start nodding my head, yes. "But, yeah, I'm really feelin New York."

"That's what's up."

"Now, don't get me wrong, I'm not sayin that I'll retire there or nothing like that." I think back to last winter for a second. "Cuz, really, the winter can kiss my high ass."

"Hahaha! Right, right."

"But, I can see myself livin there for at least five more years or so."

"Okay." I watch Queenie's eyes get wide. "Five years is a nice stack of time."

I can't help but laugh a little at the excitement dancing all over my friend's face. "Yeah, you know, the money's been really good so far workin as a massage therapist. So, I been thinkin that while I'm studying to become a Reiki Master, I might look into attending the Swedish Institute's school of Acupuncture, which means another solid four years for me fa sho."

Queenie tosses her head back. "Nanh see. That's what I'm talkin bout. The dynamic duo will be together again. What!?" She raises her hand for a high five.

"Yep, we sure will." I give her a high five.

"So, wait, how do your parents feel about you becoming the holistic mystic? I thought you were just taking a break from Xavier."

"Really? Though both of them said that they're cool with my plans, I can tell that they're a little disappointed that I'm not completing my undergrad in Business. But, I do know and can feel that they just want me to be happy."

"Right."

"And, who knows, maybe I will complete my undergraduate in Business one day. But, right now, I'm gone walk down that unbeaten path of holistic health and wellness."

"That's good, Corin. It takes a lot not to follow the sure thing. I'm proud of you, girl."

"Thanks Queenie. Means a lot. Plus, I been meaning to tell you that I've started takin some African dance classes that I'm really likin right now. It's like I'm discoverin a whole new me. I think that one day I might want to perform with a company or something."

"Oh really?"

I knew I'd catch her off guard. "Yep!"

"Heeeyyy, wait a minute. I thought you said that I was the one who was the African dancer."

I laugh at Queenie cuz sometimes I feel like she can probably tell me more about the other dimension than I can tell myself. "I know. But, I saw a flyer about a dance class at a place called Faretta about a month ago and went on a whim just to see if I could watch."

"Spontaneity. I like. Continue."

"Yeah, well, I instantly was hooked. I mean, the place doesn't look like much, but it feels magical. In fact, I think I saw your favorite teacher from the other dimension the other day – Babacar."

"Really, Corin? Someone named Babacar really exists?"

"Yep. And he teaches a style of dance called Sabar, too."

"Get the fuck outta here."

"Hahaha! I know. Crazy, right?"

Queenie doesn't answer me. She jus nods her head in agreement as she stares at the thoughts in her mind.

"Earth to Queenie. Queenie are you there?"

She looks over at me as if she jus saw a ghost. "Wow, Corin. I wonder of how much of that other dimension is gonna come to past."

"Right!?" I think about all of the possible outcomes of Queenie's statement. "Well, we know everything's not gonna come to past seein that I didn't complete Business School at Xavier. Sooo, Computel's definitely out of the question."

"Yeah. I know. But, look at you. You're actually a massage therapist, Corin. And from what you just shared about Babacar, I have a feelin that you're gonna have a lot of near coincidental and déjà vu moments in the next twelve to fourteen years."

"Humph. I guess time will tell." A thought pops into my mind. "Oh, but wait. Don't forget that I don't have herpes. So, that's somethin else from the other dimension that won't come to pass."

"Yep. Gotta give thanks for that, mama." Queenie pushes her chair back. "I'ma go to the restroom before the second half of the show starts."

When she gets up, I start lookin around at all the cool art posted up on the walls, from my chair, as I absentmindedly acknowledge Queenie. "Okay."

Just as I fix my eyes on a beautiful painting of a black woman, whose hair mimics small tree branches, wading in a river with the moon illuminating behind her, my view is obstructed by a dark, tall, slender frame. Knowing that I'm bein watched, I let my eyes linger, a while, along the torso and limbs, from the chest to the feet, admiring how the clothes perfectly fall onto the body before I finally direct my attention above the neck. Glad that I took my time, I blush a little at the warm, yet piercing smile, pointed directly at me. He raises the glass in his left hand as if he's toasting to me and then bends his body in a slight bow before walking away. I take a deep breath so that I can feel my abdomen fill up with air and hopefully direct the exhalation in such a way that it removes the sweet fluster forcing my facial muscles into an unremovable happy-go-lucky smile. *Hmmm. That was random and a lil daunting.* With my head held down, I pretend like I'm searchin for something in my purse.

"Girl, what are you cheezin at?"

Whew! Good lookin out GOD. I look up at my friend as she sits back down. Just as I was about to tell her what occurred, our waitress who's rockin the hell out of a boy-fade haircut, big looped earrings with a cute, short sundress, brings us two new drinks.

"Aw, thanks Corin. I was…"

I inadvertently cut Queenie off. "For what? I didn't order these."

"You didn't?"

Initially I look at the waitress confused before that warm piercing smile dips across my mind and the waitress starts explaining and pointin toward the bar. "The gentleman over there …" I follow her pointed finger to the guy who was standin in my view a few moments ago and smile. "…said he hopes you're still here when the show is over."

Queenie follows her finger, too. "Uhhhh, jus how long was I gone?"

I bend my head a lil and smile to myself. *Smooth move.* Then I look over at the guy and mouth 'thank you' with my cute girl smile before I acknowledge the waitress with a 'thank you'. "Girl, you wasn't gone long at all. When you left, I started lookin around at the artwork, from my seat, and before I knew it, oh boy was blockin my view."

"Oh yeah? He's cute."

"I know, right?"

"So, did he say anything to you?"

"Unh, unh. He just smiled, raised his drink toward me, and did a slight bow."

"A bow?"

"Yeah, it was kinda cute."

"I guess. I wonder why he didn't come over and say hi."

I direct my eyes to the host who is back on stage talkin about the next act. "Who knows. But, I'm likin his prelude."

"Sooo, you stayin or coming with me to the airport?"

I simply smile at my friend before I tune in fully to what the host is sayin.

"And without further ado, comin to the stage is Papa Truth."

I think, *That's an interesting stage name – Papa Truth.* Me and Queenie slowly smile at each other when my admirer steps on to the stage.

"Good evenin ladies and gentleman. How ya'll doin?"

I watch and listen to how the crowd responds to him. They're anticipating him. Hmmm, he must be good.

This piece is called "Until Proven Guilty".

I know a lot of ya'll will protest

But my words are my truth, it's a villain's world baby

I care not if you contest

I'ma straight shootin respectable brotha who's been around, fucked a lot, and know the difference between a no and a yes

So when I tell you bout this being of the female persuasion

It's important not to drink, pop a pill, or kick off the blazin

Otherwise, you'll miss the trip I'ma take you on – baggaged perception is counter-amazin

Our time together was a month and a half, maybe two

We vibed easy, connected within worlds, it was more of her that I sought to pursue

Her laughter reminded me of rainbows – colorful, big, bold

My mind repeatedly announced rose pedals at the touch of her hand, passing her slightly – within her embrace I'd easily enfold

Silence was comfortable, my space she did not crowd

Her beauty was spellbinding – rich, vibrant, loud

Shiiit, but don't let that description fool ya

Cuz, apparently, it has nothing to do with the truth or the replica

I urge you all to breathe in each moment with precise certainty

Cuz life has a way of drastically flippin yo script instantaneously

See, on this one night after debating the fate of our society, my body felt hijacked by her eyes as she walked toward me

She let me kiss her full in the mouth – her lust grabbin at my back

The heat and moisture seepin from her lavanous volcano had my mind searchin – where is my pack, where is my pack - of rubbas that is

My manhood was swellin by the second - no wish was needed by Oz or the Wiz

The grind of her pelvis released a plethora of messages

Open-ended sentences and half asked questions bee-bopped throughout my mind like savages

I follow her lead, lift up her sundress, and take her bra-less breasts in my hands

Her moans and groans direct my tongue to her nipples as they officiate my plans

Absentminded and conscious, somehow I manage to let my manhood breathe

She grabs it; she strokes it – Aw yes! Umph! I'm under her siege

Her kisses, moans, grinds become wilder as her volcano reacts to the play of my fingers

I find myself in parallel realities – one a man fuckin; the other, a spirit that lingers

My spirit stops a moment and looks at the feminine silhouette beneath me

Her eyes are rolled back for a second before they realize that I'm looking at she

I let her hungered eyes divert my attention to the package beside me

I peel it open with my teeth while searchin her soul – justified with what I see

I stop to take off my clothes and watch the heels of her feet make lines in the sheet – she can't stop movin, she must be ready to freak

The pubic hairs peeking out through her bikini propels me to pull them down with deliberate focus

But half way between her thighs and knees, I'm accosted by a grip that feels foreign and unjust

Perplexed by the uninvited action, I glance at her questioningly

She looks at me with lust-imprinted eyes, followed by an out-of-place plea

Ummm, I don't think I'm ready for this - her voice sounds out candidly

I look at her confused before I respond matter-of-factly

Luv, you need to live your life and let your actions and words seductively meet

With that she relaxes her grip, finishes the strip, I assume from her stance she retreats

But my assumption rings stupidity throughout my ears, my head – hell it knocks me off of my feet. It reminded me of that old wise tale of never to assume cuz she got my ass and now I want nothing to do with she

For, according to her, the next day on the phone, her recollection of things was skewed – awry

I cringe, hammer, and knock around my memory tryin to determine the onset of her twist

Exhausted with her view and damned by my plight, I ascertain that I mistook her actions for a motha fuckin yes

That was "Until Proven Guilty" ya'll. Thank you."

Queenie and I just look at each other as we slowly join the rest of the audience in applause. *Well, I be damn.*

"He was good, right?"

I blankly look at my friend as I slowly nod my head yes. "Unh hunh, he was good." Caught up in the truth of his words, I shy away from the humility of the victim in me and wonder about the victim in him. Shit, whether or not his poem is true, I know that there are some guys who fall victim to our, meaning females, insecure messages during lustful moments.

The host re-introduces the back-up band who fills the space up with musical notes and timely rhythms beckoning everyone to snap their fingers and sway from side to side in their seats while in thought, conversation, checkin the time, and/or sippin their drinks. Just as I'm about to share my thoughts of the poem with Queenie, Papa Truth, himself, appears before me and asks if I mind if he joins us. I look over at Queenie more out of reflex than to ask if she's okay with his company cuz I know her ass don't mind – she wants me to start dating again. So, of course, I'm not surprised when she gestures her outlaid hand toward the empty chair he's snatched from another table and nods her head in agreement.

"Sure. Have a seat," I reply.

Queenie and I both compliment him, right as he sits down. "Great poem."

She and I look at each other and giggle a little.

"Why, thank you, ladies," he responds with that slight bow he offered to me earlier.

Grateful for the intimate setting, I get a better look at his smooth, dark chocolate skin and beautiful smile. "You have a beautiful smile." Oooop, did I just say that?

Queenie smiles at me knowing of my spontaneous goof.

"Thank you, luv. I guess it's reflectin the beauty comin from ya'll." He extends his hand. "So, I'm Papa Truth."

I take his hand in mine. "Corin."

He repeats my name slowly without takin his eyes away from mine. "Co-rin."

Feelin a little uncomfortable, I start moving our hands in a handshake fashion and then gesture toward Queenie who's eatin this moment up with a big ass smile on her face. "And this is my girl, Queenie."

He directs his attention toward Queenie for a brief moment and gives her a slight bow while still holdin on to my hand.

She responds with a nod and slight bow of her own.

Finally an intelligent thought enters my mind that I don't mind speakin. "So, Papa Truth, what did your mama name you?"

He directs his full attention to me and looks in my eyes as if he's building up to something. "You know, people in this scene rarely ask me that. My name is Charles Richmond, luv."

Stunned and totally caught off guard, I look over at my friend who looks like she just saw a ghost, again. I guess time will tell if he's the Charles Richmond that was Mama May's husband. Hence, my own.

About the Author

Toshii K. D. Cooper is a child of God, a student of truth, and a teacher of self-love who is grounded in the blissful intentions of the Universe. A native and current resident of 'The Big Easy', New Orleans, Louisiana, Ms. Cooper's spirit consciously resonates here in the USA and across the waters of the African Diaspora. Her mission is acknowledging, accepting, planting, and being Infinite Wisdom always.

A former Senior Operations Specialist at Merrill Lynch, middle school Math Instructor, and professional West African dancer/performer, Ms. Cooper is currently a Massage Therapy and Continuing Education Instructor, Reiki Master, developer of the modality, Atoning Chakra Massage, and owner of Infinite Healing – A Holistic Mobile Spa (in Atlanta, GA). Her passions lie in being of service via healing and uplifting minds, bodies, and souls with her touch, energy, words, and artistic creative expressions.